INTERCESSION

The Disillusioning Art of Shell Formation
Volume III

*"I will give you a new heart and put a new spirit in you; I will remove from
you your heart of stone and give you a heart of flesh."*

– Ezekiel 36:26

A NOVEL BY

NICOLE GARBER

YELLOWPLUME

Copyright ©2014 Nicole Garber
Library of Congress: 20-13920305
ISBN: 978-0-9911774-2-4

YellowPlume
PO Box 31272
Edmond, OK 73003-0022

Cover art: Abby Stiglets aby3.com
Cover & Interior Design: ZAQ Designs

To all of my girls.

ACKNOWLEDGEMENTS

In October of last year, when I was halfway finished writing Intercession, a few circumstances changed and I was redirected. This new direction came while having coffee with a friend and hanging out at *JuiceBlendz* with a group of girls that I adore. I want to thank God for placing these people in my life and I want to thank these people (you know who you are) for inspiring me to answer through my writing the age-old question "Who am I".

As always, a thousand thanks to:

My husband, Jimmy, for understanding how important this project is to me and for supporting me fully. And thank you for picking up the slack when I've been in my writing cave for days. I love you.

Mom and Dad, you are the best. You've been my rock. Dad, thanks for being the first to read my book and thank you for taking the time to edit. Mom, for always having an ear to listen, for your editing help, and for being both a mother and a friend.

Brooks and Madison, for being exactly who you are. You are my sunshine!

Karen, for driving half way across the country to help me sell books, for spreading the word, for editing, and for hosting the signing in Alexandria. So much fun! Lucky to have you as my mother-in-law.

Marty, thank you for your words of wisdom, for hosting the signing in Bartlesville, and for your business expertise.

Abby, thanks for another beautiful painting. I think this is my favorite cover… so far. Look forward to starting the fourth.

My editor, Louis Skipper. Couldn't have done this without you. I appreciate your attention to detail.

To the bookstores that invited me for signings and placed my books on their shelves.

And thank you to all my friends who have supported me fully and encouraged me along the way.

CHAPTER ONE

I stood up slowly, legs wobbly like a newborn fawn. The little boy one row up was peeking over the top of his seat, staring at me with two wide green eyes. I regarded him sleepily. He stuck out his tongue. I returned the gesture, and he began to cry. I placed a hand on my mother's shoulder and steadied myself before squeezing by her. The man in seat 13C studied me with suspicious eyes. Still groggy, I ignored him and moved into the aisle, walking the narrow strip of blue-gray carpet toward the back of the plane. I felt a jolt and stumbled. My feet felt heavy and my head felt light. I glanced to the right. An old man sat with his arms folded across his chest; lost in thought, he was looking at the clouds. I could hear the chatter of children over the hum of the engine. I looked to my left: an experienced traveler equipped with a neck and an eye pillow. Her head was tilted back and her mouth was agape. A cough. A laugh. A workaholic hunched over her computer. A teenager with his nose buried in a book. A cowboy. Boots. Hat. Big-buckled-belt. Coming home. I felt nauseous. I hurried down the aisle, darted into the lavatory, shut the door, locked it, and pressed my back against the flimsy barrier. Inhale. Exhale. Repeat. Quick, rapid breathing. The intercom crackled overhead and the flight attendant's voice did little to calm me.

"Ladies and Gentleman, we are experiencing quite a bit of turbulence. As we begin our descent into Tulsa, I ask that you make sure your seatbacks are up and the tray tables in front of you are secured. In addition, please stow all carry-ons in the overhead bins or under the seat in front of you. It's going to be bumpy, so keep your belts fastened for the remainder of the flight."

I turned to face the small lavatory mirror. My normally olive skin was pasty white. It was no wonder I had frightened the little boy in 12E. Scared and tired eyes, ashy skin, thin frame, unruly black hair, and slumped shoulders. I looked like I had seen a ghost. No, I looked *like* a ghost. What did A-Omega see in me? How could I have accepted their offer? I wasn't good enough and the terrible dream I woke from was all the refreshing my memory needed. I splashed a bit of water on my face and patted it dry with a paper towel. I coated my lips with gloss and fluffed my tangled waves. I opened my eyes wide and stared at my reflection. "I can do this. I am strong, determined, stubborn, and kind. A-Omega told me so." If I said it out loud enough times, there was a small chance I might actually believe it.

With a slow and much steadier gate, I returned to 13E and took a seat between Alex and Sue. I looked across the aisle at the middle-aged man. Although he looked far less concerned than he did five minutes ago, he was, nevertheless, still staring at me. I looked at Alex.

"I didn't scream out loud, did I?"

Alex raised his eyebrows and exhaled audibly. "Another dream?" He pulled me in close and kissed the top of my head.

"They won't go away."

"Same one?"

"Just a different variation of the same old thing: my death," I confessed, surprised by how free I felt when I told Alex the truth. I quickly recalled the recurring nightmare I had while in Alexandria. After keeping it to myself for months, the worry over whether it might come true had nearly eaten me alive.

I heard the distinct sound of the landing gear lowering and as if on cue, Mom grabbed my left hand and gave it squeeze. "Everything's going to be just perfect, and *I'm* so glad to have you home."

Sue had definitely placed emphasis on the word *I'm,* but I didn't grasp the scope of her sentiment until I stepped off the plane and saw Will waiting for us just behind the security check at Tulsa International Airport. Alex and I walked side by side, hand in hand. Sue was lagging behind. She was toting the largest allowed carry-on so that she wouldn't have to check a bag, which didn't make sense. Both Alex and I had checked luggage, so she would still have to wait. The airport was quiet today and we were breezing through the terminal, but it felt like we were crawling. Everything was moving in slow motion, including my thoughts; I was back in Oklahoma and I was having trouble letting reality sink in.

Will's distinguishing features became more recognizable as we drew near. I felt nervous. Will was wearing a plaid shirt tucked into the waist of his blue jeans. He seemed the same, but also very different.

Fifty feet away - my limbs felt weak. I hadn't expected this. I hadn't been this anxious when I was reunited with Sue, when I returned to our cottage on the lake and found her standing in the living room. Perhaps it was because I didn't have time to think about it. I wasn't prepared for her arrival. She was just there, standing with her arms wide open, waiting for an embrace.

Forty feet away - Will was not going to be so welcoming. He had his arms folded across his chest. He was tapping his foot, keeping a steady rhythm. My gaze met his. I was still too far away to see the heavy lines below his eyes and across his forehead, but close enough to detect that his face held no expression. This was not the man I remembered. There were many things I loved about Will. He was slow to anger and quick to trust. He always saw the best in me. However, what I loved the most... what I had missed the most, was his uncanny ability to cheer me up when I was down. Never, not once in the past ten years, had I let him know he made me happy; that when he smiled, my frozen lips wanted to mimic his. And when he made a joke at his own expense to lighten the mood... my mood... I wanted to laugh... I really did. All at once, I knew what was different. Will wasn't smiling. Mom warned me that he was angry. I left him and my mother in the middle of the night and ran away with my boyfriend. It wasn't like I just hopped over to the next small town. It was major. I separated myself from Mom and Dad. I put fifteen hours, 700 miles between us. Unforgiveable. Or maybe he was angry that I had left my mother so soon after her medical emergency. A heart attack. I skipped town the next day. It sounds horrible and cold and despicable, but I left to save her life… my dad's life and according to Mom, he had come to that realization, but I didn't doubt that he was going to make me pay. I wasn't expecting complete forgiveness. But a smile… at least a smile. I gave Alex's hand a hard squeeze and he squeezed back… a silent understanding formed between us. The situation was bad. It wasn't my imagination. Alex had noticed it, too.

Twenty feet away - a smile turned the corners of Will's lips. *Finally! I knew he couldn't stay angry for long.* Instinct began to turn the corners of mine… until I realized Will wasn't looking at me, but rather past me, at Sue. Alex gave my hand an encouraging squeeze. I didn't return the gesture. Unspoken words.

Five feet away - I could smell the faint scent of Will's cologne. Grey Flannel. He had smelled the same for nineteen years, but only now did I identify with the scent. When I was living in Amsterdam, I spent the night at my friend Carly's house. I had never had many friends, and it was the first time I had ever spent the night. I was uneasy about sleeping over, but I accepted the invitation because I knew I might not get another offer. When I went home the next morning, I had forgotten my clothes on her bed. On Monday, Carly returned them to me, clean and folded. My clothes smelled like Carly's house, a scent that she was most likely unaware of because she was used to it. But I could smell the hint of vanilla lingering in the cotton fibers. It smelled like friendship. I thought about the story Alex told me when we were in Minnesota. He said he remembered the way his mom's hair smelled: like mint. Is that what absence does? Heightens your sensitivity to those things you hold dear? Grey Flannel was not my favorite cologne, but it was Dad. It was inviting. It was a warm embrace.

Three feet away - my knees shook and although delayed, Will stretched out his arms. A spark of hope. Sue fell into Will's embrace. My heart sank.

And there was the truth. It slapped me across the face so hard it stung and all at once, I was reminded that although I was coming *home*, I wasn't

Will's. I was related to Sue. She was flesh and blood… my aunt. But the man I had always called Dad, Father, wasn't really mine. He had dedicated his life to raising me, the daughter of a monster. He had raised me as his own after he had lost so much. And I repaid him by running away. I would hate me, too.

Will held Sue in his arms for the longest time while Alex and I stood uncomfortably, not knowing where to look or what to say. At long last, Sue peeled herself away from the man I used to call Dad, and Alex unlocked his hand from mine and outstretched it. A friendly gesture.

"Mr. Colbert." Alex cleared his throat, patiently waiting for Will to reciprocate the gesture. Will looked down at Alex's hand for what seemed like an eternity, then all at once, he turned his back on the both of us. Completely shocked, I watched Will walk away, heading toward the escalator. The fingers of his left hand were interlaced with my mother's and with his right hand, he gripped the handle of her carry-on. As they disappeared into the pits of the baggage claim, Alex and I stayed behind. I took Alex's outstretched hand in mine and laid my head on his chest.

"At least he looked you in the eye," I sighed.

INTERCESSION

CHAPTER TWO

We were only twenty miles outside of Tulsa and already there were open pastures dotted with grazing cows. It was several days before the official start of spring and the sun was shining, bursting through puffy white clouds, which was a bit misleading since the temperature was 42 degrees: chilly and wet. My dad rolled down the window to let in some fresh air. I shivered, pulled my sweater around my shoulders, and thought about asking him politely to put it back up. I was on thin ice and I knew it. So, I bit my lip to keep my teeth from chattering. I glanced at Cocoa sitting beside me. Her tongue hung out of the side of her mouth and her ears were perked. She seemed very pleased to be off the plane. They say a dog can always find its way back home, and I didn't doubt that Cocoa knew exactly where we were going. I glanced at Alex, who was sitting on the other side of Cocoa, gazing out the window of Will's new Ford F150. His shaggy brown hair moved with the wind. He was far away.

"A penny for your thoughts," I whispered and patted Cocoa on the head. She licked my hand, then nudged Alex with her nose. The lack of conversation was killing me and the tension in the truck was so thick, I could have cut it with a knife. Mom was reapplying her makeup in the vanity mirror. The radio was tuned to easy listening. Dad's eyes were fixed on the road. He sat so still and rigid in his leather bucket seat that he looked like a statue. Cocoa curled up in a ball and lay her head on my lap. I leaned back, letting my muscles and my mind relax. I had woken up this morning without the slightest idea of what lay ahead of me. Less than a week ago, I had accepted A-Omega's offer. A-Omega told me I was strong, but I still saw myself as weak. They told me I was kind, but I wasn't so sure. Despite my mixed emotions, I felt good about my decision. When we left the small Minnesota cottage that had been my home for nearly a year, I hadn't the foggiest idea where we were headed. A-Omega had not revealed our final destination, but that hadn't stopped me from considering the many possibilities, all of the places I had never been: Tokyo, Doha, Moscow, Rio de Janeiro. Because I didn't know whether to pack a parka or a bikini, I was hopeful A-Omega would send me everything I needed once I arrived.

I had spent a good portion of my life abroad, moving from country to country and had hated it… loathed it. I had only accepted the offer a week ago and already A-Omega had me on the move. But strangely enough, instead of feeling dread, I felt excitement, and I thought that maybe this time moving would be different because *I* was different. I thought I might even be able to love Europe if Alex was with me. Or China. Bangladesh. Canada. It didn't matter as long as Alex was by my side. But it wasn't until we arrived at Minneapolis/St. Paul International Airport and checked in at the designated counter that the mystery was unveiled and my initial shock gave way to disappointment. I had prepared myself for an extraordinary journey. I had allowed myself to believe A-Omega trusted me with something big. It made me feel important. Strong. Untouchable. I hadn't expected anything extravagant, but I did expect something a bit more exciting than this. I had anticipated something new. I had hoped for a fresh start. But A-Omega shipped me back to Bartlesville, the place I had run away from less than a year ago. I glanced down at the black steel-toed combat boots that A-Omega included in the box. They might as well have sent me a pair of cowboy boots if they were planning for me to return to the prairie. I gave the back of Will's seat a swift kick, underestimating the stiffness of the toe. He grunted and for the first time in forty-five minutes, the silence was broken.

"Sorry," I said, completely meaning it.

Living with Sue and Will was going to be tough. Is this what Pastor Joe meant when he spoke of taking the hard road? Will was definitely going to make life hard on me.

When we passed the Moose Lodge, a pre-fab metal building that sat on an acre on the edge of town, Will cleared his throat and turned down the volume on the radio. Alex and I looked at one another in unison. Dad… Will was getting ready to say something important, and we were all ears.

"I'll be taking Alex to *his* house, I presume."

I was just about to chime in, but Alex beat me to the punch.

"Yes, sir," Alex responded with haste. Maybe his hurried response was an attempt at being polite. Or maybe it was a desperate plea to get out of the car. Most likely, it was a bit of both.

"Will!" I whined. Since landing in Tulsa, I had barely spoken a word; I knew that my voice alone was enough to grab Will's attention, but I decided to be a bit more dramatic, so I laced my voice with exaggerated concern and pleaded my case. "Alex doesn't have a car. It's 4:30. It's almost dinnertime. He doesn't even have a way to get to the store for groceries."

"No worries, Mr. Col-," Alex had just begun to respond when he was interrupted.

"He has two feet," Will snapped.

Taken aback, I sucked in a deep breath. I could feel a knot rising in my throat. I wanted to say something smart aleck, but I was in no position to backtalk. I sighed and glanced at Alex, hoping to catch his eye, but he had returned his gaze out the window. His elbow was resting on the door and he was massaging his temple with his thumb, a tell-tale sign of his concern. I twirled my promise ring around my finger and began to chew on my nails, a habit I had broken while in Minnesota. Mom flipped the vanity mirror shut and fixed her eyes on the road. I couldn't believe she wasn't going to respond, that she wasn't going to stand up for me… for Alex. Her silence was betrayal. I could have sworn that just a few hours ago, she was on *my* side. I had followed A-Omega's instructions to a T. Why weren't things going my way!? I was on the right path but there was only one thing I knew for sure: Nothing about this mission was going to be easy.

CHAPTER THREE

I spent the rest of the afternoon unpacking my belongings from the three bags I brought home from Minnesota. I did a bit of wash and then began to reacquaint myself with my old bedroom. Nothing at all had changed. The same mocha colored carpet and whimsical wallpaper. I reclined on my white wrought iron bed and studied the papered walls, considering the pattern and for the first time, connecting the dots. Whimsical meant fanciful, carefree, fun. Whimsical was everything I was not. My parents were both shrinks. Were they trying to be suggestive? I laughed and shook my head in wonder, letting my eyes move from the wallpaper to the bulletin boards Will had built for me shortly after we moved in. He had secured them to the wall and Sue had filled them with pictures: castles, beaches, and mountains. Maybe my life hadn't been so bad after all. I glanced at my bookshelf. It was in the same spot and all of my books were still there. And on top of my desk sat the pack of glittery stationary collecting dust. I remember just how hard it had been to write the letter of farewell to Mom and Dad, and I remember the mixture of feelings that swelled inside of me when Alex drove down the gravel road and I caught the last glimpse of the only home I knew. I had been gone for nearly a year, but Sue and Will hadn't touched a thing. Nothing had been moved. It was comforting to return home and discover that my room was still my room, not an office or guest room. Not a home gym filled with rubber floor mats and equipment. On the other hand, the lack of change was saddening. It reminded me of the person I used to be. In the last ten months, I had made a lot of mistakes, but I had also learned a lot in the process. I was different now. More mature. More rational. On the road to recovery. Halfway between heartache and healing. I couldn't quite see the light at the end of the tunnel, but I knew it was there and I felt certain A-Omega would do everything in their strength to lead the way.

Once my belongings were clean, neatly hung inside my closet, and tucked inside my drawers, I sat down on the floor in the middle of my room and spread out the contents of *the box* on my light brown carpet, hoping each item might be more meaningful after my seven-hour journey. When I received the box from A-Omega several weeks ago, I could only be certain of what to do with three of the six items. Although I didn't understand the meaning behind the boots nor did it make sense why A-Omega would send them to me, it was fairly obvious that they wanted me to put them on my feet. And then there was the ornate and beautiful golden fleur-de-lis pin. Attached to the back of the brooch was a note that simply said: *For where your treasure is, there your heart will be also.* I pinned the golden brooch over my heart, never giving it a second thought. But in the week I had worn it, the brooch had taken on a different hue. Now more silver than gold, the color was mottled. I thought about mood rings and how the color supposedly changes based on the emotion of the one wearing it. I wondered if there was something to that and if so, was my brooch changing color based on my mood? And the phone. Everyone knew what to do with a phone and out of all the gifts from A-Omega, it was the one I had enjoyed the most... so far. As I sat cross-legged on my bedroom floor, I pulled the other three items from the box. A leather notebook with a shield on the cover. In the center of the shield was a single word: faith. I was pretty sure that I was supposed to write something inside, but what? I flipped open the cover and thumbed through the blank white pages. Confused, I closed it and set the journal down on the floor in front of me. It was heavy... thick. It would take a lifetime to fill it up. I had no idea where to start. With a gentle hand, I placed the journal back into the box and pulled out the computer software, the most obscure gift I had ever been given. To a techie, a gift like this might be exciting and possibly meaningful, but I was not computer savvy. To top it off, the software was for a Mac. It wasn't compatible with my ancient PC. I would have to buy a new computer in order to use it. I tossed it aside and pulled out the last item from the box. The list of names. I unfolded the slip of paper and began to read:

Quinn Collins
Mason Armishaw
Katelyn Cross
Terry Dunbarr
Todd Catchitore
Steven Bellamy
Gracie Abbott
Baxtor Lavine
Shae Simmons
Peter Jovorskie
These names will form a belt. The Truth will be the buckle.
Arm Yourself Well,
A-Omega Ephesians 6: 10-18

A belt? A belt of names? A buckle. Was this a riddle? I was horrible at riddles. I had asked Alex for his opinion, but he wasn't able to offer any explanation. I had also done an online search. I started with Quinn Collins but only made it to Gracie Abbott before getting frustrated and calling it quits. Too many people shared the exact the same name. I had found fourteen different people with the name Quinn Collins. Twenty-five named Katelyn Cross and twelve named Steven Bellamy. The names were no clearer now than they were when I received them two weeks ago. Confused, I placed the list of names back into the box and then for safekeeping, stood on tiptoe and slid the package onto the highest shelf of my closet. Out of sight, but not out of mind.

When I leaned over the banister the next morning, Will was stretched out in his recliner. It was 9 AM and he was sound asleep. His glasses were resting on the end of his nose and he was snoring. The morning paper was in his lap and a burnt orange, leather bound book was wedged between his hip and the chair. My best guess… he had been there a while. Lightning was piercing the sky and thunder was rumbling so loud, it was shaking the whole house. But it didn't wake Will. He was in a coma or something. Sue said that he had been sleeping quite a bit during the day, all because he didn't sleep well at night. I knew it was because of me. I wish I could say something that would help him get some shuteye, but I wasn't about to break the silence he had created. I was still hurt that he didn't hug me at the airport, that he didn't welcome *me* with open arms. I had been able to do some thinking on the plane. I thought about my real father, Carl, and all of the pain he had caused. But mostly, I thought about Will, the man I had always called Dad. A part of me could understand why he was acting the way he was. I had not been the perfect child. I had been stubborn, sneaky, cold, distant, and mixed up. I had perplexed Will, an experienced psychiatrist who worked with kids that had far greater problems than me. That's what he did. He fixed people. He tried to heal their minds. But he was never able to fix me, and I think he just gave up.

Lightning flashed outside the window and rain streaked the glass. I hoped it was true what they said about spring: in like a lion but out like a lamb. I tiptoed into the kitchen and began pulling items out of the pantry and putting them into a brown paper grocery sack. I couldn't arrive at Alex's empty handed, especially after the way Will treated him the day before. Besides, Alex had to be close to starving by now. On the way out, I saw a plate of pastries on the counter. I wrapped a few in a paper towel and placed them in the bag. I grabbed the keys to my car and made my way out the door.

It felt weird driving my old Honda again. I had driven the Wagoneer for close to a year and it was like driving a tank. My car was much smaller and fast in comparison. When I slid into the driver's seat of my Accord, I was uncertain whether it would start. According to Mom, when I left, they parked it in the garage and hadn't driven it since. So I was pleasantly surprised when I turned the key and heard the engine turn over without so much as a sputter. My car was hardly new and by no means was it fancy. It was an older model that my parents had gotten a great deal on, but compared to Alex's Jeep, it sounded like a racecar. The only thing it needed was some gas. I backed out of the garage and all at once, the quiet disappeared as large drops of rain splattered on the windshield. I turned on the radio and shifted into drive. An advertisement blasted through the speakers. A cheesy jewelry jingle that was surprisingly catchy. I tuned into a different station and when I heard a song called *Yellow*, I turned the volume up and pressed my foot down hard on the accelerator. The sudden burst of horsepower thrust me backward into the grey cloth seat, and I could hear my tires spinning wildly beneath me. I looked into the rearview mirror at our old farmhouse that sat on a hundred acres at the edge of town. After living in big cities for most of my life, it was nice to step outside and not see a single soul. Solitude. The stars were brighter in the country and the background music was serene, almost lonely at times: a symphony of coyotes and crickets instead of the bustle of city buses and the sound of sirens. It made me feel a million miles away, but surprisingly, Alex's house was only five minutes from mine. Today, however, it felt like we were on opposite sides of the world. I couldn't get there fast enough. I had spent the last nine months living so close to Alex that we had been together twenty-four/seven. We hadn't shared the *same* cottage, but his cottage was nearby… exactly fifty-four steps away from mine. He made me coffee in the morning. We spent our afternoons on the beach. When the weather got too cold to swim, we cuddled beside the fire. Even though he already knew everything about me, I had used our time together to learn more and more about him. I missed our cottage. I missed our time. I missed Alex. It had been less than twenty-four hours since Dad booted him out of the truck, and I needed him now… right now. The thought of his hazel eyes warmed my chilled skin and the thought of his lips on mine quickened my pulse.

CHAPTER FOUR

I hadn't anticipated that walking up the path to his house would bring back so many memories of new love, but it did. In the time it took me to dash from my car to his front door, I began to reminisce about the time when we were just getting to know one another. A time before I knew who he was or why he was here. A time when his mystique lured me in, and his striking unworldly features occupied my thoughts and clouded my judgment. I had known all along that Alex was different from other boys, but at the time, I couldn't have fathomed just how different he was. I took myself back to the first time we met in art class. "Hello." That was all he said, but I remember how I couldn't breathe when he said it. His voice was smooth… unsettling… intoxicating. I remember how my heart skipped a beat when I turned around to find that he had taken the open seat next to mine. I was feeling all fluttery just thinking about it. It was the most perfect, exciting time of my life. Our newness. Before we ever had a fight. Before trouble came our way. Before the secrets. Before tough decisions had to be made. Back when it was more about love than survival. It seemed like a lifetime ago. With the brown paper bag in one hand, I used my other hand to shield myself from the rain. I hurried to the front door and stood there for a moment before ringing the bell, taking a moment to consider all that we had been through in the past year and a half. This guy. He was mine. He was all I had ever wanted and he was mine. I wouldn't let myself soon forget.

I had anticipated giving him a long, slow kiss as soon as he opened up the door, but when I saw him, I set the brown paper bag down on the entry table and fell into his arms instead. I could tell he hadn't been awake for long. His hair was mussed and he was still in his pajamas: a pair of sweatpants and a tee shirt. I let my body meld to his. I felt his warmth. His arms wrapped around my waist and pulled me closer.

"It's only been sixteen hours and forty-seven minutes." His voice was raspy, sultry. "I can't believe how much I've missed you, Sunshine."

The sound of his voice stirred me. I pushed back just enough to look up into his eyes.

"I've missed you, too." With my arms wrapped loosely around his shoulders, I gave him a longer, slower kiss than I had originally intended.

"And strangely enough, I've missed this house," I told him. "It brings back memories. Good memories."

Alex bit his lip and nodded his head in agreement. We stared at each other for a comfortable moment then, resting my head on his shoulder, I closed my eyes, relishing the thought of spending a rainy day wrapped in his arms… but Alex killed the moment with an unexpected whisper.

"What's in the bag?" he asked.

I regarded him for a moment before responding. His lips no longer parted, his mouth changed from soft and supple into a thin, knowing smile. "Food," I said, kissing him on the cheek.

"You're the best. I'm starving."

"I'm sorry," I said. Lips pouty. Puppy dog eyes. "I would have come over last night and brought you something… but you know… Will."

"I know." He shrugged his shoulders. "No big deal. I found a pack of Ramen Noodles in the pantry. Only the electricity hasn't been turned on so they were a little crunchy."

"I feel terrible," I whined, then followed Alex to the kitchen table, on which sat a small stack of magazines and his laptop.

"Don't feel bad. You have enough to worry about. I'm just glad you're here." He smiled.

"Me, too." I handed him the brown paper bag. His breakfast. "What are your plans?"

Alex took a seat in the oversized wooden Windsor armchair. I climbed onto his lap and began to playfully run my fingers through his hair, smoothing it flat then mussing it up.

"You mean my plans for today?"

"Yeah."

"I have to do boring human things, like get my electricity turned on and buy groceries. Other than that, I'd thought I'd spend the day with you... unless there's something you need to do for A-Omega. It sounds like they want you to get started right away."

"Well, I haven't heard from A-Omega, and I have no plans."

"Good." Alex smiled and shoved half of the morning bun into his mouth. "So how's the house? Everything still the same?" he asked, wiping a few crumbs from his chin.

"I'd rather be here. My house isn't the friendliest place right now."

"He'll lighten up. He has to get over it, right?"

"I don't know. He can be pretty stubborn. I spent most of yesterday in my bedroom. It's the only warm room in the house."

Alex shook his head and swallowed the bite he was chewing. "Sounds like an eventful homecoming. Anything else new?" He picked up his most recent edition of *Car and Driver* magazine and began to flip through it with purpose, not stopping until he found the page he was looking for.

"Besides the chill in the air? No." I paused and took a closer look at what he was reading. "Are you car shopping?"

"After buying groceries and turning on the electricity, getting a car is number three on my list of things to do. It's not fair to ask you to cart me around."

"I don't mind."

"I do."

"So what's it going to be? Another Wagoneer?"

I sat in the chair beside Alex and tried to pretend that I was engaged in the article he was reading- "BMW's Engine of the Future."

"Not a chance. I want something fast. Something James Bond-ish.

I've been thinking a lot about it. I figure that if you're going after Carl Pierce, then the least I could do is be the getaway driver. I'll take you where you need to go in style." Alex looked up from the magazine. He was staring into thin air, imagining the color of his car and the new leather smell of the interior. All at once, he shook his head and laughed. "I still can't believe Joe wanted the Wagoneer."

"It was good of you to give it to him."

"It was the least I could do. I feel bad, though. It's going to cost a lot to keep it running."

"I don't think he minds. He wanted it for sentimental reasons."

I looked from Alex to the article, and then back to Alex. "Is this the car you want? A BMW? An M5?"

"Like Flynt's? No way." Alex's chest puffed out a bit when he said "No." I discretely covered my mouth, so he wouldn't catch me smiling. Yes, Flynt drove an M5. Yes, Flynt was his rival, but I will never forget the look on Alex's face when he first saw Flynt's M5 parked in the lot of Artist's Edge. How he ran his hand down the hood. How he stood drooling over the shiny paint and pristine interior. He was in love... until he found out who drove it. I was somewhat surprised that Alex wouldn't get the car he really wanted just because Flynt Redding drove the same make and model.

"I think I want something I can fix up. A project. Something vintage. A classic."

"That's a lot of work," I remarked.

"It's not like I have a whole lot to do."

"Sure. I guess. Whatever. Like I said before, I don't care if you use my car." I expected Alex to come back with something smart; instead, he sat staring at me while chewing nervously on his lower lip. "Why are you looking at me like that?"

Alex paused another thoughtful moment, and then licked his lips before he continued. "I know that the whole Carl thing is kind of a touchy subject," Alex said in a voice so muffled that I had to lean in to hear him. "I know that, even though you were sent here to find him or... whatever..., that you don't like talking about him much. And under normal circumstances, I might try to shield you from seeing something like this... because my job is to protect -"

"Alex! You're rambling. Just get to the point!"

"Fine." This time he spoke louder. "You're never going to guess who's on page forty-five." Alex smoothed the page flat and then held the magazine up so I could see. I stared at the article, noticing the picture before reading the text. A handsome and distinguished middle-aged man with a very pretty but much younger woman. The man was in the driver's seat of a bright red Aston Martin v12 Zagato. A smug smile spread across his face. I wasn't sure who I was looking at until I read the title.

INTERCESSION

CHAPTER FIVE

Big Boy Toys: Carl Pierce and his Priceless Collection

"Uggh." A chill stole over me. Seeing his name conjured up images I'd rather forget. Like Chloe, Carl's daughter, and my sister. I wished I could erase the memory of her death from my mind. Helpless, I had watched her body descend into a watery grave. I took another look at the picture. I stared at Carl's face and shuddered as I thought about the girls he had locked in his basement. I thought about my biological mother, Eva, and how she had risked her life to set them free. My eyes moved to the redhead bombshell leaning over the driver's side door kissing my monster of a father on the cheek. Eva was dead, but Carl didn't seem to have a problem moving on.

"I knew I shouldn't have shown you. But I just thought that since Carl is your mission, then you might want to know a little bit about your dad." I gave Alex a sharp look to let him know that he used the wrong terminology. "I mean… I thought you might want to know a little bit about… *the man* you're going after."

"He's my biological father, but you're right, I'll have to face it sooner or later. I'm glad you decided to show me."

"No secrets, right?"

"Right, no secrets."

"You know, the car he's driving is worth nearly six hundred thousand."

"Dollars?!" I gasped.

"Yes, dollars."

"Who's the woman?"

"His fiancé. Zandie Burchette."

"Figures. She's pretty."

"Not pretty like Eva. Not pretty like you."

"You're digging up dirt on Carl. You've been doing your homework."

"Not really. I was looking for a car and he just happened to be in the magazine. Seeing him in *Car and Driver* was like a sign from God. At first, I was thinking practical. I was leaning toward a small SUV, something to replace the Wagoneer, but when I saw this, I decided I needed something fast. If we're going up against Carl Pierce, then our weapons need to be just as good... just as fast as his."

"If you say so."

"I'm serious. How about you? Have you started looking into the names on your list?"

"Yeah. I did an online search. Nothing. I searched the first seven names and then gave up"

"Gave up?"

"Too many people with the exact same names. A-Omega should have given me more to go on."

Alex reached into the bag and took out another pastry. "Maybe I should give it a try."

"What are you going to find that I haven't?"

"It won't hurt for me to look, will it?"

"Have at it," I agreed, not able to hide the sarcasm in my voice. I snatched the magazine just as Alex was reaching for his laptop. Alex powered on his computer and tilted the screen so I could see as well.

"Give me a name on your list."

"Gracie Abbot," I told him. "I promise... you're not going to find anything."

Alex shot me a sidelong look. "It's worth a try. You're not going to find it sitting in the coffee shop either."

I scowled and returned to my reading while Alex's fingers moved swiftly across the keyboard.

When he let out an exasperated sigh, I was quick to respond. "Told you so," I said without looking up.

"Yeah, you're right. Too many choices. There's a Gracie Abbott in Charlotte, D.C., Burbank, Tampa. The list goes on."

"Like I said. There's nothing to do but wait."

"Give me another name."

"Okay. Todd Catchitore. Not quite so common. But still, I doubt you find a thing."

Alex began to type then paused. "How do spell the last name? C-A-T-C-H-I-T-O-R-E?"

"Yep."

"That's what I thought." Alex hit return and after studying the list of results that bounced back, he clicked on the first title.

"Humph."

"Humph what?" My eyes shot up from the article and I was now completely focused on the screen.

"I think I found a winner."

I discarded the magazine and reached for the computer, exchanging one for the other in an effortless sweep. Alex had quickly and thoughtfully highlighted the text and now the passage of interest was leaping off the screen, begging me to read it. I was speechless. I glanced at Alex through narrow, suspicious eyes. How could he have stumbled upon something so easily when I had been searching for two weeks and come up with nothing at all? I cocked my head to the side and waited for him to explain. Unspoken words between us. He knew exactly what I was thinking and responded with haste.

"The article was only posted this morning… if that makes you feel any better," he offered with a shrug of his shoulders.

With a scowl, I turned back to the screen. The caption was short, barely a paragraph. It appeared under the events section of the Urban Tulsa Weekly. I doubted that I would find out everything I needed to know about Todd Catchitore in this limited amount of text, and I was more drawn to the picture than the print - a pudgy man with a thick head of curly hair, clad in a striped shirt and a polka dot bow tie. Below the picture was the name, Todd Catchitore. Maybe Alex had found something after all. My eyes moved back up to the article and my heart rate quickened as I began to read.

Rescue to the Rescue

Join Professor Catchitore, better known as ProfC by his students, for a lecture on how to predict the future. Known by many as much more than a professor of history, ProfC, an eccentric but gifted speaker, is also the founder of Rescue, an organization that fights modern day slavery. A discussion about the past, the present, and the future; a lecture that will not disappoint. Join Professor Catchitore on Friday, March 20th at 2 PM at the Harry Kendall College of Arts and Sciences on the University of Tulsa Campus, 800 South Tucker Drive.

Slavery: a single word that I couldn't seem to escape. Funny how, for my entire life, I hadn't considered the word. So wrapped up in my own pain, I never took the time to feel the pain of others. I never thought about what it meant to be a slave or how it felt to be controlled. But on my nineteenth birthday, while I was staying in the cottage on the lake, A-Omega sent me the most unexpected gift. A first edition copy of *Uncle Tom's Cabin*. The story broke my heart while, at the same time, angering me. Months later, after reading Eva Pierce's journal, I discovered several secrets. For nineteen years, I had called Sue and Will, "Mom and Dad," but I had had it all wrong. Eva Pierce was my biological mother, Chloe was my sister, and Carl Pierce, my extremely wealthy biological father, was hiding young girls in his basement. Eva found them. She set them free. Although she never indicated in her journal why Carl was holding them hostage, one could only guess. And then just last week, when Sue showed up unexpected at the cottage, the truth, the whole truth finally came out. How could I have *not* known that my entire family was involved in the fight against human trafficking? How could I have been so blind? Why hadn't anyone bothered to tell me the truth? A-Omega wanted me to follow in my parents' footsteps. I didn't know all of the details, but I was fairly certain that A-Omega wanted me to join the cause, to fight the fight, to stand up for those who have no voice. There was no doubt in my mind that Alex had found the right Todd Catchitore. This was no coincidence. Alex had uncovered the first lead. My mind was racing. I had barely settled in. Things were moving quickly... too quickly. I had come prepared to fight, but was I ready? Was I good enough? Did I know how? Who was I to stand up against a man like Carl Pierce? I recalled the nightmare I had on the plane and I felt the color drain from my face.

I could hardly think about Carl without wondering if I was anything like him. Did I have any of my father's traits? These were my dark thoughts, and they shifted like shadows in the night. A cold sweat. A sick feeling in the pit of my stomach. I glanced at Alex; we didn't share the same expression. He had a smug look on his face. Once again, Alex was ready to fight, and I was ready to run.

"I stand corrected." I forced a smile. "You were right and I was wrong. Alex," I put on an air of enthusiasm. "You did it. You found a name on the list." My lips began to tremble.

"What would you do without me?"

I fell back into Alex's lap and wrapped my arms loosely around his neck. "So, I guess we're going to the seminar?" My voice caught in my throat. "I guess this means the mission has officially begun?"

"Unless you have something better to do."

I thought about my other option: sitting in my bedroom all alone, sifting through the contents of the box, while Sue and Will ignore me.

"Not at all." I planted a kiss on his lips hoping he hadn't felt mine tremble.

"You're not having second thoughts, are you?"

"No. It's a date," my voice quivered. He smiled. Without a doubt, I could tell that Alex was excited about this adventure. And I was too, in a way. But I was scared. Worried. And rightly so. Alex was fearless as usual. He was my strength. Maybe A-Omega had sent the package to me, but we were in this together.

The day had flown by. Alex and I were exhausted but we had accomplished a lot. Groceries: check. Gas, water, and electricity in the name of Ian Limbeaux (the fictitious name Alex used for all legal purposes): check, check, check. Plans for Friday: check. Todd Catchitore's seminar on Past, Present, and Future wasn't until Friday afternoon, but we made plans to leave for Tulsa early Friday morning so we could car shop and grab some lunch before heading to the college.

It was 5:30 when I finally left Alex's, and I made it half way home before remembering the gas light had come on when I started the car this morning. Eager to see Alex, I had put it off. Not so eager to return home, I thought now would be the perfect time to fill up. I could see the QuikTrip sign a quarter mile up the road. I continued through the stoplight, turned on my blinker, and pulled up to the pump. With stars in my eyes and my head in the clouds, I began to fill up my tank with regular unleaded. I left it to pump while I made my way into the gas station to grab a pack of gum and a newspaper. I was bombarded with emotions. Before Alex, I had very few emotions and I lived by my own set of rules. For instance, I never allowed myself to get attached to anything or anyone, because my family never stayed in one place for long. I never took risks, because I knew if I did, there was a good chance I would get hurt. I protected myself, because I had first hand knowledge of how cruel the world could be. Now, all of a sudden, I had a purpose and although I didn't know the details, I knew there was a plan. I was on the right track, the right path. I no longer had my shell, but I felt like I would be okay. Best of all, I was able to take this journey with the person I loved most: Alex. Head still in the clouds, I chose a pack of Spearmint, turned around, and was just about to head for the newspaper stand when I stopped dead in my tracks. A simple seven-letter word brought me back to reality.

MISSING

CHAPTER SIX

*F*riday came quickly. I was surprised. Where had the last four days gone? In the blink of an eye, I found myself seated at a table inside one of Tulsa's finer restaurants, staring out the window at Alex's purchase, a beat up Porsche 56 Speedster that needed new everything. Just two hours earlier, we drove the Honda from Bartlesville to an address on the north side of Tulsa, a junkyard that was selling cars for parts. Alex saw the ad online. The price was right and the car was running… barely. But Alex thought it was perfect and paid in cash.

Alex cleared his throat and began, startling me from my reverie. "You don't have much to say." He ran a hand through his wind blown hair. "Look, I know you think the car's going to be a lot of work, but I like that kind of work… " His voice faded as my thoughts moved from the rusty old hotrod to the poster I saw pinned to the corkboard in the gas station several days ago. Since seeing it, I had hardly thought of anything else. I visualized the red letters in bold caps: MISSING. They were intended to grab the attention of passersby, but the focal point of the poster was buried beneath various advertisements: items for sale, upcoming concerts, and help wanted flyers all tacked to the same bulletin board. The bold red letters had worked; I had taken notice. I had moved past the newspaper stand toward the bulletin board to get a better look. As I began to push away the other slips of paper, curious to find out what *exactly* had gone missing, I recalled a poster I had seen in Kansas last year. It was when Alex and I were en route to Minnesota. "Lost and Injured" was the title of the poster. A yellow parakeet named Freedom had vanished from a local veterinary office and was in desperate need of medical attention. There was a name and number at the bottom of the poster, along with information about the handsome reward offered to anyone who knew the whereabouts of this beloved bird. I wondered what had gone missing now. Another bird? A dog perhaps? But when I pushed away the last advertisement, I found that it was neither. A chill moved over me as I stared at the black and white image.

"It's important, Rae, that I have a dependable way to get you around." Alex's voice was fading in and out, and I was only catching bits and pieces of the conversation. "If protecting you is my *only* job, then I take it seriously."

"Huh?" I asked, glancing at Alex but not giving him my full attention. I was still thinking about the poster of a girl: Jessie Paulman.

Declared missing on February 19th.

Last seen at a fast food restaurant on Peoria.

Five foot two.

One hundred and thirty pounds.

Light brown hair.

Green eyes.

A statistic.

Contact Jackie or the Tulsa police if you have any information.

"See. You're doing it again. You're not even listening. You're here, but you're not," Alex complained.

"Sorry. I was just thinking about the poster."

"Oh." Alex smiled and waved his hand dismissively. "Don't worry about it. I'm sure they've found her." Alex picked up his menu and pursed his lips. "What sounds good?"

It was hard to sit across from Alex and worry. He had paired a clingy black tee shirt with a lightweight heather gray jacket. His hair was wild from the wind, but it looked like he meant for it to be that way. Perfect.

His eyes… intense. Like he was peering into my soul. No one but Alex could do that. I felt all warm and melty. And his mouth. Full. Soft. Gently chewing his lower lip. He had no idea what he was doing to me. No idea at all. Focus, I told myself. Focus!

"I'm not hungry," I sighed.

Alex set his menu on the table and looked me in the eye. "Quit worrying about the poster and eat."

"It's not just the poster, it's that someone covered it up. Is someone's garage sale really more important than a missing girl?" As I recalled repositioning the poster on top of the other ads and securing it with a pushpin, my anger resurfaced and I could feel my cheeks beginning to flush.

"I agree." His voice was now soft and encouraging. "I'm not trying to be insensitive. All I'm saying is that you have your work cut out for you. Your plate's full. Right now, there's nothing you can do about Jessie Paulman. Today we're in Tulsa to meet Todd Catchitore… remember…? The man on your list of names. I just think we should stay focused, that's all." Alex straightened his silverware and reached for the fresh baked bread that was artfully placed in a silver tray at the center of the table. "I'm getting the Beef Wellington and the French Onion Soup," he said, breaking the roll in half and smearing it with butter. "Have you decided?"

"The BLT."

Alex laughed. "One of the finer restaurants in town and you're ordering a bacon, lettuce, and tomato sandwich."

"It's on the menu. They wouldn't have added it to the menu if they didn't expect someone to order it."

Alex smiled. "I know everything there is to know about you, but you never cease to amaze me."

Not taking Alex's words of wisdom to heart, I continued to think about Jessie Paulman through lunch. I kept eye contact and tried to converse, but something was gnawing at me. Was it Jessie's age? By looking at the picture, I could tell that Jessie was fairly young, maybe my age, but most likely a little younger. Although a cause for concern, I didn't think it was that. Was it the date she disappeared? She was last seen on

February 19th. That was over a month ago. Statistics say that if a missing person isn't found within the first few days, the chances of finding them drop drastically. Maybe that was it. Maybe Jessie wasn't to be found. Her parents? I couldn't stop myself from thinking about how her parents were feeling and doing so made me feel even worse. Her parents felt terrible. They had to. No. Beyond terrible. I couldn't imagine. I didn't want to imagine. Not knowing. That had to be the worst. And then I realized what was bothering me, distracting me to such an extent that I couldn't enjoy a nice lunch with my boyfriend. Guilt reared its ugly head again. I had inflicted the exact same pain on Sue and Will when I ran away. I didn't do it to be mean or selfish. I caused them pain. I brought trouble. I knew it. They knew it. I did it to protect them. I left a letter, but I didn't tell them where I was going. I didn't even bother to contact them when Alex and I arrived at the cottage. Not even a simple email to let them know I was okay. They must have been worried sick. It was no wonder Will wouldn't speak to me. But then I reminded myself that I was not like Jessie Paulman, and Sue and Will were not the average mom and dad. Sue and Will hadn't hung missing person posters with my name and picture, nor had they bothered to look for me. Only now, after digging up all of the buried secrets, did I understand why. To post pictures of me across the state would have done little to help them with their cause, which was to keep me safe by keeping me hidden. I only hoped that Jessie Paulman was safe in the same way that I was safe. That she was with someone who was taking care of her. Now more than ever I realized that this world is a big, bad place. No place for a young girl to be on her own. I was so naïve and stupid. I hoped Jessie had more sense than I did. I hoped her parents found her soon.

As I followed behind Alex in my Honda, I panicked, concerned that his 56 Speedster didn't have the wherewithal to make it to the college. Making matters worse, Alex took a wrong turn and we got stuck in road construction. Because of this, we were running late for Todd Catchitore's discussion on human rights. Alex knew I was nervous about meeting Todd, and being late to the conference only added to my anxiety. This was my first lead, and already I was blowing it. By the time I pulled my Honda into the open parking slot next to Alex's new ride, I was completely irritated. With an umbrella over our heads, we scurried out of the rain and into an auditorium filled with, at the most, fifty students and professors combined. Blaming the weather for the less than satisfactory attendance, Professor Catchitore delayed the seminar a bit, hopeful that more would arrive. As he paced the stage telling stories to bide the time, Alex and I took a seat near the front and settled in. There were still a few stragglers, and I felt relieved that I was not the only one who was tardy. After fifteen minutes had passed, a lady at the back of the room shut the double doors and Todd Catchitore began his discussion on the past, present, and future of slavery.

"I'd like a show of hands. How many of you out there in the audience love history?"

Several hands lifted into the air, and I assumed they were Professor Catchitore's students and were promised class credit for attending the seminar and showing enthusiasm on the topic. I glanced around the room and noticed others in attendance sat undecided with hesitant arms wavering at their sides, wondering if perhaps ProfC was asking a trick question. Todd waited for a few more hands to rise before moving on.

"Not at all the numbers I had hoped for, but I have to say, I'm not surprised. So, if you are *not* here for a history lesson, then I'm guessing you're here because you want to know the future."

The room filled with applause and Professor Catchitore flashed a smile.

"Now, what would you say if I told you that 'history' and 'the future' are more closely related than you think?"

A hand shot into the air. ProfC pointed to a well-dressed boy sitting on the front row and nodded.

"I've always been taught that we shouldn't *dwell* on the past but that instead, we should look toward our future."

"Dwelling upon something is very different than forgetting about it. Two opposite ends of the spectrum."

Chatter rose from the crowd and I guessed everyone was thinking the same thing: *Where was the quirky professor going with this?* ProfC stepped to the edge of the stage and looked out at the audience without saying a word. With tented fingers and downcast eyes, he began to pace back and forth in front of the podium.

Finally he spoke. "As a small child, I fell in love with history. My father was a professor at a small community college in the town where I grew up. He is the most knowledgeable man I know. When I was young, he would tell me a story before bed, but it wasn't a run of the mill fairytale like most children get. Each story was a short lesson in history. The stories were not in chronological order; he skipped around quite a bit. One night, he would tell me a story about World War II and the next night, he would teach me a lesson on the French Revolution. I hung on every word my father said and after years of listening attentively, I arrived at one conclusion: History repeats itself over and over again."

The college boy in the front row raised his hand again. Appearing to appreciate his interest, ProfC smiled and motioned at the boy, giving him the go ahead to speak.

"It seems to me that if history *does* repeat itself, then we could prevent wars and economic downfall. It seems to me that we could pick up a history book and read about all of the things *not* to do."

"A boy after my own heart," ProfC chuckled. "I couldn't agree more and as a humanitarian and a defender of human rights, I have often thought the same thing." He drummed his fingers on the podium. With pursed lips and a furrowed brow, Todd Catchitore looked out at the small crowd. "If it were that simple, then why don't we? Why don't we pick up a history book? Why don't we take a look at our past so we can change our future? I'll tell you why. It has something to do with the eyes… the ears. Let me explain."

The professor stopped drumming his fingers, reached beneath the podium, and returned with a remote control. With the touch of a button, a screen began to descend slowly from the ceiling. *The eyes? The ears?* What did the professor mean when he said the eyes keep us from correcting our mistakes? I thought the professor was being rather vague, and I could hardly wait for him to explain. I wasn't the only one, either. As I glanced around the room, I noticed that everyone's attention was fixed on the stage. While waiting for the quirky history professor to resume his discussion, my mind began to wander; I began to think about how I would introduce myself to this man. His name was on my list. Did he know me? Was he expecting me?

When the professor cleared his throat, I snapped back to the present. He pushed another button and the screen changed from white to blue.

"I am getting ready to show a short film. This film is a collection of photos and short clips from four great atrocities that occurred in the last three hundred years." ProfC looked at his watch and tapped the face of it. "I could spend a year teaching about each one. Unfortunately, I only have an hour. My mother always told me that a picture is worth a thousand words, and I hope you find that to be true in this case. Let the images speak to you, and please be sure to take notice of any similarities you see between the images as well as any differences."

When ProfC nodded his head, the lady standing at the back of the auditorium dimmed the lights and a moment later, the film began to roll.

INTERCESSION

CHAPTER SEVEN

*T*he film was set to a song (an eerie melodic mixture of stringed instruments, electronica, drums, and the human voice) that perfectly joined the past with the present.

The first image to appear was a sketch of an African man on bent knee. Clad in nothing more than a white loincloth and shackles, the caption below him said, "Am I not a man and a brother?" The next image was a black and white photo of makeshift gallows where several rail thin men stood on a platform waiting to be hung. Campmates were forced to watch the execution. Below the image were the words, "Behold the fate of those who try to escape!"

A crematorium: brick machines where bodies were turned into ash.

A metal dog cage beside which sat a roll of masking tape.

A pair of shackles.

An Asian woman with her eyes closed. Cuts across her face. Bruised beyond recognition.

A huddle of filthy young children. Faces smeared with soot.

A baby blue house with boarded windows and chipping paint.

A group of children seated together on a bench. Knobby knees. Naked. Protruding ribs. Skin draped over bone. Below the image was the single word: Auschwitz.

A teenage girl of Hispanic descent. Weak smile. Sad eyes.

A heartbreaking clip of a manmade trench being filled with naked, lifeless bodies.

A little boy. Dark brown eyes. Peeking between gaps of barbed wire.

A boney forearm tattooed with a series of five numbers.

A crime scene: body bag, yellow tape, and a rundown apartment for a backdrop.

A truck stop.

A black and white image of uniformed officers looking up at a burning building. Crumpled, broken bodies on the ground.

A sign reading Dachau.

A photo of several men peering out of hollow eyes through a fence of twisted barbed wire.

A preteen girl standing on the corner. She wore a smirk on her face but her eyes told a different story: hopeless. The infected sores running up and down her arms served as her shackles. Forced dependency.

It was brutal looking at a picture of someone so damaged… so broken. I wiped a tear from my cheek and looked over at Alex in time to catch him dabbing at the corner of his eye. A girl who couldn't have been any older than thirteen; she was trying to hide her pain behind a heart of stone. The film rolled on.

A shabby room with scarred concrete walls. Layers of color showed through the chipping paint. A thin mattress lay on the floor.

An overseas cargo crate that was broken open with bodies stacked inside.

The sketch of a slave being branded. Marked by his owner.

A dark skinned girl with tear stained cheeks.

A gas chamber.

A newspaper article from 1911: One hundred and fifty perish in factory fire; women and girls trapped in ten-story building. Lost in flames or hurl themselves to death.

The last picture was a sketch of a slave being whipped by his owner while other slaves were forced to watch.

When the screen went black, light returned to the auditorium. The professor was standing behind the podium looking out at the audience.

"History is full of horrible tragedy and there is not enough time in my life to give each tragedy the attention it deserves. What I'd like to know is this: What can *you* tell me about these images?"

A single hand shot into the air, and ProfC pointed to a girl on the front row.

"I saw pictures of the Trans-Atlantic Slave Trade."

"You're correct. Anyone else?"

"Some of the pictures were from the Holocaust."

"Good. Very good. What about the other images? What about little boy missing his two front teeth? What about the cargo crate?" ProfC waited for someone to respond, but no one did. "What about the girl standing on the corner. The dog kennel?" Professor Catchitore paused to smooth his mustache. "What about the truck stop? Anyone?" I knew what answer the professor was looking for. I had heard of the dog crate case before. A fifteen-year-old girl from Phoenix had gotten into some trouble with her parents and ran away to teach them a lesson. Later that day, she hopped into the car with a friend and a boy she didn't know. She was bound with duct tape. They taped up her hands and then stuck tape over her eyes and mouth. They told her that if she screamed, they would shoot her. Shortly after arriving at her trafficker's house, she was welcomed by several men who were waiting to introduce her to the world of human trafficking. She was told that if she didn't cooperate or if she tried to escape, they would hurt her sister. To humiliate her, she was forced to curl up inside of a dog kennel. The story was all over the news. You couldn't miss it. And the image of a girl locked in a cage quickly became a symbol for child sex trafficking in the state of Arizona. ProfC exhaled deeply; his sigh echoed through the silent auditorium. "How about similarities? Did you see any similarities between the images?"

This time the response was greater. The room was filled with students who wanted to answer, and Prof C took a moment to consider who he would call on first. He pointed to a squatty girl sitting two rows up from me and to my left. She stood up slowly and smoothed her skirt.

"A victim." She paused, waiting for affirmation. "In many of the pictures, there was a victim."

"Very good," ProfC said, then moved on to the next student.

"Many of the victims were held by force!" shouted a girl somewhere at the back of the room.

"Yeah! They were held against their will," the boy next to her shouted. "The shackles. The barbed wire."

"They were shamed!" shouted another.

"They were treated inhumanely," yelled the husky boy seated beside me.

Spontaneous shouts filled the room. No longer in control of his audience, ProfC interlaced his fingers behind his back and began to pace the stage.

"They were killed while others were forced to watch."

ProfC stopped pacing and lifted a hand in the air. A hush fell over the crowd. "You're all very perceptive and all of these answers are correct, but there is one important answer that you have neglected to mention. I'm looking for a single word. Any ideas?"

I didn't realize that I would react so impulsively to his question. I wasn't the type of person that liked to respond publicly, even if I knew the correct answer. But when the professor looked at me and nodded, I realized that my hand was indeed raised, and that everyone in attendance was staring at me, waiting to hear what I had to say. I stood up slowly and locked eyes with ProfC.

"Slavery," I said, then quickly sat back down.

"You're absolutely right. Slavery is what ties all of these images together. Excellent. Now, can you tell me the differences?"

Silence. A single hand raised into the air. "The dates were different."

"Good. Now tell me this. *Who* were the victims?"

A girl seated in front of me raised a confident hand.

"Casey," ProfC said, pointing to the girl with curly blond hair. Because he knew her name, I assumed she was one of his students.

"In the sixteenth through the nineteenth centuries, the victims were Africans. They were brought to the New World on ships. Many died before they ever reached land. Many more died upon arrival. Still more died while in servitude. And after they were emancipated, hundreds of thousands of former slaves died from malnutrition, poverty, and disease. Millions of lives were lost."

The well-dressed boy on the front row raised his hand and Professor Catchitore called on him at once.

"The Industrial Revolution. Women, children, orphans, and immigrants were the victims. They worked in slave-like conditions with little or no pay. And the image of the newspaper article. I believe that was The Triangle Factory Fire of 1911. The fire took the lives of over 100 women, primarily Jewish and Italian immigrants. It was found out that the exit doors were chained shut so the women couldn't leave. They were trapped in the fire. Many decided to jump to their death rather than be burned alive."

My first impression of the boy was that he was a kiss up. Dressed in an argyle sweater and khakis, it appeared that he was attempting to mimic ProfC's style. But I had to hand it to him; he knew what he was talking about. I remembered studying about the Triangle Factory Fire in New York City. The Industrial Revolution had reached a crossroads, and the tragedy became the catalyst that would lead to reform.

"That's exactly right." The professor gave the boy an affirmative nod. "What about the other images? What about the video clips?" He waited for another hand to rise. The auditorium was silent. "Anyone?"

Finally, I saw the professor gesture. I glanced over my left shoulder and saw a slip of a girl with dark hair standing alone in the shadows at the back of the room. Holding onto the seatback in front of her, she addressed the professor.

"Some of the other images and video clips were from World War II. The victims were predominately Jewish, but others were targets, too. Homosexuals. The mentally ill. Physically handicapped. Jehovah's Witnesses. Africans. Gypsies. They were starved and beaten. They were made to live in unfit conditions. They were forced to work until they could no longer stand. They were slaves. They were murdered."

ProfC moved behind the podium. He licked his lips and smoothed his mustache. "The definition of the word 'slave' will not surprise you. A slave is a person held in servitude as the possession of another. What *will* surprise you is that slavery still exists in the world today. It is in the United States. It is in this very state."

Chatter erupted from the audience. ProfC held up his hand to silence the crowd.

"Several weeks ago, I was discussing the topic of modern day slavery in class. One student looked at me concerned, and she said, 'Slavery was abolished in the United States in 1865. It's illegal. I'm surprised to hear that it exists at all. So when did slavery return to this country?' My answer was this: 'Did it ever leave?' I am referring to human trafficking. Surely you've heard this term before." ProfC didn't wait for an answer. "Human trafficking is the tragedy that no one recognized. Human trafficking is modern day slavery. Maybe you didn't know that slavery still exists, and this is why: While slaves are treated in much the same way as they were hundreds of years ago, there is one difference. The face of slavery has changed."

"So who *are* the victims?" asked a heavyset boy with glasses seated near the back of the room.

"Human Trafficking is thought to be a 32 billion-dollar-per-year industry and that number is only getting larger. It cuts across race, gender, and age. The 'who' has changed and, are you ready for this? While certain groups of people may be more vulnerable, no one is exempt. It doesn't matter where you live or who you are. If your heart is beating, you could be the next victim of slavery in the twenty-first century. Shackles. Barbed wire and guns. Dog crates and masking tape. So while each victim might be bound in a different way, one thing remains the same: they are bound. They have *NO* control." Shocked chatter arose from the crowd and the professor patiently waited for the noise to die down before he continued.

"We can't *change* history and history can be hard to look at when the past isn't pretty. However, if we can face the past, then we *can* learn from it and use what we learn to better the future. So the question remains: Will we look at the past? Will we address the problems of the present? Will we make the world a better, safer place for our children... for our grandchildren? We can watch movies about slavery and every kind of social injustice. They might move us, but do they make us move? Does the desire to make a difference lead to action? That's the question we should be asking ourselves. Earlier, I told you that our inability to recognize the problem has a lot to do with our eyes and ears. That's because sometimes our eyes and ears just aren't enough. Sometimes we need to use our heart in order to grasp the scope of the problem. To feel the pain of others. To sympathize... to empathize."

Professor Catchitore glanced at his wrist and tapped the face of his watch. "I need to be wrapping it up, but I can give you one word of advice:

you must look at the past if you want to change the future. Darkness exists in this world. Slavery has been around since the beginning of time. We can sit in this auditorium and talk about slavery, about human trafficking. We can curse it. We can bury our heads in the sand and pretend it doesn't exist, but that doesn't make it go away. We might even be moved, but hesitant to move into action. I encourage you not to wait. Take a stand! In life I have found that it is better to light a candle than to curse the darkness."

With a single click of the remote, the screen retracted into the ceiling and ProfC ended the presentation. "I hope you will all join me for my next lecture titled 'Preying on the Weak'. I will be discussing methods of coercion and intimidation."

ProfC was a far cry from suave, but he was a dynamic speaker. He had initially captured the attention of the audience with his quirky attire - a button up plaid shirt with a bright orange bow tie. Nevertheless, it didn't take long for his passion on the topic of slavery in the 21st century to become contagious. Adults and college students alike had sat on the edge of their chairs as Professor Catchitore discussed how history repeats itself over and over again.

It was 2:15. The seminar was over and people were filing out of the auditorium. I realized that it was now or never. I needed to introduce myself. To tell the professor why I was here. How I found him. I needed to ask him why his name was on my list. ProfC descended the stairs at the side of the stage. I stood up and walked into the aisle. I took a step toward him and hesitated. Another student beat me to him. Not wanting to appear too anxious, I twirled my promise ring around my finger and waited for Professor Catchitore to finish his conversation before moving any closer. Goosebumps formed on my skin and my stomach turned. *This is crazy!* All at once, my bag began to vibrate. Thankful for the distraction, I reached inside my purse and felt around for my phone. I glanced at the professor. He was steering the student toward an information table at the back of the auditorium. With my hand still fishing around inside my purse, I moved quickly toward the stage. I was less than ten feet away when I felt the vibrating object beneath my fingers. I pulled it out and stopped short when I read the text. Completely baffled, I looked up at the professor. He was staring at me hopefully. Perhaps he was curious why I was the only person in the room who answered his question about slavery correctly. Well, if he wanted to know, then I could tell him about my family. That would be a start. I could tell him about Carl. I could tell him about A-Omega. I retrained my eyes on my phone and stared at the screen.

Wait!

I had received six text messages from A-Omega in less than fifteen seconds.

Wait!
Wait!
Wait!
Wait!
Wait!

I let my eyes wander back to the professor. I had caught his attention. I glanced at my phone. My heart was pounding in my chest. I could feel the professor's eyes on me. *Wait? Wait for what?* I wondered. I took another step toward the professor to test the waters but before my foot touched the ground, my phone began to buzz again. Another text. The exact same message.

Wait!

I moved my eyes from the phone to ProfC. No longer smiling, the professor looked confused. It seemed that A-Omega didn't want me to meet Todd Catchitore… at least not right now. *But why?* His name was on my list. Regardless, I had promised to follow their lead. So without understanding, I walked out of the auditorium and didn't look back. Alex was thoroughly confused and didn't understand my change of heart. Even after I showed him the text from A-Omega, he disagreed.

Todd Catchitore's name *was* on my list and he thought I should have, at the very least, said hello. "This is the guy," he told me. "This is the guy that can help you put Carl away."

In disagreement, we left the college. Alex wanted to look for car parts while he was in the city and insisted that his feelings would not be hurt if I decided not to join him. The weather was still cold and wet and lightning illuminated a sunless sky. As I sat inside my car watching through a rain-streaked windshield as Alex pulled away, a thought occurred to me. Alex had plans and I had nowhere to be. Absolutely nothing to do. Why not take a short detour before heading home? I wasn't too far from the Pierce estate, and I couldn't resist the temptation to drive by. I hadn't seen the mansion in a year. So I hopped on Highway 244 and drove in the direction of downtown. Twenty minutes later, I was parked in front of Carl's house. I didn't care about being discrete. Today the house looked even more ominous than it did last year. Maybe because I knew the things that happened behind these walls, and I knew the kind of man who lived within.

The mansion sat back from the road on a lot that was at least three acres, which was rare in a part of town where real estate was expensive and hard to come by. I took in the massive stone structure with its high-pitched roof and copper guttering. Heavy curtains still covered every window. Only now did I realize why Carl would want to hide behind dark panels of velvet. The good things in life could be done in the light of day, without being fearful should anyone's eyes fall upon the happenings, but what went on inside the Pierce estate was not right. It was shameful. It was wrong, and therefore, it could only be done in darkness. *I could walk up to the door right now*, I thought. *I could end this once and for all.* Sitting in front of Carl's house, I could feel my stomach start to sour and beads of sweat erupting from every pore. I turned on the air and took a deep breath. My thoughts were tangled. I was calm and nervous. Confused and certain. Scared and undaunted. Timid and bold. Hesitant and ready. My blood was boiling. If ProfC's discussion was intended to rev me up, it had accomplished just that. Now, more than ever, I had a burning desire to fight, to put Carl away, to lock him up, to make him pay for what he had done. I wanted to ruin his life in the same way he had ruined so many others. A-Omega told me my mission was Carl Pierce, but now they were telling me to wait. Were they playing games with me? *Wait!* It was the first direct message I had received since arriving in Oklahoma. I promised A-Omega I would listen and while every part of me wanted to go after Carl Pierce right now, I knew that I must follow A-Omega's lead. As I pulled slowly away from Carl's, my father's, large stone mansion, the dream I had on the airplane came back to me and understanding hit me all at once. I was no match for Carl. I was weak. Maybe that was why A-Omega wanted me to wait. I wasn't strong enough. But would I ever be?

"Why," I shouted. "Why *me*? You gave me Todd Catchitore's name. So why do you want me to wait?"

Before I even finished asking my question, my phone began to buzz. Anticipating that it might be another text from A-Omega, I picked it up and discovered I was right.

A-Omega

Better a patient man than a warrior, a man who controls his temper than one who takes a city.

CHAPTER EIGHT

*B*ecause my mission had started out with a bang, I had never taken into consideration that my patience might, at some point, be tested. I had never been a patient person and lately, I was dragging around the house with nothing to do but wait, and the waiting made me want to go after Carl even more.

Better a patient man than a warrior, a man who controls his temper than one who takes a city. What was that supposed to mean? It was the middle of April. It had been four long weeks with no direction from A-Omega, and no new leads. My thoughts were a tempest. Some days, I thought about how my mission would end. Other nights, I would lie wide-awake going over the speech ProfC made, wondering if I had missed something. I now had at least twenty-five questions that I wanted to ask him. How had he become involved with human trafficking? Had he received a box from A-Omega, too? Did he know Carl Pierce? What are the police doing to stop this atrocity? What could *I* do to help? And so on. Patience was not one of my virtues, and I couldn't understand what good it did for A-Omega to inform me of my objective if they didn't want me to do anything about it. Carl Pierce was the goal. Why not just go after him? He was my biological father. I knew where he lived. Better yet, I knew how to break into his basement. I had done it once before. Didn't A-Omega want Carl Pierce locked up?

As each minute ticked by, I thought about how many people, how many girls he was harming, how many human beings were being mistreated because of him. But instead of putting an end to his evil schemes, I was waiting, keeping my eyes open, grasping for anything that might lead me in the right direction. I felt as though A-Omega had left me hanging. They were holding out on me. They led me into a mission without any information. They told me to go on this journey, but they had forgotten to give me a map. To top it off, I had left Alexandria, my favorite place in the world, to return to this. Ever since my arrival, home was not the most hospitable place in the world. Dad spent his free time asleep in his recliner. It had been a month and we hadn't even made eye contact, much less conversed. It was depressing to see him so down, so unlike the Will I used to know. Sue and I were speaking, but she was spending so much time in the garage and the front yard preparing all of her pots for planting that she was more like a ghost than a mother. I think Will's withdrawn behavior was bothering her just as much as it was bothering me, and she was immersing herself in her favorite pastime until we all got over the hump. Maybe she thought that if the inside of the house wasn't looking pretty, she could at least create a facade. So while my mother planted and spent her time in the makeshift garage/potting shed/workshop, I did the only thing I knew to do. I pounded out my problems on the pavement. It was the only time I traded my combat boots for my Saucony's. Running was good. It gave me time to think, to sort out my feelings. To come up with a rational explanation for what I was doing here. I always returned from my run feeling emotionally lighter than when I left. Like maybe the whole world wasn't really resting on *my* shoulders.

I was lacing up my shoes when I heard a knock at my bedroom door. Cocoa's ears perked when the light rapping woke her from her nap. She was still curled up in a ball on my bed, but when Sue peeked into my room, Cocoa jumped up at once and greeted her at the door.

"Can I come in?"

"Sure," I said without enthusiasm.

Mom had a gracefulness about her when she walked. I looked up from tying my laces, and I watched her. She had the natural ability to glide across the floor and draw attention. Clearly another indication that I was not hers. I instantly began to wonder from whom I had received my clumsiness. Carl? I shuddered at the thought of him and focused on my sneakers.

"You seem a little down lately." Mom sat on the end of my bed and patted the mattress for Cocoa to join her. Cocoa wagged her tail and immediately followed instructions. Once on the bed, she rolled onto her back so Mom could scratch her belly.

I shrugged my shoulders but didn't respond.

"I know Dad's being stubborn, but he'll come around."

Mom was wearing a sleeveless shirt this morning, and I could see the long pink scar that ran down her arm. I used to trace it with my finger when I was little and she would wince as though it hurt. I closed my eyes and hugged my legs.

"What's wrong, Rae?"

"Everything." My face was resting on my knees and my voice came out a bit muffled.

"Can you narrow it down?"

"We can start with Dad, if you like."

"What about him."

"I've had time to do a lot of thinking and now that I know almost everything about my past, things are beginning to make more sense. I've come to the realization that Dad... Will never wanted to deal with me."

"Rae." The tone of my mother's voice changed, now more cool than comforting, she was warning me to watch my mouth. "That's not fair."

"I think maybe he tried... at first. But when he wasn't successful, he just brushed my problems under the carpet. Now that I'm back, it's much worse. I feel like he's brushed *me* under the carpet."

"Just give him time. I promise he'll come around. So is it *just* Dad, or is there something more? Is everything okay with Alex?"

"Everything's fine, better than fine with Alex."

"I haven't seen him around. Just thought I would ask."

I rolled my eyes. "I can't imagine why."

Sue shrugged her shoulders. "I miss him. It would be nice to see him soon." Mom placed a curled finger to her lips and tilted her head to the side. Mom was slipping into psychiatrist mode... I could tell by her expression. She couldn't help herself. It was her job to get to the bottom of things. To solve problems. But I hated when she did this, when she treated me like one of her patients instead of her daughter. "So if it's not Alex, then what else is wrong?"

I hugged my knees tighter. I was exhausted... mentally. I decided to let her have her way. Maybe she would surprise me. Maybe she could help. "When you started with A-Omega, did you ever feel unsure of yourself?"

"Sometimes... I guess." The hesitance in her voice made me question whether or not she could relate.

"I'm scared, but I think I'm ready. A-Omega told me to wait. But I don't feel like waiting."

"You remind me a lot of Nana." At these words, Sue grabbed my attention. "She always said 'If you want it done the right way, you just have to do it yourself.'"

"I agree."

"But sometimes, we just aren't strong enough, Rae. Sometimes we need help."

"Right now I'm doing nothing. Right now I want to quit."

"You can run away from a lot of things in life, but you can't run away from who you are or what you were meant to be."

"That's a great question, Mom. Who *am* I?" I don't think I know anymore. I'm not sure I ever knew."

"Things happen *to* you, so things can happen *in* you, so that things can happen *through* you. You have to be worked *in* you before you can be worked *through*." I considered what she was saying. "You'll hear something soon. Be patient."

Tears of frustration were forming against my will. I turned my head and surreptitiously moved my hand across my eyes. "I quit school," I told her, now lowering my voice as I calmed. "I came home. I'm being good. I'm doing better. I'm trying."

"And it *will* be fine. I promise." Mom ran her hand through her hair and smiled. I glanced at the scar on her arm. Mom had been through a lot, too. She knew what she was talking about. She had made it through the storm. She survived. She brought me hope.

Still hugging my knees, I looked into her eyes. "Thanks mom. Thanks for always knowing the right thing to say. For never giving up on me."

"That's what I'm here for, Sunshine."

Sunshine. The nickname she had chosen for me years ago. Considering that I was, for the most part, a dark and brooding creature, I loathed the name because it didn't fit. I can't remember many times when I felt all bright and sunny. But now that I knew the meaning behind the term of endearment, the name was growing on me, and for the first time, I didn't shudder when she said it.

Mom motioned at the window, drawing attention to the darkening sky. "If you're going to go for a run, you'd better get movin'. More severe weather on the way."

As I pounded down the gravel road, my thoughts drifted from my mother to Jessie Paulman. Why couldn't I get this girl out of my mind? Drawn to the poster like a magnet, I felt like it had been left there just for me. I was supposed to see it. And because Jessie's face had been hidden behind a slew of other ads, it was apparent that no one else had paid too much attention. I hoped Alex was right. I hoped Jessie's parents had found her. More likely than not, she was safe and sound, and I was the one who was worrying. I slowed as I reached the stop sign that marked the end of the gravel road. I looked both ways before crossing Silverlake, and then built up speed until I reached a full sprint. I thought about the day, four weeks ago, when I sat outside Carl Pierce's mansion. I could have gone up to the door, but I didn't. I tried to tell myself it was because A-Omega had told me to wait. But that wasn't the entire truth; I was scared. All at once, my stomach lurched and I felt nauseous. I reminded myself of what happened last time I went after someone who had weapons that were larger than mine. I had nearly gotten myself killed and taken Alex down with me in the process. But that was back when I was trying to protect myself. Now I was with A-Omega. I had made the decision. They promised to show me the truth. They promised me protection. All I had to do was follow their lead.

"Where are you now?" I cried out. "I don't understand why Carl is so ruthless. How could someone be that cruel? I don't understand why Will is so angry when I should be the one who is angry with him for lying. I don't understand why you brought me here when all you want me to do is wait. It doesn't make sense. Have you changed your mind about me? What do you want from me? If you do still want me, I'm here. I'm right here. I'm ready. I'm ready to go after Carl. I'm ready to fight. Please help me understand. Please," I begged. The only response was the thunder that rumbled overhead and the lightning that flashed before me.

When I returned from my run, I glanced into the living room and noticed that Will was stretched out in his recliner, as usual. He looked so serious when he slept with his lips pursed, his lids shut tight, and a wrinkle in his brow. I tiptoed across the wood floor and observed Will for a moment before I decided to sit down on the sofa beside his chair. As I gazed upon his sleeping form, I recalled a moment we shared before my high school graduation, just after I had snuck into Chloe Pierce's dungeon. I had taken his bird watching binoculars on the mission to Chloe's, and I was attempting to return them to the shelf in his office before he noticed they were gone. When he caught me, he didn't ask about the binoculars; instead, he asked me why I was holding my side. I could have told him that I fell down Chloe's basement stairs and had broken a rib or two. I could have been honest with him, but I wasn't. When he asked what was wrong with my side, I told him "nothing." He told me that he wanted to take a look at it, and I was hateful in return. He sensed that something was wrong, that I was not well, and he wanted to help. I reminded him that he was a shrink, not a real doctor. Ouch.

It was no wonder Dad brushed things under the carpet. He didn't know what else to do. It wasn't that he hadn't tried to be there for me, to fix me, to help me, to love me. He had always been there, but I had pushed him away. If someone continued to push me away, I wonder how many times I would try to get close before calling it quits. Will had tried his hardest for eighteen years. I focused on how his hands were folded across his chest. It was sort of morbid, but with his hands folded in such a fashion, it seemed he was more fit for a casket than a recliner. Had he given up? Had Will given up on me? I pulled the Merino wool blanket from the back of the sofa. Very gently, so that I wouldn't wake him, I lay the throw over the top of his body.

"Dad," I said. I waited a moment for a response, but nothing came. "Dad," I continued. "I just want you to know that I love you and that I'm sorry. I'm sorry if I let you down. I'm sorry I pushed you away whenever you tried to get close." I could feel tears welling up in my eyes and for the first time since arriving in Bartlesville, the spot on my chest just beneath my brooch felt warm and tingly, just like it did when I put it on for the very first time. Just like it did after I accepted A-Omega's offer. I grasped my chest, letting my hand envelope the pin. Hot. Hotter. I released it. How bizarre. I closed my lids and felt the wetness spill onto my cheeks. "I'm sorry that I never let you fix me. I know you tried." I waited for him to say something, anything, but not even my apology stirred him. "I love you, Dad." Will shifted in his recliner but didn't wake. I stood over him for a moment before turning around and ascending the stairs to my room. Once inside my safe haven, I shut the door and walked into my closet. On tiptoes, I reached up to the top shelf and felt for the box. Pulling it down, I grabbed the journal from inside and for the first time since receiving it, began to write on the blank pages.

April 19th

I am following Your path. I'm looking for You. I am listening for Your voice. I want to hear from You. I have all of these gifts that You have given me. They're just sitting in a box. I don't know how to use them. I need Your help, but You're quiet. Please show me how to use these gifts.

INTERCESSION

CHAPTER NINE

*I*t was the last week of April and the rain hadn't let up. I hadn't seen much sun since we touched down in Tulsa five weeks ago. There was standing water in the fields beside our house and each new inch of rain threatened to submerge the road. Will still wasn't talking to me and because of this, I couldn't imagine what life would be like trapped inside the house with him and Sue. Rough. So every night, I prayed for the sun to shine and every morning, I woke to the sound of rain pelting against my bedroom window. The weather wasn't the only thing that was bad. Just like the dreary skies, I was gloomy and as the storms worsened, so did my negative attitude. Not wanting to get out in the rain, I would sit in my bedroom and let my mind run wild. I thought about the short video I saw during ProfC's seminar. The images broke my heart. They were hard to look at. The professor said that history is hard to look at when the past isn't pretty and he was absolutely right. My past wasn't a pretty picture, and I was having trouble dealing with my own indiscretions. A-Omega wanted me to smooth the path for others. But how was I supposed to help others when I couldn't even help myself? My thoughts were gale force winds, completely destructive and creating such a racket in my brain that I couldn't hear anything else.

One night, I was complaining to Mom and she was quick to tell me a story about the Prophet Elijah who ran for his life after speaking truth to the evil King Ahab and his wife Jezebel. Elijah wanted to hear God's voice and standing on top of a mountain, Elijah waited for God to pass by. Soon Elijah found himself in the middle of a furious gale, but the Lord was not in the wind. After the wind, there was an earthquake, but the Lord was not in the earthquake. After the earthquake, there came fire. But God wasn't in the fire, either. It wasn't until everything fell still that Elijah heard the voice of God. In a gentle whisper, God told Elijah to go back the way he had come. Elijah was to return to the exact place he had run away from and follow God's lead.

I had forgotten about the story of Elijah on the run, and I was very thankful that Mom reminded me of it. It was comforting to know that even prophets of God ran away every once in a while, and that even men like Elijah got tired and wanted to quit. I wished the storms would stop so I could hear God's voice. In the meantime, I planned to make the most of things. Alex and I were going to take a little adventure. I had spent my senior year in Bartlesville and hadn't seen a single site and from what I was hearing, there was quite a bit to see.

"The shrunken heads were not only the most disgusting thing I've seen all day, but strangely enough, they were also my favorite."

"Sicko," Alex snorted.

"What was your favorite part?" I asked as Alex pulled out of the Woolaroc parking lot.

"The guns," Alex replied without elaborating.

The dark skies and rainy days were affecting Alex's mood, too. Over the past couple of days, Alex had grown distant and I was pretty sure the weather was bringing him down. I thought getting out of the house might be good for the both of us. A little excursion to lighten the mood. My plan hadn't really backfired, but it hadn't met my expectations either.

Earlier this afternoon, on the way into the park, an old man at the ticket counter named Lyle told us to take caution passing over the bridge as we drove toward the museum. "It's been raining for a solid month and a half," he told us. "The bad news is the river is up and by supper time, the road will be impassable. The good news is the visitor count is down and you'll most likely have the entire museum to yourselves." He told us that we looked like a nice couple and then gave us a card with the name of the museum manager, Wanda Carlisle, on it. He suggested that once we got inside, we ask her about the "special" tour. Lyle was right. When we parked the car and walked into the museum, we discovered that it was deserted. But it wasn't until we found Wanda that I realized just how special the tour was that we were getting ready to go on. Not only would we be guided through the museum, but through various rooms of the lodge as well, rooms that were, on any other day, off limits to visitors. Wanda was a colorful lady with a natural gift for storytelling and as she told stories of the happenings behind these walls, I felt like I was a part of the past, like I was living in the Wild Wild West. But Alex wasn't sharing in my excitement. Although cordial, he was aloof and it appeared that something was weighing heavily on his mind. After the tour, he seemed even more withdrawn than before and when I dropped into the museum gift shop to look at polished rocks, beaded necklaces, and books by local authors, he seemed indifferent about joining me and decided to swing by the concession stand to order a soda and buffalo burgers instead.

Alex put the key into the ignition and after several failed attempts, the engine finally turned over. Staring out the cracked front windshield of Alex's Speedster, I clutched the souvenir sack in my lap and considered the primitive map the gift shop cashier had drawn on the brown paper bag. She was kind of a peculiar old lady. Long stringy gray hair, crooked nose and teeth. She hadn't been able to take her eyes off my brooch and in a shaky voice, she began to ask me questions about the pin that I couldn't begin to answer. She suggested I have it appraised. She even recommended a local jeweler who specialized in that sort of thing. Although she couldn't remember his name, she knew the location of his shop. *At the corner of*

Adams and Armstrong. In scratchy handwriting, she scrawled these words below the roughly drawn map. I smoothed my finger over the dried ink and then looked out the window, letting my thoughts move from the map to the beautiful 3,700-acre wildlife preserve. Filled with roaming buffalo, the huge plot of land was once the weekend retreat of the late millionaire oilman, Frank Phillips, and according to the tour guide, the lodge that sat on the property was not only an entertainment hotspot for prestigious guests like Will Rogers, Harry Truman, E. I. Du Pont, Sir Thomas Lipton, and Herbert Hoover, but also a haven for local outlaws, bank bandits, and train robbers. I cursed the rain that prevented us from exploring. I knew that a little fresh air was exactly what we needed.

Alex shifted into drive and let his foot fall heavy on the gas pedal. Completely disregarding the speed limit sign, he let the needle of the speedometer hover just above 45 as he hastily made his way toward the exit. Now I thought I knew what was bothering him. He was irritated that we had taken our time at the museum and because the river was now flowing over the bridge, we might not make it home. Or, maybe he was upset that the fix up job on his Porsche wasn't going as planned and he was already out a couple thousand dollars.

"You know," I said smartly. "There's a good reason you're not supposed to speed through here."

"Name one," Alex snapped.

I pointed to the buffalo that was blocking the road. Alex slammed on the brakes and I gripped the side of the door as the Porsche fishtailed across the slick asphalt. Regaining control of his car, Alex skidded to a halt several yards from the only live buffalo I had ever seen.

"You've got to be kidding me." Alex gave the horn a honk but the buffalo didn't budge.

"You could just get out of the car and make him move," I suggested.

Alex looked at me sharply and then returned his eyes to the road. He pulled a little closer to the bull and gave the horn another blast.

"Careful," I warned. "Make him mad, he'll charge."

Alex responded by slamming his fist onto the horn and holding it there. Finally, the lazy buffalo showed the first signs of moving. Waiting for the bull to cross the road, Alex gave me a sidelong glance and the first smile of the day. "Find anything good in the souvenir shop?" he asked, glancing at my bag.

"As a matter of fact, I did. While you were taking your time at the buffalo burger stand," I said, pulling a paperback book out of the bag, "I had time to read a few short chapters, and according to this book, a buffalo might be the least of your concerns today. Big Foot, Alex! I'm talking about Big Foot."

"Really?" he said with a heavy dose of sarcasm. "Are you serious right now?" Alex rolled his eyes. "I thought you limited your reading to romance and mystery. This sounds more like myths and mysticism."

"Oklahoma folklore."

"Hmmm."

"It covers everything from outlaws to Bigfoot. It's a good read... so far."

"Well, let's just hope we don't run into Sasquatch."

"You never know what you'll find in the forest. You of all people should know that."

"Now that Ben's gone, I feel like the forest is a much safer place to be."

"I hope you brought you're camera, that's all I'm saying."

When Alex didn't respond, I began to worry. I had been attempting to cheer him up all day. I didn't have everything in the world to be cheerful about either. I had spent most of my life controlling things, manipulating situations to get the outcome I desired, but for the first time ever, I felt I had no control. But I wasn't complaining to him. I was trying my hardest to make the situation better, not worse.

"What's wrong," I nudged him playfully and then leaned across the console to plant a kiss on his cheek. "You seem... tense today," I whispered in his ear and then stretched a little further and kissed him on the lips. With the car still parked in the middle of the road, Alex looked in his rearview mirror, making sure no one was behind us.

"Can we talk about it?" My request was more than a plea; it was a demand.

Alex relaxed into the worn leather seat.

"Yeah, whatever. Better make it snappy, though. There's already water covering the bridge. If it gets any deeper, we won't make it out of here."

"That wouldn't be so bad, would it? To be stuck out here with me?"

"Stuck out here with you and Sasquatch. Sounds appealing."

I inched closer and lowered my voice to just above a whisper. "You need to be cheered up. You're cranky."

"Am I?"

"Yes, you are." I let my lips graze his cheek.

"Maybe a little."

"What's wrong?" I tilted my head and studied him. Alex the angel. Alex, the one who was always there to make *me* feel better. Now more man than supernatural being, I reminded myself that Alex was becoming human.

"I feel like I'm losing you." Alex bit his lip. I could tell he had more to say, but that he was holding back.

"That's ridiculous."

"I know it is and I shouldn't have said anything."

"No. I'm glad you did. I just can't imagine why you would feel that way."

"I just feel like... maybe you don't need me as much as you used to." Alex moved his hand to my cheek and then let it drift down to my chin, moving his thumb across my lower lip. "Is it bad to say that I want you? All of you... and I don't want to share."

When his voice quivered, I was reminded of the fact that I was all that Alex had. Alex had put eternity on hold to protect me, to be here with me on earth and based on the condition of the eagle spread across his chest, it was becoming more and more evident that he was here to stay. The more the eagle disappeared, the more Alex's human characteristics surfaced and the more assured I was that he wasn't going to be sucked back up to heaven... at least not anytime soon. Although the eagle was gorgeous, a piece of work created by the hand of a skilled artist, I wanted nothing more than to see it gone for good. I moved my hand over the top of his shirt.

"How's the bird?"

"Still there."

With his lips inches from mine, I could feel his breath warm on my face. I closed my eyes. I tried to put myself in his shoes. I tried my hardest to consider how he might be feeling. I had been reunited with Sue and Will. I had a home and although it was rather cold inside at the moment, we both knew that Will would warm up soon enough and that things would go back to normal before too long. Alex also had a home, but it was empty. A house that was furnished nearly twenty years ago by his mom and dad. A house where pictures of his family hung on the wall, forever reminding him of all the things he would never have again. Alex was here to love me, to protect me. He thought I took too many chances. He thought I put myself in dangerous situations. He *was* becoming human. Maybe he feared he was no longer strong enough to keep me safe. I moved my hand down his shoulder and let it rest on his bicep, feeling the strength in his arm. Strong? Yes. Supernatural….? I took a deep breath. Maybe he thought he'd fail. Maybe he thought he'd lose me and he'd be left with nothing. I knew the feeling all too well.

I unfastened my seatbelt and slid onto his lap, letting my legs hang over the console. I leaned back into his arms and gazed into his hazel eyes. Neither one of us said a word. I began to run my fingers through his hair. For a split second, I looked past his appearance and right into his soul.

Love. Pain. Needs. Worries. Loneliness. Fear.

"You have me," I assured him. "All of me. I'm not going anywhere."

"That's good to know."

In silence, his lips hovered above mine. His gaze was intense. I wondered if he were reading my mind. I hoped not. But I did wonder what he was thinking right now. I wished I knew. What was it about him that made me feel so fragile in his hands? I had known Alex on earth for nearly two years, but this moment felt like new love. I was trying to focus on Alex: his face, his eyes, his beauty, when a drop of rain landed on my forehead.

I let out the breath I was holding and smiled. "Your soft top's leaking."

Alex tenderly wiped the drop of water away with his thumb. "I know. Turns out, the car's a bigger project than I thought it would be."

"You can do it. I have faith in you. Everything you touch turns to gold."

Alex laughed. "Thanks for the vote of confidence."

"So… do you want to know more about Bigfoot?" I asked, changing the subject.

"Not really," he returned with the first real laugh of the day. Alex was pretty easy. A kiss was all it took to make things better between us.

"Alex," I asked. "Do you still believe in soul mates?"

Alex laughed again, harder this time. "From Sasquatch to soul mates. Your mind moves a thousand miles a minute."

"Well, do you?"

"Of course I do."

"Do you think everyone finds theirs?"

"Eventually, yes."

"I do, too."

"Why do you ask?"

"I just finished a book a few days ago and it has me thinking. The two leading characters are soul mates, but everything seems so hard. When I think soul mate, I think perfect, like those two words are synonymous or something. But it just seems like nothing is ever perfect." I moved my finger to his lips and let it rest on the spot where his freckle used to be. My eyes wandered back to his, and I noticed that the small scar at the corner of his left eye was fading more and more each day.

Creases formed in Alex's forehead as he considered what I was saying. "Finding your soul mate can be hard. But that isn't the hardest part."

"What do you mean?" I asked, shifting in his arms.

"The hard part comes after."

"What do you mean?" I asked again, this time with more concern.

"I just mean that because the world is hard, love can be hard in this world."

I wasn't sure how to respond, so I waited for him to elaborate, but he didn't. "Well," I said, shrugging my shoulders. "I'm just glad you came back. Against all odds, I might add."

"Yes. I did."

"But what if you hadn't?"

"But I did, so why the 'what ifs'?"

I used my finger to draw a heart in the fogged up glass. "You know, I should really be the one who's worried," I told him, changing the subject. "You could still get sucked up to heaven at any moment. And about the eagle on your chest," I said as I recalled the fading eagle I last saw in February. "I'm not sure I believe you. Maybe I should see it for myself."

INTERCESSION

CHAPTER TEN

*L*ightning flashed, a jagged finger of light that stretched from the heavens to the earth and I shivered. I was soaking wet and my teeth were chattering. I was hiking through a wet and soggy cemetery just to make Alex smile. I was always thinking of my man. As I crossed the lawn, I pulled my heavy sweater around my shoulders and shivered. I knew how to cheer Alex up and not even a storm could stop me. Lightning lit up a darkened sky and I quickened my pace, sincerely hoping that my efforts would not go unappreciated. When I made the decision to follow A-Omega, my heart began to open and subsequently, so had my eyes. Yesterday, after our visit to Woolaroc, I returned home to an empty house and began to think about Alex and really consider why he might be so down. I began to think about what I could do to cheer him up, and then, all at once, I was struck with an idea. I was impressed that I had been able to come up with something so ingenious and disgusted with myself at the same time for not thinking of it sooner. Alex had been back on earth nearly two years, and we had not celebrated his birthday once. To make matters worse, I hadn't even bothered to ask when he was born. Alex had entered into this world on two separate occasions; his celebration should be twice as big as anyone else's. Now the only thing I needed was an exact date. I knew the year: 1988. The math was easy. He was two when he died. He died in 1990. Now all I needed was the month and day.

I didn't think his gravestone would be too hard to find, (it had only been a year since my last visit), and I was pretty sure I was headed in the right direction. I recalled the last trip I made to the cemetery. A cold and wet March day. When I had set out to find Alex's tombstone, I was just beginning to understand the truth about my boyfriend, the truth about my past. A year later, now that I had uncovered most of the secrets, I thought I might feel more comfortable, more confident, as I walked toward his grave, but I didn't.

With my feet sinking into the wet lawn, I moved as fast as I could, thankful that I had on combat boots instead of All Stars. Another flash of lightning. A drop of rain on the tip of my nose. I continued on, not stopping until I saw the three white stones (two large and one small) I was looking for. I had arrived.

Today, I had the cemetery all to myself. The rain began to fall harder and thunder rumbled overhead. I suppose it wasn't the best day to visit a graveyard. With a heavy heart, I approached his stone and knelt down in front of it. Tears welled up in my eyes and I was surprised by my reaction. It was like I was seeing his grave for the very first time. Shock. Then disbelief. Followed by sadness. And finally, fear. Being here today put everything in perspective. His name was engraved on the stone. I ran my finger over it. When I saw his name last year, I remember feeling confused. Today, a new feeling rose up inside me. Appreciation. Now more than ever, I realized Alex was here for me. Alex was a gift from God. With eyes closed, I let the rain wash over my body and the tears fall down my cheeks. I felt the scope of his sacrifice. As thanks, I was throwing him a birthday party. He deserved so much more than that.

I studied the engraving:

Alex Michael Loving
1988-1990
Beloved only child of Sarah and Paul

Only the year was given. No month. No day. I stood up and turned back in the direction I had come. I could always just ask Alex. But then the party wouldn't be a surprise. There had to be a way. Think. Think. Think. Then all at once, I knew. It was time to give an old friend a call.

I let the phone ring eight times and was just about to hang up, when a raspy voice on the other end of the line answered hello.

"Joe?"

"Speaking."

"Joe, this is Rae."

"Rae!" It was as though his spirits lifted when he said my name, which was strange, because I didn't usually have that effect on people.

"Joe, you sound terrible. Is everything okay?"

The raspy whisper turned into a hearty laugh. "You never did beat around the bush did you, dear?"

"I'm sorry. That was rude. It's just, you sound... sick."

"I figure as soon as the ice melts around these parts, then my body will thaw and this irritating cold and nagging cough will go away."

"Oh," I said, recalling the misery of a Minnesota winter. Just the memory was enough to make me shiver. "If it makes you feel better, the weather isn't so great around here, either. I'd take a snowstorm over a tornado any day of the week." Joe laughed and then cleared his chest. "Well, I'm sorry you're sick. Is everything else okay? Is now a good time?"

"Now's the perfect time. It's so good to hear your voice. I've missed our little talks."

"Me, too."

"How's Alex?"

"Good. Haven't you talked to him?"

"Not as much as I had hoped."

"Joe, he seems a little down."

"That's understandable. It's hard enough knowing where to fit into this complicated world when you're human. I can only imagine how it must feel to be him."

"Why? Has he said something?" The other end of the line went silent.

"That's okay. You don't have to tell me if he did." I paused. More silence. "On a positive note, I think I have the perfect way to cheer him up."

"What's that?" Pastor Joe was obviously glad that I had changed the subject.

"A surprise birthday party. But there's only one problem. I have no idea when to have the party because I've never asked him when he was born."

"July 17th," Joe said immediately.

"Being that you're his godfather, I should have figured you would know."

"That's one date I will never forget." Joe coughed again. "How are things going with you, Rae?"

"Crappy."

The pastor laughed again, which brought on another coughing fit. When finally he cleared his chest, he began, "That's what I love about you, Rae. You say exactly what's on your mind. Tell me dear, has something happened?"

"That's part of the problem, Joe. Nothing much has happened at all. A-Omega told me to wait. So I am waiting… and waiting… and waiting."

"Waiting is a good thing."

"No, it isn't."

"Sure it is. Waiting isn't only about putting off what you'll receive at the end. It's about who you become in the process."

"I guess," I said, my voice filled with uncertainty.

"Is there something else, Rae?"

I hesitated, unsure whether or not I wanted to share with Joe my innermost feelings. My vulnerabilities. My weaknesses. "Alex isn't the only one going through an identity crisis, Joe," I blurted, surprised by how good it felt to get these feelings off my chest. As soon as the words left my mouth, it was as if a weight had been lifted from my shoulders. "A-Omega told me to wait, so I'm waiting. But while I'm waiting, I'm thinking… thinking about how unqualified I am for this task. About how I'm not strong enough… good enough."

"Don't believe everything you think. A good friend taught me that."

"I drove by Carl's a while back," I confessed. "I was sitting outside his million-dollar mansion thinking about walking up to his door. I couldn't believe how small I felt. I should have marched right up to his house in the boots A-Omega gave me and pulled him out by the collar of his expensive shirt. I don't know what's wrong with me. Sometimes I want to go after him; other times, I'm frozen with fear."

The other end of the phone was silent. I had been running my mouth, talking about the negative. I hoped I hadn't put Joe to sleep.

"That's one way to look at it." Joe finally spoke. "I'm certainly glad you didn't pull Carl Pierce out of his house by his collar. My dear, you have to focus on the positive. Keep out the bad thoughts and let in the good."

"Easier said than done."

"Where there's a will, there's a way," he fired back. Pastor Joe was old, but he was still as sharp as a tack. "Mind if I share a story?"

"Sure."

"When I was much younger, I was having thoughts like yours. I had no idea who I was or what I wanted to do with my life. My mom told me to take out a notebook and draw a line down the center of the paper, dividing it in half. On one side, she told me to write down every bad thing I thought about myself. She called this the 'list of lies'. On the other side, she told me to write down every positive thing about myself that I knew to be true. She called this side of the page, 'the truth'. So I did. I wrote down everything I loved and everything I didn't. I wrote down how I saw myself and how I thought others saw me. She was right. On the road to self-discovery, making a list is a great place to start. By the time I got to college, the list looked very different. I had not only added to the list, but I had also crossed a few things off. You see, how you view yourself and how others see you can change based on circumstance. Not sure if you knew this, but it wasn't my intention to become a pastor."

"It wasn't?"

"No. I was headed down a much different path. But then life threw me a curve ball. It was a tough transition. I was 22 years old and everything I had worked so hard for was gone in the blink of an eye. Everything that defined me no longer existed. Once again, I began to do a little soul searching. Around that same time, a good friend gave me a piece of advice that I will never forget. She told me that God doesn't change like shifting shadows. She went on to say that even though *my* opinion of myself had changed, *God's* opinion of me hadn't."

"It's weird thinking about you being anything other than a pastor. So what did you want to be?"

"A pilot."

"Well, it's good to know that I'm not the only one who has asked the question 'Who am I?'"

"Of course you're not. Even Jesus asked 'Who am I?'"

"He did?"

"Sure He did. Although… He wasn't asking because He needed reassurance. He was asking His disciples a reflective question."

"So, Jesus wanted to know who the disciples thought He was?"

"Exactly. And He asks us all the same question today."

"What about you, Joe? Who does He say you are?"

"He says I am blessed."

"And who do you say He is?"

"God is love."

Later that night, I took my journal out of the box and opened it up, staring at a blank white page. With my purple gel pen, I made a list just like Joe had done once upon a time. I divided the page in half and on the left-hand side, I started the list of lies (all of the negative thoughts I was having). When I shut my journal for the night, the 'truth' column was completely blank. I prayed that soon the storms would die down, and I prayed that I might have some words to put on the other side of the page.

CHAPTER ELEVEN

*T*he next morning, the relentless ringing of the doorbell woke me up. I wondered who it might be. Living in the country, even though we were only a few miles outside of town, we didn't get as many guests as we might otherwise have living in a neighborhood and hearing the doorbell wasn't a sound that we were used to. Not a chance it would be Alex; he vowed to steer clear of the house until Will had calmed down. I rolled onto my back and stretched. I had fallen asleep reading and my book was on the floor without a bookmark. Slowly, I crawled out of bed, moved curiously over to the window, and looked down at the circle drive below. The driveway was empty, but a cloud of dust lingered on the dirt road. Someone had come to our door, but they hadn't stayed long. I wondered if Sue and Will were home. Then I remembered it was Monday. Will was at work and because Mom had taken the Sunday night shift on the psyche ward at the hospital, she wouldn't be home for another hour or two. I watched the dust settle. Still mostly asleep, I rubbed my eyes and started down the stairs. Halfway down, a thought came to me… *a package. Maybe A-Omega had sent me another package.* Suddenly alert, I took the stairs two at a time, nearly tripping over my own feet. Once I was at the bottom, I moved toward the door and flung it open. And there it was. Just as I had hoped. Another box. A big box. I checked to see who it was addressed to and was pleasantly surprised when I saw that it was addressed to me. I wrapped my arms around it and picked it up, not only surprised by how little it weighed, but also by the return address. Abe's Electronic Warehouse out of Richmond, Virginia. A surge of excitement rushed through me. What was inside?!

Packing popcorn was flying everywhere. Finding out what was inside of the box was more exciting than nineteen Christmas mornings combined. My thoughts began to swirl when my hand hit something hard. Another box? What had A-Omega sent me this time? I slid my hand across the smooth flat surface, felt for the corner, and pulled it out. I took a moment to comprehend what I was seeing, but when everything began to register, I squealed with delight and ripped the shrink-wrap from my brand new Mac Book Pro. Realizing how rude it was to open up a gift without reading the card, even if no one was looking, I fished my hand inside the box to see if there was any sort of note and, of course, there was. It was the kind of card that is so common with online purchases: a short note that expressed the sender's feelings *in 500 words or less*. I glanced at the card. The signature told me that the gift was not from A-Omega; rather, it was from Sue and Will.

> *Rae,*
> *We are so proud of you and so glad to have you home. Thought this gift might help you on your journey and give you just the drive you need. Remember, when the storms come, when the earth shakes beneath your feet, and when the fiery trials threaten to overtake you, just listen for a gentle whisper. And when there's nothing to do but wait, appreciate the stillness. Keep your eyes open. Look around. There is a lesson to be learned in every arena of life.*
>
> *We love you Sunshine,*
> *Mom and Dad*

Now that I had a new computer, I could install the software. I waited for the phone to buzz with a new text message from A-Omega telling me to wait. It never did. Twenty minutes later, I turned onto Frank Phillips Avenue and pulled into a strip mall across the street from Starbucks. I parked in front of Collin's Repair, a drab storefront that I would have never noticed had I not found the address for the small computer repair shop online. Besides the Goodwill, which took up a large chunk of the property, most of the businesses appeared to be small and privately owned. A restaurant. A salon. A Singer Sewing Machine Shop. A karate dojo. I turned off the engine, grabbed my new computer and the antivirus box, and climbed out of the car. I was hopeful that installing the software would shed a little light on my mission.

When I walked into the store, I was relieved to find that I was the only customer and I wouldn't have to wait in line. Behind the counter was a boy in jeans and a camouflaged shirt standing on a ladder looking for something on a large metal shelf. When the door chime sounded, the twenty-something boy glanced in my direction and then descended the rungs with caution. I met him at the counter and placed my laptop and the antivirus box near the register. With less than a yard between us, I reevaluated his age. Although he had a very youthful appearance, the lines around his eyes were more indicative of someone in his late thirties or early forties. His hair was dirty blonde with patches of white at his temples. He had big, brown eyes that might have held me captive had it not been for the large scar in the hollow of his neck.

"First customer of the day." He had a bit of a southern drawl. "What can I do for you?"

I looked him in the eye. "I was wondering if you could install this software on my computer."

"For sure." He picked up my laptop and whistled. "17 inch screen. 2.66GHz Intel Core 2 Duo. 320 GB hard drive." He whistled again.

"I understand the 17 inch screen part. But everything else…"

"Gotcha," he laughed, and my eyes drifted to the scar on his neck. I quickly readjusted, forcing my eyes to meet his before he noticed I was staring. "It's not often I get to work on a computer like this. Only the junkers come through here. This is the computer graveyard. We bring out of date computers back to life. We resurrect them… so to speak." He smiled and held out his hand. "By the way, I'm Quinn."

I'm Rae," I responded, and shook his hand.

"Well, this is gonna be a piece of a cake." He picked up the software box and after reading the label, flipped it over, and glanced at the back. "And it ain't gonna take long, either. You're welcome to wait."

"Perfect. I think I will." I took a seat in one of the plastic chairs pushed up against the wall and began to play a game on my phone while watching Quinn out of the corner of my eye. He stood behind the cash register peeling the shrink-wrap off the antivirus box. There was a hand written note taped to the front of the register that I hadn't noticed on my way in. I squinted, trying to read what it said, but I was too far away. Quinn tossed the wrapping into the trash and then, instead of opening the box, moved his fingers to his throat and glanced at me. "I noticed you looking at my scar."

I felt my cheeks grow warm. I swallowed the lump in my throat. I wanted to crawl in a hole. I couldn't find the words to say, so I said nothing.

"Don't mean to put ya on the spot," he laughed. "Just want ya to know it doesn't bother me. It's a conversation starter."

I took in a deep breath and bit my lip. I looked him in the eye. "I'm really sorry."

"Don't be sorry. If you want, while you wait, I'll tell you the story about how I got it."

"Oh, you don't have to do that," I replied, hoping he couldn't *see* the redness that I could *feel* on my cheeks.

"No worries. Look, the scar makes others more uncomfortable than it makes me. Once a lady asked me if I would like the name of a good plastic surgeon. I guess she thought my scar was so disfiguring that I would want to have somethin' done about it. But I don't see it that way. Not anymore. Behind this scar's a story."

I thought about the scar on my mom's arm and how it brought back painful memories. There was a story behind that scar but growing up, we didn't talk about it, and I was fine with that. I really was. The scar reminded me of the car crash. The car crash reminded me of Laney. Laney's death reminded me of my birthday: September 13th. And my birthday reminded me of how guilty I should feel. But several weeks ago, the story had finally come out. Now I was glad I knew. I no longer looked at her scar and felt scared or uncertain. Talking about it *had* helped. Now that I knew the truth, the raised pink line that ran down her arm made me feel peace instead of fear. Innocence instead of guilt.

"You can either see the good or the bad in life. I decided to see the good and I decided that I was pretty lucky to have a life to live. Ever since then, I use the scar as proof."

"Proof of what?"

"Modern day miracles."

At the mention of the word "miracle," I had a change of heart. Now I *did* want to hear his story, and I felt myself being drawn back to the counter. I was no stranger to miracles. When Alex came back from the dead, I had experienced one of my very own. It was just that I had never met anyone else who had experienced a miracle, and I figured that after listening to what Quinn had to say, I would be one the wiser.

"The miraculous is everywhere. I just never thought about miracles when I was eighteen years old. I was thinking about girls and cars. Even after the accident, I had trouble believing the story, but I knew two truths. I should have died in Argentina and the experience I had while I was there changed my life for the better."

Quinn turned on my computer and the screen lit up. "This computer's fast like lightning. Do you mind me asking what you need such a nice computer for? I mean, what do you do? Are you in school?"

"I'm kind of in between things right now. I was in art school. But then I moved back home. I'm taking a break. Intersession."

"Well, that's okay. I know I wasn't thinking about school when I was your age. Always admired those people that had it all together, you know. The kind of person who knows exactly what they want to do with their life as soon as they come out of the womb. The gifted. Well, I wasn't one of 'em. Never too good in school. Never really found my calling. Not the best at social skills, either." Quinn laughed. "Growin' up, people always talked down to me. Said I was a bad egg, things like that. After a while, I started believin' 'em. I was a self-fulfilling prophecy, that's what I was. In the eighth grade, I started actin' out. Fighting with my parents and what not. Stayin' out too late. Not makin' the grades. My dad was never one to say things like 'I love you,' but I knew he did. No matter how bad it got, my dad believed in me, and no matter how far I drifted, there was a bond between us that couldn't be broken: We both *loved* to hunt. Just before my senior year in high school, Dad planned a hunting trip to Argentina for the two of us. Dad was hoping it would bring us closer. I was excited. Argentina has the most spectacular dove hunting in the world. With the doves having five hatches a year, the farmers were practically paying us to come and hunt them."

Quinn pulled out a CD from the box, which I assumed was the software, and inserted it into the disc drive on the side of my computer. Still looking at the screen, he continued. "I guess my dad thought I needed to travel all the way to South America to find myself. Figure out *who I was* and what I wanted to do with my life." Quinn laughed. "He was right."

Quinn's fingers moved swiftly across the keyboard, but he continued to tell his story as he typed.

"On the morning of July 23rd, we flew into Buenos Aires and from there, into Córdoba. We were staying at a nice lodge on about 8,000 acres. We settled in and everything was going perfectly. Dad and I were bonding. Somehow, I had been able to let go of all my worries and just enjoy the time. And the hunting... amazing. But on our last night at the lodge, things started to get exciting. After a long day, we stayed up late sharin' stories and laughin'. Didn't call it a night until around 1 AM. Completely exhausted, I made it back to my room, took off my boots, and was about ten steps from my bed when I felt somethin' slimy under my foot. Then came a sharp, piercing pain. When I turned on the light to see what I had stepped on, I saw a snake slithering toward the door." Quinn took a momentary break from the job at hand and looked me in the eye. "This was no ordinary snake," he said, looking at me with raised eyebrows and a twisted smile. "It was Yarara Lancehead. One of the most venomous snakes in South America and it bit me right on the top of my foot. I later found out that only one in four people survive after being bitten by this particular snake. Its venom does nasty things to the body and it's best to receive the anti-venom right away. You don't wait around to see what happens with a bite like this, if you catch my drift. Ya wait, ya die. And there was my problem. I was on an 8,000-acre ranch, and the owner of the ranch, Nicolas, had sent one of the bird boys home with the truck. The closest hospital was an hour away and we had no way to get there. The only form of transportation on the ranch was a four-wheeler…. a one-seater. So while Nicholas took off on the four-wheeler to find the truck, Dad stayed at my side. Two hours later when Nicolas returned, my foot had doubled in size and I was having trouble breathing."

Quinn shut down the computer and then rebooted it.

"I don't remember much about the ride to the hospital. After the venom is in your system for a while, your body just starts shuttin' down. You stop breathin'. You can get swellin' of the brain. According to Dad, it was four in the mornin' when we arrived at the clinic in the town of Jesus Maria. The staff spoke no English, so Nicolas was our translator. They carried me into the clinic and laid me on a cot. They started the anti-venom infusion right away." Quinn rubbed the scar at his throat. "Midway through the infusion, I stopped breathing completely. The doctor had to perform an emergency tracheotomy." Quinn touched the scar on his throat. "Very thankful I was unconscious for that. They kept me alive with a homemade ventilator. But three hours later, when the anti-venom infusion was complete and I was still unconscious, the doctor told Nicolas, 'No hope.' This was the worse case she had seen. According to my dad, the doctor washed her hands and left the room. I guess to the doctor, I was just another name. But to the nurse, I was an opportunity… for a miracle."

When Quinn referred to himself as just another name, my thoughts began to swirl. Quinn. Quinn. Why did his name sound so familiar? And then it hit me. He may have been "just another name" to the doctor, but he was not just another name to me. He was number one on the list of ten names A-Omega had given me. Collin's Repair. Quinn. Quinn Collins. When I walked into Collins's repair, I wasn't sure what I was looking for, and I was uncertain of what to expect. Now I knew. There was something in Quinn's story that A-Omega wanted me to understand. Quinn continued to talk as he worked, and I continued to listen.

"My leg had tripled in size. I had swelling of the brain. I was hooked up to a ventilator that had to be compressed eighteen times a minute just to keep me breathing… just to keep me alive. At the final hour, after even my father had given up hope, the nurse walked in with an old priest. They approached the cot. She unfastened the clasp of her chain and gave the pendant to the old man. The priest prayed and then laid the golden cross on my chest. Together, Dad, the priest, the nurse, and the other patients prayed in both Spanish and English. God heard and God healed. According to Dad, the second the cross hit my chest, I blinked my eyes. As they continued to pray, I continued to heal. Each minute brought healing. I still walk with a bit of a limp and I have this scar, but I can't complain. According to doctors, I shouldn't be here; but according to God, I should."

"You said the experience changed you. What happened after you came home?"

"Just because I changed didn't mean everyone else did. People will still say what they want to. It's just that their words didn't bother me so much anymore. When I was in South America, God told me a little somethin' about myself that I didn't know. He told me I was good. He told me I was worth somethin'. He told me I had purpose. I realized that what other people say about me is not nearly as important as what God says about me. God saw somethin' in me that no one else did."

"So no more *bad thoughts*, then? Never?"

"Sometimes I feel the bad thoughts creeping back. Sometimes I still get discouraged."

"So what do you do?"

"I remind myself of three things. First, I try not to forget who I am. You know… all of the things that make me, me. Next, I think about who Christ says I am." Quinn touched the crucifix that hung around his neck. "My life was saved in the town of Jesus Maria when a cross was laid upon my chest, and according to Jesus, I *am* good, I *am* worth it, and I *do* have purpose. And most importantly, I think about who Jesus is to me."

There was an awkward silence. The cross. The pendant. The prayers. I continued to stare. This conversation sounded a little too familiar. Just last night, Joe had given me the same advice.

"So, looks like you're all set," Quinn said, changing the subject. He handed me my laptop and the empty antivirus box.

I dug around in my bag for my wallet. "What do I owe you?"

"Seven dollars even."

I pulled out a bill and handed it to him. "Keep the change."

He opened the register and tucked the bill inside the drawer. "So, do you get a lot of viruses?"

"No."

"I just assumed... well it's good to protect your computer just in case. You know what a virus is, right? And you know how you get them?"

"Yeah, I mean... it just locks up your computer. It messes with everything."

"Right. Sometimes viruses come to you. They can be disguised as an email or as a pop-up ad. But most of the time, we invite the virus in and we don't even realize we're doing it. If you see an email you think might contain a virus, just delete it. Never open it. Never, never open it. Viruses are contagious. Not only will it affect your computer, but you'll start sending out bad emails and other people's computers will be affected, too. On a positive note, the software does a pretty good job of letting in the good stuff and keeping out the bad. But you have to do your part, too. Just be careful what you click on."

"I think I can handle that."

"You know, I never really thought about it too much." Quinn scratched his head and cleared his throat. "But computer viruses are a lot like bad thoughts. They can ruin a computer just like a negative thought can ruin the mind." He touched the gold cross that hung around his neck. I considered what he was saying but didn't respond. "I don't know. I just thought I'd throw that out there. Anything else you need while you're here?"

"No. But I know where to find you if I do."

On the way to my car, I thought about my experience at Collin's Repair. I had spent most of my life filling my mind with 'bad thoughts.' Lately, my negativity was at an all time high and my bad thoughts were threatening to take over. Consumed with worry, fear, and self-doubt, I was struggling. Then I met Quinn, and I didn't think our meeting was a coincidence. I felt this, but did he? His name was on my list. He didn't seem to recognize me, but surely he knew who I was. Halfway across the parking lot, I changed my mind and re-entered the store. Quinn was still standing behind the counter and when the bell over the door chimed, he looked up.

"Forget somethin'?"

"No. Not really." I stopped in the middle of the room and hesitated, shifting my weight uncomfortably before working up the courage to ask the question that was on my mind. "I just have to ask. Were you expecting me today?"

Quinn looked confused. "Should I have been expecting you?" He began to shuffle through his date book.

"No. Never mind. But thanks for sharing your story. It helped me out more than you know."

"I hear that a lot. I'm glad it helped you. It helped me too. It helps me every time I tell the story. It's my testimony. You can't just receive all that goodness and keep it to yourself. You have to share it." Quinn looked up from the date book and flashed a smile. "Life's a funny thing, you know. I never thought I would be working in my dad's computer repair store reviving old computers. I never thought I would be married with three kids," he said, moving his finger over his wedding band. "You can make all the plans you want for your future, but as far as purpose is concerned, God will take you where you need to go."

I was still thinking about Quinn's prescription for bad thoughts and how Joe had given me similar advice when I called him last night. Coincidence? Probably not. "Quinn. I hope you don't mind that I ask... it's just..."

"I'm an open book. Ask me anything you want."

"Well… you said it's important to know who Jesus is to you, but you never told me. Who do you say He is?"

Quinn smiled. "He's the antivirus for my mind and the anti-venom for my soul."

Before exiting the repair shop for a second time, I glanced at the handwritten note on the register. This time I was close enough to read it.

"Letting the Spirit control your mind leads to life and peace."

A million thoughts were swirling through my mind, and I needed to digest everything Quinn had relayed to me. His story was moving, and the message was exactly what I needed to hear. I was still in shock that I had stumbled upon his store.

I decided to cross the street and grab a cup of coffee. I hoped the coffee shop would be empty and that I would find a quiet place to sit where I could think, but when I pushed open the door, I heard a familiar monotone voice that I should have been able to place the second I heard it. I continued through the door and advanced to the counter. When the customer in front of me moved away from the register, I realized why the voice sounded so familiar. Now standing face to face with the barista, I recognized my old friend right away.

"Rae!" said the girl with black hair and ultra-short bangs.

"Claire!" I gasped.

CHAPTER TWELVE

When I came downstairs for breakfast, I overheard Will talking to Mom in the kitchen. He was complaining about how it was almost the first of June and the rain had yet to let up. "It's been storming for three months straight!" He was telling her that if the rain didn't stop soon, our road would be underwater within the next few weeks. I heard her try to make light of the situation and then he informed her that our road had indeed been underwater during the floods of 1986 and 2007. He went on to recommend a trip to the store to stock up on groceries... just in case. I wasn't excited about the idea of being trapped in the house with them for a prolonged period of time, so I showered and dressed, and one hour later, I was standing on Alex's doorstep with a pizza in one hand and a movie in the other.

It was still raining outside and the weatherman was preparing us for the possibility of severe weather. After you live in Oklahoma long enough, you come to realize that severe weather is another, more gentle name, for a tornado. I used my elbow to press the bell and anxiously waited for him to open the door. I glanced over my shoulder. The rain was coming down in horizontal sheets, which wasn't natural. The sky was dark. Branches were snapping and the sound of the wind was wicked. Shivering like a wet rat, I tried the door to see if it was unlocked. Not surprisingly, it was. It was early. Not quite noon. Alex had probably just rolled out of bed. I had expected to see him in his sweats with mussed up hair, but the house was quiet and he was nowhere to be found. I walked into the empty kitchen and set the pizza down on the counter. I grabbed a Diet Coke and was just about to walk into the living room when I noticed Alex's laptop on the kitchen table. I sat down behind his computer and moved my finger across the mouse pad. His screen flickered to life. No need to power it up, the laptop was already on. Hmmm. Alex had been using his computer. He was awake, but where was he now?

I was staring at the blue and white background of a popular social media site. Evidently, he had been setting up a profile page and the first thing I noticed was his profile picture. It was one I had taken of him several months ago, right after the start of my spring semester at the University of Minnesota. I loved the picture, but I could have sworn he told me he hated it. Originally, the image was inspiration for an assignment: I was supposed to paint something avant-garde, and I had come up with the idea one night when I was lying in bed thinking about Alex's feelings, trying my hardest to understand why he had started a brawl to end it all at the hockey match the night before. There was no denying that the fight between Alex and Flynt had been a long time coming. And while the animosity between the two of them was very real, I had come to the conclusion that Flynt Redding was not the only reason Alex was behaving so badly.

After what happened in the forest on Halloween night, the town had been talking. Flynt nearly lost his life at the hands of Benard Bodin and once again, Alex came to the rescue. He saved Flynt's life. But because Alex left the forest without so much as a scratch, people's suspicions were aroused. Lots of gossip. Lots of accusations. People were calling Alex a creature of the night and Alex was taking to heart what the town was saying. How ridiculous. The crazy things people come up with. But I still saw him as an angel. This only added to his conflict. I titled the painting accordingly: *Identity Crisis*. After a little convincing, he reluctantly agreed to be my subject and we found a fitted vintage suit in the back cottage that must have belonged to his dad: very 80's. I picked up a pair of angel wings at the thrift store and a set of vampire teeth from Trumm Drug. I plopped him down in the 1950's plaid sofa, molded his shaggy hair into a Mohawk, and told him to flash a fang and look at me out of the corner of his eye. It definitely fit the bill: avant-garde. He told me he was going to make me pay for the black fingernail polish, though. Apparently, he was quite fond of the picture after all. Unfortunately, I had only just begun the painting when my mom showed up. One week later, we were on a plane headed back to Oklahoma. I had to leave the painting behind. If I ever got some supplies, I might restart the project.

My eyes moved down the screen to the text.

Screen Name: Alex Loving

Relationship Status: In a relationship with Rae Colbert

I smiled and took a sip of Diet Coke. I felt sort of guilty for looking at Alex's computer without him knowing, but curiosity got the better of me and I read on.

Sex: Male

About Me: I love hockey, photography, music, writing, swimming for miles, chocolate chip cookie dough, stars, storms, love, family…

Short list. My smile turned into a thin straight line and all at once, I saw this list for what it was. Alex was trying to figure out what he liked and it occurred to me that maybe he didn't know. He was trying to figure out who he was. Well, welcome to the club, so was I. I had been asking myself that same question. And then I thought about Joe's story (his list of self-discovery) and how by sharing it with me, he was gently suggesting that I try making a list of my own. Maybe Alex had heard the story, too. My thoughts were interrupted by a loud, harsh, metallic noise. This noise was immediately followed by the sound of breaking glass. I slid the laptop back to the middle of the table and followed the noise, walking toward the door that led into the garage. Once inside the garage, I was nearly blinded by bright lights and all at once I realized what caused the commotion. Alex had set up huge spotlights in each corner of the room and one of them had fallen. Alex's Porsche was jacked up, and he was underneath. All I could see were his legs. Maybe Alex had bitten off more than he could chew, but he wasn't giving up. He was really serious about restoring this car. It didn't surprise me. Not really. Alex was good with cars. It was a natural gift. He had taken a part time job working on cars in Minnesota, but mostly he did oil changes and replaced serpentine belts and so on. The Porsche was different. It was falling apart and the exterior was just the tip of the iceberg. It needed everything. A better engine, upholstery, and the list went on and on. Instead of giving up, he had transformed the space into a state of the art service garage. Steal grey workbenches lined the west wall, while the east wall boasted bright red tool chests and cabinets.

I cleared my throat to grab his attention. Nothing. Not sure why I thought he might respond to my voice when he hadn't responded to a large metal object crashing to the ground. I approached the car and so not to startle him, I lightly touched his foot to let him know I was here. Slowly, Alex rolled out from under the car and took off his headphones, which explained why he hadn't heard me come in.

"What are you doing down there?"

Alex sat up, grabbed an old rag, and attempted to wipe the grease off his hands. "Just working." He sniffed and rubbed the back of his hand across his face.

"You have grease on your nose," I giggled.

Alex stood up, all greasy and dirty and with a menacing expression, moved slowly toward me. I looked down at my white jeans and tee shirt. I looked at his hands. "Don't even think about it."

He wiggled his fingers to taunt me. "What? No hug?" he questioned.

"Not until after you shower," I said, edging away from him with a smile on my face. Alex continued to advance.

"I brought a movie and a pizza," I told him, hoping that, if nothing else, food might be a distraction.

Alex wiggled his greasy fingers and moved closer, closing the gap between us. I inched backwards, not stopping until I ran into the heavy oak door that led back into the kitchen. I reached behind me and took hold of the doorknob. "You wouldn't."

"I would," Alex said, flashing a mischievous smile.

Alex had on a pair of old jeans, his work boots, and a vintage rock tee that he had picked up at the thrift store in Alexandria. His hair was messy. He had grease all over his hands and a streak across his nose and cheek. He definitely hadn't used a razor in a couple of days and as he drew near, I thought to myself, this is the way I like him best. Alex wet his lips and moved his hands, resting them on the door behind me. My right hand was still holding onto the doorknob. I let it fall to my side. The tornado sirens began to sound and rain pelted against the garage door windows. Wind whipped across the side of the house and rattled the gutters. He kissed me. Softly. Thoughtfully. I wrapped my arms around his neck. His lips brushed across the side of my cheek.

"I love you, Rae Colbert," he whispered.

"I love you back."

There are some things in life you know with certainty, and those feelings, those certainties make you feel secure, invincible. I was glad that Alex was my certainty and that when I was with him I felt strong enough to conquer the world.

While Alex cleaned up, I took the pizza and the movie to the basement, sat down on the sofa, and picked up an old 1989 tabloid off the coffee table. *Child Stars: Where Are They Now?* The title caught my attention. Gracing the cover was a then and now image of a star that had seen better days. I flipped halfway through the magazine before I found the feature article. It took up seven of ninety-nine pages, showcasing six child stars and highlighting their downfalls. The magazine had cleverly chosen the most adorable childhood image they could find, and then contrasted the image with a more recent, much scarier photo of the star at their weakest moment. A mug shot. An early morning, no makeup shot. A plastic surgery gone wrong shot. I skimmed the article and discovered that once again, the tabloid had done a good job of choosing only those celebs with the worst possible pasts. *Out of rehab but out of control* was the subtitle under the image of a man who had once starred in a popular sitcom. Another star was jailed after attacking her plastic surgeon and in bold text under her picture was her rebuttal: "But he injected my lips with too much collagen!" The images and the article made me think of the past. I shut the magazine just as Alex came down the stairs. Clean. Shaven. Fresh change of clothes. He fell onto the sofa and slipped his arm around me.

"You smell much better," I told him.

Alex laughed and picking up where we left off in the garage, his lips moved up the right side of my neck to the lobe of my ear.

"What movie did you get?" he murmured.

"*Bride of Fu Manchu.*"

His lips stopped in their tracks and he leaned back to look me in the eye.

"A 1960's horror flick? That's a rather odd choice, don't you think. Not that I mind, it's just that this isn't something you'd normally pick. I expected romance or mystery."

"It's not horror."

"Thriller, then." Alex grabbed the DVD case. "Is it in black and white?"

"It's in color, I think."

"Subtitles?" he tilted his head and looked at me suspiciously.

"No subtitles."

"Raaaeeee." By the tone of his voice, I knew he was onto me. "There's something you're not telling me."

"I'm busted." I sighed. "Okay, I'm ninety-nine percent sure that this is the last movie Carl Pierce watched."

No longer slouched, Alex sat bolt upright. "And how would you know that, or should I ask?"

"I ran into Claire at the coffee shop."

"*And.....*" Alex was getting angry. Probably because I had mentioned

Claire. It wasn't that Alex had any specific reason to dislike Claire, other than that she was my partner in crime. Toward the end of my senior year in high school, I broke into the Pierce's basement and snooped around their house. I had talked Claire into tagging along. It wasn't necessarily the action that Alex had been so angry about, it was the sneaking around. I had kept it a secret from him and he was furious. I promised I would never lie to him again. Maybe when I mentioned Claire's name, he thought I was backsliding, breaking my promise. By the look on Alex's face, I thought I'd better set the record straight and tell him everything I knew.

"There's not much to tell. After I left Collin's Repair, I went across the street to get a cup of coffee and think things through. I needed some quiet time. But I didn't get it. Apparently, Claire is working part time at Starbucks while she's attending a tech school in Tulsa to study cosmetology."

"*And...?*"

"*And!*... let me finish. So I was just going to grab a cup of coffee and sit down by myself, but she took a break and joined me. First, she asked me why I hadn't called. I told her I had been in Minnesota. She asked me why. I told her I was with you and I told her about art school. Then she started talking about Chloe and about how there was an article in the Tulsa World on her death. And then she mentioned Carl."

"She did?"

"Yes. She said the article made Chloe's death sound like an accident but then she went on to say that she wasn't so sure. She said she felt sorry for Carl because Chloe was all he had left."

"Did you know about the article?"

"No. Of course not."

"And what did *you* tell her?"

"Nothing! Even if I had wanted to, I wouldn't have had the chance. I couldn't get a word in edgewise."

"So what did she say?"

"She said that she thought Carl was depressed. I asked her how she would know that. She said she was at Starship Records and Tapes the other day after class and was looking at music when Carl Pierce walked in. She said he looked a mess and that he walked out of the store with a stack full of movies. I asked her if she knew which ones."

"*And...?*"

"*Annnnddddd...* she looked at me like I was a weirdo. Like, why would I care what Chloe's dad is watching? But then she said the only one she knew for sure was *The Bride of Fu Manchu,* because it was on the top of the stack."

"So that's it?"

"Yep. You have nothing to worry about. I want to watch what Carl's watching. I want to learn as much about him as possible. I want to know what makes him tick. And I don't think you realize the trouble I went through to get this. Carl must have bought the only copy in the state. I had to order it online." I hit play and let the movie roll. It was a little slow and the audio wasn't the best and by the time the movie was over, Alex was halfway asleep.

"Carl sure knows how to pick 'em." Alex let out a huge yawn, stretched, and then yawned again.

"How would you know? You didn't even watch it."

"I saw more of it than I cared to. So, are you enlightened?" Alex asked.

"I think so. All of those women trapped in Fu Manchu's cave. Held hostage. Fu Manchu reminds me of Carl Pierce. I think when going to war, it's always a good idea to know the strategy, the mindset of the enemy. After watching this, I realize that Carl Pierce knows exactly what he is, and he's *proud* of it."

Outside, the rain had let up and the sirens had finally silenced. I snuggled up close to Alex and thought about Fu Manchu, the villain of the story. Just like Fu, Carl Pierce was evil. And just like Fu Manchu, Carl had girls locked away, held prisoner against their will. Both wanted something and they were preying on someone weaker than themselves to get it. I thought about how the movie ended. With a huge twist. The girls were freed and right when I thought Fu Manchu would be captured, he escaped by the skin of his teeth. He had gotten away with evil, but the story wasn't over yet. How did I know? Because *The Trail of Fu Manchu* comes next. Carl Pierce's story had a twist in it as well. Just like Fu, Carl committed acts of atrocity and got away with them. All at once, I realized that Carl's story wasn't over either. How did I know? I WAS GOING TO MAKE SURE OF IT!

Alex shut off the TV and looked me in the eye. He brushed a piece of hair away from my face and tucked it behind my ear. The tips of his fingers moved down my neck and continued to descend, not stopping until his hand was resting on my brooch. He fumbled with the pin.

"Not sure if you've noticed, but it changes more and more everyday," he said thoughtfully. "It's nearly 50-50. Silver and gold." He used the tip of his finger to trace the detail. "You're…" Alex started to say something but then hesitated.

"What?"

"You're different too." Alex stared at my brooch, unable to look me in the eye. "You've changed."

"No, I haven't."

"Yes, you have."

"Am I 50-50, too? What does that even mean? The way you say it, you sound like you don't like the change."

"No. I like it fine. You seem happier. You're home with your parents. Chloe and Ben are out of the picture. You're with A-Omega now and as far as I know, they're all the protection you need."

"What about you? You're the only constant in my life. The only one I would die for."

"It's harder to live for someone than it is to die for them," Alex said, finally raising his eyes to mine.

I knew exactly what Alex was trying to say. While I would be willing to lose my life for him, he was *living* for me. He was gently reminding me that he wasn't supposed to be here. In a round about way, he was telling me that he was going through the ups and downs of life on earth because he loved me. "To love is to live," he said with finality.

"I feel like you're being negative. I feel like you're trying to tell me that I'm not giving enough."

"I'm just telling you how I feel. I feel like we're moving in opposite directions. I'm gold turning silver and you're silver turning gold."

I was not going to let him upset me, and I tried to consider Alex's feelings before I said any more. "You're changing, too, you know. You're becoming more human. Half angel, half boy," I teased him, trying my hardest to lighten his mood.

"I'm not an angel and I never was," he reminded me.

"Well, maybe we're both 50-50." I smiled. "We're just the same. We're in this together. We're both exactly where we need to be."

CHAPTER THIRTEEN

*M*y nightmare woke me early. Too frightened to fall back asleep, I pulled the sheets to my chin and trembled. Recurring nightmares were nothing new to me. After Chloe died, my dreams about drowning were finally laid to rest and subsequently, so was my fear of the water. Unfortunately, I had only been dream free for a few weeks before another one took its place. This time my subconscious used the sunless skies to take me someplace darker: Carl's cellar. Some nights, I was sifting through the boxes stacked against his basement wall. Other nights, I moved in slow motion across the basement floor toward Carl's workshop door, the door behind which bad things happen. I always woke up in a cold sweat, tangled in my sheets. Even though my nightmares had a way of coming true, I hadn't let myself get too concerned. I shared my newest dreams with Mom. She answered me like a psychiatrist (fascinated by dream analysis), not a mother (overcome with concern). She suggested that I had suppressed my emotions and memories to such an extent that the thoughts I couldn't entertain during the daylight hours were surfacing at night. She reminded me that I had been in Carl's basement and she told me that reading Eva's journal had probably upset me more than I knew. She was convinced that the nightmares were not a prediction of my future, and until just now, I thought she was probably right.

But the dream I just woke from was different. It was different because Carl was in my dream. Not only was he there, he spoke to me. But having a conversation with Carl was not a memory I was trying to suppress, because we had never spoken. I had never heard the sound of his voice, not once. More alarming than the sound of his voice was the expression on his face. It was raging... violent.... out of control. Anger took him over like a super virus. His growing fury was evident by the grotesque and distorted lines on his face. Slit-shaped eyes. Saliva sprayed when he spoke. I had seen pictures of Carl. I knew what he looked like. Tall, dark, and handsome. Publicity shots. All of them staged. I had never seen my biological father without a smile. Thin lips. Shiny, white teeth. In my dream, his anger had taken on a life of its own. I could feel his evil. A shiver went down my spine. Maybe this dream was not related to suppressed memories at all. Maybe this was more than just a dream. I tried to shake the vision, but Carl's grossly distorted features were seared into my mind. With my heart pounding wildly, I flung the cold wet sheet from my body and rolled onto my side, switching on my bedside lamp and checking the time: 7:30 AM. I could hear someone downstairs making breakfast.

When I finally moved out of bed and down the stairs, I found my dad in the kitchen eating oatmeal, drinking coffee, and reading the morning paper. It was the first time we had been alone in the same room since I arrived, and the silence was awkward. Although the lines of communication were finally beginning to open, neither of us knew what to say; Mom was always there to facilitate the conversation. I slipped my hands into the pockets of my robe and with sleepy eyes, shuffled over to the refrigerator.

"There's coffee in the pot." Will pointed to the coffee maker without looking up from his paper. Wire-rimmed glasses sat on the end of his nose and he looked down over them as he read the sports section. I smiled. That was more like the dad I used to know. I grabbed a mug from the cabinet. 2/3 coffee. 1/3 cream. I grabbed the sugar bowl and sat down at the table across from Will.

"No breakfast?" he asked. His tone was flat. Not the concerned father voice that lovingly encouraged me to eat. I used to hate it. Now I missed it.

But at least we were talking and although it wasn't much of a conversation, it was something. He was trying.

"Whatcha reading about?" I asked.

"Basketball. Really rooting for the Thunder. Brand new team. Good players. Want to see 'em do good this year." I took a sip of coffee. "Hey." His voice lifted and he looked up for the first time. "Aren't you following the Jessie Paulman case?"

"I guess so. But last I heard, the investigation had hit a brick wall."

"I don't know. Looks to me like they might have found something." Dad looked at me with bunched lips and concerned eyes as he pushed the paper toward me. I reached out to grab it but then all of a sudden, he had a change of heart. I guess he didn't want me to see the article after all. He tightened his grip on the paper. In response, I tightened my grip and pulled. We were playing a game of tug of war and Will showed no signs of backing down.

"Will," I huffed. "Release the paper." I looked up to find him staring at my hand. He had a hurt look on his face. He looked like a wounded animal.

"What's on your finger, Rae?"

"Oh… that." I fumbled with my words. "Um… nothing."

"Nothing?" He said sharply, dramatically. He had never used that tone with me before.

"Just something Alex gave me," I said, referring to the promise ring Alex gave me a year ago. It was not a promise to marry, which is what my dad thought, I'm sure. It was a promise to love me for eternity.

"Yeah. I'm always the last to know everything around here."

"It's not what you think," I tried to explain.

Dad shook his head, released the paper, and muttered something unintelligible. I snatched it and sure enough, Jessie's picture had made the front page. This meant the investigation *had* taken a turn, and I couldn't imagine it was for the better. I glanced at the text and began to read.

May 25, 2009
Missing Tulsa Teen Thought to be Another Victim of Human Trafficking

After reading the title, a sickening feeling spread through me. I pushed my coffee aside, unfolded the paper, smoothed it flat in front of me, and continued to read.

The disappearance of 19-year-old Jessie Paulman had been written off as another unsolved missing person's case until new information brought to the attention of OSBI suggested the possible link between this Tulsa teen's disappearance and a multi-state human trafficking ring. The 19-year-old girl, who likes to play the guitar and sing, is described by friends and family as a lover of life. "She always sees the best in others. She loves animals and art and is excited about finishing up her senior year and attending art school," her mother said. She was supposed to meet a friend after school then be home in time for dinner, but Jessie Paulman, clad in a tartan wool coat, never arrived.

I refolded the paper and flipped it over. "I knew it. I knew it when I saw her poster hanging in the gas station. I was supposed to see that poster, and I have a feeling that Jessie's a part of my mission."

"That's certainly a possibility."

"I have a feeling Carl has something to do with this!"

"Trust your instincts." After seeing the ring on my finger, Will was doing his best to hide his hurt, but I could still hear a hint of sadness in his voice.

"Well, I hope my instincts aren't right about this," I returned. I was about to push the paper back in his direction when an advertisement caught my attention. Armishaw Jewelers. I had heard the jingle on the radio at least a hundred times, but I never paid much attention to the words. Seeing the lyrics written out before me elicited a much different response. At the bottom of the advertisement was a simple map showing a cross street. Below the map was a one-line catchphrase.

At the corner of Adams and Armstrong.

I stood up and grabbed my coffee. "Mind if I borrow this?" I asked and without waiting for him to respond, I snatched the paper and hurried up the stairs. As if on a mission, I pulled the crumpled souvenir bag out of my nightstand and smoothed it out a bit. I laid it on my desk next to the newspaper. The maps matched up. This was the jewelry store the souvenir lady recommended. She couldn't remember the name of the store, she only knew it was at the corner of Adams and Armstrong. I showered, dressed, and put on a hint of make up and a squirt of perfume. I fastened the old brooch over my heart. Now 8:30, I dialed Alex. He answered with a groggy voice.

"Alex!"

"Rae?" His voice was heavy with sleep. "It's eight-thirty in the morning. Is something the matter?"

"Alex, I think I found another name on my list. Be ready to go by 9:30!"

CHAPTER FOURTEEN

I had seen the billboards for months, and the catchy jewelry jingle on the radio had gotten its fair share of airtime. I was so focused on the rhythm of this mediocre melody that I hadn't considered what they were saying, what they were selling. Seeing the lyrics written in the paper was what finally caught my attention. This morning when I saw the words "antique brooch" and the name "Armishaw" in the same advertisement, my mind began cranking at once.

> If you have a piece of gold
> Something passed down something old
> Armishaw's is the place to come
> Our experts can tell you what year it's from
> A unique treasure? An ornate brooch?
> Armishaw's has the best approach.
> A precious alloy from the earth
> We can tell you what it's worth!
> At Armishaw's

An antique brooch. Armishaw's could tell me what it's worth. They could even tell me when it was made. I unpinned the brooch from my tee shirt and studied the ornate detail. A-Omega hadn't instructed me to do anything with the brooch other than to keep it pinned to my chest at all times. But what if...? What if I was supposed to learn something about the brooch that could help me? Quinn Collins hadn't helped me much with Carl Pierce, but his story had taught me a lesson on how to conquer my negative thoughts and now the antivirus software didn't seem like such a strange gift after all. An antivirus for the mind. Some anti-venom for the soul. There was a Mason Armishaw on my list of names; he had to be affiliated with Armishaw jewelers. I recalled the scripture on the slip of paper attached to the pin.

For where your *treasure* is, your heart will be also.

A unique *treasure*? An ornate *brooch*?

Was the scripture directing me to the jewelry shop? Was the scripture advice? Regardless, there were just too many similarities to ignore.

I jumped in the car and drove to Alex's. Showered, dressed, and waiting for me on the front porch, he was ready. At precisely ten o'clock, we pulled up to a small building on the corner of Adams and Armstrong.

"You sure this is it?"

"It has to be. It's the only building here."

Based on the jingle and the amount of airtime it received, I figured the store had a rather large budget for advertisement and therefore, I assumed the building would be rather impressive. It wasn't. A run down house with a damaged sign, Armishaw jewelers was not what I expected.

Upon closer inspection, the old house took on a more commercial feel. I noticed the residential style entry door had been replaced with an all glass version. The store name was spelled out in black stickers across the glass; the "A", the "H", and the "J" were peeling off. I parked my car in the small lot in front of the store. Equally intrigued by the possibilities, Alex was excited to tag along and as we advanced toward the jewelry shop, the feeling that I was in the right place grew stronger. Mason Armishaw was here. I just knew it. As this feeling of certainty began to escalate, my excitement to hear what he had to say about the brooch did as well.

When I opened the glass door, a bell jingled and a pudgy man with a full white beard swiveled in his chair to acknowledge us. Realizing that his vision was distorted by the huge magnifying lens covering his eyes, he pushed the loupe to the top of his head, gave Alex and me a good look up and down, then swiveled in his chair and returned to what he was doing. "Be with you in a moment."

I walked over to a neighboring counter and looked inside the glass case at the unique jeweled rings and other antique treasures. Alex joined me but when he realized the case was filled with engagement rings, he took a step backward and began playing a game on his phone.

The old man sat with his back facing me as he worked with a small pick, attempting to pry a diamond loose from its setting. "What can I help you with today?" he asked.

"I saw an ad for your store. I have an old brooch. I was hoping you might be able to tell me something about it."

Pushing the loupe to his forehead for a second time, the man turned in his chair and bellied up to the counter. "My name's Mason Armishaw." Suddenly interested, Alex moved up to the counter as the man extended his hand in greeting. "I've been in the business of antique jewelry and appraisal for the past fifty years, and I have found that there's more to a piece of jewelry than precious metal and stones. Behind every piece of jewelry, there's a story. Before I take a look, do you mind telling me what you know about the brooch?"

"Well, that's why I'm here. I don't know anything about it other than it looks old. Really old," I told him, not wanting to share the details about how it arrived at our Minnesota cottage in a box that also contained a list of names, one of which was his.

"May I?" The jeweler motioned to the pin on my tee shirt.

"Oh, of course," I said, unpinning it at once and placing it in the palm of his hand. We were silent as he studied the antique piece. The pin was gorgeous, silver and gold adorned with beautiful stones. I expected an immediate response, a gasp, an ooooh, an ahhh. I could hardly go into town to run an errand without someone commenting on how beautiful it was. It had become a conversation piece and I was surprised that

Mason's initial reaction was quite the opposite. Mason moved his finger along the pin of the brooch. "Sharp enough to prick a finger. Sharp enough to pick a *lock*."

"So what do you think?" I prompted.

"I've never seen anything quite like this. It's old. You're right about that."

"The color of the metal is weird," I told him. "When I first received it, it was gold, no doubt, but when I pinned it to my shirt, it quickly changed. It's now silver and gold. Over the past couple weeks, I've noticed that little flecks of gold are gradually returning. It's the strangest thing."

"It's both actually. Both silver and gold. It's called electrum," he said, eyeing the piece in quiet disbelief. "Have you ever heard of it?"

"Can't say that I have."

"That's probably because it hasn't been produced in almost 1500 years. It's often called the forgotten precious metal; however, it's not a pure metal at all. Not gold. Not silver. Because it hasn't been refined, it's actually an alloy of the two. It can range in color from a pale yellow or yellowish white to a deep yellow. The color variation depends on the gold to silver ratio. Electrum was used to make the earliest coins. It's harder and more durable than gold. Plus, thousands of years ago, refining gold was very labor intensive. I think most people assume that gold just comes out of the ground as a precious metal, but that isn't the case. It's always filled with impurities and to remove them, the craftsman would have to put the alloy into a fire of around 1000 degrees Celsius. Never leaving the flames, he would stir the gold and skim away the impurities. The craftsman knew the refining was complete when he could see his reflection in his work. The word Electrum was also used in ancient writing to describe the precious stone *amber*," he said, pointing to the gems set into the fleur-de-lis design of my brooch. "One reason the alloy and the stone shared the same name is because they share a similar color; both are the color of liquid sunshine. But the similarities don't stop there; both were thought to have healing and protective powers. Amber is actually tree blood. It's the substance a tree uses to repair itself... to heal from the inside out. The alloy electrum was used as armor in ancient times... to protect the body in battle. But when put together in a piece like this, they both heal *and* protect. This brooch has a rich history indeed." Mr. Armishaw, lost in the moment, inspected the brooch closely, pulling his loupe down over his eyes so he could see it more clearly. "Absolutely amazing. Simply unbelievable." The old man flipped the broach over to have another look at the back. "Unbelievable. Un-be-lieve-able."

"What about the color?" I asked. "Does gold have symbolic meaning?"

"Of course. Gold is a symbol of eternity, perfection, purification, and divine love."

"What about silver," Alex interjected.

"Silver is a symbol of strength and atonement. It can withstand extremes: weather, heat, and many kinds of abuse. Regardless of the trials it goes through, it still has the ability to be shaped into a desired form."

"Electrum sounds a bit like electricity to me," Alex chimed in.

Returning the magnifier to the top of his head, Mr. Armishaw began right where he left off. "And that's an excellent hunch. Indeed, both amber and electrum are excellent conductors of heat... of electricity."

"So are you telling me that based on the composition alone, you know this brooch is old... ancient?"

"That's exactly what I'm saying. This brooch is at least fifteen hundred years old."

I tried to speak, but the words wouldn't come. Alex, apparently reading my mind, asked the question that, still stunned, I could not: "Then it must be worth a fortune."

"There's nothing to compare it to. I would say it's priceless."

"What about the fleur-de-lis? Is there a story behind that?" My voice finally returned.

"Fleur-de-lis is French for the lily flower. The three petals represent the Holy Trinity: The Father, The Son, and The Holy Spirit. The fleur-de-lis symbolizes the search for spiritual truth."

The bearded man looked up from the brooch and arched his eyebrows hopefully. "I'd be willing to take this off your hands if you're looking for a buyer."

"It's not for sale. I'm sorry. In fact, I rarely take it off."

"I didn't think so, but it was worth a shot. Is there anything else I can help you with? Anything I can show you, perhaps?"

"Oh, no. I don't think so. We really just came in to ask you about the brooch."

"I've been in the jewelry business for years, and I think I can tell when a girl sees something she likes. Still seated in his chair, Mason rolled over to the glass case where my eyes had indeed been wandering, and then he reached into his pocket and produced a set of keys. Gingerly, he sorted through the keys until he found the one he was looking for. Mason looked up at me and smiled.

"Getting engaged is such a happy time and the engagement is just the beginning of a wonderful rest of your life. My wife, Penny, and I were married for fifty years before she passed."

"Oh. I'm sorry."

"No need to be sorry. We had a long and wonderful life together." The old man inserted the key into the lock and slid open the glass door.

"I think you've misinterpreted our visit," Alex fumbled with his words. "We didn't come to look at rings."

"Once you find that special someone, you never want to let them go," the man returned without acknowledging Alex's previous statement. "Oh how I wish I could have back some of those years with my Penny." Without looking up at me, the old man reached into the case that held at least a hundred different rings and plucked the shiny engagement ring from the velvet bed where it had been resting and presented it to me.

"Wow. You're good," I told him. "How did you know which one I was looking at?"

"Like I told you before, I've been doing this for years. Would you like to try it on?"

Of course I wanted to try it on, but before responding, I glanced in Alex's direction to check for his response.

"Well, while we're here," he sighed. "and he already has it out of the case, we might as well see how it looks on your hand."

Not moving my eyes from Alex, a smile spread across my face as Mason gently pushed the ring onto my finger.

"It's beautiful," Alex whispered. "I'm guessing it's old. Is there a story behind it?"

"As with every antique piece, there is a story behind the ring as well. There's a history with jewelry. Generally, I hear stories about mothers wanting to pass down a special piece to their children. It connects that child to their loved one. It gives them something to remember them by."

I knew exactly what he meant. I had a similar experience with the silver locket. The necklace had been in my family for years. It had belonged to my nana, then my mother, then Laney. When I was thirteen, the locket was given to me. When I wore it, I felt a connection to the past.

"In the same way, all of the items in my store have stories. Each piece had an owner once upon a time. I believe the story of the original owner should be passed on to the future owner and has the potential to impact their lives in positive and beautiful ways."

I studied the shiny princess cut diamond. Surrounded by smaller diamonds, the solitaire was set into a platinum band.

"Don't you want something bigger?" Alex asked. "How many carats are we looking at, Mr. Armishaw?"

"It's a half carat in the center. With the surrounding diamonds, the total weight is just over a carat."

"It's perfect. Can you tell us the story behind it?" I asked.

"I hope you're not offended, but I save the story for the person who will be wearing the ring for a lifetime. It's not a money thing. I hardly care about that. I think there's a special ring for everyone. The story behind the ring is also very special, and I share it only once."

"Okay. That's understandable. Thanks so much, Mr. Armishaw, for helping me with my brooch," I said, taking the beautiful ring off my finger and handing it back to the old man.

Mr. Armishaw looked past me and focused on Alex. "If there is anything I can help you with in the future... anything at all, you know where to find me."

Alex began to tug at his shirt and fan himself as we exited the store. "Is it me, or was it was hot in there?"

"It would be nice to hear the story." I nudged him gently in the side.

Before closing the door behind me, I looked over my shoulder and noticed a piece of cardstock that had been taped to the register. *For where your treasure is, there your heart will be also.*

We had definitely come to the right place.

50-50. Mason Armishaw confirmed it. My brooch was changing. Alex was right. But was he right about me? Was I changing, too? And if so, was that necessarily a bad thing? Changing? It was a word that perplexed me. I never really knew who I was before and with all that was going on now, how was I supposed to know what I was turning into? Who is Rae Colbert? "Who am I," I asked myself. I was reminded of Alex's short list of defining characteristics on the social media site. We were more alike than he knew. I was making lists, too. He was making a list of truths, while I was making a list of lies. I pulled my new laptop off my desk and carried it over to my bed. I flopped down on my stomach and began to set up profile pages on various social media sites, just like Alex had done. *Name. Sex. Relationship status.* Then came the hard part. *About me.* What did I love? What made me, me? I started with the obvious.

Alex. He was what I loved most.

Then I moved on, surprised by how easily the list was coming together.

My family. Coffee. Books. Sleep. Cocoa. Talking to my mom. Reading. Music. My iPhone. Vintage. Spaghetti. Lip Gloss. Jeans with holes. My boots. Painting. Purple. Looking at old scrapbooks. Minnesota. Peanut butter and honey sandwiches. A-Omega. Lattes. Bookstores. Romance. Running. Boy Miro and Miro. My robe. The lake. Ice hockey. Dates. The Sun.

Maybe I knew myself better than I thought.

CHAPTER FIFTEEN

I went to bed thinking about Mason Armishaw, with his fluffy white beard and the loupe that rested on his forehead. This in turn led me to consider the brooch and what it was made of. Electrum. A mixture of silver and gold. An alloy known for its protective powers. I was even more drawn to the story of how gold is derived from electrum. Heated in the pits of the fire, the goldsmith skimmed away the impurities until only gold remained. The goldsmith knew the process was complete when he saw his reflection in his work. And the stones that were set into the brooch. Amber. Tree blood. Healing from the inside out. Even the pin's design held meaning. The *fleur-de-lis*: a symbol that represents the search for spiritual truth. I considered my brooch. Gold when I received it but appearing more silver when I pinned it to my chest. Although still more silver than gold, it was slowly regaining some of its original color, and I wondered if perhaps I was being refined. I definitely felt like I had been placed in the midst of the flames. Nothing was going the way I wanted it to, and yet I forged on.

Just before nodding off for the night, my mind drifted to the engagement rings in the case, and more specifically, the one I slid onto my finger. I wished I knew the story behind it. I was dying to find out. But when my eyes fell shut, darkness invaded my pleasant thoughts and my dreams became a nightmare: I found myself in Carl's basement. The room was dark and dank and a familiar smell filled the air around me. I fished my hand into my pocket and reached for the LED flashlight that I thought to bring along. With a trembling hand, I pushed the button and a narrow beam of light shone onto a row of boxes stacked against a concrete wall. I moved the flashlight up toward the ceiling and back down. Boxes. Boxes. Boxes. Each box was labeled with a name. Then I saw a name that was familiar. My flashlight haloed the word Abbott. A last name. I moved the beam of light a fraction of an inch until the first name came into view. "Gracie." A sinking feeling developed in the pit of my stomach. I glanced at the stairs I had crept up exactly one year ago, but instead of ascending into the Pierce's living room as I had previously done, I inched my way across the concrete floor toward Carl's workshop door. Moving through the darkness, my pathway lit by a single beam of light, I came to a stop in front of the door that marked the entrance to his workshop. My hand swept over the concrete wall, searching for the switch I knew was there, and when I found it, I flicked it on. Light poured out from beneath the door. I gave the knob a cautious twist. It was unlocked. I started to push open the door, when I heard the sound of a chiming doorbell. I stood stock-still and listened. I could hear the sound of a door being opened somewhere in the distance. Then the sound of voices. I returned my attention to the unlocked workshop door, gave the knob a full turn, and pushed it open. The light inside was so bright, I couldn't see a thing. My eyes were still adjusting when I heard the sound of footsteps. With each second, they grew louder. So close, they were nearly upon me now. Then came the sound of the turning of a doorknob. Silence. My heart was pounding hard in my chest. Silence. A warm hand on my chilled skin. Tight. Gripping. Noooooo!!!!!!!!!!

My eyes shot open and I drew a startled breath. I sat up with a start, arms flailing. Mom stumbled backward, but caught herself on my bedside table.

"Well, God bless America," she gasped.

It took a moment for me to realize that I was not in a dark basement; rather, I was surrounded by all the comforts of home. My colorful batik duvet had been tossed to the floor, a tell-tale sign of restless sleep. I sat in silence for a moment, still trying to convince myself that I was not in Carl Pierce's basement; but rather, I was having another vivid nightmare. Caught off guard by my violent waking, Mom approached me for a second time and carefully sat down on the edge of my bed, studying me curiously.

"There are some dreams we never want to wake up from and others we can't wake up from fast enough. Another nightmare?"

I exhaled and fell back onto my soft feather pillow. "Thanks for waking me." I rolled over onto my side and studied her perfect features. Soft brown hair. Perfect pixie cut. Clear blue eyes. A small mouth with full lips, the corners of which were always turned upward in a smile. Porcelain skin, close to translucent. She was holding a large envelope in her hands.

"Do you mind me asking what *this* dream was about?"

I gave her a sharp look. Being that Sue and Will were both shrinks, analyzing dreams was one of their favorite pastimes and their preferred method for psychodiagnosis; however, more recently she was very careful to walk the tightrope between psychiatrist and Mom.

"Same as the last one."

Still seated at the end of my bed, she set the envelope down beside my pillow. "The delivery man punched the bell at least five times. I did my best to make it to the door before it woke you up. But…." my mother hesitated. "When I saw that the envelope was addressed to you, I just had to show you. I knew you'd want to open it right away."

I sat up and rubbed my eyes before taking the envelope in both my hands. Eyes still bleary, I looked for a return address. There was none. Still half asleep, I looked at her confused.

"Why don't you come downstairs and open it. I made breakfast… and coffee. You look like you might need a kick-start this morning. Come on," she urged. "It's French toast. I made it just for you."

"I guess I *could* eat something."

Mom hurried down the stairs, but I wasn't quite as energetic as she was. Still groggy, I climbed out of bed and slipped on my robe before joining her in the kitchen. It was a beautiful morning. The sun was shining. No rain pelting against my window. Were the storms finally over?

"Well…?" she said in a singsong voice. Mom was standing in front of the stove, scrambling some eggs to go along with the toast. I took a seat on the barstool and rubbed my eyes before glancing at the envelope. I was confident that she and I shared the same hunch: this letter was from A-Omega. Mom had anxious eyes and was paying more attention to the envelope than to her cooking. I was surprised by her interest. Ever since I was a child, she had done her best to keep me from the clutches of Carl Pierce. And now, A-Omega was sending me after the man that she and Will had spent a good part of their lives trying to protect me from and she was excited about it? It didn't make sense. The kitchen television was turned on and as I ripped open the envelope, Mom switched the channel from a cooking show to the news. She set the remote on the counter, flipped a piece of French toast onto a plate, and doused it with maple syrup. A piece of paper. I held it in my hands, staring at it, remembering how A-Omega had contacted me in the past, and wondering why they might be trying to make contact with me now. I hadn't heard from them in months. I could feel my mother's eyes boring into me as she finished putting my breakfast on the plate. She scooped up a huge helping of eggs. Missing my plate completely, she dropped them onto the floor.

"Okay. Now all you have to do is unfold the piece of paper," she snorted as she stooped over to clean up the mess. I could tell she was growing impatient.

"You do it," I said. "I feel sick to my stomach."

Mom stood up, wiped her hands off on a dishtowel, and made a second attempt to scoop some eggs onto my plate. She slid my breakfast across the counter. My mom had never been much of a cook, so I wasn't sure what had gotten into her while I was away. She still loved to work in the garden, but baking had become her new favorite pass time. I glanced at the mixing bowl on the counter and the empty packaging beside it. Eggshells. An empty bag of chocolate chips. The wrapping from a stick of butter. Chocolate chip cookies! Mom was making dessert before I had even finished breakfast.

Sue was still looking at me with eager eyes. We made the exchange. I grabbed the plate. She grabbed the letter. I took a bite of French toast while she unfolded the piece of paper.

"It's an itinerary, of course." She looked up and raised her eyebrows.
"Is it from A-Omega?"

"Yes."

"Looks like they have me on the run again," I sighed.

Mom chuckled. "Settle down. No reason to get worked up just yet."

I cut the French toast into bite-sized pieces and shoved another forkful into my mouth. "So where am I going this time?"

"It's not ladylike to talk with your mouthful. Houston. You're going to Houston," she replied and pushed the itinerary back in my direction. I set my fork down and picked up the piece of paper. This time there were no instructions. Just an itinerary. Very official. I was to fly out of Tulsa International Airport on the 18th of July and I would be returning on the 21st. Not a very long stay, I thought. I looked at the bottom of the page and saw that the ticket had been paid for in advance. The responsible party, A-Omega. Ticket. Just one.

Telling Alex about the package was the first thing on my mind, but after looking at the cuckoo clock hanging on the kitchen wall, I was reminded that it wasn't even 9 o'clock. Alex's sleeping habits had drastically changed since we arrived. While in Minnesota, Alex was often up at dawn, and taking a morning swim in the ice-cold water of Lake L'homme Dieu had become his morning ritual. Alex had a lust for life. He used to be the kind of guy who didn't like to miss a thing. He hadn't wanted to rest while the world was going on around him. But not anymore. Alex liked to stay up late working on his Porsche and then sleep the day away. In reality, Alex's sleeping habits were not the only thing that had changed. He was changing, too. I first began to notice the subtle changes in Alex on New Year's Day; after spending New Year's Eve playing in the snow, Alex had caught his first cold, but it wasn't until two month later, when I saw the eagle spread across his chest, that I put two and two together. Alex was becoming human. Of course he needed more sleep.

I knew how much I despised being woken before I was ready. I got up from the barstool, snuck a huge spoonful of cookie dough, and made my way upstairs. I took a shower to kill time. Even though the air was still cool, the sun was shining. Summer. Finally. So I dried off, slipped on some jean shorts, and rolled them up an inch and a half to make them shorter. I paired the denim with a long sleeved black and white striped t-shirt and of course, the black combat boots from A-Omega. I picked up my robe, which I had thrown on the ground, and hung it on the hook in my bathroom. I turned toward the vanity and stared into the mirror at my reflection. The bathroom light was off, but the sun beaming in through my bedroom window provided just enough light to make out my distinctive features. Tall. Skinny. Long black hair. High cheekbones. Alex said I had changed, but I thought I still looked the same. I flicked on the light switch and held my face several inches from the mirror. Maybe there was something different. If so, it was subtle. Hmmm.

It didn't bother me that Alex thought I had changed, but I didn't like hearing him say it. It wasn't what he said, but how he said it. There was disappointment in his voice. A hint of sadness, maybe. What did he expect? How could anyone go through the things I had been through and remain the same? Did he want me to go back inside my shell? I didn't want to go back. I was surprised how much I enjoyed *feeling*. Even though *feeling* could hurt sometimes, the ability to feel made me feel free. And I would rather hurt than feel nothing at all. I shrugged, pulled out the vanity drawer and rummaged through it, searching for my powder. I brushed a generous amount across my face and then coated my lips with a tinted gloss that smelled like cupcakes. I pinned my brooch over my heart and finished lacing up my boots. Complete. I switched off the bathroom light.

Even though I had successfully convinced Alex that my Dad was at work and not at home, I still had to bribe him to get him to come over. After promising to share with him some cookie dough and a bit of exciting news, he promised that he was on his way. I slipped my cell phone into my pocket and returned to the kitchen to find my mother spooning dough balls onto a cookie sheet.

"Alex is coming over and I promised to save him some dough."

"I saved some back for you, too. You look thinner than ever, Rae. You need to put a little meat on your bones." Mom looked me up and down. "Still a little chilly for shorts, don't you think?"

"I'm fine Mom," I reassured her. I took a seat on the barstool, the perfect place to watch Mom cook. I crossed my legs and planted my elbows on the counter. I leaned forward, letting my chin rest on my hands, and silently watched Sue at work. The news was still on and the weatherman was going on about a cold front that was heading our way and how we could expect another couple inches of rain.

"If you say so." Mom shrugged her shoulders and returned her attention to the cookie sheet. "Do you think he's going to be upset?" Mom asked, changing the subject.

"Huh? Who? Alex? Why would he be upset?" I folded my arms across my chest and straightened my back.

"There isn't an airline ticket for him."

"Oh…" My voice trailed off as I remembered the conversation Alex and I had at Woolaroc. Alex was still bound and determined to protect me, and he didn't like feeling left out. "Good point." How was Alex going to protect me if he wasn't there? "It'll be fine. I'm sure Alex will just buy a ticket and try to get on my flight. There's no way he's going to let me go all by myself."

My mom bit her lower lip and turned her attention back to the dough, using an ice cream scoop to plop an extra large, perfectly shaped dough ball onto the cookie sheet.

"Mom? Why are you making that face? Why aren't you saying anything?" Still sitting cross-legged on the stool, I began to bounce my foot up and down.

"Well. A-Omega would have…." Mom started to explain, but she was interrupted by a noise on the TV. The sound of rolling drums followed by a high-pitched note on the synthesizer. Late breaking news. In one swift motion, I swapped my fork for the remote and turned up the volume. "Hold that thought. I want to see this."

"I don't know what's gotten into you, Rae. You never used to care about the news."

"Shhh," I told her, trying to catch what the pretty brunette anchorwoman was saying.

"I'm here this morning to report a terrible discovery. Police found a body floating in Lake Keystone. Phillipa Jenkins, News 4 Crime Tracker, has been following this breaking story all morning and she joins us now. Phillipa:" The camera panned in on a reporter: a woman of Hispanic descent.

"Jessica, both Sand Springs Police and OSBI have cleared the area, but they spent most of last night and this morning scouring the shore near the lake and the surrounding woods looking for evidence. Police tell us a couple discovered the body near the shoreline just east of the turnpike at around 6:30 last evening and called the police."

The camera focused on Jack Schwartz, Sand Springs' police chief.

"We are unsure of the deceased's identity. It appears the body has been here for several days. Any person who has seen suspicious activity around the Keystone Lake area in the last two weeks, please contact authorities. This would be very valuable to our investigation."

The camera zoomed in on Phillipa.

"The body was taken to the morgue last night and a medical examiner is performing a complete autopsy. We are hopeful that they will be able to make a positive ID later this afternoon. Reporting live in Sand Springs, I'm Phillipa Jenkins."

"All right Phillipa, Sand Springs police are checking with other police departments around the metro to see if there are any missing person cases that might be related. We will keep you updated as news breaks."

I switched off the TV. "It's Jessie. I just know it is, Mom."

"Well, I think you're jumping to conclusions. They didn't even say if the body they found belonged to a man or a woman."

"But I just know it is. Have you ever had that feeling? When there's no evidence to prove it, but you just feel it in your bones."

"I do know what you mean. When your dad and I were in Asia, w-"

Mom had just started into a story when she was interrupted once again. This time it wasn't the signature sound of late breaking news that diverted our attention. Instead, it was a loud and booming noise that startled us both.

"Do you hear that?"

"Yes. Yes, I do? It sounds like something's coming down from the sky!" Mom abandoned the dough on the counter and looked out the kitchen window. "I don't see anything, Rae." Mom was leaning over the kitchen sink; her nose was pressed against the glass. "Wait a minute. I see dust. I think someone's coming up the road."

Mom looked at me in disbelief.

"Alex!" We said in unison.

With stocking feet, she slid across the wood floors into the dining room where she could get a better view. I hopped off the stool and followed suit. Sure enough, we were right. Alex was flying down the road in his '56 Speedster.

Mom and I exchanged looks of astonishment. "He thinks he's James Bond," I tried to explain.

The car was old and of course, the stereo system was subpar. Upgrading the audio was definitely on Alex's *want* list, I knew that, but I just figured he would take care of some of the more functional items first, like, for instance, the leaky soft-top. As Alex pulled into our circle drive, Mom and I moved from the dining room to the front porch to greet him. After the dust settled, Alex opened the car door and stepped out.

"So, what do you think?"

"It's a classic. Beautiful," Mom said as she descended the steps and approached the vintage Porsche. "Looks like it still needs a lot of work, though." Mom ran her hand across the chipped paint. Alex noticed what she noticed and he interjected. "It's what's inside that counts," Alex smiled. "I've spent most of my time under the hood. You wanna see?" Alex raised his eyebrows hopefully.

"Sure," Mom said, shrugging her shoulders.

Alex moved to the rear of the Porsche, opened what appeared to be the lid of the trunk, and stood proudly beside his work in progress.

"Engine's in the back, huh? I would like to say I know a little bit about cars, but I don't. It does look impressive, though." Mom studied his license plate. "And what is this? A personalized plate!"

I scrambled down the stairs and joined my mother at the rear of the car. My jaw dropped. "Really, Alex? NLIMBO?" Alex smiled a toothy smile. "You're taking your new name seriously."

"I figure if A-Omega put the name on my passport, then I should use it."

"Actually, the name is very James Bond-ish. Ian Limbeaux fits right in there with Miss Moneypenny."

Alex ignored my sarcasm, moved to the front of the car, and lifted what should have been the hood, revealing a large speaker that completely filled the small trunk. "And this ladies, is my baby... the bazooka tube... aka, a subwoofer."

"That explains why we could hear you coming down the road before we could see you," Mom said, moving around to the driver's side door and opening it. "You don't mind, do you?"

"Of course not. You can take it for a spin, if you like."

"No. Not now. I have cookies in the oven," she said, situating herself in the aged leather seat. "It's a piece of art. It really is. I can't wait to see it when it's finished."

Alex rested his arm on the driver's side door and leaned the rest of his body in the car, going over the details of what he had already done, and what he still had left to do.

"This is a lot of car, Alex."

"I figure that with Rae working for A-Omega, I can put it to good use. I came to the conclusion that if I was going to keep Rae safe, then I was going to need something fast. I loved the Wagoneer, but it just wouldn't have stood a chance against Carl Pierce's collection of hotrods."

Mom gave me a sidelong look. "He has a collection? I guess you know more about Carl than I do," Mom said, still looking at me out of the corner of her eye.

"Yes, a big collection."

"If you say so, Ian Limbeaux. Well, I guess I'll leave you two alone. I have to finish up in the kitchen. Maybe I'll take it for a spin another time." Halfway to the front door, Mom stopped and turned toward us. "It's good to have you back at the house, Alex." Mom's smile was warm and full of meaning.

"It's good to be back, Mrs. Colbert."

"And Rae, I have a big surprise for you when you get home. So don't be too long."

As soon as Mom shut the door, Alex turned to me with hopeful eyes. "So which do I get first, a cookie or the good news?"

"How about we go for a drive?"

INTERCESSION

CHAPTER SIXTEEN

*T*en minutes later, I was lying on top of a patchwork quilt in the middle of the park, using my colored pencils to draw pictures of Alex in my sketchbook. It couldn't have been a more perfect day and from where we were, I could see the bridge and hear the creek water gurgling underneath. Alex was sitting on the edge of the blanket eating one of Sue's cookies.

"I received correspondence today," I informed Alex, breaking the silence.

Alex swallowed a mouthful of cookie and looked at me with his big, green eyes. "From A-Omega? Is that the news?"

"Yes, from A-Omega."

"That's great news! What did they say?"

I rolled over on my side and Alex joined me, using his elbow to support the weight of his upper body. With our faces aligned, I noticed the gentleness of his eyes. Among other things, Alex's eyes had changed, not in the way that they looked (hazel green pinwheels), but *I* felt different when I looked into them. I no longer felt the need to be protected; I felt the need to protect.

"They sent another letter."

"And?"

"Houston."

"When do they want us there? I'm ready to start right away. I never thought I'd hear myself saying this after what happened with Chloe and Ben, but I'm ready for another adventure."

"July 18th. It's still a ways out. But there's one little issue." My mother's words were fresh in my mind. I began to wonder how Alex would take the news. "There was only one plane ticket."

It took a moment for Alex to process what I was saying and what this meant for him, but when realization finally hit him, he looked hurt, angry, and confused. I felt guilty.

"I don't get it."

"I don't either." Through sympathetic eyes, I looked at Alex. He relaxed onto his back and looked up at the sky. "I'm sorry. Maybe you could just buy a plane ticket and hop on the same flight. I could use the company."

Alex was still looking skyward. "No. They must not want me there. They must have a reason."

"If it makes you feel any better, I don't really want to go alone. I'm scared."

Alex reached into the plastic baggie and grabbed another cookie.

"Well, it doesn't. It doesn't make me feel any better. But you trust them, right?"

"I trust them. I am so ready to trust in something. I just have this overwhelming feeling that they know best. Do you know what I mean?"

"No," Alex returned with sharpness in his tone that chilled me.

"It's not something that I can really explain."

"Try."

"I've grown up hearing about A-Omega because of Mom and Dad and Nana and Papa. My parents have always been with A-Omega. They know them well. I think they would give their lives for A-Omega, should it come to that. I'm not sure how it's possible, but I feel like A-Omega knows me better than I know myself. On the other hand, I feel like I'm just getting to know them. A part of me is scared because I realize things might change. I haven't been back long and already things are changing. It scares me because I look at all the moving my parents did because A-Omega told them to. I don't want to move all over the place. I'd kind of like to settle down for once in my life. And leaving you isn't an option. Not even for a couple of days. I really wish you'd consider buying a ticket and coming with me."

Alex was staring at the clouds with a blank expression on his face.

"A penny for your thoughts."

Still looking upward, Alex didn't respond.

"Alex?"

Reluctantly, he rolled back onto his side and looked me in the eye. "What?"

"What are you thinking about?"

Alex wet his lips and ran a hand through his hair. "Guitars."

A bit caught off guard by his response, my voice took on a quizzical tone. "What? Really? That's random. *Really?*" I asked, slightly offended that I had shared some of my most heartfelt feelings, that I had just said things out loud that had previously only been present in the quietest portions of my mind, and all Alex was thinking about was guitars. Had he even heard me? "Guitars?"

"I'm thinking about buying a guitar and teaching myself to play."

"Okay. And this just came to you?"

"No. I've been thinking about it for a while. Just wasn't sure when I would fit it in. But the Speedster is getting close to being finished. Two months, tops. With your new career, it looks like I might have a little free time on my hands."

"That's awesome," I fumbled with my words. "Electric or acoustic?" I didn't know what to say or how to say it. I was prepared to make an apology. I had come up with a rather short speech about how everything was going to be okay between us, even if I was gone for a bit here and there. I was ready to remind him that we had already been through so much and here we were, still together, still happy, but in less than one minute, he had already moved on. He had already erased me from his calendar and filled the blank spot with something else.

"Maybe both. But I found an acoustic guitar on Craig's list. I'm going to start out with that. He's only asking 75 dollars for it, and it's practically new. I think I'll call the guy and see if I can look at it tonight."

"I'm sure you'll be great," I said. I loved that Alex wrote lyrics, and I didn't doubt that he would excel in playing an instrument, but I couldn't deny that we seemed to be moving in opposite directions, and that scared me more than anything else. When we were in Minnesota, we had different opinions on how to handle Chloe and Ben, but at least we were aiming for the same goal. Now that I was with A-Omega, things seemed different between us.

"So what are you going to do if you get in trouble?" All seriousness returned to Alex.

"You mean if I get in trouble in Houston?"

"Of course that's what I mean."

"I don't know. The other day when I went to Collin's repair, I saw a dojo. Maybe I should look into karate classes."

"Karate class? Are you serious?"

"Of course I'm serious!"

Alex moved a hand though his shaggy brown hair. "You say you're scared, but you seem hell-bent on going after Carl. That's trouble any way you look at it."

"It is my mission. Besides, things are only getting worse. Did you hear about the body they found floating in Lake Keystone?"

"No."

"They haven't identified it yet, but I'd be willing to bet that it's Jessie Paulman. I'd also be willing to bet that Carl Pierce had something to do with her death."

"You're turning into a conspiracy theorist."

"It's just a hunch."

"If you are right, that further proves my point. Carl is dangerous."

"Of course he's dangerous, but I thought you agreed that going after Carl was a good idea. I thought you agreed that he belongs in prison."

"That's when I thought I'd be going with you."

"Are you trying to tell me something?" I laughed and snuggled up to Alex. "That I'm puny?" I giggled.

Alex moved his hand up my arm and enclosed it around my entire bicep. Then he raised his eyebrows. With one simple gesture, he had proven his point.

"You don't have faith in me? Is that it?"

"Faith? Are you kidding me? After all the messes you've gotten yourself into," Alex scoffed, and I could tell that he was no longer joking. "You're so flippant about your well-being. I came here to protect you." Alex shook his head in disgust. "Do you even realize what I have given up to be here?"

"*Every day*," I whispered.

"I'm sorry. That came out wrong." Alex took a deep breath and pulled me to him. His lips brushed across the top of my head, and he wound his fingers through my hair. "I want to be on earth because you're here. That's the *only* reason, Rae. I'll do whatever it takes to stay. But if something happens to you then I don't know what I…."

"Stop," I interrupted and looked him in the eyes. "Nothing is going to happen to me."

"Yes. I forgot. You're going to take karate. Rae, the black belt," Alex laughed.

"What's so funny?" I smacked his arm playfully. Alex got up from the blanket and gave me his hand.

"Come on," he urged, pulling me off the ground with a single tug. "Let's go for a walk." Alex folded up the blanket and placed it on top of the subwoofer in the trunk of his car. "I was out here the other day and saw the coolest thing ever."

Alex took my hand and started toward the trees. I felt a little anxious as we stepped into the woods. Nothing good had ever happened to me in the forest. Alex could sense my unease and he asked, "What's wrong?"

"I'm just thinking about what happened on this path last year. I was just going for a run. The next thing I know, Benard Bodin has me pinned to the ground, trying to kill me." I felt a chill as I thought of Ben.

"And I saved you, remember?"

I exhaled but didn't respond.

"Come on. You have nothing to worry about today. Like I said before, the forest is a safer place now that Ben's gone." Alex stopped, looked over his shoulder then glanced at me and smiled. "Unless you're still worried about Bigfoot."

"*Worried?* I never said I was worried about Bigfoot. I said *you* should be worried about Bigfoot." I tried to sound convincing. "But I'm serious, Alex. What happened last year doesn't seem real. But it was real. It seems like it happened in another life. But it happened just last year." How could I forget the feel of Ben's hands wrapped around my neck? Unable to breath, I thought I was dying.

"Do you ever think about her?"

"About Chloe?"

"Yes."

"I try not to. It's weird. For years, I thought Laney was my sister, and because she died on the day that I was born, I just knew I was responsible for her death. If I could have wished for anything, I would have wished to meet her. I wanted a sister so badly. Then after a crazy turn of events, I found out that I had a sister after all. Chloe. Not quite the sister I had in mind. I'm not sure what hurts worse, losing Chloe or knowing that my own sister wanted me dead."

We had barely gone a quarter of a mile before Alex released my hand, veered off the concrete, and began to make a path of his own through the forest. I turned sideways and squeezed through an opening between the branches. Trying my best to keep up with him, I trudged across the swampy ground. It had been raining nonstop since we arrived in Oklahoma, and it appeared that all the rainwater had drained into the low-lying portion of the forest where Alex was headed. Although the sun was shining, the wind was nippy and it whistled through the branches of the trees. As goose bumps formed on my legs, I began to wish I had listened to my mom's advice and picked jeans instead of shorts.

"Just a little bit further."

"Ummhum. Next you're going to tell me to trust you."

Alex looked over his shoulder and smirked. "Trust me." Then he stretched out his hand and I grabbed hold.

"You do remember that I almost died... right here. In this forest. Actually, I think it was a little to the west."

"Rae...."

"Yes."

"Trust me. It will be worth it. I promise."

I followed Alex deeper into the woods. After another fifty yards, he let go of my hand and walked ahead of me. He came to a stop under a tree.

"We're here," he informed me, reaching his hands into the sky.

"Where? Where are we, Alex?"

"Look closely." When Alex lifted his hands into the air, his short-sleeved tee shirt slid up his arm and I couldn't help but notice his well-defined bicep.

"Am I supposed to be looking at you or the tree?" I teased.

Alex took off his backpack and unzipped it. "The tree, Rae, the tree," he said as he pulled out his dad's old camera and began to snap close ups of the leaves, the bark, the branches.

"You're taking pictures of tree bark, Alex. You *have* been bored. Maybe getting a guitar *is* a good idea."

Alex snapped another picture and then pointed at a leaf directly above his head, begging me to take a closer look.

I joined Alex beneath its branches. "Now, what am I supposed to be looking at?" I jeered. Still pointing at the leaf, Alex rolled his eyes. "I don't see anything. I feel like I'm five years old sitting in the dentist's office looking at a Highlights magazine. You know, the page with the hidden pictures."

"If I remember correctly, you loved those magazines and that was your favorite page."

"You're right," I said. "But I wasn't very good at finding the hidden objects. Mom always had to help me."

"I'll give you a hint, then. What you're looking for is kind of… almond shaped."

All at once, my eyes went wide with realization. "It's a cocoon!" I shouted. "I see it!"

"Not just a single cocoon. The entire tree is filled with them."

"You're kidding me. I've never seen anything like this. They're camouflaged."

"Some of the cocoons are green and some are brown."

"When will the butterflies come out?"

"It depends on what type of butterfly it is. If I had to guess, I would say that they're black swallowtails."

"Is there anything you don't know?"

"The swallowtail is the state butterfly. It's just a guess, but if I'm right, the park will be filled with them soon."

I stood on my tiptoes and grabbed hold of a branch, pulling it down in order to take a closer look at the cocoon that was fastened to the leaf. "They're not very pretty."

"The most beautiful butterflies emerge from the ugliest cocoons."

"Is that true?" I asked as I released the limb, watching it spring upward.

"It is."

I turned around to find Alex looking at me through the lens of his camera. I started to move toward him when he stopped me.

"Don't move another inch." My muscles went taut with surprise.

Alex grinned and looked me up and down. "You look so perfect. Just like that. Right where you are. I have to take a picture."

"Fine," I pouted and shifted my weight.

"I mean it. Don't move a muscle." Alex pressed his face against the camera and began to focus the lens. "The light is absolutely perfect. You have a halo around you. It's a perfect yellow halo. You look like an angel."

"A dark angel, maybe." I flashed a mischievous smile. "Do you want me to pose?"

"No," Alex's voice was so soft, it was as if he was talking to himself. "Just do exactly what you're doing."

It was weird to see Alex looking at me like he was. Like I was something foreign to him, something to be explored. While I did hate having my picture taken, I kind of liked being Alex's subject, the focus of his attention. Alex knew everything about me. There wasn't much I could do to surprise him. He had seen me grow up. He had watched my life from up above. But when he looked through his camera, it was like he was seeing something new, something fascinating that he had never noticed before. He was discovering me. I loved that there was something about me that could still surprise him, allure him, and hold him captive.

CHAPTER SEVENTEEN

A big surprise! Mom wasn't lying. She had spent the last two months hiding away in the small workshop off the garage. I thought she was planting flowers. I thought she needed alone time. If only I had known what she was really doing. Mom had converted my dad's garage workshop into a bona fide art studio. She had painted the walls candy apple green and covered dad's tool bench and the cabinets above with black chalkboard paint. Gone were the old rusty pulls. In their place were shiny silver knobs. She had written on the front of each cabinet door in chalk. I opened the door labeled "oils" and was taken aback. Not only had she bought huge tubes of oil paint in every color, but she had also taken the time to arrange them neatly. I shut the cabinet door and glanced at the others. There was a door marked "acrylics and watercolors," a door marked "brushes," a door marked "oil pastels/ nupastels/ pencils/ markers," and a door marked "gesso." On top of the tool bench was a pair owl bookends; books about famous artists and museums were positioned between the two birds. On the other side of the workbench was a small television and an iPod docking station with speakers.

"So what do you think? Did I do good?"

"Too good. I thought Dad was mad before. He'll *never* talk to me again when he finds out I've taken over his workshop."

"It was his idea, you know."

"Really?" I returned, a trifle surprised. I walked over to the window and sat down on the stool in front of my old easel. I tilted my head to the side and studied the landscape painting in front of me. "This is horrible," I laughed. "I remember when I went through that landscape phase. The only thing I wanted to paint were trees and flowers, but I couldn't seem to get it right. I probably went through ten canvases."

"More like fifteen. And they weren't horrible. You were learning. You hadn't found your niche."

"Come on, Mom. They're terrible. Just admit it."

"I thought you could add to them. You never know. If not," Mom said, pointing to the cabinet marked 'gesso,' "you can always cover the canvas with gesso and start fresh. What ever you decide, there's enough here to keep you busy for a while."

I stood up and walked around my new studio. Mom had taken my childhood artwork, had it framed, and hung it on the walls. "Do you like it?"

"Mom. I'm pretty sure no one has ever done anything this nice for me. I can't believe you kept all my old artwork. I think I painted that one when I was five. I used finger paints instead of oils."

"You're very talented… just like Eva." Mom sniffled and dried her eye. "I really hated to pull you out of your college art class, but I'm so glad you're home."

"I don't need to go to school to be an artist, Mom. Besides, now that I'm with A-Omega, who knows what lies ahead."

"I'd love to see you take some classes this fall. Just consider this an extended intersession."

"We'll see."

"I guess I'll leave you to it. Do you have everything you need?"

"Are you kidding? I have air conditioning, a heater, a TV, paints, music, and my laptop. If I had a refrigerator and a coffee pot, you'd never see me again."

"Don't you know I thought of that?"

When Mom left the studio, I flicked on the TV. Ready to get started at once, I grabbed a bottle of gesso off the shelf and used the remote to change the channel to the news, one of the many signs that I *was* changing. Less than a year ago, I would barely glance at a newspaper. I didn't want to know what was going on in the world unless it was something good. Like the other day when I was reading the paper, I saw an article that made me smile. *Sperm Whales Adopt a Deformed Dolphin.* I thought to myself, this is the *only* kind of story I would have read about last year. How strange that the only acts of kindness found in the daily paper were performed by sea life. Depressing and inspiring at the same time. If whales could be nice, then why couldn't humans?

But this evening, I wasn't looking for inspiration; I was hoping the five o'clock news might shed some light on the missing person case. I was curious if they had identified the body found on the shore of Lake Keystone. I cracked open the gesso and took a big whiff. The smell of paint made me feel artistic and holding a brush in my hand made me feel like I could conquer the world. I listened to the news as I brushed on the first coat of gesso. Just when I thought the storms were over, the meteorologist was predicting more rain. In other news, a young baseball player was killed in a car crash, the stock market tanks, layoffs continue, the economy is down, and unemployment rises. Negative. Negative. Negative.

As I finished coating the canvas with a thick layer of gesso, I wondered what it would feel like to be a canvas and have a fresh start. Why couldn't life be that easy? I stood up and stared at my progress. Blemish free. When the gesso was dry, I could begin my masterpiece. While the thought of starting a brand new painting was exciting, I didn't want to forget what was underneath the gesso. If I wanted to, I could run my finger across the surface and feel the bumps and scars of my mistakes. The mistakes added character, texture, definition, and depth, but they were no longer the primary focus. I left the canvas to dry then set my brush down, pulled out my laptop, switched it on, and logged onto the popular social media site where I had created an account. No new notifications. I frowned. Alex had not accepted my friend request. I scowled and began to search for friends. I typed in "Alex Loving" and when his picture popped up, I clicked on it and was taken to his profile page.

"He has 10 friends!" I gasped. "How does *he* have more friends than I do? He's dead!" I clicked on Alex's *friend's* icon to see exactly who he was acquainted with. Alex was friends with a few of the guys from the Redhawks, the hockey team he played for last winter: Danny Westbrook, Terrance Hawking, and Dustin Whitamaker. I assumed there were no hard feelings. Just like a guy - Have a disagreement, get in a fight, throw a punch, and magically, everything's better. Not like girls who act like cats and use you as a scratching post… for the rest of your life. Meow. I think I'd rather take a punch. My eyes moved down the screen and my mouth fell open in shock when I saw that Corrine Harvey was one of Alex's friends. *What?* I glanced at her profile picture: Corrine was posed with her lips pressed against the cheek of her latest boyfriend. Surprise, surprise. But the thumbnail was too small to see the details. I clicked on the image to enlarge it. There, that was better. Now larger, I could see who she was kissing. Athletic. Blonde. Handsome. Sun kissed skin. Rock star hair. *No way*. Corrine Harvey's lips were locked to Flynt Redding's cheek. Mouth still agape, my chin was resting on the stained concrete floor of my new studio. Still not believing it, I clicked on her About Page.

Screen Name: Corrine Harvey

Sex: Yes

Relationship Status: Flynt Redding

Gag!

About me: I love to party and hang out with my friends. I love the sun and lazy days on the beach. Rules I live my life by: YOLO (you only live once).

"Well, I guess I got exactly what I asked for," I sighed as I vividly recalled trying to set Flynt and Corrine up on a blind date last October. I scrolled through her photos. They were all about the same. No originality. Corrine holding up her phone, taking a picture of herself in the bathroom mirror. Corrine making kissy lips. Another self-portrait. Corrine at a party, a group shot with friends. Corrine frolicking on the beach in a skimpy bikini. Gag. Gag. Gag. Bored, and a little curious, I clicked on Flynt's page and let out a sigh of relief when I saw his profile picture. It was just Flynt. He was taking a slap shot into the hockey net. I clicked on "About."

Screen Name: Flynt Redding

Sex: Male

Relationship Status: Single for now

Whew. I felt myself relax. Not really sure why I cared. I guess I just wanted Flynt to end up with a good girl. Not someone like Corrine Harvey, someone who would ultimately hurt him. I glanced at his status updates.

Zac Brophy-> Flynt Redding: Congrats Bro. You'll do great in the pros. Go Wild!!!!!

127 likes 14 comments

What? Really? The Minnesota Wild? His dream had come true. He was going pro. Not only that, he was playing for his dream team. No wonder Corrine suddenly found him so appealing.

Cassie Johnson -> Flynt Redding: Yay! You did it. I always knew you would. You were never one to let anything or anyone stand in your way.

148 Likes 25 comments

Jacob Martin -> Flynt Redding: Save me a few tickets, Bud. Rink side. Don't forget about me when you're rich and famous.

42 Likes 4 Comments

And so on and so on and so on. There were more comments than I wanted to count. So Flynt had finally done it. Accomplished artist. Entrepreneur. Competitor for my affection. Corrine Harvey's boyfriend (according to Corrine). And the newest addition to his list of accomplishments: right-winger for the Minnesota Wild. Wow. I was both impressed and ecstatic. Flynt had overcome a lot to get where he was, to fulfill his dreams.

"Good for you, Flynt." I said. I left Flynt's page and began to search around for some of my long lost friends. Without much trouble, I was able to find both Carly, "Crazy Carly" as my parents called her, my bestie from Amsterdam who was now living in Houston, and Claire Kirpowski, my partner in crime. I sent them a friend request and continued to search. I sent a request to Terrance Hawking. Besides Alex and Flynt, he was the only Redhawks team member who wasn't pompous and rowdy. I thought about sending a request to Flynt, but then decided against it. After all of Flynt's inappropriate advances toward me, being friends with Flynt would be unforgivable in Alex's book.

I turned back to my canvas and had just put a finger to it to check if the gesso was drying, when the *breaking news* sound effect grabbed my attention. I moved my eyes from the canvas to the screen of the small television in the corner of the room.

"This is Eyewitness 4. I'm Bree Jones and right now, we are following late breaking news coming in from the Tulsa County Medical Examiner's office. We begin this afternoon with new information on the disappearance of a local teenager, Jessie Paulman."

At the mention of her name, I was covered in goose bumps and the hairs on my arms stood on end. I jumped up and moved closer to the TV. I turned up the volume and stood captivated in front of the screen.

On February 19th, the parents of Jessie Paulman filed a missing persons report after their daughter failed to return home from school. Phillipa Jenkins is on location with the details. Could you tell us what you have learned, Phillipa?"

The camera panned in on the dark headed anchor. "Thank you, Bree. Police have made a positive ID on the body found floating near the shore of Lake Keystone last night."

My stomach lurched. I knew what was coming next.

"Investigators now say the body has been identified as nineteen year old Jessie Paulman."

The petite woman was paid to hold her composure in situations like these, but I could detect a tremble in her voice, and I knew she was fighting back tears because as the camera zoomed in, I saw her chin begin to quiver.

"I'm standing just outside Tulsa police department with Detective Baxtor Lavine. Detective Lavine, can you shed any light on why both the OSBI and the FBI are involved?"

"Well, Phillipa, we are still in the early stages of this investigation. At this time, we are unable to reveal any specific details. I can say that there was evidence surrounding the crime scene to suggest a link between this homicide and several other homicides within forty-five miles of the I-44 corridor that stretches from St. Louis to Dallas. Dental records were used to identify the body, but the initial cause of death is yet to be determined. The Paulman family is coping with this recent finding and is mourning the loss of their daughter. We are making every effort to respect their privacy by releasing only that information pertinent to the case."

"Let me ask you this, Detective. Have any arrests been made?"

"Like I said, Phillipa, the investigation is still in the early stages. At this time, there is not enough information to make an arrest."

"Thank you. Bree, back to you."

I flicked off the TV and stared at my canvas. I was shaking. I knew it. I had a feeling and that feeling was right. Emotions flooded my body, and I was on the brink of tears. I couldn't push the image of Jessie Paulman from my mind. The picture shown on the news was in color and the image much sharper, clearly showing the exact shade of her hair and the freckles that spread across her cheeks. But it was the black and white image on the poster in the gas station that I couldn't shake. The confident smile. The squinty eyes. Even though the bright red letters that spelled out "MISSING" initially captured my attention, it was Jessie's face that I couldn't forget. Not a day went by that Jessie didn't cross my mind. I had seen posters for missing children before, but I had never paid much attention. So why had this poster left such an impression on me? Was it because I had read about similar stories in Eva's journal? Although I didn't know exactly why the girls were being held captive in the Pierce's basement, I had a pretty good idea. What I did know was this: not one of them wanted to be there. Looking at Jessie's poster made me feel uneasy, just like I felt after reading Eva's journal: a sickening feeling in the pit of my stomach that wouldn't go away. But it wasn't just the news report that left me feeling edgy. It was the detective who was reporting it. Tall. Dark. Handsome. I was pretty sure I had just found a name on my list.

Without another thought, I bolted out of my studio door, leaving my gesso-coated canvas to dry on the easel. As I plowed through the kitchen en route to my bedroom, I startled my mother who was busy working on one of her new culinary creations. I didn't take the time to check her expression. When I reached the stairs, I took them two at a time. The box A-Omega sent to me was on the top shelf in my closet, and I couldn't get to it fast enough. Once inside my room, I opened my closet door and stood on tiptoe to reach it. I moved it to the edge of the shelf with my fingers before taking hold of it and pulling it down. My shaking hands fumbled with the tape holding the lid shut. Still trembling, I pulled out the slip of paper to review the list of names:

Quinn Collins
Mason Armishaw
Katelyn Cross
Terry Dunbarr
Todd Catchitore
Steven Bellamy
Gracie Abbott
My heart stopped beating in my chest. Number 8...........
Baxtor Lavine

CHAPTER EIGHTEEN

I will never forget my thirteenth Christmas. Mom had cleverly wrapped a gift and put it under the tree. Because we moved around a lot and didn't have much space, I usually only received one present on Christmas morning. That year, I had asked for a pair of shoes. They weren't just any shoes, either. Red perforated suede. Peep toes. Tiny kitten heels. They were the most amazing shoes I had ever seen. Imagine that. Me, the one who couldn't care less about fashion. But I wanted them… bad. The package Mom put under the tree was the exact size and shape of a shoebox, so I was pretty sure the bright red heels were inside. On Christmas morning, I pulled the gift out from under the tree and peeled back the paper. Instead of a shoebox, I found another layer of wrap. Mom had written notes all over the paper and before tearing it off, I read each one. It took me thirty minutes to open the present. There were boxes inside of boxes and layers and layers of wrapping paper; each layer was covered in sentiment. Mom knew I was having trouble adjusting to my new school, and she filled each layer with love. Terms of endearment that I so desperately *needed* to hear. Inspiring quotes by inspiring people. Her hopes and wishes for me. Little cartoon drawings that made me laugh. When I took off the last piece of wrapping paper, I was holding a box that fit in the palm of my hand. It wasn't the shoes I wanted. It was my Nana's silver locket.

My mission with A-Omega was beginning to remind me a lot of my thirteenth Christmas. Each item in the box was like one of my mother's handmade pieces of wrap, leading me not to what I expected, but to what I needed most. Healing. In the same way that I expected the red shoes to be inside the box, I expected the gifts from A-Omega to help me lock up Carl. Instead, the gifts were words of wisdom to heal my mind and mend my heart. Then, just when I was beginning to think my mission had nothing at all to do with Carl, I was led to Baxtor Lavine. Things were finally beginning to fall into place. Not in the way I imagined they would, but things were definitely coming together. And even though the items in the box had yet to help me put Carl away, I still had hope that my mission would end with his incarceration.

I spent the rest of the evening Googling the eighth name on my list: Baxtor Lavine. Apparently, Mr. Lavine was a part of the belt, the chain of names. And the buckle? The buckle was the truth of which I knew very little. The buckle of a belt connects, but I wasn't getting the connection. How were the ten names on my list connected? But A-Omega promised to help me find the truth. And I did trust them. Seeing Jessie's poster at the gas station wasn't a coincidence, and I was still convinced that Carl Pierce was responsible for her death. I couldn't prove it, but I could feel it in my bones. Baxtor Lavine was a detective for the Tulsa Police, but I wanted to know more than his title. I wanted to know him. What was he like? What was his history? After finding three of the ten names on my list, I had learned that there was a lesson to be learned from each person. So what was Lavine going to teach me? How might he lead me to Carl? How could I help him put Carl in jail? I had every intention of meeting him, but I wanted to be prepared. I wanted to know what made him tick, so I dug a little deeper, sifting through article after article until I found one that raised a red flag.

September 13th, 1990
Local Billionaire Jailed

Self-made billionaire Carl Pierce of Tulsa Oklahoma was arrested late last night after being accused of harboring three young girls in the basement of his Tulsa mansion.

I paused when I came across a name I didn't recognize. Monica Bradley? According to the article, Monica Bradley was a nineteen-year-old girl from Memphis, Tennessee, who was brought into police headquarters by a "Good Samaritan" after they found her at the intersection of 10th and Denver in downtown Tulsa. From what I was reading, she was disoriented and badly beaten. Still, I didn't put two and two together until I read the next line.

Monica had nothing in her possession besides a small sum of cash and a cell phone that was linked to Eva Pierce, wife of Carl Pierce.

I gasped. "Monica Bradley was one of the girls in Carl's basement!" My eyes moved down the screen, reading the words faster than I could comprehend them.

Monica Bradley confirmed that a woman fitting the description of Eva Pierce gave her the phone before freeing her and two other girls from the basement of the Pierce's mansion.

Monica Bradley was a witness. "If there was a witness, then why wasn't Carl in jail?" I mumbled. The article suggested that Carl was involved in a nationwide human trafficking ring. The accusations didn't stop there, either. Baxtor Lavine had named Carl the kingpin. *Baxtor Lavine must have been pretty sure of himself to make a statement like that*, I thought. The closing paragraph stated that Moncia Bradley was in police protection and that Lavine was hopeful Eva Pierce would be another credible witness.

I bookmarked the article, and moved on the next.

September 15th, 1990
Detective Lavine, Out of Jurisdiction and Out of Line.

What?! Detective Baxtor Lavine flew into Minneapolis to look for Eva Pierce! I couldn't believe my eyes. Why hadn't Sue mentioned this?

"Wait a minute," I said out loud. "Why is Sue's name in this article?" I was growing angry thinking about how Sue might still be keeping secrets. I wanted to shut off my computer, but I read on.

Eva Pierce was pronounced dead when the Colbert's car collided with oncoming traffic.

The more I read, the more bizarre the story became.

Lavine, a former combat medic, used his background in emergency medicine to save lives at the scene of the deadly car crash.

September 18th, 1990
Minnesota Police accuse Oklahoma Detective, Baxtor Lavine, of tampering with evidence at the scene of Thursday's fatal accident.

September 20th, 1990
Key Witness, Monica Bradley, Found Dead in a Southside Home.

September 21st, 1990
Detective Lavine Jumps the Gun Again

The murder of key witness, Monica Bradley, and the untimely death of Eva Pierce, left Baxtor Lavine grasping at straws, and the unauthorized search of the Pierce estate might just cost him his badge.

September 22nd, 1990
Police Detective Makes One Last, Desperate Attempt To Lock Up Local Celebrity.

September 25th, 1990
Detective Lavine Ostracized by the Very People Who Supported His Efforts

Just as I suspected! Although very weak, there was a link between Jessie Paulman and Carl Pierce and his name was Baxtor Lavine. It was 9:30. Just as the meteorologist predicted, rain had begun to fall and drops were splatting against my bedroom window. I could hear the cadence of conversation taking place below me in the kitchen, but it was only a single voice. Sue's. She was on the phone, and I could hear her laughter mixed with the clatter of dishes. I bet she was talking to Papa, and I was getting ready to bust up her party. I had shown her the list of names A-Omega included in the box, and I had asked her if any of them looked familiar. She flat out told me no. I slammed my laptop shut and with only one thing on my mind, stormed down the stairs, fuming as I walked into the kitchen.

Sue took one look at the expression on my face and hung up the phone without saying goodbye. She set the phone on the counter and opened her mouth to speak, but I beat her to the punch. Not giving Sue a chance and without using better judgment, words flew from my mouth.

"No more lies. None. Why can't you just tell me a simple truth?"

"I have no idea what you're talking about, Rae!"

"Baxtor Lavine. I asked you if you knew him. You said no."

"And I'm telling you no, again."

"Then how did your name wind up in the same newspaper article as his?" I knew that the article did not say that Baxtor and my mother had met, nor did it say that they were working as a team, but what were the chances? "You're trying to tell me that you had no idea Baxtor Lavine, the Tulsa police detective that was after Carl Pierce, was at the scene of the accident on the night of September 13th. Bull. Bull bull bull."

"Rae, that's enough."

"I'm scraping by mom. I asked you for help, not hindrance. All you had to say was that you knew the name. I don't understand why you keep lying to me."

"She's telling the truth," Will's husky voice came from behind me, and I spun around on the wood floor and looked into his eyes, waiting for him to shed new light on the question I had been asking myself for years: What really happened on the night of September 13th? Why had I survived?

"Didn't you find it strange that we would drive 2 ½ hours to the cottage in Alexandria only to stay a single night. Did you not wonder why we left so soon or how we were tipped off that the Bodin's were coming for us?"

Looking over my shoulder, I glanced at Mom who shared my baffled expression. I looked Will in the eyes. He was right. I did have a lot of questions. There were a lot of grey areas and plenty of things that didn't add up. Portions of the story that just didn't make sense. Truths that I thought died with those who lost their lives in the crash. Was he getting ready to tell all? Would he be willing to connect the dots?

CHAPTER NINETEEN

*U*nfortunately, the new information came at a most inopportune time. If I had uncovered this finding hours earlier, I might have been able to make it to the Tulsa Police Headquarters before Lavine left for the night. But now it was 10:30, and I was left with nothing to do but think. I tossed and turned. I replayed the conversation that took place between Will and me.

Of course, I had thought it was strange that my parents would take Eva to the cabin in Minnesota and stay only a day before leaving again. Of course, I wondered how they had known Marion Bodin was hunting them. How had they known they were in danger and that it was time to leave the cottage? But after Mom showed up in Alexandria and told us the story of what happened that night, I didn't question it any further. She simply said that they had received word that the Bodin's were on their way. I wrongfully assumed the warning came from A-Omega. When Will told another side of the story, I was a bit taken aback by the unexpected twist. It seemed improbable, but the newspaper articles I found online did support what Will was saying. I had no choice but to believe him. And when Dad told me about the tall and handsome, dark skinned stranger who showed up at the cabin late on the night of September 13th, without even telling me his name, I knew the man was Baxtor Lavine.

According to the newspaper, in a final and desperate attempt to track down Eva Pierce, Baxtor had hopped on a plane bound for Minneapolis. Fortunately, in the midst of chaos, the Colberts and the Lovings left a few breadcrumbs behind and Lavine was able to follow the trail all the way to the cottage. According to Will, their introduction was quick and the exchange of information was rushed. He told the story like this: Just as he was getting ready for bed, there was a knock at the door. It was rainy and cold that night. Will switched on the porch light and saw a man standing on the stoop. The stranger introduced himself, flashed his badge, relayed the warning, then returned to his car while Will woke up the cottage and packed the bags. Thirty minutes later, they were headed out of town.

Will spoke fondly of Lavine; he gave him credit for saving their lives and blessing them with a daughter. Trained as a combat medic in his early twenties, Lavine had used his medical knowledge to save me from Eva's dying womb. So after all that Lavine had done for my family, why did Sue still consider him a stranger? How could she not have known? Was she lying? I thought about the accident. Sue had been injured. I knew this because of the scar that ran down her arm and because of the letter I found in Nana's scrapbook. But while we were staying at the cottage, Alex added to the story and told me his version of what happened on that fateful night: Sue was not only injured but also very disoriented, stumbling through the wreckage, cradling two lifeless children in her arms.

But Sue and Will's relationship with Lavine had extended beyond the night of the crash. According to Will, Baxtor had helped them in many ways. For instance, when I was seven, when Carl discovered that I was alive, Lavine helped Sue and Will leave the country. How could Sue not have known about that? And then I remembered something Sue had told me during my senior year in high school. She had said that after Laney died, she did her best to take care of me, but that most of the time, she couldn't pull herself out of bed. She told me that for the first seven years, Will took care of everything. So maybe she wasn't lying. Perhaps she was telling the truth. I wanted to believe her. I wanted to trust her. I did. But it was hard to trust when they had been lying to me for nineteen years. Negative thoughts (or bad thoughts, as Quinn liked to call them) were trying their hardest to creep back in, and I could feel myself slipping into that dark, familiar place. I didn't want to dwell in the darkness. An antivirus for my mind, some anti-venom for my soul. Remembering what Quinn did to extinguish his bad thoughts, I began to think about his cross pendant and I began to pray. When I began to dwell on the truth instead of the lies, the darkness slithered back into the shadows, and I could feel the light. I am strong, I am stubborn, I am persistent, and I am kind. I focused only on the truth until I fell asleep.

With a queasy stomach and tired eyes from little rest, I jumped into my car first thing the next morning and headed out of town without even thinking to call Alex. I started out on Highway 75. When I reached the heart of Tulsa, I took the Denver Street exit, and proceeded north. I rolled through the light on 8th and came to a stop at the intersection of 7th and Denver. The streets were empty and the downtown seemed deserted, but still I looked both ways before taking a right onto 7th and heading west. I drove slowly, reading the street signs as I passed them. Elwood Avenue. I kept going. I checked the address that was lying in the passenger seat and then looked back up for direction. Civic Center Drive. I had arrived. I took a right and found myself on a street lined with concrete buildings. The many patrol vehicles confirmed that I was at the right address. I maneuvered my Honda into a tight parallel spot in front of the building and said a short prayer before unlocking my door.

The precinct was exactly what I had expected; it looked just like they do on TV. Similar to the exterior, the walls inside the police headquarters were made of concrete and gave the building a cold, official feel. Once inside the lobby, I found that, *unlike* the outside of the building, the inside was swarming. Turning a full circle, I wondered where in the world I might find Detective Lavine. Unsure of what to do next, I took fifty steps toward the service desk and found a short, uniformed officer on the other side of a thick glass window. She had a large birthmark on the side of her neck that was only partially hidden by her strawberry blond bob. Completely ignoring me, the officer continued to talk to her coworker. I placed my elbows on the counter and rested my head in my hands, making it apparent that I was growing intolerant of her rude behavior. Still not catching her attention, I rang the service bell on the desk. She turned toward me with snarled lip.

"Can I help you?"

"I'm here to see Detective Lavine."

"Do you have an appointment?" she asked smartly. She was irritated because I had just interrupted her gossip session.

"No."

"I can't help you then. Lavine's out all morning. Don't expect him back 'till later this afternoon."

"Do you mind if I wait?"

"You can do whatever you want." She scratched her head with her long fake nails. "But so that you don't waste your time and his, I suggest you make an appointment and let him know what business you'd like to discuss."

"Thanks for the advice. If you don't mind, I think I will wait, because my business can't."

The short woman, whose name was Rose, curled her lip and with a stiff hand, motioned to a row of wooden chairs in the lobby. I followed the line of her arm and took a seat where she suggested, waiting for the off chance that Baxtor Lavine would walk through the front door and invite me back to his office. His name was on my list. We had important business. But unlike Quinn Collins, Todd Catchitore, and Mason Armishaw, Baxtor Lavine knew who I was. He brought me into this world, but would he recognize me? Was he expecting me? Would he give me the time of day? I was pretty sure that I was supposed to be here. When I hopped in the car this morning, there was no text from A-Omega telling me to wait. I was going to trust my instincts and stay. Besides, I had driven too far to turn around and go home now.

I took the seat closest to the door and farthest from the service desk, and then I began to look around. I spent a majority of the morning watching a variety of colorful and occasionally resistant individuals enter the station in cuffs. To bide the time, I played a game called "guilty or innocent," wrote in my journal, and thought about Jessie Paulman, Carl Pierce, and Gracie Abbot. Was Gracie Abbot one of the three girls in Carl's basement? Is that why I kept seeing her name on a box in my dreams? Did Lavine know who she was? Would he be able to lead me to Gracie, the seventh name on my list?

I popped my shoulders, stretched, and reached into my bag. Pulling out my phone to check the time, I realized I had been sitting on the hard wooden chair for nearly three hours. It was almost 1:00 and my stomach was beginning to growl. He should be here by now, I thought. Had I missed the detective? Had he slipped by while I was writing in my journal? Impossible. It would be hard to miss a man of his stature. Even on TV, his appearance was overpowering. Towering over the reporter who stood at least 5' 8", Baxtor Lavine was just shy of seven foot. Eye-catching smile. Deep set eyes. Plus, he was a sharp dresser. He didn't really blend in with the riff-raff coming in and out of the precinct. There was no way I could have missed him. Again, the image of Jessie Paulman flashed in my mind. I had to believe that if I were patient, Lavine would show.

I began to worry about the introduction. Would I tell him that A-Omega had given me his name? I had to prepare myself for the fact that I might sound crazy if I told him the truth. Or I could just start by telling him that my father was Carl Pierce and that I believed Carl was responsible for the death of the Tulsa teen. Crazy. He's going to think I'm crazy. No, sitting here waiting for the detective to show is crazy. Maybe Rose was right: I should have made an appointment. I had nearly decided to call the whole thing off when out of the corner of my eye, I detected the flashing of lights. It was the most excitement I had seen since my arrival. I stood up, slung my bag over my shoulder, and walked toward the entrance.

Initially, I thought the flashing lights were coming from one of the many cop cars parked in front of police headquarters but upon closer inspection, I discovered the true source of the excitement. As I neared the plate glass windows, I realized it was the flashing of cameras that had caught my eye. I made it to the door in time to see Detective Lavine pushing his way through a crowd of journalists. The press was bombarding him with questions and despite his size, he seemed to be struggling to fight them off. When Lavine finally made it through the door, I backed off a bit to give him space. Keeping several yards between us, I judged his mood. Once inside the lobby, the detective let out a long sigh and moved the palm of his right hand across his forehead. Lavine was exhausted and right now was probably not the most opportune time to approach him.

The expression on the detective's face was easy to read. He felt like he had just found shelter from the storm. The lobby of police headquarters was his home base. No one could touch him here. Yet here I was, with information that could cause the ground beneath his feet to shake. I had things in my possession that could change everything. Lavine let out another sigh as I approached. I hated to burst his bubble, but rest was not in his future. Even though I knew he would be interested in what I had to show him, I was still incredibly nervous. Lavine was slightly intimidating, with his statuesque build and important position, but that wasn't why I was on edge. I was uneasy because I knew that this was it. For months, I had complained about my mission: things were happening too fast, or things were happening too slow. I knew that once I acquainted myself with Lavine, my mission would begin to soar and there was a pretty good chance that I would have less control over the situation than I did now. My life was about to change; was I ready? I approached Lavine and stood in front of his towering figure. He twisted his mouth slightly as he studied my face, searching for recognition. I had one chance to grab his attention and being that circumstances were not working in my favor, I knew I would have to shock him if I wanted him to listen.

"I believe you know me." I was shaking. I moved a trembling hand over my hair to smooth it. "I'm Carl Pierce's daughter." My voice quivered. "I think Carl was involved in the murder of Jessie Paulman. I want to help you put him away."

CHAPTER TWENTY

Detective Lavine sat behind his desk, sipping a cup of lukewarm coffee and popping the knuckles of his right hand. His eyes never left me, but he didn't say a word. No longer quite as anxious, I broke from his stare and began to study the personal items on his desk. There weren't many. There was, however, a picture of his family but by the looks of it, it was an old one. I surreptitiously glanced at his left hand, checking for a wedding band. There wasn't one. My eyes scanned the white plaster walls. Besides a single plaque, the walls were completely bare. Engraved on the plaque's bronze colored metal was a scripture.

The weapons we fight with are not the weapons of the world. 2 Corinthians 10:4

My eyes moved to the shelf behind his desk where I noticed a small, decorative cross and a pair of praying hands bookends. Before I could draw any detailed conclusions, Lavine interrupted my train of thought.

"You cut right to the chase, don't you?"

I cleared my throat and let our eyes meet once again. "I didn't know how else to grab your attention. To be honest, I might have exaggerated a little bit. I *am* Carl Pierce's daughter, but I don't have any evidence to put him away. At least not yet. I'm just going to be straight with you. I think there's something we need to discuss before this conversation goes any further. I know what you did for Sue and Will."

The detective looked taken aback. "Sue and Will Colbert?" he said with a drawn out breath, as if he were pulling those names out of his bank of memories.

"Yes. Sue and Will Colbert. The man and woman who raised me. You must remember them?"

Lavine started as if he had seen a ghost and then chuckled. "Well I'll be." He chuckled again. "And I thought I was talking with Chloe Pierce, Tulsa's princess. You can now understand why I seemed so edgy. I heard that Chloe met her demise, and I was sitting here thinking that either the newspapers had it all wrong or I was having a conversation with a ghost. I was sincerely hoping there was a newspaper misprint." All seriousness returned to his face. "It has been known to happen before."

"Well, they were right this time. Chloe's dead. I saw her die, so I know it's true." I watched his eyes grow large like saucers. "Honestly, Baxtor-"

"Detective Lavine."

"Sorry, Detective Levine, but I would prefer not to talk about Chloe… if you don't mind."

"I understand. I was being rather insensitive. It's just…" his voice broke off in apology, and I picked up the pieces of the conversation to ease the awkwardness.

"It's no worry. Chloe was my sister and I'd like to leave it at that."

"Fair enough. So tell me this. When I lost the case against Carl, I temporarily lost my job and my credibility. What I did for Sue and Will could have gotten me into even more trouble. It could have cost me everything. Will knew this. His silence about all that happened was an expression of his gratitude. So how did you find out? How did you find *me*?"

I swallowed the lump in my throat and contemplated whether or not to share with the detective my mission and all of the circumstances leading up to the arrival of the box and my decision to work for A-Omega.

"I've spent most of my life lying." I started out slow, still slightly hesitant about sharing with this stranger such personal information, such intimate details. Trust, I reminded myself. His name was on my list. I needed to trust, to open up. Maybe there would be something in my story that could help him. Besides, I felt comfortable around him. I glanced up to the plaque hanging on the wall and read the scripture for a second time. I bit my lip and looked again at the detective. "I've lied to myself for years. I had no problem justifying the lies I told myself, because I thought I was the only one getting hurt. Then I started lying to others, and I found that hurting other people wasn't as easy to justify. I could tell you a story that would explain everything, a story that is easy to digest, easy to believe. You'd be happy, and I wouldn't look crazy. But it wouldn't be the truth," I continued. My voice was now strong and confident. "You're name was on a list I received from A-Omega, detective."

I held my breath, waiting for him to chuckle again. I was waiting for him to dismiss me from his office without letting me explain why I was here, without letting me hand over the evidence I had in my possession.

"A-Omega." Lavine nodded his head. "Understood."

I waited for him to follow this statement with something more, but instead, his expression changed and, as tears began to form , he tented his hands and held the tips of his fingers to his eyes. He looked like he was praying so I sat in silence, remembering how awkward it was when I had interrupted Pastor Joe while he was in the middle of talking to God and how guilty I felt afterward. I was a different person now. Rarely did I fly off the handle, and I was beginning to think about other people besides myself. A fly buzzed around my head, making the silence more obvious. With a trembling hand, I took hold of the coffee mug and sipped the lukewarm liquid. I wanted Lavine to respond immediately, but he didn't. Thankfully, I was becoming very good at waiting. After a moment, the handsome detective wiped away the wetness from his cheeks with one quick sweep and stared at me with bunched lips and a furrowed brow.

"Carl Pierce?" he licked his lips. "You're going right for the shark himself. I have to ask… is this some sort of personal vendetta?"

"Not exactly. I just don't want to waste any time, that's all. I have a few things that might help you and then I have something else… something a little more… it's not evidence per se, but it's a start."

"I used to know someone like you," he sighed. "It didn't end well for that person." Lavine looked at me with knowing eyes and all at once, I recalled the articles I had read online the other day. Lavine had paid the price for going after Carl Pierce. Although it was only temporary, he had lost his badge. His wedding band was missing from his ring finger. By the looks of it, he had lost his family, too. It took years to regain the title he once had and here I was asking him to risk it all again. "I'm assuming that if you took the trouble to come to headquarters and spend the day waiting for me to return that you must have done your homework."

"I know enough."

Lavine set his cup of coffee on the desk and rested his head in the palm of his hand. "You can understand why I might have reservations about pursuing Carl Pierce."

"Reservations. Yes. I understand. Do you think I might also have reservations about putting my father away?"

Without hesitation, the detective gave an affirmative nod. "Yes. I do."

"Well, you're wrong. I have NO reservations. The sooner Carl Pierce is behind bars, the better."

"You walk into my precinct and introduce yourself as Carl Pierce's daughter. You tell me you think he's involved in the Paulman case, which you must know that I'm working on. You also tell me that you want him convicted. Is there something I've missed? Because I feel like I've missed something."

I lifted my eyes and focused on the plaque that hung on his wall. I re-read the scripture. Without a word, I reached into my bag and pulled out Eva's journal. I flipped to her last entry and laid it in front of him.

"I thought maybe you could use this as evidence."

Lavine studied me carefully before shifting his gaze to the journal. I spent the next five minutes watching him read, thankful that I could let Eva do all the explaining. It was bad enough thinking about what had happened to the girls in Carl's basement; I didn't think I could make any comments on the subject at the moment. When he was finished reading the entry, Baxtor gave me an ambiguous look.

"This might have come in handy twenty years ago. Where did you get it?"

"I found it in the Pierce's basement when I broke in last year."

"Why doesn't that surprise me?" Lavine muttered. "You and I have more in common than I thought. Carl Pierce is trouble, Rae. Sometimes you just can't touch a man with money. Are you willing to take the risk?"

"Of course I am. I made the decision to follow A-Omega, and I don't go back on my word. I've been told that I'm stubborn."

"Oh, I don't doubt that." Lavine bit his lip and shook his head. "Listen, I hear what you're saying, but do you hear what I'm saying?"

"Loud and clear. If I told you the things I've been through in the past year and a half, the stories would chill you to the bone. My life has not been a cake walk, Detective, but I believe that everything in life prepares you for something greater."

"That's fine, and honorable even, but you haven't given me anything that I can use."

"What about the entries in Eva's journal? That's proof. What about the cell phone? Surely-"

"The cell phone," he interrupted. "The infamous cell phone. I thought I had finally put this case to rest, but I think it will haunt me for the rest of my life. Look, Carl Pierce was tried and found not guilty. This case isn't just closed, it no longer exists. Ever heard of Double Jeopardy? Carl can't be tried for the same crime twice. Doesn't matter if there *is* new evidence."

"You're right. But you have to look at the past if you want to change the future," I said, repeating ProfC's words of wisdom. "Maybe you can learn something from the journal that will help you in the Paulman case. Tell me this. Monica was your key witness in the case. She was murdered. What do you know about the other two girls in Carl's basement? Do you know where they are now?"

"Heaven only knows," he scoffed. "But not a day goes by that I don't think about them."

"What were their names? Do you know that?"

"Monica gave us the names and ages of the other two girls, but because we never found them, I had no way of knowing whether her tip was credible. Besides that-"

"Before you say anymore, detective," I interrupted. "I want you to know that your name wasn't the only name on the list from A-Omega. There were others. Terry Dunbarr and Gracie Abbot. Do either of those names sound familiar?"

Baxtor looked at me shocked beyond belief. He opened his mouth to speak but nothing came out.

"I've been thinking a lot about it, sir, and I'd be willing to bet that those were the two girls in the basement with Monica Bradley."

Finally, the detective found his words. "Monica Bradley, Theresa Ann Dunbarr - Terry -, and Isla Martinez. Nineteen, twelve, and five."

Nineteen, twelve, and five? Now I was at a loss for words. Both saddened and stunned by this unexpected finding, I felt tears beginning to well up.

"I recognize the name Terry Dunbarr, but not Gracie Abbot. I'm sorry." Lavine began to jot something down on a pad of paper. "Gracie with an 'ie' at the end?"

"Yes," I managed to return. I wiped a tear from my cheek. "Nineteen, twelve, and five? Five?" I asked, hoping that I hadn't heard him correctly.

Lavine wore a twisted expression as he shook his head. After twenty years, it seemed that the shock and horror had not worn off. "Hard to imagine, huh? Listen, I'll keep my ears and eyes open. If anything comes across my desk relating to a Gracie Abbot, I'll let you know. And if by a miracle you happen to run into Terry Dunbarr... let *me* know. She might be able to help in some unforeseen way. Regardless, I would sleep better at night just knowing she's alive."

"I will detective. And thanks for taking the time to talk to me today. I know you're a busy man." I jotted down my name and number on a scrap of paper I found in my purse and pushed it across the desk toward him. "Detective..."

He nodded his head for me to continue. I chewed on my lip, contemplating how to ask the question that was on my mind, contemplating whether or not I wanted to know the answer, the details.

"The newspaper said you tampered with evidence at the scene of the accident."

Lavine smiled, as though he had been expecting the question all along. My heart was racing as I considered the accident, as I considered Eva no longer alive, as I considered myself... born into the world on the night of the crash. He laced his fingers behind his head and leaned back into his chair.

"I don't want any details. I really don't. But I just need to know... was I the evidence?"

"Yes."

My body trembled. The answer to my questions and to everything it implied was "Yes."

My knees shook as I stood. I regarded the man who gave me life. The man who made it possible for Sue and Will to raise me. Why? Why had he done this for me? Why had he risked it all for Sue and Will? I wanted to ask him these questions, but the words wouldn't leave my lips.

"Thank you, detective." I grabbed my bag and turned to leave.

"Rae -"

I stopped short and turned to face him.

"I know what you're thinking. You want to know why I did it. Just so you know, you're not the only one who hangs on every word A-Omega speaks. You call him A-Omega. I call him God. I call him Provider."

I followed his eyes to the plaque on the wall.

"I received my box eighteen years ago, so I'm familiar with your journey. I lost a whole lot more than the Pierce case. My job. My family. My respect. I finally accepted the gift from A-Omega that had been right in front of me all along. I began to listen to the Truth." Still looking at the plaque, Lavine nodded to the wall.

"So what kind of weapons do you use now?" I asked.

"Now days, I only use one weapon - prayer."

I took a moment to consider the larger than life bond that the two of us shared. We were in this together, like two links in a belt for which only the truth could be the buckle.

INTERCESSION

CHAPTER TWENTY-ONE

*T*he month of June went by in a hurry. I divided the month between the karate dojo and my art studio. While I trained, I imagined I was sparring against Carl. This pushed me even harder. I had a feeling that I would be meeting my biological father on my trip to Houston, and I wanted to be in tiptop shape. When I wasn't at the dojo, I was painting and while painting, I thought about Jessie Paulman. I just knew Carl Pierce had something to do with Jessie's disappearance, but how would I prove it? And what about Gracie Abbot? I had convinced myself that Gracie was one of the girls Carl had locked away, but Lavine had proven my theory wrong; Gracie was *not* one of the three girls that Eva helped escape. But Terry Dunbarr *was* and her name was on my list as well. I thought about my meeting with Lavine. It hadn't gone as smoothly as I had hoped. I had walked into his office with Eva's journal and high hopes. I left with nothing more than a feeling of defeat. I thought about the plaque that hung on Lavine's wall. *The weapons we fight with are not the weapons of the world.* According to Lavine, I was wasting my time in the dojo; no matter how hard I trained, physical strength might not be quite as useful as I thought. Lavine suggested I take another route: prayer. I found it hard to believe that words have the strength to win a war… especially a war like this.

Mid-June, I was struck with a new idea. Maybe Carl wouldn't meet his demise by the click of a gun… but maybe by the click of a camera. And I thought it would be wise to listen to Lavine's advice as well. So I *prayed* that a camera would capture something good, something that would convict Carl. When I called Alex and shared my plan with him, I thought he'd be excited and that he'd want to come along. Instead, he was still offended that I had run off to meet the detective without thinking to call, and rather than agreeing to come with me, he said he would just stay at home and work on the song he was writing. He was really taking this guitar thing seriously. He had even given his guitar a name: Stella. With Alex out, I considered my only other alternative: Claire Kirpowski. She might have been second fiddle to Alex but the more I thought about it, the more she seemed the perfect choice. I recalled how much she enjoyed our last excursion. She loved the detective work just as much as I did. She lived for this sort of thing. And I was glad to have her in my company because truth be told, I was too scared to go alone. With Alex already on the defensive, I didn't dare ask to borrow his camera, so I decided to use Will's instead.

I was glad that Claire and I had exchanged numbers at the coffee shop; it made getting in contact with her easy and just as I suspected, she was eager to come along. After telling her a little bit about my mission, it was settled. Claire was going to help me keep tabs on Carl Pierce. She couldn't resist. She was going to help me play detective and unlike Alex, she was excited about it. Claire had school in Tulsa twice a week, and I agreed to drive to the city every Tuesday so we could meet up after her class. We had met twice now, usually at a sandwich shop on Cherry Street. We'd sit for an hour, sometimes longer, discussing surveillance techniques and strategy. I usually sipped on a cup of soup while Claire shared her concerns about breaking into the Pierce mansion and her opinion on the best spot to keep watch on Carl's house.

It was raining when I awoke and the dark summer sky masked the time of day. It was the first of July. Where was the sun? I glanced at the clock. It was 6 AM. I climbed out of bed, stretched, and slipped on a pair of leggings and a plain white tee shirt and wrapped a colorful scarf around my neck. I could have used the weather as a perfect excuse to stay in my pajamas and paint. But this morning, I wasn't thinking about my candy apple green studio nor was I thinking about the umpteen canvases that needed a fresh coat of gesso.

Claire and I were supposed to meet later this afternoon. So far, we hadn't collected any incriminating information against Carl, but this would be our third time to meet, and I was hoping the third time would be a charm.

I wasn't expected at the sandwich shop until five and I was glad for that because I had plenty of things to do in the meantime. For starters, ProfC was having an early morning seminar on human rights and I didn't want to miss it. This time, the professor would be discussing how traffickers use the U.S. highway system to transport their victims and he would be sharing his thoughts on why selling *people* is quickly becoming more lucrative than selling *drugs*. After the seminar, I planned to do a little birthday shopping. Alex's party was only a week away, and I still hadn't thought of anything to give him. I wanted a gift that was special... thoughtful and if I hurried, I'd have time to do a little shopping between ProfC's seminar and meeting Claire.

It was 8 AM. Showered and dressed, I started out my bedroom door. Dad had the day off, and I knew he would be crashed out in his recliner. He still wasn't sleeping so well at night. I looked over the banister into the living room below and found that I was right. Dad was where I expected him to be. His arms were folded across his chest and his glasses were resting on the tip of his nose. He had a copy of *The Bell Jar* resting in his lap. Quietly, I crept down the stairs so that I wouldn't wake him. I grabbed my purse off the hook in the foyer, snuck into his office, and snatched his digital camera. I left a note on the kitchen counter that simply said: *Going to Tulsa. Be home tonight.* Quietly, I opened the front door and shut it behind me.

It rained hard all the way to the city, but I didn't let the weather discourage me. Today would be the day; Claire and I were going to stumble upon something good. We were going to find the connection between Carl Pierce and Jessie Paulman. I could feel it in my bones.

After a very informative discussion on human trafficking and after a half day of shopping, I hurried through the rain into the sandwich shop and was welcomed by the smell of warm broccoli cheese soup. I walked up to the counter and a girl named Frannie took my order. She had mousy brown hair that was complemented with subtle highlights of rich chocolate. She had a bright red bandana tied around her head and a small stud in her left nostril. I paid her, took my number, and then grabbed a discarded copy of the Tulsa World from a table that was ready to be bussed. It wasn't hard to find a place to sit; the restaurant was quiet and empty. The rain was keeping everyone at home. I unfolded the paper, spread it out in front of me, and gasped when I saw the headline:

Grizzly New Details in the Death of Missing Tulsa Teen

The Jessie Paulman case was front page. My heart skipped a beat. It felt like a heavy stone had been placed on my chest. Last year I would have looked the other way. I wouldn't have read the article. But today I did. Jessie seemed to be calling, shouting my name from the grave. I looked out the window and tears began to fall. "How could someone have done this?" The rain was still coming down. "I promise you, Jessie," I whispered and wiped a tear from my eye. "I will find whoever did this to you and I will make them pay."

Two hours later, after thoroughly reviewing the details of our stakeout, Claire parked her car on a side street a quarter mile away from the Pierce estate. We walked through the pouring rain and found a soggy spot on the grass behind a thick row of hedges. Claire had picked the spot and it was perfect; we could spy on Carl through breaks in the branches without getting caught. It was only 8 o'clock, but the sky was darker than usual because of the heavy clouds and pouring rain. While feeling cold and wet wasn't necessarily comfortable, Claire and I decided that the weather was working to our advantage. The grey skies allowed us to detect a faint light coming from Carl's basement that would have gone unnoticed on a sunny day. Something was going on down there, I just knew it, and even though our previous stakeouts had been worthless, I had a hunch that today would be different. Wet and cold, I shivered and pulled the sleeves of my coat down over my hands to warm them. My dad's camera was around my neck and tucked inside my jacket to protect it from the rain, keeping it dry until I was ready to use it. We had been sitting in the rain for nearly an hour to no avail. Light was still visible in the basement, but we hadn't seen any sign of Carl. But he *was* home. I knew that for a fact. Access to Carl's twelve-car garage was at the back of the house and we had the perfect view. Carl had forgotten to shut one of the overhead doors, and I could see his bright red Aston Martin parked inside. I thought about Alex and how he would love to see it for himself.

Completely focused on the mission, Claire and I sat in silence. We didn't dare let our guard down for a second for fear we might miss something important. With eyes glued to the mansion, our conversation was limited to complaints about the weather, annoyances over having wet rear ends, and suggestions about how we should think about bringing something to sit on next time. Neither one of us wanted to say it, but I knew we were both thinking the same thing. *What if?* What if there was something sinister going on in the basement? What if we went home with nothing? What if we got caught? I didn't need to refresh Claire's memory about what had happened last time we snuck into the basement. We had escaped by the skin of our teeth. When Claire's voice had sounded through the speaker of my walkie-talkie, I panicked. "They're home," she informed me. Her warning had sent me running. I fled the Pierce's living room and scrambled down the basement stairs, intending to exit the mansion through the same cellar door I had entered. But when I neared the bottom step, I lost my balance. The next thing I knew, I was airborne. I landed with a thud on the basement floor, breaking a couple of ribs and losing my walkie-talkie in the process. On a positive note, Claire and I hadn't got caught and I had thought our secret was safe, but I was wrong. Chloe found my walkie-talkie in the basement and left it lying on the kitchen counter in my Minnesota cottage with a note. "I have returned something of yours. Now return what is rightfully mine."

"I'm going to move around to the front." When Claire broke the silence, two things startled me at once: Claire's voice and the sudden burst of light that came from the cellar as the double doors flung open.

Claire had already started to stand up, but I caught the sleeve of her coat just in time. "No. Stop. Sit." I demanded. Claire had been looking at me instead of the cellar door and she had missed this recent development. But sensing the seriousness of my tone, she didn't argue. Slowly, her eyes joined mine in looking at the now open cellar door.

Without a word, Claire peeked through the gap in the hedge and gasped. A figure was moving out of the basement and into the backyard.

"What is he holding?" Even from a distance, we could tell that the person emerging from the cellar was a man. With a tall, sturdy frame and a dark head of hair, there wasn't a doubt in my mind that it was Carl.

"I don't know. A bag?"

"He's coming toward us," Claire gasped.

"Shhhh."

This time Claire didn't listen and she continued to run her mouth. "What's he doing? Taking out the garbage?"

"Claire. Shut up," I warned again.

"Who takes the garbage out in the pouring rain? Something's up. Snap a picture, Rae."

"Fine." I fished my camera out of my jacket, pulled off the cap, and focused the lens.

"Turn off the flash."

"I'm not an idiot, Claire."

Carl was moving closer, but he didn't seem to be in a hurry. Dressed in casual attire, he walked through the rain at a leisurely pace.

"Something's not adding up," Claire continued.

Carl approached the ally and set the large black garbage sack down by the edge of his driveway. Then, instead of returning to the basement, he stood beside the bag with his hand on his hip.

"What's he doing now?"

"I don't know."

"You take out the garbage. You go back inside. You don't stand in the pouring rain waiting for the garbage collector. Besides, it's eight o'clock… too late for the trash truck." Claire had made a good point. I lifted the camera and took a close up of Carl. "Something fishy's going on. As soon as he goes back inside, we should go through that bag."

"I'm not going through his trash," I said in disgust.

Claire and I were bickering over what could possibly be in the bag when we heard a car rolling up the alleyway. The sound of tires splashing through a puddle pulled us back to our mission at once. Our eyes returned to the scene in time to see Carl moving away from the bag and back to the basement. A shiny, white sedan came to a stop in front of his driveway.

"Are you getting this?" Claire whispered.

Instead of responding, I took more pictures. The man driving the white sedan got out. *Snap.* Unfortunately, his back was to me so I was unable to get a shot of his face. He picked up the bag. *Snap.* This time, I thought I was able to get a fairly decent picture of his profile. The trunk popped. *Snap.* The man disappeared behind the lid. *Snap.* He slammed the trunk shut. *Snap.* Another image. He was now moving to the front of the car, and I had the perfect shot. I zoomed in quickly and took a picture of his face before he slid into the driver seat. *Snap.* As the sedan pulled away from the curb, I took a picture of the license plate. It was a little blurry but with some enhancing, I hoped it would be clear enough to read.

INTERCESSION

CHAPTER TWENTY-TWO

I woke to a sunny sky and a runny nose. That's what happens when you sit outside in the pouring rain for an hour and a half. After coming home last night and taking a hot shower to thaw, I transferred the pictures over to my computer and was fairly satisfied with the way they turned out. Without a flash, the shot of the driver's face hadn't turned out as good as I had hoped, but the one of the license plate was nearly perfect. I had captured all but one character, and I thought that if I sent this information to Lavine, he might find it very useful. Although I had been completely opposed to going through Carl Pierce's garbage at the time, I was now wishing we had had the opportunity. I had a sneaking suspicion that my biological father was getting rid of evidence, something that might incriminate him. I pulled the blankets up around my face and sniffled. I made a mental list of things I needed to do. First on the list: Take something for my cold. Second: Email Lavine the pictures from last night and pray that he might be able to use them. Third: Call Pastor Joe and confirm that he was still flying to Oklahoma for Alex's surprise party. And last, but not least, call Alex and see if he wanted to spend the day at the park. The weather was beautiful. Not a cloud in the sky, and I was hopeful things were finally looking up.

Two hours later, I was at the park, lying on a blanket, sipping a soda, and watching Alex play his guitar. The butterflies had finally emerged from their cocoons and the park was filled with colorful, fluttering insects. Just a little over a month ago, Alex seemed excited about the cocoons attached to the tree, about the new life inside, about the idea of something beautiful emerging from something ugly. He had taken at least fifty pictures, and I thought that based on his previous enthusiasm, he might at least comment on the colorful creatures, but he didn't mention them at all. This wasn't exactly surprising. Alex wasn't commenting on much lately. I turned my attention away from the butterfly that had landed on the edge of our blanket and regarded Alex. Straight-faced and completely focused, he dropped the tuning down on his guitar and began to pick the strings as he sang the lyrics to one of his favorite Nirvana songs. I fell back onto the blanket and closed my eyes. There was tension between the two of us, and I had no idea why. It made me feel uneasy. Sick to my stomach. I wanted to fix it, but I didn't know how. I hoped the surprise party might help. It was right around the corner, and I was relieved that I was ahead of the game. I had already found Alex the perfect gift. A ukulele. I just knew he would love it. To make the party even better, I was having dinner catered by Dink's, the local barbeque joint that Alex loved. So it looked like the only thing I had left to do was bake the cake. I wasn't great at making cakes, but I had found a recipe online that looked easy and yummy. No way I could mess it up. Mom had talked Papa (Mom's father from Missouri) into coming early, and he would be arriving in a few days. Papa had heard so much about Alex and vice versa. I couldn't wait for them to finally meet. And as far as I knew, Pastor Joe was still planning to attend. Alex would be so excited.

I returned my attention to Alex. His voice hovered just above a whisper as he sang. He's sad about something, I thought. But what? I wished I could tell him about the party. I knew that would cheer him up. For years, I had been so good at keeping secrets. Now I was having trouble not spilling the beans. I studied Alex's fingers while he played. They moved with ease, like he had been playing all his life. I loved his hands, but it had been a while since I had felt his touch, and I began to wish he were holding me instead of Stella. Stella was beautiful. Originally, Alex had only intended on spending seventy-five dollars. But when the guy from Craig's List didn't show, he went to the local guitar store instead. A 15 ½-inch cutaway made from Tasmanian Blackwood and Adirondack Spruce, the high-end guitar had a Mahogany neck with bird inlays. It was absolutely gorgeous.

"Mind if I try?"

"Sure." Finally he spoke. Alex stopped playing and put the pick between his teeth. With the utmost care, he put the strap over my head and positioned it on my shoulder. I ran my fingers across the shiny finish.

"Teach me something."

"Mmmm... Okay."

Alex moved behind me. His hands grazed my shoulders, and I could feel his breath on the back of my neck. He leaned over my shoulder to position my fingers on the strings. At that moment, I realized just how much I missed his touch. We had both been so busy; while I had been diving into my mission, my purpose, he had been busy with his car, with his guitar, with his song writing. I closed my eyes and relished the moment.

"Loosen up a bit," he whispered. With my eyes still closed, I began to relax. I began to think more about the scent of his cologne than the chord I was getting ready to play.

"Now strum."

With my right hand, I moved my thumb down the strings.

"That was a G. Not bad."

He began to manipulate my fingers and once again, my thoughts began to drift. Now I was thinking more about *his* fingers than mine.

"How about now? Does that feel all right?"

"Umhum," I returned in a voice so dreamy it grabbed his attention.

Alex cleared his throat. "The guitar, Rae. How does it feel?"

I opened my eyes and refocused. "Um. Good. I guess."

"Okay. Perfect. Now you're playing a C."

Ready to move onto another subject, I removed the strap from my neck and set Stella down on the blanket beside me. Alex carefully picked her back up.

"I know you didn't ask, but I thought I would let you know that the stakeout went well."

"Good."

"Carl's up to something."

"He's up to no good. That's what."

"I know. He was getting rid of evidence."

"Did you get pictures?"

"Yes."

"I assume you sent them to Lavine."

"I did… but I haven't heard back." I waited a moment to see if Alex would respond. When he didn't, I moved the conversation in an entirely different direction. "I talked to Pastor Joe this morning."

Alex began strumming his guitar and didn't respond. While I waited for him to say something, I pulled out my phone and checked my email. I was anxious to see if Lavine had received the photos I had sent. I was dying to know what he thought. Unfortunately, my inbox was empty. I sighed.

"Pastor Joe," Alex finally replied. "What did he have to say?"

"He's concerned about you." I slid my phone back into my bag. "He wanted to know why you haven't called."

"I've called."

"Not in a month."

"Is that all he had to say?" Alex continued to strum. I recognized the song at once. "Yellow" by Coldplay.

"No," I said, observing the butterfly that had returned to the edge of our blanket. "He talked a lot about God."

"He *does* like to talk about God, doesn't he," Alex said curtly.

"Well, he is a pastor, so I guess it's understandable."

"So what about God?"

"He said that you can see God in nature… even in the smallest creations."

"Is that right?" Alex's tone of voice was condescending.

"I'm beginning to understand what he means."

Alex used to talk about heaven, about God, about things that brought me hope. I'd ask him to tell me the story of *us*, the *heavenly us*. Just a little over a year ago, when Alex found me in the cemetery standing in front of his gravestone, he didn't hesitate to talk about God... about heaven. At the time, I didn't really want to hear it, but I did now. As the days passed, he became more and more closed off. Personally, I thought it was a bit selfish that he had all of this knowledge and was keeping it to himself. I had never really thought too much about God until now. I guess I thought of God like this: If He was real, then He either didn't know I existed or He just didn't care. I had never seen any real evidence of God working for me in my life, but of course, I hadn't really gone looking for Him, either. And now, when strange and spiritual circumstances were surrounding me, Alex could not... would not enlighten me.

"No comment?"

"I have nothing to say."

"About God or nature?"

"Both."

"You used to."

"Yeah. I did," Alex said, still strumming. "But I don't remember much about Him anymore."

"What about heaven? What about us? The *heavenly us*?" At this point, I was nearly begging.

"I don't remember much about that, either." Alex put the guitar down, leaned back onto the blanket, and supported himself with his elbow. He looked at me with wild indignation. "Don't look so surprised. I told you this would happen," he snorted.

"You can talk to me about it... if you want," I offered.

"There's nothing to talk about."

"But if you want, you can talk to me about how you feel."

"I don't want to talk to you about it, okay. Drop it. Done."

"Fine. It doesn't seem like you want to talk about much of anything any more."

I held out my hand and as if on cue, a butterfly landed on the tip of my finger. "Do you want to know what I think?"

"Sure. Let's hear it. Lay it all out, Sunshine."

"Sometimes I wonder if you resent me. Life is hard and I'm the reason you're here."

"I *said* just drop it."

"Fine. I will."

And just like that, the conversation was over. Alex and I were moving in opposite directions. We were meant to be together. I knew that. We were soul mates. We were cosmic. But then I remembered what he said on our trip to Woolaroc. When I asked him if he thought everyone found his or her soul mate, he said yes. He said sometimes finding your soul mate is the easy part. It's the staying together that can be tricky. I hadn't really considered what he might be saying to me. Was he trying to tell me that life was hard or that I was hard? His words hurt so bad I wanted to cry. Perhaps I was being oversensitive. Maybe I had made a mistake inviting Joe to the party. I couldn't let Joe see him like this. The party was in two weeks. Maybe I shouldn't have planned a party at all.

Disheartened, I left the park. I returned to my house and Alex returned to his. I pulled into an empty garage, slung my bag over my shoulder, and walked into the kitchen. I made a peanut butter and honey sandwich and poured a glass of milk. Once in my room, I placed my lunch on my desk and pulled out my laptop. I switched it on and surfed around a bit, landing on a popular celebrity news site with a startling image spread across the home page like a banner. *Ten-year-old photos resurface and send this star running for the hills.* Once again, I thought about the past. I thought about what Todd Catchitore said about history. "People don't want to look at the past when the past isn't pretty." Todd was right, people don't want to look at the past when *their* past isn't pretty, but he failed to mention that the need to look at and judge everyone else's past is human nature. A bit disgusted, I logged onto my profile page. Fifteen new notifications! What? It seemed that all of my requests had been accepted. 16 Friends. Who knew? And to top it off, I had a friend request. I wondered who wanted to be friends with me; I clicked on the icon at the top of the page to find out.

Athletic. Handsome. Blonde. Rock star hair. Flynt Redding had friended me. Turmoil. Alex was already mad at me. How would Alex feel about this? Should I accept? Decisions... decisions. I hesitated a moment, wondering how Alex would react. Then I moved the arrow over "accept" and clicked. It was done. I was friends with Flynt Redding, my boyfriend's greatest rival.

A box popped up at the bottom of the screen. We had been friend for less than a minute and already Flynt had sent me a message.

Flynt Redding: Just wanted to say hey! I know a lot has happened between us. Just wanted you to know that it's all water under the bridge. I miss you. BTW, where are you now? It's like you just fell off the face of the earth.

I began to thoughtfully type out my response.

Rae Colbert: Not sure what to say, Flynt. Sorry about everything. I miss you too and wish you well. I'm back in Oklahoma.

I hit return and then began to add photos to an album I labeled "Alexandria." Several moments later, Flynt came back with another message. I read the text inside the box.

Flynt Redding: You still with Boy Miro?

Rae Colbert: Of course. And a little bird told me you were seeing Corrine.

I smiled the first smile of the day.

Flynt Redding: Nothing serious. Keeping my options open. Unless.... you'd like to reconsider.

I made no comment

Flynt Redding: Only joking. I'm happy for you and Boy Miro. You make a ... nice couple. I mean... you're cosmic, right.

Rae Colbert: Yes, cosmic. That was a weird night.

Flynt Redding: No joke

Rae Colbert: I feel like I should apologize, but it looks like it worked out for you and Corrine after all.

Flynt Redding: You know you're still the only one for me.

I ignored him. I shut my computer off and glanced down at the ring on my finger, the promise ring Alex had given me. A symbol of our love. I twirled the ring around my finger as I considered what it meant to be cosmic. If we were cosmic, why did it seem like Alex no longer wanted to be with me? There was tension in our time together. He bottled up his feelings. He was short and snappy. He was pushing me away.

CHAPTER TWENTY-THREE

I went completely overboard, just like I had planned. Much to my mother's surprise, I had cleaned the house from top to bottom. Gifts had been wrapped. My dad was on his way to Tulsa to pick up Pastor Joe from the airport. Papa had been here for nearly a week. Mom used the party as the perfect excuse to get him to come for a visit and once he was here, she had begged him to stay indefinitely, promising him that under no circumstances would he wear out his welcome. Although he was reluctant at first, afraid that he might mess up our daily routine, she didn't really have to twist his arm. Truth be told, despite the strong front that Papa put up, he missed my Nana terribly and was growing more and more lonely everyday. Papa was sitting on the sofa watching the news and as I finished up with the dusting, Mom walked into the living room carrying a large silver serving tray on top of which sat a cup of tea, two cups of coffee, and an assortment of cookies.

"Have time for a break, Rae?"

I pulled my phone out of my pocket and checked the time. "Ummm. I don't know. I only have three hours before the party, and I still haven't made the cake."

"I told you I'd help you bake the cake."

"No. I want to do it."

"Are you sure you want to attempt it? Maybe it's something we could work on together."

"Mom. I have everything under control. It's a fail proof cake. No way I can mess it up."

"Sit down. Have a cup of coffee and talk to your Papa."

I repositioned the bandana on my head and sat down beside my grandpa. Mom handed me a mug, and I stirred in some cream and then a big spoonful of sugar.

"Sue tells me you've been busy," Papa sipped his tea and took a bite of a fresh baked Madeline.

"Well, I don't know about that."

"You're being modest, Sunshine." Sue returned her cup to the saucer and added a bit of sugar to the joe. "You leave for Houston tomorrow. Why don't you tell Papa a little bit about what you'll be doing there," she encouraged.

"You know just as much as I do."

"Dad," Mom suggested. "Why don't you give her a few words of wisdom? And while you're at it, maybe you could give me a few as well. Truthfully, I think I'm more concerned about Rae's trip than she is."

"That's easy. I can give my two favorite girls the same piece of advice. Keep you eyes open. Not everything is what it seems. Keep your heart open. There are many ways to love. Keep your mind open. This world is full of possibilities. And most importantly, have faith. Because we know that in all things God works for the good of those who love Him."

I couldn't figure out what I had done wrong. I followed the recipe to a T. I had even tasted the batter and it was amazing. Frustrated, I thought about the lopsided cake as I stood over the stove and stirred together the sugar and corn syrup. Sadly, the mixture looked like a ball of slime instead of the salted caramel frosting in the picture. With five minutes left on the timer, I was hopeful that it might come together after all. Still stirring, I glanced over my shoulder at the topsy-turvy, two-layered cake I had displayed on the crystal stand. It looked horrible and the frosting was the only chance I had of saving it. If the mixture didn't turn into caramel soon, then I was in trouble. When there was a minute left on the timer, the mixture turned into a smooth, pourable frosting. I turned off the burner but continued to stir. I was supposed to wait for it to cool, but I was running behind schedule, so I dumped it directly onto the cake and watched it drip down the sides. As I stood back to evaluate, I heard the sound of the front door opening. Dad was back with Pastor Joe. I glanced at the cuckoo clock on the wall. Only an hour and a half till Alex arrives.

"Something smells good," a voice hollered from the entryway.

I heard one pair of feet moving quickly into the kitchen and another pair of feet shuffling behind. With my head cocked to the side, I was studying my creation when Will walked in with Pastor Joe. I squealed when I saw Alex's godfather. "Joe!" I ran over and gave him a hug. "It's so good to see you!"

"You've been busy," Will remarked. Mimicking *my* previous posture, he now stood with *his* head cocked. Just like me, he probably thought that if he shifted his eyes a bit, the cake might have a better chance of looking balanced.

"I know. I know. It looks like the Leaning Tower of Pisa," I laughed.

"No, it looks like a cheeseburger." Will walked up to the cake and stuck his finger in the frosting.

"Dad!"

"I was thinking it looked more like a piece of chicken fried steak with gravy over the top," Joe chuckled.

"Oh well," I sighed. "Let's just hope it doesn't taste like one."

"Where's Charlie?" Dad asked.

"Papa's taking a nap. And I hate to run up to my room right after you get here, but I have a party to get ready for. A girl's gotta look good." I gave Joe another hug, then walked across the wood floors toward the stairs.

When I glanced at him over my shoulder, I smiled. Wearing the same navy suit and leather oxfords he always wore, Joe stood in complete confidence. Joe was just Joe. He was constant. Always the same. He didn't try to pretend he was someone else. He knew exactly who he was and he was happy.

"Alex is going to be so excited to see you, Joe!" I hollered on my way out of the kitchen.

"She doesn't seem like the same girl," I heard Joe whisper to Will.

"I know. She does seem happy, doesn't she?" Will whispered back.

I shut my door on the conversation. Joe was right. I was different. I was happy. I unpinned the ancient brooch from my shirt and set it on my dresser. The gold was slowly returning, and the brooch was taking on a beautiful caramel hue. I turned on some music, shed my clothes, and tossed them into the hamper. I stepped into the shower and as the water washed over me, started to worry. I told Alex that he was coming over tonight so we could say goodbye before I left for Houston. Will and Alex hadn't had any contact since mid-March when Will booted him out of the truck. What if things don't go as planned? I pushed these thoughts out of my mind and thought of cheerful things instead. *Tonight was going to be perfect. Alex is going to be so excited. So surprised.* I knew we weren't supposed to keep secrets, but I also knew he would totally understand.

I had never been more wrong. At precisely 7 PM, the bell rang. I hesitated a moment before answering, making sure the party was hidden from view. Alex thought he was coming over to tell me goodbye, to say farewell, bon voyage. To wish me luck on my journey. Little did he know, tonight was all about him. I twisted the knob and pulled open the door. And there he was dressed in his usual jeans, blue and black vans, and V-neck tee. I bit my lip. Alex moved toward me with watery eyes.

"Don't go," he whispered. "Please don't go," he begged.

"HAPPY BIRTHDAY!!!!!!"

Alex looked taken aback. The party moved into view, and my mom switched on the music. Alex stood stunned in the foyer, and I stood in front of him, looking at his sad face. Maybe tonight was not the best night for a party and all at once, I wished that we were all alone.

I looked out of my bedroom window and let my eyes wander up the country road, remembering how just a year ago I could count on seeing Alex's Wagoneer parked off to the side. He was determined to protect me. To stand guard over my house, making sure that I was safe. Tonight, the road was empty and after a turbulent evening, the house had become very quiet. When Alex stormed out the door at 8:30, less than two hours after he arrived, Joe, Papa, Mom, and Dad had decided to call it a night. I wiped a tear from my eye as I gazed out at the empty country road, wishing that things between us could go back to the way they were before. Wishing Alex could be the way he used to be. Wishing he wasn't sad and confused. Wishing he wasn't so lonely. Wishing that Joe hadn't been here to see us fight. Wishing Joe hadn't traveled 700 miles to see him storm out the front door only an hour and a half after he arrived.

I moved from the window and began to throw enough clothes into my duffel to last three days. How could he leave it like this? How could he start a fight when I was supposed to hop on a plane tomorrow? Thinking that a good book might take my mind off my troubles, I had just tossed a mystery novel into my bag when a soft knock sounded on my bedroom door.

"It's open," I muttered.

The door creaked and I looked up from my duffle bag just as Dad peeked his head into my room. Expecting to see Mom, I was startled when I saw him.

"Dad!" I zipped up the duffle and gave Will my full attention. His ratty bathrobe hung on his sturdy frame, draping loosely over his red plaid pajama bottoms and white cotton tee shirt. As he shuffled across the carpet toward me, I noticed his eyes. His eyes, which always sparkled, looked tired. Dad stopped in the middle of the room, pausing directly below my ceiling fan and looked up at the spinning blades. He pursed his lips and scratched his head.

"You didn't hang up your yellow bird."

"Yeah, I know."

"You loved that bird. I remember the day we bought it." Dad paused. "You know, the yellow bird is a very symbolic creature."

"It is?"

"It represents love."

"It does? I had no idea." I lay down on the floor beside my bed and looked up at the ceiling fan, the spot where my little bird used to hang.

"It represents sacrifice. Miners used yellow birds in coal mines to warn them of danger. Yellow birds are delicate. They're so tiny, toxic gasses kill them more quickly than humans. If the bird died or got sick, the miners knew it was time to get out. In a way, the yellow bird is clearing the path for others. Taking on pain and suffering so that others might have life."

There was a long and awkward silence. I was pretty sure Dad didn't come up to my room at 1 AM to discuss my little yellow bird. For the past three months, he had been giving me the silent treatment, and now, just hours before departing on my first mission for A-Omega, he wanted to talk.

"You're a good girl, Rae. You never asked for much, and that made me want to give you the world."

There was another long and awkward silence. I was certainly not prepared for heartfelt emotions. Not at this hour and certainly not from Will. I had come to the conclusion that he absolutely despised me... that he resented who I was and where I had come from. Dad's eyes were now fixed on his feet. He began to brush his sheepskin house shoe back and forth across the carpet nervously.

"Dad?"

"Hum?" He looked up from his slipper and into my eyes.

"You gave me enough. You gave me plenty." No longer lying on the carpet, I was now leaning against the side of the bed.

"But I didn't give you the truth."

"I guess I can understand why you didn't."

"It doesn't make it okay."

"I'm okay with it now."

"I want you to know that I'm also human. I make mistakes and I'm sorry." Dad moved his hand across his face, rubbing his eyes first then he began to massage his whiskery chin. I had never seen him look so tired. "Even the best man is only a man at best."

"I know. And I'm sorry, too. I'm sorry for running away."

Dad tilted his head back and gave a modest chuckle. "I guess I can understand why you did."

"But it doesn't make it okay." I smiled.

Dad let another muffled laugh escape him, then completed his journey across my spacious bedroom and sat down on the corner of my bed. Still seated on the floor, I looked up into his eyes. Although they still looked tired, the sparkle had returned.

"I've always loved your taste," he said as he smoothed his hand across my duvet cover. "What do they call this print?"

"Batik."

"Batik. That's right. You have impeccable taste."

"Except in boys, right."

The drastic change in my father's expression and the furrow in his brow told me that I had hit the nail on the head.

"I love Alex, and I hate to see him this way," my father responded without a moment's pause. His comment was completely unexpected and I was caught off guard. Did he really just use the word *love*? I wanted to remind him that actions speak louder than words, but I decided to keep my mouth shut and let him finish.

"He's the son I never had."

"I didn't realize you felt that way."

"I do. However, what he did was wrong. That was not a gentlemanly thing to do. He should have…"

"Are you talking about tonight? The way he stormed out of the house without saying thank you or goodbye?"

"No. I'm talking about how he took you away to Alexandria without consulting us first."

"What he did saved your life," I reminded him. "And Mom's life."

"I'm not trying to insult Alex's strength or make little of where he came from. Miraculous, no doubt. These things don't just happen… and yet, he's here. He's the protection your mother and I prayed for. But…."

"But what? You prayed for my protection and God delivered. We did what we needed to do."

"It was selfish," Dad snapped.

"Just so you know. It was my fault... not his. Alex wanted to tell you everything. He wanted to tell you about us. He wanted to tell you about himself. You are the *parents* he'll never have."

"I can see that. Alex is a good kid."

"Then what? Everything worked out, didn't it?"

"Maybe my own pride is getting in the way, Rae. I took pride in providing for you and your mother. For eighteen years, I kept you safe. When I prayed for your protection, I had no idea that God was going to deliver an extremely handsome and insanely strong young man to replace me. After Alex arrived, I was no longer the hero. I was just the guy with the hairy back. What was it that you called me?"

"Woolybooger."

"Ah, yes. Woolybooger. Every dad prepares himself for the day his daughter falls in love and no longer looks at him with the same adoring eyes. I believe that some dads pull away early because they can't bear to think of the loss. They'd rather leave than be left. At any rate, it was hard enough knowing I no longer held that special place in your heart. But when you left, it felt like you stabbed me in the back and Alex gave the knife a final twist."

"I never meant to hurt you."

"I thought I would never see you again."

"I guess all I have left to do is say I'm sorry and try to make it up to you," I said, repeating Dad's words from a moment ago.

Dad hung his head and resumed his previous smoothing of my duvet. If he kept it up, the colorful batik cover would be threadbare.

"I presume you had a... *nice* time at the cottage."

"Nice. Yes. And eventful."

"Pleasant *accommodations*, I'm guessing."

I could have gone on and on about the pleasantries of the little cottages on L'homme Dieu, but I knew it would be better to give him an answer that was short and to the point.

"Pleasant, yes."

"And there was plenty of space there for the two of you?"

"Dad, I know the direction you're steering this conversation and the answer is NO! Can we *not* talk about this?"

"So you're saying that… Alex was a gentleman?"

"Of course he was," I huffed.

"It's a legitimate question. You've become a very beautiful young woman. And Alex… well… supernatural or not, he's a man."

"Dad. We didn't do anything. Nothing. Alex wouldn't touch me with a ten foot pole."

Dad looked taken aback. "A ten foot pole? Really?"

"I practically had to beg to get a kiss."

When his eyes finally met mine, a smug smile spread across his face. "I always knew Alex Loving was a good boy. Just had a feeling about him."

"Okay, Dad." I yawned and glanced at the clock. Dad didn't take the hint. "I hate to cut you short, but I have to be up in three hours."

"Oh, right. I guess if I'm taking you to the airport, I need to get some shuteye myself." Dad stood up at the foot of my bed, slipped his hands deep into the pockets of his robe, shifted all of his weight to his right side, and then back to his left. "Is there anything else bothering you, Sunshine?"

I was exhausted, but I realized that Dad still wanted to talk. So I yawned, sat up straight, and tried to catch my second wind. I thought about what he was asking me. Yes. There was something else bothering me. I was a little scared about the trip. What would happen? I pondered his question a moment longer before responding. "I feel like nothing is going my way. I keep running into roadblocks. A-Omega is taking their time and I have no idea where I'm going."

"You're going to Houston."

"I know, but what if I get there and they tell me to wait. Then what?"

"Then I guess you wait."

"That's not all. Alex is growing distant."

"Any idea why?"

"No, but at least *you're* talking to me now. One step forward, two steps back. I'm trying to do the right thing, but as I get close to the truth, I feel darkness nipping at my heels, trying to drag me back."

"Reminds me of a short novella I read the other day. About an old fisherman who hadn't brought in a good catch in 84 days."

"Are you talking about *The Old Man and the Sea*?"

"You've read it?"

"Yes. Hemingway."

"As a shrink, I could pick the book apart and analyze every paragraph. Many accept the autobiographical reading of the novella and believe that Hemingway is telling *his* story through the old man. If this is true, then I could tell you that the cramp the fisherman got in his left hand while out at sea was symbolic of Hemingway's writer's block and that the old man's desire to bring in a big catch was symbolic of Hemingway's need to write a best selling novel. It's a story that ends well for the old man."

"No it didn't. It took him a long time to catch the marlin and when he did, the sharks ate his prize."

"I learned two life lessons from this story. First of all, the sharks won't attack unless you're onto something good… and the old fisherman *was* onto something good. And secondly, maybe it's not so much about the fish as it is about the journey. It's not about the tangible prize rather the change that takes place inside as you travel down the path.. or across the ocean. It's about the people's lives you touch along the way. The old man was a hero to the young boy. Although many would say the old man lost it all, I say, he was not defeated."

As Dad moved to the door, I turned onto my side and pulled the duvet up to my chin.

"Rae."

"Yes, Dad."

"He loves you, Rae. Alex loves you." Dad's hand was resting on the doorknob. He was staring at his slippers. "He loves you more than he loves himself, and that's a kind of love you don't find everyday." He opened the door. "He wouldn't touch you with a ten foot pole, huh?" Dad laughed and closed the door behind him.

I felt like a mac truck had hit me. Every inch of my body ached. Dad kept me up late talking and I was tired, but once the lights were out and my head finally hit the pillow, I found it impossible to extinguish the worries that were igniting in my mind. Where was A-Omega sending me, and how was I going to make it on my own? How was I going to make it without Alex?

INTERCESSION

CHAPTER TWENTY-FOUR

*I*t was late, and I was spent. Thirty hours in Houston and no luck… no leads. I had absolutely no idea where I was going or what I was doing here. Because I hadn't heard from A-Omega, I spent the morning and most of the afternoon with Crazy Carly. We grabbed brunch and went shopping on Westheimer near River Oaks. Carly brightened my day and lifted my sprits. She just had that way about her. With her long red curls and freckled face, Carly had been my first *real* friend. She understood me when no one else did. How could I feel discouraged around Carly? As usual, she kept me entertained with tall tales, but this time I had a few stories of my own. She told me I seemed different. I told her it wasn't the first time I had heard that, and then I asked her "How so?" Her response was immediate. She told me my color was different. She told me my aura had changed. When she first met me, I radiated the color brown. Yikes. But now, I was starting to look a little yellow.

After a full day of shopping, laughing, and reminiscing with a good friend, I returned to the posh hotel where A-Omega had housed me. Couldn't complain about that either. The beds were soft and I had Wi-Fi. I pulled out my brand new silver computer, pushed the power button and in an instant, I was online. I vividly recalled my old laptop. It was a dinosaur. I spent more time waiting for it to turn on than I did using it. I clicked on the free Wi-Fi and then decided that my first order of business was to find some dinner. I hadn't eaten since late this morning and my stomach had been growling for the past hour and a half. Nothing sounded good besides Chinese, so I searched for a nearby restaurant and finally decided on Kam's because it had a five star rating and because they delivered. I called in for curried chicken and shrimp with pineapple, one of their specialties, and then decided to check my email while I waited, hoping that A-Omega might have sent me something... anything that might give me a clue as to what I was doing in Houston. It made absolutely no sense. None of it. I had been waiting a long time for this trip, this mission. I had prepared myself physically by running a couple of extra miles a day and doubling up on karate. Plus, I was praying, just like Baxtor and Quinn suggested. My email account popped up, but there was nothing from A-Omega in my inbox. But there was something from Alex. I hadn't talked to him since he stormed out of my house and my fingers trembled as I opened the email. I missed him. I was worried that he was still upset. I wanted him here. I needed to see him. But if I couldn't, then getting an email from him was the next best thing. Alex's email consisted of four short lines that were centered on the page. A poem. If Alex was writing me poetry, then there was no way he could still be upset. My heart fluttered as I anticipated his words, but when I read the first line, it sunk.

Your presence isn't what it used to be

What was that supposed to mean? I wanted to shut off my computer and pout; instead, I continued to read.

You've put me at a distance.
When I try to touch you
All I get is your resistance

"Are you kidding?!" I shouted at the screen like he could hear me. "Where did this come from?" I felt an overwhelming urge to pick up my cellphone and give him an earful, when I noticed that, on my email homepage under chat, the dot beside Alex's name was green. He was online. If this was the way Alex wanted to communicate, then I was going to give him a taste of his own medicine. I clicked on his name and waited for the chat box to pop up. I placed my fingers on the keyboard but they wouldn't move. Why was I angry? Why did his little poem aggravate me? Was it because he hadn't said it to my face? Was it because he was right? Maybe I had distanced myself from Alex, but he had been distant, too. And just because I had a lot going on didn't mean that I loved him any less. Now more than ever I needed him. I closed my eyes and tried to put myself in his shoes. All along, he had wanted to come on this trip with me. He had counted on it. I couldn't erase from my memory the hurt look on his face when I told him A-Omega had sent only one ticket. Alex felt left out. I had to rethink this. Instead of lashing out as I had intended to do, I was going to simply explain myself. I was going to tell him how I felt, and I was going to attempt to make it rhyme, just as he had. I began to type.

> Really? You think I don't like your touch?
> To feel your fingers on my skin?
> I come to you with everything
> But you won't let me in
> I always wanted *you* more…
> Even from the start
> Now you prefer the strings of your guitar
> To the strings of my heart

I waited for a response, but nothing came. I knew he had seen what I had typed. I was pretty proud that I had been able to express myself poetically. But what would he think? Was it too harsh? My words were no harsher than his. After several minutes, my computer beeped with Alex's response.

> Yeah, but I'm not just talking about your body
> I was referring to your mind
> Even when you're right beside me
> You're kind of hard to find

Now that was just insulting. I hadn't flown off the handle as I had wanted to, but right now I was very close. How could he say that? We talked. We talked all the time. Besides, he was the one pushing me away. I felt the need to further defend myself. This time the words came easy. Short and sweet.

> You don't know my dilemma
> My past can't be undone

Two short sentences. How strange that my life could be summed up in ten words or less. My computer beeped again. This time, it only took a second for him to respond.

> But somehow I've been left with nothing
> And you've been given more than one.

Fourteen words. That's all it took to break my heart. Tears formed in my eyes against my will. I knew exactly what he was talking about. He was no longer talking about our relationship. He was talking about the father he never had, the father he found in Will. He was talking about my biological father, Carl, and how, when he turned out to be a creep, God gave me another. He was talking about my biological mother Eva and how, after she died, God gave me Sue. Even though Alex never verbally referred to Sue and Will as his mother and father, I knew he felt that way by the genial way he spoke of them. He was always quick to remind me of their caring nature. Will was the only father figure in Alex's life, and Will had brushed him off. I was thankful for the conversation that I had with Dad just before I left, and I was thankful that I had tried my hardest to clear Alex's name. It was comforting to know that I had set the record straight. It was helpful to know that Dad felt the very same way about Alex.

Will's not mad anymore. Go talk to him.

NO! Alex's response was immediate and non lyrical. His verbiage no longer rhymed.

He says he loves you. He told me that you're the son he never had.

Really?

Yes, really. So get over yourself and go talk to the man.

I'll think about it.

You'd better. I want to hear that you talked to Will. And when I come home in a couple of days, I want to see that the two of you are getting along.

I'll think about it.

Goodbye

No. Goodnight.

Goodnight, Alex. I love you.

XOXO

I closed Gmail and went to my favorite store's homepage. I had just begun scrolling through the sale section when the phone on my bedside table rang, startling me. I picked it up.

"Hello."

"Hi. Is this Ms. Colbert?"

"Yes."

"Did you order in Chinese?" The hotel receptionist asked.

"Yes."

"Could you come down to the lobby to pick up your order?"

"Can you just have them bring it on up?"

"I'm afraid not. You have to come down to the lobby. It's hotel policy."

"Okay. I'll be right down."

My stomach growled at the thought of food. Quickly, I changed into something more presentable and made my way to the elevator. Once in the lobby, I paid the deliveryman, stepped back into the elevator, and pushed the button for the tenth floor. I decided to eat my fortune cookie on the way up. I fished my hand inside the bag and pulled it out. Was it bad luck to read your fortune before you ate your meal? Na. I broke open the cookie and ate half of it before opening up the sliver of paper. When I saw my fortune, the half-chewed cookie nearly fell out of my mouth.

You don't have to know where you're going to be headed in the right direction

I read the lucky numbers below the fortune.

Lucky Numbers 7, 20, 20, 09, 13: 15

I turned over the slip of paper to read the other side.

Lobby
大厅 (dà tīng)

CHAPTER TWENTY-FIVE

*N*eedless to say, I got no sleep at all, which was a complete waste of a fancy hotel room with a mattress more comfortable than the one I had at home. As soon as my head hit the pillow, I began to think about my fortune. A simple sentence that might mean nothing to someone else, yet it meant something to me. Before ordering Chinese, I had absolutely no idea where I was going or why A-Omega had sent me here. I had assumed that I was here to find information that would incriminate Carl Pierce. But if that was the case, why hadn't I found anything? And then, just as I'm about to enjoy my dinner, I open up a cookie that gives me a frustrating fortune. It was frustrating because I knew that it was meant for me and even more frustrating because the cookie held encouraging words, but not an answer. After tossing and turning for hours, I crawled out of bed. I flicked on the bedside lamp and a dim light illuminated the room. I rubbed my eyes and waited for them to adjust. If I was going to continue to think about the fortune cookie, I might as well give it another look. I closed the lid of the Styrofoam box to stifle the strong smell of leftover curried chicken and shrimp. The fortune was under the takeout box. I picked it up and took it back to bed with me. Now more interested in the numbers than the fortune, I began to wonder if there was something I was missing. I had eaten plenty of Chinese food and opened enough fortune cookies to know that there was something odd about this set of numbers. I held it under the lamp and leaned in for a closer look.

Lucky Numbers 7, 20, 20, 09, 13: 15

This fortune had two twenties. Was it a typo? I laid the slip of paper on the bedside table, rubbed my eyes again, and flicked on the TV just in time to see a rerun of 20/20 entitled lotto money/lotto problems. Okay, this was bizarre. "20, 20" on the fortune cookie. 20/20 on TV. It was an episode about the lives of lottery winners after coming into a fortune. I caught the middle of Henry's story. They were interviewing him in his home, a trailer somewhere in the middle of New Mexico. He won three million dollars and had nothing to show for it. The interviewer, Barry, was an attractive middle-aged man with salt and pepper hair. His skin was tight over his cheekbones, but loose around his eyes. When he spoke to Henry, you got the impression that he truly cared. There was a degree of sympathy in his voice that I thought was genuine. Barry wanted to know how Henry had squandered his money so quickly. Henry shook his head and said that a better question was why he had won the lottery in the first place.

"Money only brought me trouble," Henry said. "I lost everything in my life that was true when I won the lotto. Money is good… it can be good that is." Henry went on with his story about how he opted to take the lump sum and how he squandered it all on drugs. I drifted in and out of sleep, but was startled awake when I heard weeping. Henry was still answering questions, but Barry must have struck a nerve. Henry had tears running down his face.

"I just didn't know what to do with all of that money," Henry sniffed. "I guess I thought I was finally something because I had it. You can see where money got me. You're lookin' at the real Henry now."

When 20/20 took a commercial break, I nodded off to sleep, drifting in and out of advertisements for heart medication and Nestle Tollhouse cookies. When the program returned, Barry was in Carmel, Indiana, talking with Tina, a lotto winner with an experience very different from Henry's.

"Now I have heard that there's a story behind how you won the lotto."

"Absolutely," Tina professed. "It was my first time to play. So my winning could be attributed to beginner's luck. But I like to think that it had more to do with the numbers I chose."

"Do you mind sharing with us those numbers and why you chose them?"

"The week I won the lotto was the worst and the best week of my life. I was in the middle of a divorce and my ex-husband was playing hardball. I was living with my mother because my husband booted me out and moved his girlfriend in. The story gets much worse before it gets better. The week I won the lotto, I was diagnosed with cancer. I tried to stay upbeat. The day before I won, I remember thinking to myself, 'At least I still have my job.' But that morning, I walked into work and was fired. It wasn't because I had performed badly; it was because my company was trying to cut costs by outsourcing. I remember thinking to myself, 'I'm going to die.' I had just been diagnosed with cancer, and I no longer had insurance. And to be completely honest with you, I felt like dying. I'm going to bring up my faith here, Barry, if you don't mind."

Barry shifted in his seat, and made a gesture with his hand for her to continue. "Certainly. Certainly."

"As a child, I was told that God would never give me more than I could handle, but I was a thirty-three-year-old woman living… and dying, in my mother's house. I can remember feeling that my circumstances had far surpassed what I could handle."

"So what did you do? It's obvious that your luck began to change."

"It wasn't luck that pulled me out of the pit I was in; I know that for sure. Sometimes you have to be completely broken before you can be truly healed. That night, I went to bed and prayed. Praying was nothing new to me, but this prayer was different. It wasn't an 'I have to squeeze everything in before I fall asleep' kind of prayer. The prayer lasted into the next morning. It wasn't an 'Ask for what I want' kind of prayer, either. I didn't ask for a thing. Instead, I told God how I felt. I told him I felt abandoned, unloved, and overlooked. I talked to him like I would talk to my mother, but I told him things that I would never dream of telling her.

I told him that despite everything that had happened, I did want to live and that despite the hurt that I had experienced, I did love life."

"Did he… respond?" Barry's body went rigid and I noticed a degree of discomfort that was not present during his other interview.

"Verbally, no. But I felt peace in knowing that everything was going to be okay, and in knowing that I was going to be healed. The next morning, after only a couple hours of sleep, I got out of bed and went into the kitchen. Barry, have you ever had a feeling like the universe is leading you in a specific direction?"

"I can't say that I have, Tina."

"That's what happened to me. I had never cared about the lotto, and I had never known anyone who had won a dime from playing. But as soon as I woke up the next morning, I couldn't turn around without hearing about the lottery. It was on the radio and the TV. I went out to get a few things at the store and I saw the ad on billboards. I'm not a gambler Barry, but for some reason I just decided to give it a try. I also made the decision to pick my own numbers. I picked numbers that meant something to me. I chose my birthday, I chose the date that I was diagnosed with cancer, and I chose the date that I anticipated being completely healed."

"And you won millions with those numbers."

"I did, Barry!"

"That's the kind of story you don't hear everyday."

"And you haven't even heard the clincher. On December 14th, after enduring nearly a year and a half of chemotherapy, my doctor shared with me the good news. I was cancer free."

"I've had the pleasure of spending a full day at your home, Tina. You have a beautiful house, but nothing extravagant. In fact, if I didn't know your story, I would never suspect that you had millions. I hope you don't mind that I ask, but I am rather curious. What do you do with your money?"

"God speaks in mysterious ways and I do believe that the money I won was a blessing. I also believe that blessings are meant to be shared. Sometimes, we hear God's voice the loudest while we're in the midst of the most pain. Other times, his voice comes in a gentle whisper. God wants to comfort us while we're in pain, and He wants to bless us. But not so that we can keep all of God's goodness to ourselves. It's so we can share with others the goodness that God showed us. When I was at my lowest point, there was one and only one word I could use to describe how I felt. That word was hopeless. So to answer your question, Barry, I started a foundation to help those who are down and out, those who are feeling as hopeless as I felt."

Barry wiped his eyes, and I noticed that the skin below his eyes was now red, puffy, and taut. "You have a much different story to tell than other lotto winners I have interviewed. What makes you different?"

"I never forget a blessing. Every time God blesses me, whether big or small, I write it down in this book." Tina held up a purple journal and began to leaf through the pages. "It's getting pretty full. So, I guess you could say that I'm blessed."

I shut off the TV and closed my eyes. I felt sort of guilty that I had just heard one of the most inspiring stories of my life, yet all I could think about were numbers. Numbers. The numbers on my fortune cookie. The numbers on Tina's winning lotto ticket. Her numbers meant something to her. Did my numbers mean something as well? Numbers. Two Twenties. Dates. That's it. I sprung out of bed and held the fortune to the light. The first number was a seven. A date. I sat up straight.

"The seventh month of the year is July," I said aloud. Today was July 19th. Perhaps the numbers did represent a specific date. I glanced at the second number. It was a 20. A 7 and a 20. I felt like I was finally getting somewhere. July 20th. That's tomorrow. I glanced at the next number. It was another 20 and I felt like I had hit a brick wall. I couldn't figure out what to do with the third number, another 20. I moved on to the fourth number: 09. I glanced back at the first number: 7. 7 and 09. Both integers. But the nine had a zero in front of it and the seven didn't. I hopped out of bed only to return seconds later with my purple gel pen. I opened the drawer of the nightstand and pulled out a small pad of paper. On the paper, I wrote the number 20 and the number 09. I stared at them with wide eyes.

2009

Of course, the answer was so obvious. I couldn't believe that I hadn't seen it before. The first four numbers on the fortune cookie represented tomorrow's date. I moved onto the last two numbers.

13: 15

There was only one peculiarity with this set of numbers. Instead of a comma separating the thirteen from the fifteen, there was a colon. Now that I was warmed up, it only took me a second to understand what the last two numbers stood for. 13:15 was military time for 1:15. I copied my fortune onto a pad of paper with my purple gel pen.

You don't have to know where you're going to be headed in the right direction

Next, I copied down my lucky numbers in the form of a date and a time.

July 20th, 2009 at 1:15 PM

I flipped the fortune over and looked at the word on the back.

Lobby

大厅 (dà tīng)

My mind flashed back to the interview on 20/20, when Tina asked Barry if he had ever had the feeling that the entire universe was leading him in a specific direction. At that moment, I knew exactly how Tina felt. I had been looking for signs all day, but found nothing. Just when I was ready to throw in the towel, I received direction. A-Omega? It had to be. But how had they managed it? How would they have known I was going to call Kam's for takeout? It wasn't possible. Was I so tired that I was turning my fortune into something it wasn't? Was I so desperate for an answer that I was willing to look anywhere, even inside a cookie? No. This was no coincidence, and I was leaning toward another option. A-Omega was *much* bigger than I thought.

CHAPTER TWENTY-SIX

*A*fter my fortune cookie discovery, I was pretty sure that even if I did close my eyes, I wouldn't be able to sleep. My mind was racing. My thoughts were swirling, but when my alarm sounded at 11:30, waking me from a very deep sleep, I was relieved that I had gotten some shuteye. While I slept, I dreamt of digits and when I awoke, numbers were the first thing on my mind. In less than two hours, it would be 1:15. What was I going to do? Was there something waiting for me in the hotel lobby? If so, what was it? Even if it turned out to be nothing more than my overactive imagination, I thought I should at least check it out, but if I was going to leave this room, I needed to get cleaned up, eat some breakfast, and I definitely needed a large coffee. I thought I would start off the morning by taking full advantage of the amenities: the jetted tub, the lavender bath crystals, the assortment of spa lotions and oils, the plush white robes with Zaza embroidered onto the terrycloth, and of course, room service. I ordered a vegetarian breakfast burrito, a large orange juice, and a carafe of coffee with cream and sugar. After breakfast, I ran a hot bath and dropped a handful of crystals into the water. Thirty minutes later, I emerged from the tub feeling refreshed and ready for whatever the day might bring. I pressed an oversized towel against my face and inhaled the scent of lavender. I was surprised how calm I felt at a time when I should feel very anxious. This could turn out to be a very big day, I thought. I began to wonder what I should wear. Of course the boots. I had to wear the boots. I dug around in my suitcase and I pulled out a pair of black jeans and a vintage rock tee. I stood in front of the mirror and applied a bit of powder and some lip gloss. I fluffed my hair and stood back to look at my reflection. I am strong. I am determined. I am stubborn. I am kind. I am ready to go.

It was 12:50 when I hopped on the elevator. When I reached the lobby, I was surprised to find it empty. This is crazy, I thought. I am crazy. Receiving directions from a fortune cookie? What was I thinking? I'm sleep deprived, I told myself. Discouraged, I glanced at my phone. 12:53. I was early. I turned a full circle, hoping that something or someone might catch my eye.

"Can I help you, Miss?"

I jumped and turned around to find the bellboy smiling at me.

"No. I'm just waiting for someone."

"What's their name? You can take a seat and I'll inform you when they arrive."

And there it was. Once again, it appeared as though I was nutty. Should I tell him about my divine appointment with who knows who and that my invitation arrived via a fortune cookie late last night? I think not. Should I tell him that I was on a special mission for A-Omega and there was no way that he could possibly help? No!

"You know what? I think I'll just have a seat and keep my eye out, but thanks anyway."

The bellboy nodded his head and lingered a moment longer. "Well, if you need anything, my name's Raoul. Just let me know," he said with a sparkle in his eyes.

I sunk into a surprisingly comfortable zebra print chair with a red seat cushion and exhaled. Following A-Omega was tiring... mentally. I had run for miles and never felt this exhausted. With my eyes glued to the lobby entrance, my mind began to drift. Did I have a liaison? I wondered.

If so, who would it be? It could be anyone, if there was a liaison at all. They could be young or old, tall or short, male or female, comrade or enemy. Maybe there wasn't a liaison. Maybe I was in the lobby to observe. Maybe there was something that A-Omega wanted... needed for me to see. I looked over my shoulder taking notice of a couple in the corner. They were smooching while waiting on the elevator. If I had to guess, I would say they were both in their early thirties. Didn't look like anything fishy was going on. Nothing out of the ordinary about a couple in love. I heard the elevator chime and watched the man take hold of the woman's bag. With his free hand, he took her hand in his. The diamond she had on her ring finger was so big I could see it clearly from a distance. Possibly newlyweds. I twisted my promise ring around my finger and turned my attention back to the door. I was surprised to find that, besides the bellboy, the concierge, and the women behind the check-in-desk, the lobby was still empty. I glanced at my phone to check the time. 1:07. Just a few minutes to go. I checked my e-mail. Out of five new messages, three were spam, one was from my mom, and the other was from Alex. I opened my mother's first.

Just checking in with you. Wondering how things are going. Keep your chin up and remember you are on the right path. Call me when you get a chance.

I touched the trashcan to delete the email, made a mental note to call her later, then clicked on the message from Alex.

I miss you like crazy, Sunshine.

I smiled and could feel my cheeks warming, amazed that a simple email from Alex could release butterflies in my stomach. I hit reply and typed: *I miss you too, Mr. Limbeaux.* I had just hit send when I felt a tap on my shoulder. It was Raoul, the bellboy.

"I'm sorry to bother you again, but there's a taxi driver outside requesting a Miss Rae Colbert."

I glanced at the time on my phone. 1:15. Not a minute early. Not a minute late.

"I'm Rae Colbert." My voice quivered despite my attempt to keep it steady and strong.

I felt my heart accelerate when Raoul gestured with a curl of his finger to the cabbie waiting in front of the hotel. Was this really happening? I began to think of all the bad things that could happen if I hopped into the cab. Where was he planning to take me? What if something happens? Alex isn't here to protect me. Am I really strong enough to protect myself?

"Um, Miss Colbert, shall I hold the cab for you?" Raoul's voice interrupted my negative thoughts, and I realized I had been staring at the boy, wide-eyed, for over a minute. It's meant to be, I thought. I closed my eyes and reminded myself of all the ways A-Omega had led me thus far. I was standing at a crossroad. I could go or I could stay. I knew I was supposed to get into the taxi, but I was scared. Jumping into the cab would take a leap of faith. So was my faith stronger than my fear?

"Miss Colbert?"

Lucky Numbers 7, 20, 20, 09, 13: 15. It was no coincidence. A-Omega had sent me to Houston, and I trusted them. I would go. I rose from the comfortable chair to discover my legs were shaking, and followed the bellboy through the hotel entrance. Raoul walked toward the cab and opened the back door. I stood on the sidewalk filled with indecision. *What if this is the wrong choice*, I wondered. *Houston is the fourth largest city in the U.S., both in size and population,* I reminded myself. What if I get hurt? What if I die? What if this is the right way and Carl is waiting for me at my destination? What if he kills me? Raoul was motioning for me to get in. It felt right, but I was still unsure. Slowly, I stepped off the curb. As I walked toward the cab, I caught a glimpse of the license plate. Jer2911. I slid into the yellow cab and Raoul shut the door behind me. I took notice of the man behind the wheel. He wore a baseball cap with the bill twisted sideways. His skin was dark and smooth. The planes of his cheeks were flat. His lips were full and well defined. When his hand moved to the steering wheel, I took notice of his neat cuticles and manicured nails. Then my gaze fell to the plaque beside the radio. His name was Steven Bellamy - number 6 on my list of names. My eyes met his horn-rimmed sunglasses in the rearview mirror. He flashed a smile but didn't say a word.

I was fairly competent at reading body language, and I knew that many times I could learn the most about a person when they were silent. This guy was okay. I was okay. Relaxing into the seat, I closed my eyes and felt the car pull away from the curb. I was not at all surprised when he didn't ask where I was going. I figured he knew. That's how A-Omega worked. I was always the last to know. It's trust. It's faith. I felt the car slow to a stop and moments later rebuild speed as we moved through the city. Steven took a sharp right, and I opened my eyes as he pulled onto one of the main thoroughfares. Gone were the museums and mansions surrounding my hotel and in their place, a long string of small, poor houses. Bars on the windows, sofas on the porches. I glanced at the clock on the radio. It was 1:45. In less than thirty minutes, the scenery had drastically changed. His eyes moved from the road to the rearview mirror in order to catch my expression. I forced a smile despite my pounding heart. My mind drifted to his license plate: Jer2911. I wondered what it meant. I pulled my phone out of my bag and Googled it. 218,000 results bounced back and as far as I could tell, the content was the same. It was a verse from the Bible: Jeremiah 29:11.

"For I know the plans I have for you," declares the LORD, "plans to prosper you and not to harm you, plans to give you hope and a future."

I slipped my phone into my pocket then shut my eyes and trusted. Everything was going to be okay. I listened to the music on the radio and tried to relax, but when the taxi came to a stop moments later, I opened my eyes and gasped. "Oh, God, no!" I said just above a whisper when Steven shifted into park.

"This is the end of the line for me." His voice was void of emotion, and I felt the blood drain from my face. My voice caught in my throat.

"You're going to wait, right?" I asked, noticing how he had not switched off the meter.

"Take your time."

I slid out of the car and stood on trembling legs. I shut the taxi door and began to panic. I had no idea where I was going. Luckily, Steven rolled down the window and pointed through the alleyway at the rundown apartment complex in the distance. "Apartment 414."

"You're sure it's apartment 414?" I asked. "How do you know?"

Steven picked up a newspaper from the passenger seat. "The reservation was made online," he said without looking at me. "I'm just doing what I'm told."

When I didn't move, Steven turned to me and lowered his voice. "Lady, I'm going to give you a helpful piece of advice. If I were you, I would let those boots take me where I was goin' and I would let them take me there fast."

"You said apartment 414, right?" I asked, pulling out my phone so I could enter the apartment number into my notes. I was so nervous, I knew I would forget.

"Nice phone," he remarked without looking up from the article. "I'd tuck that thing away before I took another step. Just sayin'. And that pin on your shirt. I might put that away too." Bellamy eyed my purse and shook his head but didn't say a word.

I caught his drift and obliged, slipping the phone into my pocket, but I left the pin in place, over my heart, right where it was supposed to be. I slung my bag over my shoulder and on feeble legs, made my way toward the dark, narrow alley, trying to remind myself of what it meant to work for A-Omega. Remembering stories my parents told me of close calls. Like the time my dad rescued a woman out of an abandoned building in Dewallen, a red-light district in Amsterdam. A bomb went off just moments after he helped her escape. He hadn't been hurt, not seriously, anyway. And the night of September 13th. Out of everyone involved, my parents had been the only ones who survived. Mom, however, had been injured in the accident and the scar on her arm was proof. My heart rate climbed higher as I approached the alley, a long narrow hall of broken brick and darkness. When I stepped onto the pathway between the two buildings, I recalled what Pastor Joe said about taking the right path. He said that it might get dark at times, but that there would always be a lamp to light my way. To my left, I caught a glimpse of a figure pacing back and forth. I looked to my right: A woman with wrinkled skin sat hunched over against the brick wall. Small packages passed between filthy palms. With my eyes still focused on the complex just fifty yards ahead, I stood up straight and quickened my pace. I was fast, and I knew I could run if I needed to. As I continued to forge ahead, the pacing figure to my left moved closer. He was no longer a shadow, he was a man. Short and muscular. Black hair, slicked back. A goatee. He wasn't wearing a shirt and I could see a gun tucked into the waistband of his pants. All at once, I realized there were things that moved faster than my feet. Bullets. I continued to focus on the building in front of me, and I prayed as I walked. He inched closer. He was walking beside me, looking me up and down. I thought about all I had learned in my self-defense class. First and foremost, be aware of your surroundings and always avoid dark alleyways. Great. I had already failed. Step 2: form a plan. What will I do if he tries to attack me? I could hightail it to the apartment complex, or I could run back to the cab. I wasn't excited about either option. Step 3: be prepared to resist. How could I resist? I didn't have any weapons. What did I have that I could use against him? My self-defense training? My steel-toed boots? I considered what Lavine said about weapons. The weapons we fight with are not the weapons of the world. Prayer. Yes. As I began to pray, the goateed man gripped his gun and began to speak in a language I didn't understand. With smoothness in his step, he quickened his pace and before I knew it, he was standing in front of me. Unable to advance, I stopped in my tracks. Fear could have taken over; instead, confidence came to me all at once. I held my ground. For the first time in my life, I wasn't taking the *flight* option. I was on a mission and I was prepared to fight. I looked him square in the face. He bit his lip. He had a wide face and small, greedy eyes. He stood in front of me, smoothing his goatee. He smiled: a mouth full of narrow, whittled down teeth from poor hygiene. He resembled a shark and all at once, I remembered what Dad said about *The Old Man and the Sea.* "The sharks won't attack unless you're onto something good." Was I onto something good? If so, what was I going to find in apartment 414? My phone vibrated in my pocket. I wanted to slip my hand inside and pull it out, but I knew that in a situation like this, it was best not to make any sudden movements. But what if this was important? Was the text was from A-Omega? Slowly, I moved my right hand into the pocket of my jeans. My fingers had just made contact with my phone when a tiny voice came from behind me.

"Hey, you. Lady in yellow."

With my right hand in the pocket of my jeans, I stood frozen, my eyes not moving off the man with the gun. I noticed he was no longer looking me up and down; instead, he was looking over my shoulder. He seemed shaken. Slowly, he began to back away. I pulled my phone out and read the text.

So do not fear, for I am with *you*; do not be dismayed, for I am *your* God.

I returned the phone to my pocket. My brooch began to quiver. I looked over my shoulder and saw a little girl approaching me. She was holding her hand out in front of her. Was she talking to me? I glanced at my attire. I was wearing all black. I returned my attention to the goateed man. Hand on his gun, he continued to back away. I felt a warm hand on mine. I jumped. The little girl was standing beside me, her small hand in mine. Her long, dark hair braided into seven neat rows. She was wearing a pair of shorts and a tank top. "Just a second ago," I said. "Were you talking to me?" My voice quivered.

"Yes."

"But I'm wearing black, not yellow."

"I know, but you *are* yellow. You're all yellow like sunshine." She smiled. Her two front teeth were missing, but the permanent teeth were starting to show. "Just walk with me, lady, and you'll be okay."

I nodded and swallowed the lump in my throat. I looked up from the little girl, expecting to see the goateed man, but he was gone. All I could see was my destination.

"What's your name?" I asked the little girl?"

"Shae." She smiled. "Shae Simmons."

A tear fell down my cheek as I recalled something Baxtor Lavine said in passing several weeks ago. "You call Him A-Omega. I call him God." An hour ago, I would have never considered this part of town a safe haven, but as I held hands with Shae Simmons (number nine on my list of names), as I thought about the text A-Omega sent just moments ago, I realized now, more than ever before, that there was an eye in the sky and He was looking out for me. So I tried to see the world around me in a different light. Holding the little girl's hand, I felt safe. And as I began to feel safe in the situation and as I began to trust the one who was in control, I began to see things I hadn't seen before. I began to see all of the good amongst the rubble. I focused on the clothes that hung from lines outside the windows and the women who were drawing them in. I focused on the flowers in the planter that hung below a broken window. A concrete wall with graffiti: the painting of a woman singing. Beside her was the word "HOPE." Shae stopped just outside the entrance to the apartment building.

"I'm glad you came." She smiled. "I've gotta go now, okay." She looked over her shoulder and then back at me.

"Okay. It was nice to meet you, Shae." I placed my hand on the heavy metal door and noticed the bullet holes that pocked the dull surface. I took in a deep breath and pushed the door open. 414. I hesitated before stepping over the threshold. I looked up at the building that stood before me. Sixty feet tall and twice as wide. Even though I knew God was looking out for me, I was still a little scared.

Once inside, I stood at the bottom of the stairs looking up. The flickering fluorescents drew attention to the building's neglected interior, illuminating the graffitied walls and the broken glass on the floors. I hurried up the stairs, not stopping until I reached the fourth floor. I took note of the number on the door at the top of the stairwell: 424. To the left, the numbers got larger. I needed 414, so I turned right and began to walk down the dimly lit hall. 422... 420... 418... 416... . The door swung open. A wide-faced woman with a child at her side emerged from apartment 416. The woman regarded me suspiciously. With my feet rooted to the floor, I managed to let a few words escape me.

"I'm looking for 414."

The wide-face woman looked at me through untrusting eyes, then pointed to the next apartment. I turned my attention to the boy, noticing *his* eyes. Big and brown. Full of emotion. Full of childlike wonder.

"Boots, mama. Boots," the toddler said to his mother as he pointed to my feet. She scooped him up and placed him on her hip, shook her head, and walked toward the stairs.

I stood outside apartment 414 for a moment before gathering the courage to knock. My first knock was soft. I waited. I began to chew on my nails. What was inside apartment 414? Was it good? Was it bad? Was Carl here? If I needed to, could I still escape? Four flights of stairs. Half a block back to the car. How long should I wait outside this door? I raised my hand to knock again but before my knuckles met the metal surface, I heard someone turn the lock. The door opened a crack. A chain stretched between the door and frame. I saw an eye peeking at me through the narrow opening.

"Who sent you here?" She slurred when she spoke.

"A-Omega." The words came out of my mouth without intention. The words were not my own.

The door closed for a second and I heard the chain rattling, then it opened again, but just wide enough for me to step in.

CHAPTER TWENTY-SEVEN

*T*here was a bed in the middle of the living room, and I sat on a folding chair across from the fragile woman who was sitting in a mess of tangled sheets. Resting her elbows on her knees, she made a steeple with her fingers. Her eyes fell shut for a moment, then snapped back open, untrusting. A dingy light pushed through a foil-covered window revealing the scars that ran up and down her arms. Mascara stained the skin beneath her eyes. Silence usually prompted my mouth to run, but not today. I was still unsure of why I was here. I began to wonder if the cabbie would be waiting for me. I began to wonder how long this would take. The woman spoke first.

"Why?"

Her head was in her hands and her voice was muffled; however, I was amazed that by using a single word she could ask so many questions.

I glanced around the room, unsure of what to say. Years of nicotine stained the peeling wallpaper. A roach scurried across the top of my boot and I shook it off. A small lamp pressed a yellow circle on the dingy sheets. A pill bottle was tipped over on a small table near the mattress and a half-empty glass of water was beside it. I wondered where to start. Should I start with A-Omega or should I get right to the point? I was here to put an end to Carl Pierce.

"I should be asking you the same question," I told her. "Why?"

The woman looked up at me with the first hint of emotion that I had seen thus far.

Her mouth fell open and her eyes held a spark of recognition, but then the spark extinguished and with her palms open, she let her head fall into her hands.

"I'm afraid I can't help you," she whispered.

She had shut down. I had said the wrong thing. Think of something. Think of something. Suddenly, I was struck with an idea. Quinn Collin's story came to my mind. When he told me his story, he had shared more than a miracle. He instilled in me the importance of sharing with others. He told me he had received goodness from God and that it would be unfair to keep all that goodness to himself. I looked at the woman sitting on the bed, hugging her knees. She looked like she could use some goodness. I wondered what I could share with her. I pulled out my phone, hoping A-Omega had sent me a text, hoping they had given some clue as to what I was supposed to say. Nothing. I slipped the phone back into my pocket and suddenly, I knew exactly what I needed to do.

"Do you mind if I tell you a story?" I began.

The woman looked up. Dirty blond hair fell into her eyes. "What time is it?" she asked.

I shifted my weight and pulled my phone back out of the pocket.

"2:10."

"You have thirty minutes."

"Okay... it won't take fifteen."

The woman hugged her legs tight and rested her head on her knees.

"Ten years ago, I was a different person." I wasn't exactly sure why I started my story out this way. I wasn't here to talk about myself. I was here to get to the bottom of it all, but the words wouldn't stop. I had no control over what I was saying. "Different than I am today. I felt different from everyone else. I wore different clothes. Lived in different places. I didn't fit in. Something was missing. I was afraid of the world. I was afraid of pain. I felt like I was the one to blame for my sister's death. I just knew she died because of me. I spent ten years inside a shell that I had made all by myself. I shut out my parents. I shut out the world. I suffered in silence. And then two years ago, things started to change."

My brooch began to warm as I told the fragile woman about Alex and where he had come from. I told her about the car crash. I told her that Alex had come back to earth to keep me safe, to protect me.

"An angel," she muttered and then looked me square in the eye.

"Not an angel; a boy who was given a second shot at life. The kind of boy who could help a girl like me face the world."

She began to twirl a silver bracelet around her tiny wrist. Her eyes grew wide with disbelief and then they filled with tears.

"Noooo. *You* are the angel." Her words were running together. She shivered and hugged her body.

"I'm sorry. I didn't mean to…"

"Stop." Her body began to sway and she braced herself with her arm. She looked sleepy. "Yoooou told meeeee your story." She paused and closed her eyes. "Now let me tell you mmmmmine." Her eyes snapped open, alarmed, and then they fell shut again. "Whatime isit?" She slurred.

"2:25."

"My story is short but not very sweeeeet," she spoke slowly, trying her best to pronounce each word clearly, so that I could receive her message. "I atea whole bottleooooofpills… justa minutefore youknocked." She let her head fall back into her hands. She was taking her time with each syllable. There was something she needed me to understand. "You know how God sent Alex into your life?" Her head snapped up and her eyes popped open. "Well, I think God just sent you into mine." She fell back onto the bed and curled up into a ball.

I covered her with a thin blanket and pushed the hair away from her eyes. "I could have never found you on my own," I whispered.

"I juswanna go to sleepa little while," she whispered back. "AnI juswanna make it go away."

The ambulance arrived twenty minutes after I called. I could hear sirens coming from outside the window. The woman was lying on the bed, lost in a sleepy oblivion. Every so often, her body shook violently and she let out a whimper, a cry that came from deep within her soul. I peeled the foil away from the window and watched the medics approach. I looked at the time. *Hurry up. Hurry up.* The alleyway that had been abundant with illicit exchange on my way into the building was now deserted, leaving a clear path for the medical personnel to maneuver the gurney across the cracked walkway. They disappeared into the building and moments later, there was a knock at the door.

Coming out of the darkness, it took a moment for my eyes to adjust. The sun shone on the woman's face drawing attention to certain qualities the dreary room had softened. Behind her dull eyes and bad skin was a story that darkness had tried to keep hidden for years, but I believed the sun was stronger. As we moved toward the ambulance, a policeman approached me and began asking questions and writing down my answers in a black notebook that fit in the palm of his hand. He wanted to know the woman's name and how I knew her. What I was doing in the neighborhood… things like that. Once again, I was at a loss for words. He asked me where I lived, and I told him. He asked me where I was staying. I said the ZaZa. He looked me up and down and frowned. Then he asked me one last time what I was doing in apartment 414. There was only one thing I could say, "Someone told me she needed help."

The broken woman was on a stretcher in the back of an ambulance. I glanced down the deserted alleyway. The taxi was gone and so was Steven Bellamy.

"Would it be too much trouble for me to ride with her to the hospital?" I asked the medic after noticing my cabbie was MIA.

"Typically we only allow family, but… it doesn't look like she has anyone else. Maybe you can answer a few questions on the way. Her life may depend on it."

Who was this woman and why had I been sent to Houston to save her life?

"I'll do my best," I told him.

"Let's start with the basics," he said as he helped me into the back of the ambulance. "Do you know her name? The apartment was registered to a Dimitri Baskov, and she doesn't look like a Dimitri to me."

I let my eyes fall on the woman. There was an IV in her arm. A bag of saline was hung and an oxygen mask covered her face. I was hoping that a name might pop into my head, but nothing came. I wanted to help her, but how?

"I don't know her name."

"Any idea what she's on?"

"Oh my gosh. I can't believe I forgot." I reached into my bag and handed the EMT the empty pill bottle. "I found this beside her bed. She told me she took a whole bottle of pills just before I arrived. That was about thirty-five minutes ago."

He thanked me and studied the bottle. "Good. Good. This is a start."

When the sirens began to wail and the ambulance began to roll, I shut my eyes and started to replay all that had happened. I had only been awake for a few hours, but I was exhausted... mentally, emotionally, and physically. I could hardly remember what I had said, yet my story brought her hope and just being there saved her life. That was all. My eyes popped open when I heard the driver shout over the sirens, "Where are we taking her?"

"University. She ain't got no insurance."

"I'm going to let them know we're on our way. Do we have a name, yet?"

"The bottle of pills is prescribed to a Terry Dunbarr." My heart stopped beating in my chest for a moment. "But you know how it works. False name. Borrowed drugs. Bottle says Lortab, but we're not one hundred percent that's what she's on. The chance that this is Terry Dunbarr is one in a million."

"Not one in million," I whispered. "Terry Dunbarr is number four of ten."

My intention was to call a cab once I arrived at the hospital, but I had a sneaking suspicion that my work here wasn't quite finished. However, because Terry was still incoherent, I was in for a long wait. I took a seat near triage, anxious for an update on Terry's condition. My eyes roved the lobby. In the past year and a half, I had been to the ER three times - twice in Bartlesville and once in Minnesota - and this was my fourth. I recalled how it felt waiting on Flynt, uncertain if he was going to make it. I felt the same sort of desperation as I waited for news on Terry's condition. I picked up a two-year-old copy of People magazine and forced myself to look at the pictures. Seconds later, my eyes drifted to the vending machines. A tall man was buying a cup of coffee and I watched as the hot liquid shot into a plastic cup. I was growing more and more impatient. I approached the counter and introduced myself to the nurses. I reminded both the receptionist and triage nurse why I was here and who I had come with. They promised to keep me posted and assured me that I would be the first to know should her condition change.

Besides the tall man sipping on his coffee, the waiting room was empty and time left me with nothing to do but think. The first thing that came to mind was the show I had seen on TV the night before. Two people won the same game, but the prize ruined one person's life and saved the other's. I thought about Tina the lottery winner. She had a journal similar to mine. She wrote down every blessing in her book. My mind drifted to the journal in my bag, the journal A-Omega had given me. I slipped my hand into my purse and pulled it out. The word "Faith" was stamped into the leather. I knew what I needed to do. Starting with Alex's arrival on earth, I was going to write down all of my supernatural experiences, I was going to make detailed journal entries on all of the events in my life where God had intervened. Faith. Was it faith that allowed me to get into the cab? Was it faith that gave me the courage to walk through the alleyway and climb to the fourth floor of a rundown apartment building in a bad part of town? Slipping my hand into my bag for a second time, I felt around for my purple gel pen. I considered the events of the day and how they unfolded and as I began to write, tears began to well up in my eyes.

I thought about the obscure details of how I arrived at Terry's door and how I had shared a simple story that might have saved her life. I hadn't done much, but I was there when she needed me and that must have been enough. I thought about the show I watched the night before. I thought about what Tina, the lottery winner, told Barry, the host of the show: "Sometimes we hear God's voice the loudest while we're in the midst of the most pain. God wants to comfort us while we're in pain, and He wants to bless us. Not so we can keep God's goodness to ourselves, but so we can share with others the goodness that God has shown us." It wasn't the first time I had heard those words of wisdom. I thought about how Manila Crow and Quinn Collins had also shared the same message. Miracles. God's goodness. I couldn't believe that I had found Terry Dunbarr. That was a miracle. Nineteen years ago, Eva helped Terry escape from Carl's basement. She got her life back, but she didn't want to live.

"Rae Colbert." A mousy voice interrupted my thoughts. I looked up at the nurse standing in the doorway. "I have an update."

I snapped my journal shut and returned it to my bag. I approached the tiny woman. She had paired hot pink scrubs with navy blue clogs. A royal blue stethoscope hung around her neck. Her tag read Katelyn, RN.

"I know you were hoping to see Terry." Katelyn got right to the point. "Unfortunately, because it's a police matter now, no one's allowed back."

"What's going on?"

"I'm afraid I can make no comment."

"How is she?"

"Listen. My hands are tied. There's very little I can say. On the other hand, I recognize that you saved this girl's life." Katelyn lowered her voice to a whisper. "This is what I can tell you. She got to the ER in enough time. She's going to make it. That's the good news. The bad news is she needs help."

"But why are the police involved?"

Katelyn looked over her shoulder. Convinced that no one was within earshot, she proceeded. "Not a word to anyone, okay."

I nodded, which seemed to be all the assurance she needed.

"I see girls like Terry all time. Drug abusers. Prostitutes. No one cares. No one takes the time to look at the underlying issue. No one bothers to ask how they got here." Katelyn looked over her shoulder again before continuing. "Sadly, it wasn't Terry or Terry's condition that led to the police getting involved." I had to lean in to hear what she was saying. "It had to do with where she was when she overdosed. I can't say anymore, but I'm sure you can connect the dots." Katelyn sighed, and when the volume of her voice rose, I realized this conversation was over.

"Nursing is thankless work. I save peoples lives, but sometimes, it's more than the body that needs saving… sometimes it's the soul. I am going to do my best to get Terry the help she needs." Katelyn paused and stared at me with wonder in her expression and appreciation in her eyes. "I don't know how you came to be at Terry's door in her time of need."

I opened my mouth to explain, but the words were stuck in my throat. Katelyn touched the silver cross that hung around her neck and when she did, it was like she was trying to tell me something. Cross. Katelyn. Katelyn Cross: number three on my list of names.

"There are just some things in life that cannot be explained. Let's just agree that this is one of them." Katelyn reached into her pocket and handed me a card. I expected to find her nursing credentials and the name and number for the hospital printed across the front; instead, I found the word R.E.S.C.U.E. in bold, red print at the top of the card and her name and number below in a smaller font size. "That's my cell." Katelyn nodded her head and turned to leave. No other words were needed.

"Katelyn." When I spoke, I was surprised by how desperate I sounded. "Can you give Terry something for me?"

The small nurse stood still, cocked her head to the side, and waited for me to continue. I slipped my hand inside my bag and produced a pen and my journal. Quickly, I scrawled out my name, number, and address. I tore the piece of paper from the journal and handed it to Katelyn. "I just want her to know where she can reach me… if she wants to."

"I'll make sure she gets this. Thank you. For everything." Katelyn stepped through the double doors and I watched them close behind her.

The ride back to the hotel was not a supernatural experience. I simply called for a cab and the cab arrived. I told him where I wanted to go and he took me there, which was a relief. I wasn't trying to be ungrateful. A supernaturally arranged cab ride was exciting, but it was nice to know where I was going. I needed time to process all that had happened before I took on another mission. I closed my eyes and relaxed into the seat, not opening them until the cab pulled to a stop in front of the ZaZa. I paid him with my own money and slipped out of the door. Stepping into the lobby, I felt like I was moving out of one world and into another.

INTERCESSION

CHAPTER TWENTY-EIGHT

When the plane touched down in Tulsa, I felt a rush of excitement come over me. Three days ago, when I left on my mission, Alex and I were not on the best of terms. Still, I started to miss him before my plane even made it to Houston. While being away had been hard, my three days in Texas had been amazing, action packed, scary, enlightening, and life changing. I was finally getting to know God. I was finally beginning to feel purpose, but I was torn. Alex told me that he was here to protect me. He told me that keeping me safe was *his* purpose. And the more protection I received from A-Omega, the less useful Alex felt.

The Boeing 737 put its brakes on hard and threw me forward in my seat. "I'm home," I said looking out the oval-shaped window of the plane. I could feel the hot, humid air coming through the overhead vents. "I'm home."

Once off the plane, I did my best to keep from running through the terminal. There was a mob of people waiting behind the security check for passengers to arrive, and I thought I might have a little trouble finding Alex among the crowd. It took me a moment to recognize him. I was looking for shaggy brown hair, but Alex had gotten a haircut. He smiled, and I pushed through the crowd, moving toward him. I looked him up and down, appreciating every inch of the man I loved. His eyes. His lips.

His cologne. Just him. Surrounded by strangers, I fell into his arms. In the middle of a crowded airport, he held me tight.

"I've missed you so much," he whispered.

I let my head rest on his shoulder. "I've missed you, too." With my right arm still wrapped around his neck, I took my left hand and began to run it through his hair. It was razor cut up the back, but there was still a little length in the front.

"Promise not to leave me again."

"I'll do my best."

I didn't recognize Alex's car. In just three days, he had repaired the soft top and given the Speedster a fresh coat of paint. It looked brand new. It looked expensive. He had even brought Stella along for the ride; she was resting comfortably in her case in the backseat, and I had to push it aside to make room for my duffle. I slipped into the car and when Alex turned over the ignition, I was startled by the sound. Instead of a sputtering engine, a smooth, purring noise came from under the hood. Alex had been busy while I was gone. He shifted into drive and pulled out of the parking garage. He handed the cashier his ticket, paid for his parking, and took the exit out of the airport, but instead of taking 11 West toward Bartlesville, he took 11 East.

"We're not going home?"

"No. Not yet."

"Where are we going, then?" I glanced over my shoulder at the tiny back seat and saw Stella. "Where are we going, Alex?"

"Let's just say you're not the only one who's been busy."

"What are you talking about and why are you in such a hurry?" Alex normally liked to get where he was going fast, but tonight his foot was especially heavy.

"I have a little something up my sleeve."

"I love and hate it when you say that. Am I going to like it?"

"I'm not sure," Alex confessed. "But I hope so."

"You're not going to tell me, are you?"

"Nope."

"You are *so* unfair."

"Just sit back and enjoy the ride. We're getting close," he said as he merged onto 75 South.

Fifteen minutes later, Alex exited off the highway onto Peoria. I called my parents and told them I would be a little late, but Alex had already spoken with them. They said to take my time. When I hung up, I took in my surroundings. Boutique restaurants. High-end stores. I saw a sign in the distance that read "Brook." The sign was black with white letters and neon green accents. Before we made it to the light on 36th street, Alex took a sharp left into the parking lot of a small venue. I tried not to look disappointed. I was hungry and the establishment did not look like a restaurant. Besides, the music was loud - I could hear it before we even got out of the car - and I had a headache. I had hoped that Alex and I could have a quiet evening alone. I had so many things to tell him. So much had happened in the past couple of days, and I had planned to start by telling him the fortune cookie story.

"You ready for this?"

"Ready for what?"

Alex opened his door, slid out, and grabbed Stella from the backseat. I opened the passenger door and hurried around the side of the car to meet him.

"Alex! You didn't!"

"I did."

"You got a gig?"

"I wouldn't go so far to say that. It's amateur night and I have a new song I want to try out. It's not a gig. It's practice."

"You're being modest." I grabbed the guitar case out of his hands, set Stella on the ground, and jumped into his arms. "From a hockey star to a rock star. I'm so, so proud of you." I took a breath between kisses and leaned back to look him in the eyes. "So, do you have a name?"

"NLimBo." Alex looked at me with knowing eyes.

"Why am I not surprised?"

Alex laughed. "You ready?" he asked.

"Lead the way." I followed Alex up the sidewalk to the front door of the venue. "Are you nervous?"

"No. Not really." Alex reached for the door to open it.

"I would be if I we-" I stopped mid-sentence, pushed the door shut, and pointed to a flyer taped to the glass: one of my sketches of Alex. NLimBo was printed across the top. At the bottom of the poster was today's date. "You used my artwork." I had done at least a dozen sketches of Alex at the park. If I had known that he was going to use them for his first concert flyer, I would have put in a little more effort. "That wasn't even my best sketch."

"It was the one I liked the most."

There were other flyers posted on the side of the building, but the NLimBo flyer was the largest and most colorful. It stood out from the rest.

"It does look good."

Alex opened the door and I walked inside. I stopped short. I was still so hung up on the fact that Alex had gotten his first gig that I hadn't taken time to consider what the inside of the building would like or that there might be other people there.

Still standing by the front door, I took in everything at once. It was a full house. I looked at the crowd. Trendy. Hipsters. I looked at what I was wearing. Knowing that I was going to be on a plane, I had dressed for comfort - a pair of running shorts and a tee shirt - not a concert. I wanted to hide in a hole. "Alex, give me the keys to your car."

"Why?"

"I'm changing."

"Why? You look great."

"You could have at least warned me that I was getting ready to go to your first gig. I would have dressed for the occasion. I look like a cheerleader, Alex, not a rock star's girlfriend."

"You look fine!" Alex shouted over the music.

"Just give me the keys," I told him. "I won't take long. Besides, you still have to set up. I won't miss a thing. I promise."

"Fine." Alex reached into his pocket and produced the keys to the Porsche. He tossed them to me and smiled. "Don't take too long. I don't want you to miss *our* first song."

"Our?" I said on the way out the door. Alex just smiled.

I grabbed my duffle out of the backseat and dug through it. I grabbed a pair of tapered jeans, my favorite tee shirt, and my boots, then stuffed my makeup essentials into my purse: black mascara, blush, powder, and light pink lip-gloss. Too full to zip, I clutched my bag so the contents wouldn't spill out and hurried into the bathroom to change. By the looks of it, the bathroom hadn't been cleaned in a while, and I cringed when I had to take off my boots to slip on my jeans, but if this is what it took to look good for Alex's first show, then changing inside a small dirty bathroom was totally worth it. I stood in front of the small mirror that hung on the wall, pulled out my ponytail, and shook my head to fluff my hair. Perfect. I touched up my makeup and ten minutes later, I sat down at the round table near the stage while Alex was still setting up. He plugged in his guitar and strummed it a few times. He did a quick mike check before introducing himself to the crowd.

"Hey. I'm NLimBo." The mike screeched. Feedback. Alex made some adjustments then started again. "Like I said, I'm NLimBo and I came here tonight to try out a new song."

The crowd cheered and I noticed that most of the praise was coming from the female population. *Great*, I thought. Why was I not surprised? Alex wasn't lying when he said he wasn't nervous. He loved the attention. He was eating it up. I was glad it was him up there and not me.

"But I'm afraid I can't take credit for all of the lyrics and I think I'm going to need a little help on this one." Alex looked at me. A mischievous smile spread across his face. "I would like you all to meet my girlfriend, Rae. She wrote half the song."

The crowd continued to cheer and clap. It was like they understood exactly what he was talking about. I, however, was not so quick to catch on and still seated in my chair, I began to look around the room, dumbfounded.

"Come on up, Rae," Alex continued.

All of a sudden, realization hit me like a ton of bricks. The email. My email response to Alex had rhymed. I thought I was being witty, now I was kicking myself for being creative. I felt like I was going to throw up. I shook my head in silent opposition. I looked at Alex with pleading eyes, begging him to stop. This was cruel. I hated being the center of attention. I hated when people stared at me. I hated singing because I thought I had a horrible voice. But I was familiar with Alex's expression; he wasn't going to stop until I joined him. The crowd continued to cheer and I stood slowly. Alex stretched out his hand to help me on stage. As I turned to face the crowd, I realized that I couldn't breath. My chest was tight. I really was going to throw up. I just knew it. Alex handed me an extra mike. I didn't have a choice but to accept it. I took in a shallow breath and as I exhaled, my entire body quivered. I felt lightheaded.

"Hi, everyone. I'm Rae." My voice shook. "And right now I'm mad at my boyfriend for dragging me up here." I gave Alex a stern look.

The audience responded to my voice, but their approval did little to put me at ease. Alex moved a bar stool up to the front of the stage and motioned for me to sit down. He grabbed another one for himself.

"The other night I was missing, Rae. She went on a top-secret mission and left me behind. So I was feeling lonely and I decided to send her an email to tell how I felt."

The crowd ooohed and ahhed, which only encouraged him. Alex loved the attention.

"I didn't expect her response to be the second stanza of a beautiful song."

When I realized that I couldn't remember what I wrote, I put my hand over the mike so that I could talk to Alex in private. "Alex. I don't remember the words," I whispered.

Alex placed his hand over the microphone. "Don't worry. I already thought of that." Alex produced a folded piece of paper from the pocket of his jeans and handed it to me. I stared at it a moment before unfolding it and silently reading the lyrics. Besides my horrible voice, I could come up with no reasonable excuse as to why I could not perform.

Alex began to strum his guitar. I swallowed hard. I had to get through this. When I heard Alex's voice, I fixed my eyes on him. If I didn't have to look at the crowd, I thought I might be able to pull this off.

> Your presence isn't what it used to be
> You've put me at a distance.
> When I try to touch you
> All I get is your resistance

With my eyes trained on Alex, I waited for my cue. Just a little off key, I began. I closed my eyes and tried not to think about anything other than the lyrics and how I felt when I wrote them. I channeled my energy into the song. Not looking at the paper, I began to sing.

> Really? You think I don't like your touch?
> To feel your fingers on my skin?
> I come to you with everything
> But you won't let me in
> I always wanted *you* more…
> Even from the start
> Now you prefer the strings of your guitar
> To the strings of my heart

With my eyes still closed, I listened to Alex's voice pick up where mine left off.

> Yeah, but I'm not just talking about your body
> I was referring to your mind
> Even when you're right beside me
> You're kind of hard to find

Now more relaxed, I knew it was my turn by listening to the rhythm instead of looking for his cue.

You don't know my dilemma
My past can't be undone

Alex ended the song with a sultry drawn out voice that made the crowd feel sorry for him.

But somehow I've been left with nothing
And you've been given more than one.

Alex turned off the highway, drove a quarter mile up the mile long road leading to my house, and stopped. He put the car into park, shut off the engine, and put the convertible top down.

"You said you wanted a quiet place to talk."

"Yeah, I did, didn't I? But right now my trip to Houston is the last thing on my mind."

"You haven't said a word since we left Tulsa. What are you thinking about?"

"Things."

"Good things, I hope."

I unbuckled my seatbelt and leaned across the console for a kiss. "I was thinking about your new hair cut," I said as I ran my fingers up the back of his neck where his hair was clipped short - soft and silky to the touch. "I love it. And I was thinking about your Porsche."

"You were?"

"Yes. The Porsche is fast, but I still like the Wagoneer better. It was a little roomier."

"You're right. I should see if Pastor Joe would give it back." Alex brushed his hand across my cheek. "I missed you."

"You did?" I teased. 'You've been spending so much time with Stella, I didn't know if you would have had time to think about missing me."

"Stella *has* been pretty demanding." Alex's lips brushed across the base of my neck, then moved up slowly.

"I hope I don't have anything to worry about," I chided.

"Not a thing. I promise."

"Good."

"And your trip went well? Are you going to tell me all about it?"

"I told you, I don't want to talk about my trip right now. I want to talk about how you embarrassed me tonight and also, how it's one of the most romantic things you've ever done."

"Sorry about that. If I would have told you beforehand, you would have refused."

"You're right. I would have."

"So, are you more attracted to Alex Loving, or Ian Limbeaux?"

"That's tough. I don't know. Alex Loving the angel/ star hockey player or Ian Limbeaux the rock star. I like you both. I love you both."

"Really?"

"Is that bad?"

"No."

"It's just that Alex is so perfect. I'm in awe of Alex. Ian's kind of dark and moody."

"Is he really?"

"Yes, and sometimes I think that maybe Ian and I don't want the same things. I just feel like Ian's backing away a little."

"So I'm moody *and* distant. This just keeps getting better." Alex rolled his eyes.

"It's just that Ian has so many emotions. I used to be the one with all the problems and you used to be the one who cheered me up, but I like it better this way. You're nearly human. You're more like me... not so perfect after all."

"I've always wanted what you want, Rae." Alex's fingers moved down my neck toward my shoulder. "And I still do."

"While we're on the subject of you becoming human, how's the bird?" I asked, referring to the eagle on his chest.

"Barely there," he returned.

"So it's faded even more?"

"Do you want to see it?" Without waiting for me to respond, Alex tugged at the hem of his shirt and lifted it just enough to reveal the faded eagle spread across his chest.

I sat up in shock, my body immediately responding to what I was seeing. It had been months since I had last seen the eagle. Alex had mentioned that the marking was nearly gone, but hearing about it was different than seeing it for myself. I leaned back to examine the smooth skin of his chest.

"Well?"

"I guess I should be happy."

"Are you?" he asked, letting the hem of his shirt fall back to his waist.

"Yes. I'm happy. Now that I know what it means, I'm happy." I ran my finger across his tee shirt. "It's amazing, you know. There's not even a trace of where it used to be. Not even a hint."

"Amazing... yes," he said, stroking my hair. "Enough about the Eagle. Are you going to tell me about your trip or not?"

I spent the next forty-five minutes debriefing Alex on all that had happened. Tears streamed down my cheeks when I spoke of Terry Dunbar. Her story was hard to talk about, but I didn't leave out a single detail.

"So it went smoothly?"

"Yes and no. I'm still alive, which is good, but I'm no closer to putting Carl away."

"But you met Terry Dunbarr, Steven Bellamy, Katelyn Cross, and Shae Simmons. You met more names on your list. That's more good news."

"I guess so, but I wanted Carl locked up yesterday."

"You're impatient."

"I know," I agreed then began to fidget with my ring.

"Evil takes care of evil, Rae."

"How so?" I asked, as I continued to twirl the diamond-encrusted band.

"It's a law of nature. It's a universal truth. Carl can only do wrong so many times before it catches up with him. He'll slip. Eventually he'll get caught, with or without your help."

"I guess so." I shrugged my shoulders and changed the subject. "So, besides playing your guitar and working on the Speedster, what else did you do while I was gone?"

I looked up to meet a pair of raised eyebrows and a wide grin. I nodded, waiting for him to elaborate. In response, Alex reached into the backseat and picked up a newspaper.

"What's this?" I asked.

Alex turned the pages until he found the life and leisure section of the Tulsa World. On the front page was a picture of man with round cheeks and a full head of curly hair. Around his neck, he wore a bow tie.

"It's Todd Catchitore!" Just above the picture was the title of the article: Damsels in Distress Benefit Ball. An event to raise money to fight human trafficking. I read the entire article. "A benefit ball?"

"And *we* are going. It's at the end of August."

"In the Crystal Ballroom at the Mayo Hotel? I thought it was closed."

"It was. It was abandoned for twenty years before someone bought it. Took another eight years to restore. They're getting ready to reopen. It'll be the first event in years."

"I'm guessing this is fancy… a black tie event?"

"I'd say so based on the price of the tickets."

"How much were they?"

"A lot, but it's going to a good cause."

"Trafficking?"

"More specifically, a safe house. A place for girls to go after they've been rescued."

"A place like that must already exist."

"Not in the state of Oklahoma."

I couldn't believe what I was hearing. I thought about Monica Bradley and all the what if's. She had been under witness protection, but that hadn't been enough. After Eva's death, Monica was the only witness that could confirm the allegations Lavine made against Carl. Because of what she knew, she was murdered. What if she had been somewhere safe? What if she could have testified? That was nearly twenty years ago. I couldn't believe that in a span of twenty years, no measures had been taken to ensure the safety of girls in the same position as Monica. I thought about Terry Dunbarr, only five years old when Eva freed her from Carl's basement. She had escaped with her life, but the memories of where she had been still haunted her. Where had she gone after Eva freed her? Had anyone helped her? Did she have a safe place to go? What was her story? Tears welled up in my eyes as I remembered her sitting on the bed in that dingy apartment. Her sallow skin. Hunched over... hugging her knees. Close to death. Thirty-two years old, but she looked fifty. The pain and everything she had done to cover it up had taken a toll.

"You'll need to buy a dress."

"Huh?" Alex pulled me from my thoughts. I wiped a tear from my cheek. A dress? I hated dressing up. I loathed itchy gowns and frilly formals. During my senior year, Alex tried to convince me to go to the Masquerade Ball on Halloween night. I convinced him that we should make other plans instead. We wound up sitting on top of the water tower watching the stars. It had been the most perfect night. He also tried to persuade me to go to Prom. Once again, I turned him down, but I was looking forward to the benefit ball. As far as my purpose was concerned, I hadn't really done all that much and if attending the event meant wearing an itchy dress and getting fussed over, then I thought that was the least I could do.

"That's not going to be a problem. Mom will be all over that."

"That's what I thought. Oh, and I bought you a little something for the occasion. It's not much. It's really more symbolic than anything."

I smiled. "You bought me a present, Alex Loving?"

Alex stretched over me and opened up the glove box. He pulled out a package wrapped in bright yellow paper, and handed it to me.

"There's just this one other thing," he said as I began to peel the paper away from the box. "There's a chance that Carl Pierce is going to be at the benefit as well."

"What?" I gasped. "You're kidding me, right? Don't you think that's a conflict of interest?"

"The more money Carl pours into the cause, the less he'll be suspected."

"The case went to trial, Alex. Don't people remember?"

"That was nearly twenty years ago."

"Still, people must remember."

"Suspected. Tried. Cleared. His name is *not* muddied in this town."

"I guess I'm going to have to face him at some point," I said, tossing the wrapping paper on the floor and opening the box.

"You're more ready than you think."

"Alex!" I was breathless. "It's beautiful," I said as I regarded the ornate red and black butterfly.

"It's for your hair. I didn't know what color of dress you would choose for the benefit, but I thought black and red would go with almost anything."

"It's so pretty," I told him, gingerly taking it into my hand.

"The butterfly reminds me of you, Rae." I looked up at Alex for understanding. "I know you get mad at me when I tell you you've changed, but you have. You've transformed. And I mean that in the best possible way."

Alex took the clip from my trembling fingers. With one hand, he smoothed back my wavy locks and with the other, he fastened the clip in my hair. "You're a new creation. You've come out of your cocoon. You're free now. You're beautiful, inside and out. And I love you. I need you to know that."

"I love you, too." I touched the tip of my finger to the butterfly and held it there. "Alex."

"Yeah?"

"Did you worry I wouldn't come back? Did you worry that I might get into trouble while I was gone, and that I might need your help?"

Alex leaned back and gazed into my eyes. "Of course I did, but there was nothing I could do. It was out of my hands," he said, all seriousness returning to his voice. "I just figured, if you love someone, set them free.... if they ever come back, they're yours." Alex cupped his hands around my face. "You came back, Sunshine. That's all that matters now."

While I was away, he had poured his heart out to me in an email, and I had poured mine out to him. We had cleared the air between us. We had written a song. And performing it together on stage was an even deeper, more meaningful expression of our feelings. There seemed to be an understanding between us now. Alex and I were both confused and trying to find ourselves in this big world, but we were not drifting apart. For the first time since meeting Alex Loving, I thought that we were finally in the same phase of life. Finally, we were sharing the same emotions, the same wants, the same needs, and the same weaknesses. I pulled Alex in close so that I could feel the heat of his body and the beat of his heart. I laid my head on his shoulder and looked up at the sky. A warm summer breeze was blowing my hair. The background music was crickets and frogs. The sky was clear and the stars were shining bright.

"This would be my heaven moment," I whispered to Alex.

"Mine too," he whispered back.

CHAPTER TWENTY-NINE

"*T*he perfect dress is out there, Rae, and today is the day we're going to find it."

"I hope so. It's Wednesday. The benefit is on Friday."

"We should have started looking sooner."

"I guess."

Taking her focus off the road for a moment, Mom glanced at me from the corner of her eye. "You don't seem very excited."

"I am excited… about the benefit, but you know how I feel about getting dressed up."

"I know. It's all itchy and uncomfortable, right."

"It's not just that. I don't like being fussed over."

"You owe me, Sunshine. I never got to help you pick out a prom dress. That's a big deal for a mom. Did you know that?"

"I had no idea, and I'm sorry I robbed you of that experience. But in my defense, I had more than one reason for not wanting to go."

"You don't have to apologize. Just let me enjoy the day."

"Fine. Is this better?" I asked, plastering a super fake smile on my face.

"I'll take whatever I can get, but I was hoping you'd have a little fun too. I had full intentions of spoiling you rotten," she said as she pulled up next to the drive-thru speaker at Starbucks and ordered our usual.

Mom drove forward to the window, handed the barista her debit card, grabbed our drinks and pastries, and handed me my latte. With her iced coffee in hand, she continued. "I want to start at Miss Jackson's. The dresses there are stunning. After that, lunch at Queenie's. Their chicken salad is to die for. Then after lunch, we'll run over to Saks. I have a 12:15 makeup appointment at the Mac counter." Mom continued to ramble on as she took her receipt from the girl at the window. I was thankful Claire wasn't working today. Mom looked at me with wide eyes then shifted into drive. "Of course, you're so young that you don't *need* makeup, but sometimes it's fun to put a little on, anyway. Maybe just some eye shadow and a liner. You have the biggest, bluest eyes. We could do something really dramatic. Maybe go for that smoky look. Or sparkly."

"You know I'm going to be wearing a mask," I reminded her.

Mom looked at me confused. After a moment, understanding hit her. "Oh yeah." She nodded her head. "The mask Alex brought over with the ticket. What's that all about?"

"Each ticket came with a white plaster mask and each guest is supposed to decorate the mask in a way that best represents them."

"How are you going to decorate yours?"

"I haven't decided. It's all very weird, if you ask me."

"The mask or the task?"

I considered how the ticket was packaged: inside a small wooden box. Nestled in a bed of velvet was the mask, the ticket for the ball, and instructions in the form of a short poem.

An event to support the cause of human trafficking
A plain white mask you'll find inside the packaging
You are probably wondering why
A clue: it will answer the question "who am I"
So Embellish! Create! Reveal! Design a mask that is ravishing.

I considered the question. "The task, I guess. The mask is easy. It'll be fun to make and fun to wear, but there's meaning in making the mask. It seems like R.E.S.C.U.E is asking every guest to answer the question,

"Who AM I?"

"Why is that strange? I think it's a normal question. Most people ask that question at least once in their lives. Besides, I'm sure there's a reason why they're having you do this."

"It's not the question that's strange, it's the timing. Ever since I've been back in Oklahoma, I've been asking myself that exact same question. 'Who am I'? I can't seem to escape the question. It's coming at me from every direction."

"So have you figured it out?"

"Who I am? No, not yet. I've been talking to Pastor Joe about it, though." I laughed. "So in the next two days, I not only have to figure out who I am, but also express it artistically."

"That's perfect. You're artistic. I'm sure you'll think of something great."

"But you can't rush creativity."

"I remember a time when I was asking myself the question 'Who am I?' It was right before your Dad and I left for Asia. I felt completely unqualified. I had plenty of doubts. I was scared. I didn't feel good enough, experienced enough. I was feeling a lot of the same things you are right now."

"Really?"

Mom nodded. "Maybe sometime I'll tell you the story."

"So what did you do?"

"I listened to your Nana's advice."

"And."

"She said that it's important to know who we are, but it's essential to know who *God* says we are."

"That's exactly what Joe and Quinn said."

"They're wise."

Mom set the cruise control to 70 and turned on the radio. I glanced at the rearview mirror and the neon number in the upper right hand corner: 97. I looked at the clock: 10:05. It wasn't even noon and the temperature was already nearing 100 degrees.

Mom took another sip of her iced latte and then took her eyes off the road to flash me a smile. "Not to change the subject, but how are things with Alex?"

Still looking at me hopefully, Mom crossed the centerline and then swerved back quickly.

"Mom!" I shrieked.

"Sorry. I can't take my eyes off the road for a second." Mom grasped the wheel with both hands and faced forward.

"He's good."

"After his birthday party… I just wasn't sure."

"Everything's fine. He's taken up the guitar."

"I was wondering why you bought him a ukulele for his birthday. How's he doing with the guitar?"

"He's an expert already, of course. He's good at everything he does."

"A hockey player one day and a musician the next."

"I think he's making up for lost time."

"I think you're lucky."

"I know," I said shrugging my shoulders.

"The two of you make the perfect couple. Ah, young love." Mom relaxed into her seat. "I remember when Will and I were dating."

"You and Dad are perfect, though, right?"

"Better than perfect. It's just a different… deeper kind of love. We used to spend our time discovering one another. Now we read each other's minds."

Mom began to tell me about the love of *her* life and how she felt when she first laid eyes on Will. She told me the story of how they met. She told me how she felt when she knew Will was the one. Then there was the proposal story, which was more amusing than it was romantic. I couldn't believe that we had never talked like this before, that she had never confided in me. I was nineteen years old and I felt like I was just getting to know her. I liked Sue a lot, not just as a mom but also as a person. She shared with me how disappointing it was to plan a wedding and have her own sister refuse to be the bridesmaid, refuse to be a part. This story made me feel a little guilty since Sue's sister, Eva, was also my biological mother.

Sensing my discomfort, she began to ask questions about Alex and how I felt the first time I saw him. I told her that I got butterflies in my stomach every time I looked at him, but she wanted to know more. Since Alex was truly my soul mate, since he had returned to earth to protect me, since I had known him for an eternity, she wanted to know if Alex seemed *familiar* to me when I saw him for the first time. I told her, "Yes, he did." But then I explained how it was very confusing to be so strongly attracted to someone and not know why. I told her how conflicting it was to feel like I had known him my whole life, yet we had never met... we had never even spoken. I told her how comforting it was to uncover the truth about our history, and how irritating it was to discover that while I had been in the dark, Alex had know about us all along.

Mom and I were still talking about the different kinds of love as we pulled into Utica Square. "It's going to be a good day. I can feel it," she said, taking the last spot in front of the department store. Gold letters spelled out *Miss Jackson's* across the front.

"Looks fancy."

"It is. And expensive, too."

I slid out of the cool car onto the hot asphalt.

"What color of dress were you thinking about, Rae?" Excitement shone in her eyes, and she continued without giving me a chance to answer. "I was thinking of something colorful. Maybe bright pink or a nice yellow."

"I don't think I'm supposed to draw a lot of attention to myself, Mom."

"Look at that one in the window," she said, pointing to the most horrible dress I had ever seen.

"It looks like a flamingo dress," I voiced my opinion, commenting on the hot pink formal with a tiered skirt and a slit up the side. "Besides, I don't do sequins. They itch. I was thinking of something more along the lines of the one next to it."

"Black?" Mom rolled her eyes.

"Black will go with my boots."

"I was planning on buying you some new shoes to go with the dress."

"I'm wearing the boots," I said, holding my ground.

"We're getting off to a *great* start." Mom grumbled and opened the heavy glass door. I sighed and followed her inside. The short walk from the car to the front door of Miss Jackson's had already caused me to break out in a sweat, so when I stepped into the store, I welcomed the air conditioning.

"They have the best displays. Look at this, Rae." Mom said, pointing to bridal registry in the back corner. "Maybe in a few years we'll come back for another reason."

"I wouldn't count on that."

"Rae. I know a promise ring when I see one." She looked at the diamond-encrusted band on my finger.

"This is a different kind of promise," I tried to explain. "This is an eternal promise."

"Do you have something against marriage?"

"No, but Alex does. He's the one who doesn't want a wedding. He's made that perfectly clear and I don't want to talk about it."

Mom stopped in her tracks and turned to face me. With a worried expression, she looked me in the eye. "He's not planning on leaving… earth anytime soon, is he? I thought that he was here to stay."

"It's not that. Alex thinks marriage is worldly and mundane."

"I have heard of men trying to weasel their way out of getting married, but that's one line I've never heard before." Mom moved to the escalator and ran a hand through her short hair as we ascended to the second floor. "Still, I predict a wedding in the near future."

"I'm not even twenty, Mom. There's plenty of time."

"But when you've found that special someone -"

"Don't get your hopes up, that's all I'm saying." I interrupted.

In order to try on the black dress I saw in the window, I had to humor Mom and try on a few colorful choices as well: a lemon yellow, a bright orange strapless, and the hideous hot pink number we saw on the way in. I slipped into the yellow dress first. Mom zipped me up and told me to spin around. I was thankful when she shook her head *no*. We both agreed that I looked like Belle from Beauty and the Beast. Next up was the hot pink

number. Thirty seconds later, it was back on the hanger. Mom liked it…
a lot, but I refused. "No way," I told her. When I grabbed the black dress,
Mom rolled her eyes. "Try the orange one on first," she said.

"Fine," I groaned. I slipped into the satin formal and Mom helped me
button it up the side.

"It looks great with your hair," she told me. I glanced at myself in the
mirror, noticing how my shiny black hair stood out against the bright
orange fabric.

"I look like Halloween."

"Ummm…. maybe a little. Okay, try on the black one."

Mom put the orange spaghetti strapped gown back on the hanger.
With a smile on my face, I gazed at the black dress and sighed. "It's so
pretty. It's so perfect."

"You haven't even tried it on," she reminded me as she unzipped the
back so I could step into it. "If I agree to buy this dress, just make me one
promise. Wear white on your wedding day."

"I promise I will wear white on my wedding day, Mom."

"Good," Mom said, zipping me up. She took several steps back and
stared at me with her hand on her hip. "Well, will you look at that? You
have cleavage."

I stood sideways gazing at my profile in the mirror, then turned to
face it. "Hmmm." She was right. I *did* have cleavage.

"It looks too tight. You don't want to look like you had to stuff yourself
inside."

"It is a little tight." I examined myself in the mirror. "But the skirt's
flowy, so it's fine."

Mom shifted her weight and studied my reflection. "You look like
you're going to a funeral, not a benefit ball."

"Maybe, but you have to admit, it's the best dress I've tried on yet."

"Well, at least it's long enough to cover up those boots." Mom began
to fluff the tulle on the skirt. "I still think a brightly colored dress would
look best with your black hair."

"This is the one, Mom."

"You do look beautiful." Mom was now standing between the mirror and me. She twisted her mouth and shook her head. "You look like a woman, and I'm not sure I like that. I just don't know where my little girl has gone."

"I'm twenty in two months, Mom. I look like a woman because I am one."

"Okay. Just make me happy and do one last thing. There's another dress I want you to try. If you don't like it, we'll go with the black. I promise."

"Fine," I sighed.

Mom exited the dressing room. When she shut the door, I posed in front of the mirror. I turned sideways and studied my womanly curves. I twirled and watched the skirt rise to my knees and then return gracefully to my feet. I made kissy lips in the mirror, flipped my hair behind my shoulder, and decided to give the dress one last spin. I was stopped mid-twirl by a knock at the fitting room door.

"Are you decent?"

At the sound of Sue's voice, I opened the door, fully prepared to hate the dress she had returned with, but I didn't. As she stood in the doorway, I stood spellbound with my eyes fixed on the beautiful gown. The corset was yellow-green ombre with a white lace overlay. The skirt was made from strips of layered white tulle that reminded me of feathers on a bird.

"Well, are you going to try it on?"

"This is it," I whispered.

Mom tried not to show her surprise over the fact that we had actually agreed on something. "Well, slip it on and see if it fits. The gala is in two days. No time to have it altered."

Mom returned the black dress to the hanger, and I stepped into the timeless, multicolored gown. The dress fastened up the back and Mom helped me with the buttons. I looked like a colorful bird and as I stood staring at my reflection and the white feathery tulle that fell from my waist, I had an epiphany: I was reminded of both the yellow bird and my purpose. Just like the yellow bird that cleared a path for the miners, I too was supposed to clear a path for others. A-Omega told me so.

"It couldn't fit you any better. Rae, I think it's perfect. What do you think?"

I couldn't find the words. The dress *was* complete perfection. It was *me*. The feathery skirt and the yellow at the top of the corset gave me the perfect idea for my mask. So strange that finding the perfect dress could make everything else crystal clear.

"This is it, Mom."

"Are you sure?"

"Positive."

After lunch at Queenie's and a full day of shopping, I was exhausted and thankful that we were finally headed home. It was a forty-five minute drive and Mom talked the entire way, sharing her thoughts on the benefit ball and how exciting she thought it would be. She rambled on about makeup, shoes, and how she thought I could learn a lot from Todd Catchitore. Her voice drifted in and out; I was paying just enough attention to answer all of her questions appropriately, but I wasn't adding much to the conversation because my mind was elsewhere. This morning on the way to Tulsa, I was stressing out thinking about the mask and how I could transform it into something unique expressing who I was, but after having found the perfect dress and after having an epiphany while in Miss Jackson's looking at the feathery tulle on the skirt of the ball gown, my thoughts now had wings and I was soaring with creativity. So many things were coming together at once, and I finally knew what to do with the mask. It wouldn't be a symbol of who *I* thought I was; instead, it would represent who *God* says I am. The mask would be a yellow bird. Staring out the window, I began to think about my yellow bird and how, when I saw it hanging in a storefront in Amsterdam, I knew I had to have it. The bird reminded me of me: a tiny creature in constant flight. How was I to know the yellow bird was something greater, a symbol of love and sacrifice? Maybe the yellow bird was stronger than I thought. Maybe I was, too.

Mom was still rambling on about how I should have bought a pair of heels to go with my fancy gown when I interrupted her. "Mom. Who does A-Omega… who does God say *you* are?"

Sue took her eyes off the road and met my gaze. Although it didn't show, I knew the pain she held inside. I remember her telling me that, after Laney died, all she wanted to do was sleep. She couldn't face reality, life without her little girl. She told me God had helped her through it.

"He calls me resilient and faith-filled."

"Who do you say *God* is?" I asked as I looked out the passenger window at the highway sign in the distance. Bartlesville - 15 miles.

Mom smiled. "I call Him Healer," she said without hesitation. "What does God call you, Rae?" I looked my mother in the eye. I thought of all the things I used to be. Scared. Insecure. Tired. Cold. Distant. I had spent half of my life letting my thoughts hold me captive. I had listened to lies for too long. I was ready to listen to the truth.

"He says I'm like a little yellow bird. He says that I am love and that I am loved."

CHAPTER THIRTY

"**W**ell, don't you look dapper, Mr. Limbeaux."

"And you look… absolutely breathtaking."

"Thank you." The hard work had paid off. An excruciating day of shopping and two full days spent in my studio transforming my white plaster mask into my little yellow bird. The mask was beautiful. I had given the white plaster a base coat of metallic yellow paint and then used a craft blade to shape the sides of the mask into wings.

"Shall we?"

"You're not going anywhere without a picture. Why don't the two of you get over there in front of the living room window? Will, do you have the camera ready?"

"Mom!"

"Let her have her fun." Alex looked at my mom and smiled. "Besides," Alex said while very discreetly admiring every detail of my dress. "I may not get another chance to see you dressed like this. I'll need a picture to remember it."

"Smile!" Mom said in a singsong voice.

Alex slipped his arm around my waist and I looked up at him, sneaking a quick peek while Dad adjusted the lens on his camera. He was wearing a slim fit tuxedo. His slacks were tapered and his jacket hugged his torso, accentuating his broad shoulders. With a serious look on his face, he straightened his black bow tie and then returned my gaze. His mouth transformed into a lopsided smile. I had never seen him look so handsome. I heard a click and saw a flash of light.

"Rae!" Mom said. "You weren't even looking. Take another one, Will."

I sighed. "Really?"

Alex turned his head and whispered in my ear, "Just cooperate, Sunshine."

"Fine," I scowled.

"Pretty face," Mom encouraged.

I forced a smile. Snap.

Mom pulled the camera away from Dad and looked at the screen. "Okay. This is just not going to do. Rae, your eyes were closed. Alex, make her behave."

"Behave," Alex said and softly pinched my waist. "The sooner she gets the shot, the sooner we get to leave."

I obliged and produced the most natural looking smile I could under pressure. Snap. Now Mom and Dad were both studying the screen. They talked amongst themselves then all at once, Mom said, "Now that was a good one."

"Great. Can we go now?"

"Not just yet. One more with your masks on."

Alex and I positioned our masks, and Dad snapped a couple more pictures. I wasn't surprised by Alex's mask. Half angel, half creature of the night, Alex was still hung up on what people called him after the fight on Halloween night. In the woods across from our Minnesota cottage, he fought off Ben and saved Flynt's life... my life. While I saw him as an angel, others labeled him a vampire... a werewolf, and it seemed as though he still believed the lies.

"Now can we go?" I sighed.

"Yes. You're free to go." Mom scampered toward me, the gracefulness gone from her step. Standing on tiptoes, she kissed my forehead and ran her hand across my hair to smooth it.

"Just a couple fly-aways."

"Thanks Mom," I said, making my way to the door in a hurry.

"Goodnight, Sue…Will." Alex waved, smiling at my dad.

"Be careful, Rae."

"I will."

"Take care of her, Alex."

"I always do."

"And have fun," Mom added.

Once outside, my irritation was subdued, but inside the Speedster, anxiety began to set in. Forty-five minutes to Tulsa. I had no idea what I was in for. Carl would be there. But with everyone wearing masks, would I be able to tell him apart from anyone else? What if he recognized me? What would he do?

"Well, you look stunning tonight and very… very yellow." Alex said, lifting his mask first, then mine. He leaned in for a kiss. "Are you nervous?" he whispered.

My dress felt tighter through the bust than it did when I tried it at the store, and I couldn't breathe. Yes, I was nervous and my pulse had quickened so that I thought my heart would burst right through my chest. I wiped a bead of perspiration from my forehead and tried to take a deep breath.

"I'm worried that I'm not ready. What if Carl's there?"

"Don't worry about it. You'll be fine. We'll be fine."

"I love you, Alex. If I don't make it out of this alive, I want you to know I love you and I'm sorry I kept you here on earth. You belong someplace better and I'm selfish for having you stay. I'm also sorry for lying to you over and over again. I never should have done that."

"Rae, you have nothing to worry about."

"But just in case, I had to get that off my chest." I touched a tissue to my forehead to absorb the perspiration without smearing my makeup. Alex cranked up the air and positioned the vent so that the air was blowing directly on my face.

Once on the highway, he pressed his foot down hard on the pedal and I felt myself being pushed back into the seat.

"Now close your eyes and relax," Alex instructed as he turned on the music.

Following his suggestion, I closed my eyes and thought of only those things that brought me comfort. I went over my journal entries one by one, trying to remind myself that A-Omega… God… was there for me, there to guide me, protect me, and to warn me of danger. I placed a trembling hand on my fleur-de-lis brooch pinned to my gown. My heart was beating wildly beneath it. I let my mind wander to the fortune cookie and the message inside. Like following a trail of breadcrumbs, I retraced the steps I took in Houston until I found myself in front of apartment 414, knocking on the door. The shadow of a woman peeking through a narrow space. A shabby apartment. Sharing stories. Brushing the hair away from the eyes of a broken girl. Comfort. Love.

I had been led to Terry Dunbarr so that I could save her life. I had taken a leap of faith. I had made the decision to trust, and I had been protected. I can do this, I told myself. I am strong. I am determined. I am stubborn. I am kind. I felt myself relax and all at once, my dress didn't feel so binding. I took a deep breath. "I am love and I am loved," I whispered. "I am a yellow bird."

Forty-five minutes later, Alex rolled through downtown Tulsa. When I opened my eyes, I could see the red, neon Mayo sign glowing in the distance. A bit of history returned to the Tulsa skyline. The hotel, built in the 1920's, was once a gathering place for Tulsa's upper crust, with former guests like Charlie Chaplin, John F. Kennedy, Babe Ruth, and May West. However, when Tulsa, the oil capital of the world, went from boom to bust, the Mayo was stripped of many of its architectural features and was left abandoned for nearly twenty years. Then, at the turn of the century, the hotel was bought for pennies on the dollar. After nine years and millions in renovations, the grand hotel was restored to its former glory. Alex continued through the intersection of Boulder and 5th, then pulled up in front of the Mayo and took his place behind a long string of luxury cars and limousines waiting for the valet.

When Alex moved to the front of the line, he shifted into park and slid his mask down over his face. "Are you ready?"

I flipped down the vanity mirror and gave my lips a coat of gloss before hiding my worry behind the yellow bird. "As ready as I'll ever be."

When Alex came around and opened the door for me, my heart jumped back into my throat and it felt like my dress was being cinched. Moving my eyes from Alex, I looked at the edifice that stretched eighteen stories above me. The Sullivanesque style building had a terracotta façade with an accent of stone trim. As I watched ornately garbed men and women exiting their vehicles and making their way through the two story Doric columns and into the hotel lobby, I felt as though I had slipped back in time.

"Quit worrying," Alex told me. "Everything is going to be okay. Just remember, no one will know who you are. In that respect, the masks were a great idea."

"How do you know I'm worrying?"

"You're biting your nails."

"I was just thinking."

"About what?"

"You know how you can sometimes spot a person without seeing their face. You recognize other features like their hair, or their gait, or even certain mannerisms… not even a mask can hide their identity."

"Yeah, I guess so."

"Well, I've never seen Carl in person. If he is here, I wonder if I'll recognize him."

"He'll stand out. I promise you. A man like Carl wants to be noticed."

I took in another shallow breath and adjusted my mask.

"You look beautiful," Alex whispered, and then offered me his hand. As we approached the white columns at the entrance, the doorman, clad in a freshly starched white shirt embellished with a golden "M," stepped forward and led us through the double entry doors into the lobby. It was magnificent, breathtaking, and the restoration was flawless. Black and white marble floors led up to a sweeping staircase. The designer had incorporated colorful and modern circular sofas with several reproduction period pieces, mixing perfectly the past with the present. Above the lobby was a mezzanine where masked guests conversed. My gown was just as elegant as anyone else's, yet I felt out of place. Never in my life had I been to an event so extravagant. I had to pinch my arm to remind myself the reason I had come. I was not a debutant. I was not a part of high society. I was here because Todd Catchitore was going to share his vision for R.E.S.C.U.E and the new direction his organization was taking to fight human trafficking. This evening was not only a chance to bring awareness to the cause, but it was also a way to raise funds for the safe house on which R.E.S.C.U.E was hoping to break ground by the first of next year.

I continued to stand with my feet rooted to the ground, observing the wide array of masks, each one unique and so very telling. Many of the women's masks were adorned with large rhinestones to represent what everyone already knew: they were made of money. Still others were more unique. My favorite character of the night was the mime: a tall gentleman standing in the mezzanine with a plump Mary Antoinette on his arm. He had used the color of the mask to his advantage. With a stark white background, he only needed to shadow the eyes in black and fill in the lips with red to achieve the look he desired. He wore a pair of suspenders over a black and white striped shirt. Instead of a traditional tuxedo jacket, he wore a black vest and on top of his head, a simple black beret. As Alex made small talk with the bellhop, I watched the mime perform. Releasing his arm from Mary Antoinette's, he began to express himself with his hands. Unable to interpret his gestures, I let my eyes wander to a woman who was wearing a cat mask. Great care had been taken to cut away the bottom portion of the mask just below her nose. Soft white fur covered a delicate face and ears, and long white whiskers completed the effect. It was the most beautiful mask of the night. Her thick blond hair was pulled back into a tight bun. Her dress was solid black and was fitted to her tall, slender frame. Embroidered in sparkly yellow thread on the front of her gown, right over her stomach, was a tiny bird giving the illusion that she had just gobbled up her little feathered friend. As she glided around the room with her hands in prayer position, I wondered if she was trying to ask for forgiveness. Was she feeling guilty for doing something that came so naturally? Well aware that I looked very much like a bird this evening, I decided to steer clear of the kitty, just in case she fell into temptation.

"May I show you to the elevator?"

While I had been admiring the many masks, Alex had been discussing the hotel's renovation with the bellboy and telling him how lucky he felt to attend the first event since the hotel's reopening.

"The Crystal Ballroom is on the eighteenth floor," he continued, showing us to a short row of shiny silver elevators and pushing the "up" button. "You'll check in to receive your table assignment. You still have about an hour before dinner is served. Feel free to mingle."

"This whole thing is so bizarre and so much fun," I whispered into Alex's ear.

"Did you see the mime?" Alex asked when the doors to the elevator shut.

"Yeah, but I couldn't tell what he was trying to say."

Alex stiffened his arms and touched his pointer finger to his thumb to make it appear that he was holding a slender object. With one swift movement, he made a gentle slicing motion over his heart. "I think he was telling people what he did for a living. He's a cardiologist… a heart surgeon."

"Very good, Alex. Maybe in his spare time he's a mime. Or maybe he's just the quiet type."

"Any sign of Carl?" Even though we were the only ones in the elevator, Alex lowered his voice when he asked the question.

"No sign of him yet." A prickly sensation that started at my toes moved up my body and spread to the tips of my fingers. *I could end up standing right next to Carl and not even know it*, I thought.

When the elevator opened, Alex walked up to the ballroom doors with purpose. After checking us in under the names Sunshine Jones and Ian Limbeaux, he was handed two information packets and a seating assignment. When I asked Alex why he had registered me under an alias, he told me that since he had an alias, I should, too. Sunshine Jones was my detective name.

"We're at table 3," he told me, pulling a chart out of the packet and studying it before entering the ballroom. Alex didn't seem too impressed, but I had to stop and stare. Just moments ago when I stepped into the lobby of The Mayo, my breath had been taken away by its beauty; but stepping into the Crystal Ballroom was a different experience all together, and I knew at once why the room had been given that name. The room was named for the pair of chandeliers that hung from the ceiling. I had read somewhere that it took eight months to remove eighty years of tarnish beneath the lacquer. They had been completely disassembled, cleaned in phosphoric acid, re-lacquered, and put back together. It can be hard work getting things back the way they used to be, but by looking at the chandeliers, I realized that it was not impossible. When my eyes finally moved away from the chandeliers, I took in the rest of the room. White plaster walls with ornate detail. Cornices and ornamental moldings. The tall windows that stretched from the floor to ceiling were adorned with sage green draperies that had been drawn back to reveal an illuminated Tulsa skyline. Crystal sconces hung on the walls and contributed to the soft glow in the room. There was a stage at the front and to the right of the stage, a five piece band that included drums, an acoustic guitar, a saxophone, a piano, and a viola. I took a closer look at the stage, expecting to see a podium behind which Todd Catchitore would thank us all for coming and go into the details of R.E.S.C.U.E.'s goals for the next year. Instead, I found a long rectangular table filled with an array of paintbrushes and several different hues of paint. I felt Alex's hand on my shoulder.

"Should we find our seats?"

"Of course," I replied. Still intrigued with the setup, my eyes were fixed on the stage when Alex nudged me with his elbow. I looked at him with wide eyes and as he leaned in close so that he could whisper, he cupped his hand around my ear.

"He's here, Rae. Carl's here."

CHAPTER THIRTY-ONE

Although I didn't ask, I did wonder how Alex could be so sure. Because the guests were wearing masks that covered their faces, I felt fairly confident that he could be mistaken. I trained my eyes on Alex until he gave me the signal to look; I glanced over his shoulder at the man at the back of the room near the bar. He was holding a crystal tumbler in one hand and stirring the drink with the other. He must have sensed me staring because as soon as my eyes moved from the drink in his hand to his mask, he turned in my direction. I gasped as realization hit me. "It's Fu Manchu," I told Alex.

"I told you that you wouldn't be able to miss him."

"Wait a minute. I think I recognize the woman he's with."

Dressed in a fitted white gown, the pale woman's unruly red curls were separated with gel, accentuated so that her head looked like a nest of snakes. The gossamer veil attached to the front of her mask fell over heavily shadowed eyes and a stoic smile. Beside Carl stood Zandie Burchette, Carl's fiancé, the woman I had seen in the March edition of *Car and Driver* magazine. In the picture above the article, the slender redhead bombshell was standing beside my biological father and his pride and joy: an Aston Martin V12 Zagato. Tonight as I gazed upon the bride of Fu Manchu, I wondered if she understood the meaning of her costume and all that it implied. I looked from the tall redhead back to the statuesque man who stood beside her. Alex was right. It had to be Carl. I couldn't think of anyone else who would come to a benefit ball for human trafficking dressed like Fu Manchu. I only knew of one man who could possibly be so brazen. My chest began to tighten and I could feel my cheeks growing hot behind my mask.

"It'll be okay," Alex assured me. "Remember, our faces are covered and there's no way Carl could possibly recognize us." Alex slipped a protective arm around my waist. "Come on. Let's find our table."

Following Alex, I took in the rest of the room, savoring every ornate detail. It was magnificent. Fifty white clothed tables were scattered across the floor and adorning each one was a spray of flowers and a golden candlestick. At the front near the stage was a dance floor and several couples were moving to the music. The guitarist was also the singer, a petite man with delicate features. I expected his vocals to be similar to his stature: small. But when I heard his voice, I was surprised by how well it carried, filling the room with a low and lusty rendition of "My Funny Valentine." I followed Alex across the room on wobbly legs, and I was thankful that his arm was around my waist to keep me steady. I felt lightheaded. The color had drained from my face. My heart was pounding. Thinking about Carl made me feel cold and clammy. I felt tangled in the feathery tulle of my gown and trapped in its shrinking corset. I couldn't breath.

"What do you think they're going to do with all that paint?" I asked with a trembling voice, hoping small talk might ease my mind. If I couldn't quit thinking about Carl, there was no way I would make it through the night.

"Your guess is as good as mine," he returned. "Ah, there's table three." Alex pointed to an empty table at the front of the room and with my hand in his, I let him lead the way. We found our nameplates - Ian Limbeaux and Sunshine Jones.

Alex started to pull out my chair for me, but then he changed his mind. "You look beautiful tonight, Miss Jones. I'd really hate to see you sitting in that chair all evening. No one will be able to see your dress. I was wondering if I could trouble you for a dance." Alex cajoled.

"Not a chance I'm getting on the dance floor."

"I'm not taking no for an answer."

"I'm nervous enough as is. My legs are still shaking. Carl's less than fifty feet away," I reminded him. "The last thing I want to do is draw attention to myself... to us."

"Just one dance... for me. You turned me down when I invited you to the Masquerade Ball during your senior year and you rejected me again when I asked you to Prom. You owe me, Sunshine."

"I'm never going to hear the end of this, am I? Mom has already laid the guilt on thick. Now you?"

Alex tilted his head and flashed a charming smile. "You're not going to turn me down again, are you?"

"Ahhh.... Fine... One dance."

I guess Alex thought if he waited too long, I might change my mind. So without hesitation, he placed his hand on the small of my back and steered me toward the dance floor just as the band was finishing up.

"So good to have you here at the Mayo on this beautiful summer night," said the petite man with the deep voice. "So many beautiful gowns. So many wonderful masks. But this song goes out to a little yellow bird."

I stiffened at once when I realized he was talking about me.

Alex laughed and kissed the top of my head. "Looks like I'm not the only one you're making an impression on tonight, Miss Jones."

"This is a disaster, Alex. Everyone's staring. I hate it when people stare. I just know they are. I can feel their beady eyes."

"Good thing you're wearing a mask."

Alex was right. At least I was wearing a mask. When the music started, I began to relax and as the dance floor began to fill up, I felt much more comfortable. I closed my eyes and imagined that it was just the two of us. I put my head on Alex's shoulder. He smelled good. He looked good. He was holding me. Maybe dancing with him wasn't so bad after all. But halfway through the song, Alex startled me with some unexpected news.

"Don't look now," he whispered, "but your father and Zandie Burchette are sitting at our table."

"No way," I interrupted and completely disregarding Alex's warning, looked over my shoulder to see for myself. At that moment, I realized why Alex had cautioned me to wait. Seated in a chair directly across the table from mine, Carl was leaned back with one leg crossed over the other, stirring his drink. I quickly turned back to Alex.

"He's looking at us," I whispered.

"I know," Alex sighed. "That's what I was trying to tell you."

"I can't sit there."

"Just calm down. Play it smooth. One more dance and then we'll go back to the table."

"I told you, I will *not* sit there. I'm shaking like a leaf."

"You have to."

"No! I can't, Alex." My voice trembled.

"One more dance. You'll be fine, I promise."

I had committed to one dance and one dance only, but being locked in Alex's arms, swaying to the music, was so much better than conversing with Carl.

"I feel like I'm going to throw up."

"Just listen to the music."

"Hold me tight so I stop shaking."

The band made a smooth transition into "The Way You Look Tonight" and just as I requested, Alex held me close. Then trying to sooth me even further, he began to whisper the first stanza into my ear. I tried my hardest to think about the lyrics instead of the enemy who was waiting for me less than fifty feet away. I tried to let my body relax to his touch but in the blink of an eye, the song was over and I followed Alex off the dance floor on a pair of shaky legs. In the time it took for the band to play two short songs, table number three had gone from empty to full and as I drew closer, I noticed that the cat lady and her dashing date were assigned the pair of seats right next to Alex and me. This did little to ease my anxiety. Dressed in a skintight black dress with an embroidered birdie on her belly, I thought that if Carl didn't eat me alive, then she would definitely gobble me up. As I approached the table, I took notice of Carl... Fu Manchu... my father. He was seated directly across from me. Next to him sat his fiancé, the bride of Fu Manchu. Wearing the same stoic smile, her expression remained unchanged. She looked more like a mannequin than a person, more like a fixture than Carl's fiancée. As if sedated, she sat utterly still, staring into space while my father was deep in a conversation with the portly fellow seated next to him. With both of them distracted in their own ways, neither Fu Manchu nor his bride-to-be had seen us approach. I was thankful for that and as Alex slid my chair out from under the table, I quickly took a seat and hid myself behind the giant spray of flowers. My legs felt like Jell-O and I graciously accepted the opportunity to sit down and regain a bit of strength.

Through the arrangement of stems and petals, I studied the portly fellow conversing with my father. Clad in an elegant white tux with tails, he wore the mask of a dove. I felt relieved that I was not the only bird at the table and because bird watching was one of Will's favorite pass times, I had a little bit of insight into the character of my plump feathered friend: a symbol of peace and unconditional love, a celestial messenger, a bird that is intimately aware of his surroundings. The dove fidgeted with his white linen napkin while shifting uncomfortably in his seat. I thought that the mask definitely fit the man. Although very cordial and willing to participate in conversation with Carl, the dove was keenly aware of his environment, and it appeared that my father was making him uneasy. All at once, I realized that the portly man and I shared much more than the same kingdom, phylum, and class; we were both nervous nellies when Carl Pierce was in our presence. I was thankful that I had a friend at the table.

Still partially hidden behind the large floral centerpiece, I listened to the conversation that was taking place between Fu Manchu and the dove and occasionally took the opportunity to peek at Carl out of the corner of my eye. This was not the Carl of my dreams. This was Publicity-Shot-Carl. Carefree Carl. Celebrity Carl. His shiny white teeth were revealed when his two thin lips stretched wide into a movie star smile. Although the majority of his face was hidden, I could still see his dark brown eyes peering out from behind his mask. I looked through the spray of flowers. Carl was rattling on about his upcoming trip to New York

City. Casually reclined in his chair with his legs crossed, Carl agitated the ice in his crystal tumbler with a slender glass swizzle stick. Although I was now able to catch my breath, my heart was still thumping wildly in my chest. I was taking it all in. Assessing the situation. A woman walked by, touched Carl gently on the shoulder, and whispered something softly into his ear. Carl laughed, flashed a smile, and dismissed her quickly. I had only seen pictures of Carl. I had never seen him in action. When Alex first mentioned that Carl might attend, I couldn't imagine that he would receive a warm welcome considering that his criminal nature conflicted with the cause the ball was supporting. But I was absolutely wrong and I was revolted that the majority of the guests seemed enamored by him. Everyone wanted a piece of Carl. Some of his time. Some of his money. Some of his attention. Alex's words rang fresh in my ears: "Suspected. Tried. Cleared. His name is *not* muddied in this town." Rich. Handsome. Charismatic. He had them *all* fooled. Ugh! Disgusting, I thought. Carl had nearly everyone in attendance under his spell but I would not be one of them. I turned my attention to Alex and felt my heart rate finally begin to slow. If Carl was busy talking with others, there was less of a chance that he would try to make conversation with me. This thought became the flicker of hope that would get me through the evening. Unfortunately, when the servers came around to deliver the first course, everyone shifted their attention from casual conversation to their petite beefsteak salads. Everyone but Carl, that is. Having taken a quick sip of water to quench my thirst, I set my glass down and peeked through the arrangement just in time to see Carl motioning a server over to our table. The next thing I knew, the server was removing the centerpiece... my camouflage.

"I appreciate you, Elliot." Carl thanked the server in a gravely voice. "There. Much better," Carl exhaled loudly and smiled. "It feels criminal to sit at this lovely table and not be able to see *all* of the guests."

"I couldn't agree more," the cat woman said with a smile.

Carl only halfway returned the pleasantry, flashing a toothy smile, without bothering to look her in the eye. His attention was elsewhere. He was staring at Alex. He was staring at me. I used my glass as a distraction and took another sip of water.

"Sunshine Jones and Ian Limbeaux." His voice was deep, gravely, distinguished. "You are a couple. Am I right?"

He uttered my name before I had the chance to swallow. All at once, I choked up and nearly sprayed a mouthful of water across the table. Luckily, Alex took the lead and answered. He was so calm. So collected. "Yes. We've been together for quite some time," he returned.

"Hmm." Carl ran a delicate finger over pursed lips. "You both look so young. Not married," Carl said, glancing at my finger. "But engaged, correct?"

"Promised to one another until the end of time."

Carl shook his head and considered Alex's answer for a moment before changing pace. "So tell me, Ian Limbeaux," Carl laughed. "What do you do for a living? How do you plan to support the lovely lady next to you?"

I couldn't believe it! Carl was quizzing Alex like a father quizzes the boyfriend before he leaves on a date with his daughter. Apparently, Alex was as taken aback by the question as I was because his response did not come quickly. I began to worry about what Alex might say and I remembered a time last year when we were sitting at the dinner table with Flynt and Corrine. Alex seemed eager to divulge as much about our relationship as possible and got as close to the line as he could without crossing it. If Flynt and Corrine had discovered who Alex was or why we were at the cottage, it would have been a minor inconvenience and worst-case scenario, we would have had to move. But tonight the stakes were higher. If Carl discovered our true identity my cover would be blown. My mission would be compromised.

"Um. I'm a mechanic."

I gave a quiet sigh of relief and then took notice of Carl who now tilted his head with interest.

"Really. What's your specialty?"

"I love classics. I just finished a 56 Speedster."

"Is that so?" Alex had piqued Carl's interest and I was glad the heat was finally off of me. "I'm a bit of a car aficionado myself. I have quite the collection. In fact, I'm traveling to New York late next week. I'll be the keynote speaker at a vintage car auction. The profits from the auction support a great cause."

Of course, I thought. Carl was all about image.

"Quite the statement, the two of you." He had changed the direction of the conversation once again.

"Excuse me?" All at once, I had found my voice.

Carl laughed. "I was beginning to think the yellow bird couldn't chirp." My father smiled, but this time it wasn't a toothy smile, it was more of a smirk. "Half angel, half creature of the night. I'm not even going to try to guess." Carl licked his lips. "And you come here with a little yellow bird. A symbol of love and sacrifice. Not really sure how the two of you fit together." The smoothness was gone from Carl's voice and his eyes narrowed as he looked out from behind his mask. This was more like the Nightmare Carl, the Carl I saw in my dreams. Carl was getting angry. But why? I glanced at Alex. I couldn't see any steam coming out of his ears yet, but I knew that he was fuming. Alex was angry, too. Had I missed something?

"And I don't think your costume is very tactful." Alex usually played it so smooth. And with the exception of the brawl at the hockey tournament last year, he was generally in control of his emotions. I gave Alex's hand a squeeze. Unspoken words. When Alex didn't squeeze back, I knew exactly where the conversation was headed. "I mean really? The bride of Fu Manchu might not be the best movie to pattern your mask after considering tonight's cause."

Carl was just about to make a rebuttal when Todd Catchitore took the stage. Followed by six women dressed in white, he came to a stop behind the table. Almost immediately, I noticed that their masks were different from ours. While ours were painted with designs and intricate detail, theirs were pure white, untouched. I now realized what they were going to do with the paint.

The women stood next to him, three on each side, and when one of the women at Todd's left stepped forward, the room went silent. With confidence, she picked up the microphone in one hand and with the other, she removed her mask. Her face was youthful and I didn't think she could be any older than fifteen or sixteen.

"My name is Monique," she said with a weak smile, setting the mask down on the table and picking up a brush. Carefully, she dabbed the tip of the brush into the red and painted two rosy circles on each cheek. "I blush when I'm embarrassed."

Moving to the mouth of the mask, she added a smile with the same red paint. "And I smile when I think of my family back home in Croatia. I smile when I think about how R.E.S.C.U.E is making it possible for me to see them again. My name is Monique and I am a human being."

Monique stepped back into line and the short sturdy girl next to her stepped forward. Without a word, the girl picked up a paintbrush, dipped it in blue, and painted a single tear beneath her eye. With a different brush, she put a black circle around the teardrop and for the finishing touch, she put a line through the circle.

"My name is Sheree. I was abducted from a bus stop in New Jersey. I was moved across the country and sold for sex. I used to cry out for someone to save me. Thanks to R.E.S.C.U.E., I now have a face." Sheree slipped on the mask. "My name is Sheree and I am a human being."

The tall, slim girl standing next to Todd took two steps forward, pulled off her mask, and placed it on the table. She picked up a brush and dipped it into the purple paint. She repeated the process with a brush dipped in green, and then she looked up.

"My name is Bilyana. After being promised work in a hair salon in Italy, I was trafficked from Bulgaria to the United States and sold as a slave to a wealthy family in Maryland. I was forced to provide services for the family without pay. I was not allowed to leave. I was not allowed to call home. I was not paid. I was held against my will. I was told that if I tried to escape, my family would be murdered and I would be put in jail. Thanks to a woman named Katelyn from R.E.S.C.U.E., I did escape. I now have a face. I am Bilyana Dimova. I am a human being." Bilyana raised the mask to her face, revealing the purple rose and green stem. She stepped back into line and a girl on the right of Todd stepped out, took off her mask, and began to paint. Her name was Jessica. Sheree, Bilyana, and Monique's stories were troubling, but Jessica's story was even more heart wrenching. At the age of six, her father sold her into trafficking. Now fourteen, she stood before us, small in stature but strong in spirit. She lifted the painted mask to her face, revealing a yellow and red butterfly.

"Like a butterfly, I used to live in a dark cocoon. Thank you R.E.S.C.U.E. for loving me and showing me that, even though I once lived in darkness, I belong in the light. Thank you R.E.S.C.U.E. for giving me a face. I am Jessica Smith and I am a human being."

After the final two girls gave their testimonies, Todd removed his mask and stepped up to the table. With a swift hand, he dipped his brush in paint and moved it over the mask.

"Before you came tonight, you were asked to paint your own identity onto your mask. Some of you painted a picture of how you think others perceive you, while others of you created a mask that portrays how you see yourself. I have to admit, many of you were very creative. Through this fun and simple exercise, I hope I have made a point. Victims of human trafficking have no identity and no self worth. They are treated as property, not people. They have no face. Our goal at R.E.S.C.U.E. is not only to pull men, women, and children out of trafficking, but also to help them discover themselves and the abilities that make them unique. Our job is to help them see the face they were born with, the face that God gave them. Rescue. Shelter. Counsel. Uplift. Empower. I am Todd Catchitore. I have a face. I am an abolitionist. I am a human being." With his final statement, Todd held the mask to his face for all to see.

CHAPTER THIRTY-TWO

Several days after the gala, I began to consider something that seemed completely irrational, absolutely risky, and totally absurd. If I was going to stop Carl, I was going to have to sneak back into his basement. Claire and I had been busy. We had been snapping pictures left and right. We had caught Carl in the act of eating dinner with some pretty shady characters, but each time I sent Lavine new evidence, the detective would dismiss the photos. Circumstantial evidence, he would say. "So, Carl had dinner with the man in the white car. That's no crime," he told me, but I wasn't so sure. I reminded him that it was the same man I had seen making the exchange with Carl Pierce: the large black trash sack that went into the trunk of his shiny white sedan.

And my nightmares had not gotten better; instead, they had only gotten worse. As they became more frequent, I grew to fear Carl more and more. With each dream, his rage increased, and each night when I closed my eyes, the more lifelike the dreams became. Mom was certain my nightmare about Carl was a result of suppressed emotions and repressed memories. Now more than ever, I was convinced that she was wrong. Initially, I thought Gracie Abbot was one of the three girls locked in Carl's basement twenty years ago, but Lavine had squashed that theory. He hadn't heard of Gracie Abbott. So I was back to square one and after a little consideration, I thought I had it figured out. In my dreams, I had seen a box with her name on it. My dreams always foretold the future, and this was no exception. Gracie Abbot wasn't a part of the past, and I had to prepare myself for the fact that I might find more than I bargained for in Carl's basement; there was a chance Gracie Abbott was in his basement, too. Her name was all over my nightmares, and if I wanted to find her, then I must go back down into the dungeon.

Carl was evil. He had to be stopped. Lavine told me he would continue to investigate, but I hadn't heard anything. My mom told me to be patient, but I was growing weary waiting. I was not a patient person; anyone who knew me, knew that. I just knew there had to be some way to get to Carl. To convict him. To lock him away for good. With my purple gel pen, I began to jot down all that I knew about the 1990 trafficking case. There were four witnesses: Eva Pierce, deceased; Monica Bradley, deceased; Terry Dunbarr, in rehab refusing to talk. And last but not least, Isla Martinez, missing. I was at a loss. I considered the other names on the list A-Omega had given me. I had found eight of the ten. There were only two left. Peter Javorskie and Gracie Abbott. I wasn't sure about Peter, but I just knew Gracie was the missing link. She was the girl who could help me put Carl behind bars.

I switched off the lamp and rolled onto my back with a sigh. As I lay in silence, a single thought tore through my mind like a tornado - the Pierce basement. There had to be something in Carl's basement that I had overlooked on my first trip. Last year, the basement was filled with boxes. I had taken plenty of pictures. And then a thought struck me like a bolt of lightning. Pictures. When I received the MacBook Pro from Mom and Dad, I moved the pictures from my old computer onto my new laptop. I still had access to pictures I hadn't looked at in over a year. Faster than the thought occurred to me, I leapt from my bed and took a seat at my desk. With the push of a button, my computer lit up and moments later, I was scrolling through images that reminded me of the horrible night I spent in Carl's basement over a year ago. I could remember the feel of cold concrete and freshly broken ribs like it was yesterday. All at once, I stopped scrolling and let the mouse rest on a single image, an image that brought back memories: a stack of labeled boxes: Missouri. England. France. Holland. Croatia. Germany. Czech Republic. Italy. Oklahoma. Every place I had ever lived. With Chloe approaching the house, I had very little time to investigate my finding. In a rush to get out of the basement, I had quickly reached inside, pulled out a journal, and stuffed it into my bag. Then I did the next best thing; I snapped a picture. When I looked at the picture the next morning, I realized the flash had captured something my eyes had not. In the dark corners of Carl's basement, there were many boxes stacked against the wall. My dream was telling me to investigate the boxes. Of course! Why hadn't I thought of this before? This was huge. Frustrated because the letters on the boxes were too small to read, I zoomed in for a closer look. Much better. Names with dates.

Cory Caswell 1987
Jordan Michelson 1987
Melanie Jackson 1988
Portia Pertrova 1990
Danica Delucy 1990
But no Gracie Abbot.

The boxes were stacked high and spanned the entire wall. At least 150. If only I had thought to take more pictures. If only I could see all of the boxes now. With Lavine refusing to help me, I was left with only one choice. I was going to have to venture into Carl's dungeon and risk my nightmare coming true. It was the only way. I thought about the day Claire and I sat outside his mansion and watched as he handed off a bag of garbage to a man driving a white sedan. I smelled a rat. Carl was disposing of evidence, I just knew it. Will told me to trust my gut, and that's exactly what I planned to do. I had a feeling there was a box in Carl's basement with Gracie's name on it, and I needed to get to it before it was destroyed. Even worse, I had a feeling that Gracie was in his basement, too.

INTERCESSION

CHAPTER THIRTY-THREE

*I*t didn't take much convincing to get Alex to come along. There was no way he was going to let me break into the Pierce mansion without his protection. Besides, after putting the finishing touches on his 56 Speedster, he looked for any excuse to take his hotrod out on highway 75, a long, straight stretch of road where he could put the numbers on the speedometer to the test. Would his car really reach 200 miles per hour? Alex agreed to go on one condition: We would have to be absolutely certain Carl was away from home when we went in. "And this," he said, "will take a little planning." But I didn't want to plan. I didn't want to wait. Hearing Professor Catchitore speak always got me revved up. ProfC might be quirky, but he was a gifted speaker and you couldn't leave one of his seminars without feeling a burning desire to protect the rights of others. People's lives were on the line. I was ready to hop in the car and go now! So I tried to argue the issue from a different angle. I tried to convince Alex that *waiting* would cost people their lives and then I reminded him that there was a good chance Gracie was in Carl's basement. Alex was quick with a comeback and eager to refresh my memory. "Our lives are on the line too, Rae."

I wasn't completely convinced and absolutely refused to budge until he brought up the fact that Carl would be in New York on business later in the week and that if we could somehow verify his plans to leave the state, then our wait would not be long. With a bit of reluctance, I not only agreed to hold off on the operation for a few days, but also to let Alex do all the planning. I hated the lack of control.

Two days later, Alex showed up at my house with a copy of the Tulsa World. Very proud of himself, he pointed to the featured article in the Sunday morning paper. The title grabbed my attention: "Self-Made Mogul to visit New York City." I went on to read the story and although I now felt more ready than ever, I was appalled that the journalist, Daria Tandee, made Carl into a Saint. "A man from humble beginnings... A rich man with a big heart." Was I the only one who saw Carl for what he really was? Daria went on to call him "A positive role model." Gag. "A team player." Please. "Not afraid to get his hands dirty." Oh, he had dirty hands all right, and I was going to prove it. And when I did, I was going to suggest Daria Tandee write up the article on his arrest. She'd soon be singing a different tune. The thought of it made me feel *slightly* better.

With the stakeout still a week away, Alex wanted to spend all of our time planning. So, I spent sleepless nights in bed, tucked under my batik duvet, with a pad of paper on my lap and my faithful purple gel pen in my hand. I was making a list of my concerns, a list of things to look for in Carl's basement, and yet another list of items we should consider taking along. I was running on fumes: adrenaline and plenty of caffeine. I had bitten my nails down to nothing. Planning was not my forte and this *process* was driving me crazy! I was a fly by the seat of my pants kind of girl and if it was up to me, I would take matters into my own hands. I would not be lying in bed taking notes, that's for sure.

I thought back to the snowy day in March. After reading Eva's journal, I hopped in the Wagoneer and headed to the Bodin's home in the middle of a snowstorm without taking the time to think things through. Instead of planning, I just let my emotions take me there. I didn't need to remind myself of what happened. I would never forget that day. But this time things *were* different. This wasn't just about me. We were fighting for the poster of a girl: strawberry blond hair and freckled cheeks. We were fighting for Jessie Paulman. For Gracie Abbott, whoever she might be. We were fighting for Terry Dunbarr. Monica Bradley. We were fighting for those who were yet to be freed. And Alex was right; we needed to plan. What good were we if Carl caught us? How could we help if we were dead?

Finally, the day had arrived. I stood in the kitchen with Mom and Dad, looking out the window, eagerly watching for headlights coming up the dark gravel road, while they offered me words of wisdom. "Call us as soon as you get to Tulsa," they instructed. "And let us know what you find," my father added.

"Don't forget to bring a flashlight," Mom suggested. "It's dark out there."

I turned to them and forced a weak smile. "I'm going to be fine. Alex is coming with me. He's protected me in the past and he'll protect me now."

Although they were pretending not to be worried, I could see the concern in their eyes.

"Well, take lots of pictures." Dad handed me his expensive Canon digital SLR.

"Alex is bringing his camera," I told him.

"Take it." Dad hung the camera around my neck. "Alex's camera's great, but it's old. I guess it's okay if you want to wait for the film to be developed."

"Fine."

"And are you sure that's what you want to wear?" Mom asked. "Those pants are so tight. I just don't see how you can move in them."

"They're leggings, Mom. They're stretchy. And I'm fine."

Mom gave me an encouraging smile. Dad gave me a hug. Mom offered food. I refused, explaining to her that my stomach was a bit uneasy. Dad said he understood and then went on to tell me about the first time he ever felt like someone else's life was in his hands. It was comforting to know that I was not the only one who had felt this way before.

It was a quarter till nine when we moved the conversation to the front porch. Alex was on his way. We could hear him before we could see his headlights. His music was turned up and bass was blasting from his speakers.

Dad looked at me concerned. "I'm not trying to tell you what to do," Dad began. "But if Alex wants to get the two of you into Carl's basement unnoticed, he's going to have to turn that music down. And the car? Not very inconspicuous. It's flashy."

Standing in the glow of the front porch light, Dad shook his head and folded his arms across his chest. He looked worried and I noticed that Mom shared his expression. "I just don't know about this. Alex is a smart guy, but you're my daughter and I'm beginning to wonder what he's thinking."

"Dad, it'll be fine… I promise."

"Well, just make sure he adjusts the volume."

"I will."

When Alex turned up the driveway, he turned down the stereo and when he pulled in front of the house, I gave Mom and Dad a hug, slung my bag over my shoulder, and descended the porch stairs. Alex opened the car door for me but before sliding in, I looked over at my parents. Dad gave me the thumbs up and a smile. Mom pretended she was holding a phone to her ear and mouthed the words "Call me." I nodded and mouthed back, "I will."

Once on the highway, Alex put the convertible top down. I adjusted the volume on the stereo, relaxed into the plush leather seat, and closed my eyes. I let the wind blow through my hair. *I have purpose*, I thought. *I have never felt so alive.*

Breaking into Carl's basement was just as easy as the last time I did it. Alex was concerned there might be an alarm and he was completely prepared to disarm it, if need be. While I was *relieved* that sirens didn't blare as soon as we lifted the cellar doors, Alex was growing more and more suspicious.

"I'm not sure this is a good idea," he whispered. "No one leaves information in their basement... information that could put them away for life, and then just leaves the door wide open. Especially while out of state on business."

"It wasn't wide open," I reminded him as I moved down the cellar stairs into the basement. "There was a lock on it."

"But no alarm. This doesn't feel right, Rae. We should go... *now*."

"No. We're not going."

"Rae..."

"Alex, it was like this last time. Except last time there wasn't a lock," I said as my feet touched the concrete floor.

"I still don't like it, Rae. It's too easy. Something's off." His voice was warning.

Ignoring him, I pulled the flashlight out of my bag. By the time Alex made it down the stairs into the basement, I had already found the boxes stacked against the wall. I turned to him with a smile on my face.

"The boxes are still here, just like I remember. It doesn't look like he's touched a thing. We'll be in and out of here in less than five minutes. I promise."

I shone my flashlight on Alex. He nervously stood with my dad's Cannon SLR hung around his neck. I reached into my bag and handed him a flashlight. Reluctantly, he accepted it.

"This is just all too perfect. We need to go... now, Rae. Let the police deal with this."

"Do you not see what I'm standing in front of, Alex?" I shone my flashlight on the boxes. Stacked high, there were at least a hundred. Alex turned on his flashlight and moved in for a closer look. He took off the lens cap and began snapping pictures.

"All of the boxes have names and dates on them," he remarked.

"I told you that before we came down here."

"I know you did. It's just that seeing it is something different," he said as he snapped another picture. "Why do you think he labels everything?"

With the camera in his hands, it seemed that Alex had relaxed a bit. "Don't you think that's a little incriminating?"

"Carl's proud. He doesn't think he's going to get caught," I whispered as I pulled a box away from the wall and began to peel off the tape.

"Wait. Before you open it, let me take a picture of the front."

I stepped back and watched Alex at work. Alex was right. Hearing about the boxes and talking about the boxes was so much different than seeing the boxes. In Carl's basement, the cardboard came to life. They represented the girl whose name was printed across the front.

Alex wiped his hand across his eye and sniffed. "There's so much dust."

"God only knows how long this stuff has been down here," I reminded him.

When I saw a flash of light, I knew Alex had captured the image. Standing in the darkness, he was looking at the picture on the LED screen. "Yolanda Ponce. 1986. This box has been down here for over twenty years."

When Alex stepped back, I advanced. A wide strip of tape was holding the lid together. I felt for the end of the tape, wishing I had my nails back so I could easily lift up a corner, but with a little persistence, I caught the edge and ripped it off in one quick yank. Alex aimed his flashlight inside the box, and I began rummaging through it. Clothes. Shoes. A small plastic bag containing jewelry. An I.D. A pack of gum. A pack of Lucky Strikes. A lighter. "These boxes are Carl's trophies, Alex. This is what each girl was wearing when they were abducted. He keeps all of this so he can remember each girl."

"He's sick."

"Yeah. This is worse than I thought it would be."

"There's no way we can go through all of these boxes. You know that, right."

"I know. I'm just looking for two names, right now. Jessie Paulman and Gracie Abbot. That's the whole reason we came. But take as many pictures as you can. Get close ups of all the names. Anything will help. I want to present the perfect case to Lavine. I don't want any loose ends."

"Is he still hesitant about going after Carl?"

"Yes and no. Lavine's onto Carl. It's just that he has his ways and I have mine."

Alex continued to snap pictures. He started at the south end of the room while I started at the north. Fifteen minutes later, my persistence paid off.

"Alex. Come here."

"Did you find something?"

"I found Jessie's box!"

I could hear Alex moving toward me.

"It's the box on top. I think I can pull it down if you give me a boost." I raised the beam of light, moving it up the wall toward the ceiling.

"I can't believe this," Alex whispered as he approached. "We have to get it down. Do you think you could reach it standing on my shoulders?"

"I think so."

"Okay. Let's do this."

Alex got down on one knee and lifted bent arms into the air. I placed my hands in his. I put one foot on his shoulder and then the other.

"Here's the plan." Alex grimaced as I adjusted my feet. He let go of my hands and wrapped his arms around my lower legs to hold me steady. "We need to get the box down, look inside, and take some pictures. But then I think we need to get out."

"What about Gracie?" I whispered. "Her box is here. I can feel it. What if she's here too?"

"I don't think Gracie's here, Rae. We would have heard something by now. It's quiet. Are you doing okay up there?"

"Yeah. If you're sure you have me, then I think I have the box."

"Grab it. I have you."

"The box is heavy, Alex. Are you sure?"

"I'm sure." I could hear him straining.

"Okay. On the count of three I'm going to grab it."

"I'll be fine," he promised. "Okay. On the count of three."

"This box weighs at least twenty pounds. Maybe thirty. Are you sure you're okay?"

"And you're not getting any lighter, Sunshine. The heels of your combat boots are leaving permanent marks on my shoulders."

"Sorry." I set the flashlight down on the edge of a neighboring box.

"Okay. One. Two. Three." I grasped Jessie's box and pulled it off the stack.

"I've got it," I told him. I had done my part, but when Alex didn't respond, and when I felt his left hand slip from my lower leg, I realized he might not be able to follow through like he had promised. Not strong enough to hold the weight of the box and me, he began to stumble. Trying to recover, he returned his left hand to my calf to keep me steady, but it was too late. When he lost his grip, I lost my balance. With the heavy box in my arms, I began to sway back and forth.

CRASH!

The sound came from below but it wasn't until I saw the beam of light shining across the basement floor that I realized what had happened. Standing on Alex's shoulders, waving like a tree in the wind, I had knocked the flashlight off the box where I had placed it. It was the beginning of the end; the box was the next thing to go, and as I felt it slip from my grasp, I tried to warn Alex of what was coming, but before the words could leave my mouth, the plummeting box made contact with the hard ground, creating a loud, dull thud.

Startled, Alex jolted. His hand was all that was keeping me on his shoulders, and when I felt it slip away, I lost my balance completely and just like the box and the flashlight before it, I started to fall. Grasping in the dark, I reached out for anything that might break my fall, upsetting Carl's wall of trophies in the process. The next thing I knew, I was sprawled out on the hard concrete floor among the contents of at least a dozen different boxes.

"Are you okay? I'm so sorry." Alex was at my side in an instant.

"I think I broke something," I groaned.

"I'm so sorry."

"I told you the box was heavy."

"Can I help you up?"

"No. Just let me lie here for a minute."

Alex picked up the flashlight and shone it across the floor. "Well, I think we've found what we were looking for."

Slowly, I sat up and let my eyes follow the halo of light. A backpack. A pair of boots. A pair of socks. A hat. Gloves. "Stop!" I nearly shouted when my eyes fell on a tartan piece of cloth. As I crawled over to the object, I flashed back to a morning several months ago when I joined my dad for breakfast in the kitchen. I had been sipping on a cup of coffee when he suggested that I read the article on the front page. The article about Jessie Paulman, the missing Tulsa teen.

But Jessie Paulman, clad in a tartan wool coat, never arrived.

"Jessie's coat," I whispered. "Grab my bag, Al-"

"Shhh. Did you hear that?" Alex interjected.

"What? NO. Grab my bag."

Alex hesitated but finally obliged.

"It sounded like someone was opening a door."

"No one's here Alex. Carl's in New York, remember." I stuffed Jessie's coat and a few of her other personal items into my bag.

"I remember… but."

Then I heard it too. Alex stood up at once and completely disregarding the pain in my right arm, I followed suit.

"No, it doesn't sound like a door. It's a soft thumping noise that I'm hearing, Alex."

"Where's it coming from?"

A chill swept over my body.

"Maybe the noise is coming from Carl's workshop." When realization hit me, the sickness that developed in the pit of my stomach grew stronger than the pain I was experiencing as a result of the fall. Maybe I wasn't supposed to find Gracie Abbott's box, I thought. Maybe I was supposed to find Gracie Abbott. Carl's workshop was in the basement, but where in the basement? I had only seen it in my dreams and read about it in Eva's journal. I closed my eyes and tried to take myself there. I focused on listening.

"I think the noise is coming from over here, Alex." I reached for the flashlight and aimed it at a door on the other side of the room. I thought about Eva's journal entry. The light switch was beside the door, outside of the room. "I think the noise is coming from behind that door. I think that's Carl's workshop!"

I expected Alex to affirm my assumption. I expected to hear his smooth, honey like voice; instead, I saw a light in my peripheral vision and when I turned toward it, two things happened almost at once: I heard the sound of a door opening and I saw a man standing in the hallway at the top of the stairs.

CHAPTER THIRTY-FOUR

"**M**y workshop?" At the sound of his gravely voice, I felt my blood go cold. "Is that what you like to call it? That's what Eva liked to call it, too."

Carl paused a moment before continuing. "And what exactly do you think you'll find in there?" he asked as he casually descended the stairs.

Still frozen to the floor in fear, neither Alex nor I could respond. Why was I shocked? Why was I surprised? My nightmare had warned me this would happen. But Carl was supposed to be in New York, and we were supposed to have the house all to ourselves.

Out of habit, Alex moved to my side and put a protective arm around my waist. *This cannot be happening*, I thought. As Carl moved in on us, I began to wonder why Alex wasn't doing anything to help. Why wasn't he fighting? To make matters worse, I could feel him trembling. In a moment's time, Carl was standing in front of me, looking far less impressive than he did on the cover of Forbes. Alex released his arm from around my waist and moved in front of me, using his body to guard me, using himself as a shield to protect me from my father. I placed my hands on his shoulders, keeping him close.

"I have often thought about how nice it would be to have both of my daughters at home, under the same roof at the same time." His voice cracked and he cleared his throat. "Your March 16th message was received... loud and clear, Sunshine. Or are you going by Miss Jones now?" He laughed. "I think you should know something about me, Rae. I've never settled for less. If I can't have it all, then I want nothing. I never look back and I never leave behind anything that will remind me of failure." Carl licked his lips and reached into the pocket of his jacket. "Do you get my drift? Do you understand what I'm saying?"

March 16th? What was he talking about? Then all at once, I remembered. That was the day Chloe died. I knew exactly what he was trying to say. If he couldn't have the both of us, if the three of us couldn't live together as one happy family, then he didn't want a family at all. I was a reminder of all he had lost. He thought if he got rid of me, then he could rid himself of the pain he felt over losing Chloe. No. Not pain. Failure. When Chloe died, his plan was thwarted. He didn't want a family in the way most people want a family. He wanted possessions. He wanted trophies. I killed his dream. I was a reminder of his failure. Now he wanted me dead.

"Do you understand what I'm saying?"

I could feel tears welling up in my eyes and a hard lump forming in my throat. I nodded my head as Carl drew closer and pulled a shiny silver object from his pocket, pointing it in our direction.

"On the floor. Starting with you Ian Limbeaux."

My hands were still on Alex's shoulders and I felt his muscles tighten. I thought he was preparing to fight back. I thought he was getting ready to attack Carl with the same force that he had used on Ben. Instead, I felt him sinking slowly to the floor.

What are you doing!? I wanted to scream. *What's going on?* I wanted to ask him. Where is my Alex? I watched in horror as Alex slumped to the floor of the basement in defeat. Where was my warrior? Carl aimed the small revolver in my direction and then used it to motion me to the floor beside my boyfriend. I fell to my hands and knees, joining Alex on the hard concrete. Was this a part of Alex's plan? Did he have something up his sleeve?

In the past, whenever Alex sensed I was in danger, he didn't hesitate. But now, Alex was cooperating with Carl. Surely he knew what he was doing, but I didn't think that this was the time or place to be trying out a new defense strategy. I lifted my head and glanced in Alex's direction. When he wouldn't look me in the eye, I knew we were in trouble. Scanning the room, I took notice of the cellar door Alex had closed on our way in. With the door shut, no one could hear me scream. Escape felt a million miles away. All at once, I thought of my cell phone. Discretely, I slipped my hand into the pocket of my jacket and felt for the object that might very well be our only hope.

"Head down and hands out of your pocket," Carl barked. I felt a rush of adrenaline as he pressed the barrel of the gun against the back of my head, and then an even greater wave of panic when I heard him pull back the hammer. "I think you've done enough looking around for one day. You are so much like your mother. She was always going through my personal items."

As he continued to rant, Carl moved the gun away from the base of my skull and pointed it in Alex's direction. "I gave her everything she ever wanted. But she wanted more. So self-righteous," he said, disgusted. "Always suspicious. Oh, and just so you know. Your cell phone won't work down here. Not a chance."

My thoughts were a swirling tornado of fear and regret. There were so many things I wanted to say in Eva's defense. I now understood why she felt so trapped. He was controlling. She was scared. Scared to leave and scared to stay. Now more than ever, I realized the strength it took to do what Eva did. The courage it took to take a stand… to do what was right in the face of wrong. Carl hit Alex in the back of the head with the butt of the gun, sending him from his hands and knees onto his stomach. Carl kicked him, forcing him over onto his back then pointed the weapon at Alex's head, giving him no other choice than to look down the barrel of the gun. Alex held his eyes open wide and faced his eminent death head on, but I couldn't bear to look. I couldn't witness what was about to happen. Eyes closed tight, I was just about to accept our fate when the click of an empty chamber reverberated throughout the basement. It took a moment to appreciate what this sound meant for the two of us: Alex was still alive, and Carl was out of bullets.

"What do you know? I haven't used a gun in years. I'm a bit rusty. I generally don't do the dirty work myself." Carl sighed. "Okay, this is what's going to happen. Without any resistance, the both of you are going to stand up."

Was this a second chance? Carl's empty chamber had bought us some time. With my feet still rooted to the basement floor in fear, I began to think of our options. If only I had thought to bring a weapon. I was defenseless. Or maybe not. All at once, I thought of Detective Lavine and the plaque that hung on his wall. The scripture was burned into my memory and I recited it silently to myself.

The weapons we fight with are not the weapons of the world. 2 Corinthians 10:4.

Prayer. Before this moment, I had prayed, but I had been hesitant to trust in prayer alone. Perhaps because I was accustomed to taking care of myself. Maybe it was because I was stubborn and wanted to do things my own way. But I did want to trust. I did want to believe. So maybe it had more to do with the fact that I just didn't know how to let go.

Still crouched on the floor, I closed my eyes and began to reflect on the few times I had spoken to God and the amazing ways He had answered. My prayers always started out the same: "God, are you listening?" But tonight I didn't need to ask, because I knew God was here and that He *was* listening. I could feel my brooch beginning to warm as I began to talk to God. And strangely enough, as Carl continued to speak, I barely heard him. As Carl moved us toward his workshop door, I continued to pray silently. Carl opened the door and switched on the light. It had taken fifty-five steps to get there, but I barely remember the walk. Without warning or delay, I was thrown across the room. When my body made contact with the basement wall, the air was forced from my lungs. Crumpled on the floor, I gasped for breath, but never stopped praying. I heard another bone crushing thud and without even having to look, I realized Alex and I had arrived at the same destination and that we were about to experience the same fate. I opened my eyes in time to see Carl standing before us, sweeping his arm across his desolate workshop.

"Welcome to my humble abode. Consider this your own private room for the time being. I hope it's cozy." Reaching into the drawer of the file cabinet, Carl retrieved a sizable knife and began to move toward us. I stared into Carl's eyes, not allowing him the satisfaction of intimidating me, not even for a moment.

Sharper than any double edge sword, I thought, *is the word of God.*

As if he could hear my thoughts, Carl staggered backward, stumbling over his feet. With a look of confusion, he studied the large knife in his right hand, and then let it drop to the ground. His eyes filled with anger. His face changed from olive to crimson red as he shifted his focus to me. With a snarled lip, he moved toward us once again; however, with less finesse. He looked shaken, like he had just received an unexpected punch to the gut from an invisible bystander. Alex was moaning quietly on the floor beside me, but I didn't dare take my eyes off my father as he approached. With a quick hand, Carl grabbed me roughly, gripping me by my hair and pulling me to my feet.

"While I have your attention, I wanted to tell you a little story." He still had hold of my hair and unable to move, I could do nothing but listen to what he had to say. I cringed at the sound of his voice, the gravely sound of a man who had smoked heavily for years. He leaned in, hovering just inches above me. I could smell smoke on his clothes and liquor on his breath. The overpowering smell filled my nostrils, and I began to cough and gag, which was enough to halt Carl; however, he did not back away.

"It was a cold and rainy night about seven years ago," he began in a throaty whisper. "I was in Prague checking on one of my overseas branches. I had just locked up for the night when a little girl stumbled into the alleyway. Soaking wet and carrying her schoolbooks under her arm, I backed into the shadows to see where she was going. She stood for a moment in the middle of the street looking to her left and then her right. My first thought was that she was lost and that she was trying to get her bearings. I was just about to continue on my way when the girl walked over to my office and looked into the window. Well, now she really had my attention. Still hidden in the shadows, I continued to watch the girl as she peered through the glass. The office was furnished with a desk. On top of the desk sat a typewriter. So I began to wonder what the girl was looking at. That's when I realized she was looking at her own reflection. Although the night was dark, the lamppost in the distance shone onto the glass and I could see the little girl's face as clearly as if she were looking into a mirror." Carl cleared his throat, studying me for a moment, checking for my reaction. I thought that even a simple change of expression would have pleased him, so I held my lips in a tight pinch. Shaking on the inside, I tried to control the emotions that were flowing through me. Carl cleared his throat and continued.

"You can't imagine how I felt when I saw the angel of my dead wife staring back at me." He leaned in closer. I could feel his breath on my ear. "I couldn't help myself. I had to know for sure. But when I moved toward the girl, she fled. I did my best to follow her, but I lost her in the shadows. I swore to myself that if I ever found her again, I wouldn't let her go. I would bring her home. I would finally have both of my daughters." Carl's tone changed. "But that's not possible now, is it? If you think you can slip away again, you're wrong. I don't trust you any further than I could throw a stick. I have in mind a better way to keep you where I want you."

I could not do this on my own. I shut my eyes tight and continued to pray. I felt Carl's hand tighten around my wrist and then he lifted my arm into the air. Body weak, but spirit strong, I trembled and continued to pray, to silently cry out for help. Anticipating excruciating pain, I was taken aback when I felt something hard and cold take the place of Carl's smooth hand. A wave of relief washed over me. But when the weight of the object around my wrist brought my weak body to the floor, I looked down to find that I had been shackled. An old-fashioned steel shackle was fastened around my wrist, securing me to the wall of Carl's workshop with a heavy chain. With an iron key, Carl locked me into a heavy cuff. When I began to resist, he spoke.

"Don't fight it." His tone was steely. "You won't believe how much trouble it was to get these shackles and you wouldn't believe the thousands of people that these exact shackles have bound. Not in my day of course. These shackles are over 200 years old. You should feel like you're a part of history."

CHAPTER THIRTY-FIVE

I tucked my knees to my chest and began to shake. As lies began to fill my mind, I began to fight them with the truth. "God," I whispered. "You wouldn't have brought me this far to fail. You have always been there for me, just like you are now. I'm so tired of doing everything in my own strength. I can't do this." I looked up to find Carl repeating the same process with Alex, fastening him to the wall of the basement with little hope of escape. Alex continued to moan, but showed no signs of resistance. Once Alex was locked in, Carl held out his gun and moved backward toward the door.

"I'll be back shortly," Carl snorted. "Just long enough for you two love birds to say your goodbyes. I can't believe I'm out of bullets," he laughed. "Don't worry about screaming for help. No one will hear you. I've gone to a lot of trouble to make sure no one on the outside can hear the activities that take place in this room. You can try to use your cell phone, but it won't work. No reception. Move around all you want, but you'll only bruise your wrists. Those iron shackles are heavy."

With that, Carl switched off the light and slammed the door, not bothering to lock it from the outside. Ever since I saw Carl's hazy figure standing at the top of the basement stairs, I hadn't allowed myself to take a single breath. Now that he was gone, I took in a greedy gasp of air and cringed. The pain reminded me that I had fallen. With my back against the wall, I looked at Alex, who was still lying on his side, but no longer moaning. With my left hand, I reached out to touch him and felt his body flinch beneath my fingers. I wanted nothing more than to cry. For what? For everything. To see the man that I loved defenseless. To realize the man that I had put up on a pedestal was only human. He could no more save me than I could save myself. Neither one of us could break free on our own. I wanted to cry for his injured pride. Without knowing it, I placed upon him expectations and whether the words were said or not, he felt more defeated over the fact that he could not protect me than he did over the possibility of losing his own life.

"I am so sorry," his voice cracked.

Tears were rolling down my cheeks. "For what?"

"I've failed you."

"No. No, you haven't."

"I don't belong here."

"I know you don't, and I shouldn't have dragged you into this mess. I'm the one who's sorry. Carl Pierce is my father, my mission. This is my battle, not yours."

But when he said he didn't belong, I knew Alex wasn't talking about Carl Pierce's basement, he was talking about the world in which he didn't seem to fit.

"There's a line that separates this world from the next. I moved backwards. I crossed that line. I went the wrong way down a one-way street... for you, Rae. For you." Alex's voice trailed off. He sounded sleepy.

"Alex?"

He didn't respond, and seeing him defeated, broke me into a thousand different pieces. He had developed fears of his own and he had let those fears control him.

The room was dark, but still I closed my eyes, hopeful that merely shutting them would erase the gruesome images from my mind, the images of the girls who were locked in this exact room twenty years ago. I wondered if any other girls had shared this room since then. I could almost hear the same screams that Eva heard when I was still inside her womb. *Help!* Was that even possible? My body ached and with my free hand, I rotated the heavy shackle on my left wrist, moving it away from the bony prominence where it had already worn away the skin.

With my free hand, I pulled my phone from my pocket and checked for a signal. Carl was right. I had absolutely no reception. Slipping the phone back into my jacket, I hugged my legs, and rested my head on my knees. With the palm of my left hand, I felt for the antique broach that was pinned above my heart, remembering how on occasion, I had felt it quiver beneath my fingers.

"You sent me on a mission and my objective was Carl Pierce. But every time I take a step forward, I take two steps back. Every path leads to a dead end. You told me to ask for help when I come to a crossroads. I have done this and still I wind up in the wrong place at the wrong time. What is the truth? I know all about my truth. And I know all about lies. I thought I was supposed to lock Carl up; instead, I'm the one in chains. Is there something I'm missing? Is there something else you want from me?"

A vibration from my jacket pocket interrupted my train of thought. I had received a new text. Surely not. Carl said there was no reception in the basement. Slowly, I pulled out my phone and read the text.

It's not what I want FROM you, it's what I want FOR you, Rae.

With a trembling hand, I began to type my response into the phone.

Do you want me to be locked in chains?

I hit send.

The shackle around your wrist is not what I'm referring to. I'm more troubled by the one around your heart.

I'm trying and I'm failing.

Why don't you let me try?

I typed my response; the only answer there was to give.

Okay.

When I pushed send, the brooch on my chest began to shake with such force that I dropped my phone and held my heart. The pin was warm to the touch and as I cupped my hand around it, the temperature began to rise exponentially until the metal was nearly too hot to hold. Not letting go, I felt the heat radiate inward, filling me with a warmth that was surprisingly satisfying. My jaw was no longer quivering. The cold, damp basement no longer had an effect on me.

How am I going to get out of this mess? How do I let go? How do I let you? How am I going to break free?

My phone lit up with a new text message. Still holding onto the brooch, I picked up the phone and read:

Then you will know the truth, and the truth will set you free.

As my brooch continued to quiver, I recalled the visit I paid to the jeweler. How could I forget the expression of disbelief that formed on Mason Armishaw's face as he inspected the priceless gift? His words rang loud and clear. "This brooch is at least fifteen hundred years old. This symbol is representative of the holy trinity: the father, the son, and the Holy Spirit. The fleur-de-lis symbolizes the search for spiritual truth. TRUTH."

There was something more. I pushed myself to remember everything I could about the conversation I had with Mr. Armishaw. With my eyes shut tightly, I tried to remember not only his words, but also his simple gestures. I tried to visualize him holding the brooch and the special attention he paid to the detail of the clasp. A shadow in my memory, Mason flipped the breastpin over to study the back. Delicately lifting the pin on the back of the brooch with tip of his finger, he admired the craftsmanship. "Sharp enough to prick a finger, sharp enough to pick a lock," he said.

I gasped and sat bolt upright. "Alex," I shouted. "I've got it. I've got our way out."

When Alex didn't respond, I began to worry. He had taken a pretty hard blow to the head. I was shaking with anticipation and revelation but thankfully, my hands were steady. Quickly, I unpinned the brooch from my shirt and held the pin between my forefinger and thumb. I had never picked a lock before, much less the lock of an ancient shackle, but I was about to give it a try and I had a feeling it would work. With a delicate hand, I inserted the pin into the keyhole and began to move it around, hoping for a little bit of luck. Carl had placed me in shackles that were ancient, but A-Omega, God, had given me a gift that was much older than that. The lock was strong, but the shaft of my pin was stronger. Finally, I heard the artifact click as it unlocked, and the shackle fell loose. My wrist was sore, but I was free. I scrambled to my feet and fell at Alex's side. My presence startled him and he looked at me with wild apprehension. Gazing into my eyes, he stared at me in awe. I held out the fleur-de-lis pin and he nodded his head in sudden acknowledgement. He didn't speak, nor did he ask any questions, he simply extended his arm so the pin could free him as well.

I removed the shackle from his wrist but Alex showed no signs of moving. Turning my back on him, I pushed open the door and rushed out of the workshop and up the concrete steps to the cellar doors. Using all my strength, I heaved them open. How long had we been in Carl's basement? It was nighttime when we went in, and it was still dark. Still and quiet. The moon was full and the stars were shining. Racing back down the steps, I grabbed Alex and pulled relentlessly.

"Alex. Please, please, get up. We have to go. Now." I knelt down and kissed his cheek. "Please, please, please." Tears were rolling down my face when he finally opened his eyes. "Come on, babe. We have to get out of here."

I kissed his forehead and then his lips. I held his head in my lap and smoothed his hair.

"Please God," I prayed aloud. "Please help him get up. Please, God. Don't be far from us. Trouble is near and there's no one to help."

I held my eyes closed in prayer until finally Alex stirred. With all the strength I had, I helped him to his feet. I led him to the steps and out of the basement. We stood at the mouth of the cellar. The night air was chilly and the cool breeze that blew across Alex's face brought him back to me. Slowly, Alex moved toward me and grabbed my face in his hands. He pressed his lips to mine. I could feel his trembling. "Thank you," he whispered. "Thank you for saving me." His voice was ragged with emotion. Hand in hand, we ran from Carl Pierce's dungeon, leaving my darkness behind.

CHAPTER THIRTY-SIX

*T*he close call in Carl's basement was completely worth it. I still didn't know the identity of Gracie Abbot, but I had everything I needed to prove Carl was a crook, a thief, a murderer, and that he had a hand in the disappearance of Jessie Paulman. I had Jessie's belongings in my bag. Her wallet. Her earrings. Her lip gloss. Her tartan wool coat. I cursed the long drive to Tulsa. What I had to say, what I needed to show Detective Lavine had the ability to lock Carl Pierce up for good. I was still thirty minutes from the precinct. I could hardly wait. I pressed my foot down hard on the accelerator, hoping and praying I wouldn't get a ticket on the way. I turned the music down so I could think. Carl knew exactly what I discovered in his basement; the evidence was spread across his basement floor. He also knew I suspected his involvement in the Jessie Paulman case. This made things more complicated. As far as evidence was concerned, what I managed to escape with was only the tip of the iceberg. There were so many boxes. The lives of so many different girls. It was a race against time. I had to get this information to Lavine before Carl disposed of any evidence.

Each box was a life and with each life, there was a family aching for answers... for closure. Plus, I couldn't help but think about my life, Alex's life. Because we knew too much, we were now in danger. I thought about what happened to Monica Bradley when she agreed to testify against Carl Pierce. She was put under witness protection, but still she wound up dead. I thought about my parents. They were in danger, too. I glanced at the highway sign. Seventeen miles to Tulsa. Getting close. I thought about the drive home from Tulsa last night. Long and quiet. When Alex pulled into the circle drive in front of our house, Mom and Dad were waiting for us on the front porch. Both Alex and I had taken a beating and we were sore. I had pain in both my chest and arm from when Alex dropped me, and my wrist was already beginning to bruise from the heavy shackle. Alex didn't look so great himself. His left eye was swollen shut and already black and blue, and there was a large gash just below his eyebrow. Cuts to the face always bleed profusely and although the cut *was* deep, his bloodstained shirt made the injury look much worse than it actually was.

The porch light was on and we could see Sue and Will, but standing in the darkness, Alex and I were shadows in the night. We were figures moving toward them; they had no idea of the condition we were in. Mom had her hand on her hip and Dad's arms were folded across his chest. I hadn't called like I had promised. I left them waiting and they were mad; their body language was obvious. Alex and I hobbled up the brick stairs, toward the front door. Now standing in front of them with the light shining down on our injuries, they began to sing a different tune. No longer angry, Mom started to cry. Arms no longer folded across his chest, Dad went into survival mode. He helped us into the house and then he set up a makeshift triage in the living room. He began preparing ice packs. He used a penlight to look into Alex eyes, and was relieved that Alex's pupils were the normal size, even after the hard blow he had taken to the head. No permanent damage had been done. I was holding my side. The pain came in throbbing waves. Dad asked me what was wrong and this time I told him. Dad tried to help me, to fix me… this time I let him. My mom fought back tears and as she and my dad began dressing our wounds, Alex and I shared with them the events of the night the best we could remember. Sue and Will were kind. The kindest people I had ever met. I was lucky to call them Mom and Dad. Their lives were on the line as well. They were not exempt from Carl's wrath. Their lives had been in jeopardy once before and I had run away to protect them. But this time, I wasn't running. I was holding my ground. I was ready to fight and I had all the ammo I needed in my bag.

An hour later, I was at the police station and although it hurt to do so, I stood in the doorway of Detective Lavine's office yelling at the top of my lungs.

"I don't understand why!" I was screaming and my broken ribs were screaming back. I had taken great stakes breaking into Carl's basement, and I had escaped with enough evidence for Lavine to make an arrest. "Why won't this hold up in court?" I shouted.

"We can start with Breaking and Entering, if you like," Lavine began.

He rose to his feet and walked over to the door and shut it quietly, trying to keep the conversation between the two of us. But through the glass, I could see the many eyes staring back and I realized at once that my shouts had caught the attention of everyone at the station.

"I've been looking into these files for years, but like I told you before, we have to do things the right way. Carl Pierce is a prominent figure and there are many people here that believe he's an innocent man. I'm not saying I'm one of them, but let's not stir the pot until we're sure we have the right ingredients. Do you get what I'm trying to say?" the detective asked as he walked back to his desk. "Twenty years ago Carl Pierce was charged with a heinous crime. He was tried and acquitted."

"But what about Terry. You don't seem to care that I found her."

"I care, but you're forgetting Double Jeopardy. You can't be charged for the same crime twice."

"Maybe, but what if she could attest to the kind of man Carl is."

"Terry doesn't want to talk, Rae."

"Because she's scared."

"Probably."

"Because after she leaves rehab, she has no safe place to go."

"Right again."

"Then do something. Protect her. Don't let Terry become another Monica Bradley."

The detective shrugged his shoulders in defeat and shook his head.

"Look, Lavine, there are at least one hundred boxes in Carl's basement filled with items just like these. There you have it, all of your missing persons' cases solved in one raid."

"Believe me, the evidence is tempting," Lavine said while sipping on a cup of coffee. "But I'm bound. There's nothing I can do."

"Less than forty-eight hours ago, I was locked in shackles and chained to Carl's workshop wall. Please don't speak to *me* about being bound. Nothing is impossible."

"Your ideas are great, but it's easier said than done."

"Where there's a will there's a way."

"I'm sorry, Rae. I'm on this case, believe me, but right now there is nothing *I* can do," Lavine raised his voice while putting emphasis on the word "I".

"I came here so that you could hear my story and let me know my options. What I'm hearing you say is that I have none. Have you ever wanted something so badly you could taste it?"

"Yes. And the lesson I learned is not one I'll soon forget. I'm a firm believer in patience. When you go out meddling, you begin to disrupt the natural order of things. There are plenty of detectives that would debate this issue, but I believe the bad get what they deserve. I believe you reap what you sow. If you plant bad seeds, you'll get a bad harvest. Carl is a criminal, but he's rich and well respected. I've ruined my reputation chasing this man before. Only recently has the public given me any slack. I don't plan on going down that road again."

"It's your job. You have to go down that road."

"Carl Pierce has been sowing bad seeds for twenty years, at least. Sin has a way of catching up with the sinner. Carl's been slipping up. He's not being as careful as he once was. Off the record, my gut feeling is that he's the man responsible for the murder of Jessie Paulman, if not directly then indirectly. It's nearly harvest time. I can feel it. I'm just going to wait it out and see what grows. If there's one thing I've learned in life, it's that things have to be done the right way or no way at all."

"I'm not a patient person, Baxtor."

"I don't mean to be brash, but where did your impatience get you?"

I was holding my side, my broken ribs. Same mistake. Same basement. Same injury. Was God trying to be symbolic?

"Good point. So we wait?" I sighed.

"We wait. And we pray."

CHAPTER THIRTY-SEVEN

*D*isenchanted, I returned home, pulled my car into the garage, and stepped into an empty kitchen. When I left, Mom was in the middle of making Madelines. A sweet smell in the air was a hint that the last of the cookies had come out of the oven. The plate full of goodies sitting on the counter was confirmation. I poured myself a glass of milk, grabbed a petite cake, and sat down at the table. My mouth was full when my mom entered the kitchen. I didn't have to look up to know that she was studying me as she made her way to the stove. She turned on the gas, heating up the water in the silver and black kettle. Not really wanting to talk, I stuffed another Madeline into my mouth.

"You look upset."

I swallowed the bite I was chewing and let out a frustrated sigh. "Confused is more like it."

"Anything I can help with?"

"No. I don't think so. Lavine won't be able to use any of the evidence." I rolled my eyes. "I guess I'm just discouraged. One step forward, two steps back."

"I think I know something that'll make you feel a little better. I never did tell you what was in the box A-Omega sent *me*." I looked at mom with hopeful eyes. "Come on. I want to show you something."

Intrigued, I followed Mom to her bedroom. She disappeared into the closet and I took a seat on her bed, waiting for her to return. After several moments, she returned holding a medium sized box in her hands.

"I've received many packages from A-Omega, but this was the first." She placed the box on the edge of the bed and took a seat beside me. "Just like you, I accepted A-Omega's offer. I knew about A-Omega and I understood what they were offering, but I didn't *know* them. I wanted to, though. And when I made the decision to follow A-Omega, I had no idea what the rest of my life would look like, but I trusted. When I opened the box, I looked at each item inside as something to enjoy. I hadn't considered the fact that maybe I was supposed to learn something from the items in the box. Nor had I considered that each of the six items could teach me a lesson that could be applied to an even larger truth."

"About the Truth," I said. "A-Omega told me that the list of names would form a belt and the Truth would be the buckle. At first, I couldn't figure it out. I thought these people should all know each other. When I realized that not only did they not know each other, but that they didn't know me, I had to reconsider. I started looking for the common denominator. The one thing that each person had in common. I finally figured it out while I was in Houston. Jeremiah 29:11 on the back of Steven Bellamy's license plate. Isaiah 41:10 on my phone just before I met Shae Simmons. Scripture."

"God's word."

"It's the Truth."

Mom nodded her head, "I know."

"Then why couldn't you have just told me about the Truth?"

"Telling and experiencing are two different things. You know that. I could tell you what it's like to be in love. Depending on what I said about love, you might want to experience it for yourself. You might think you have an understanding of love based on my experience… but you wouldn't really know love until you found it, till you felt it. I can tell you about the Truth. I'll tell you about my journey, but you have a journey of your own to live and it's the Truth you learn that will pull you out of the hard times, that will help you stand on solid ground when the world around you won't stop shaking. And when you come into the purpose for your life and everything in the world is telling you to quit. When darkness comes in from every side, it's the Truth that will keep you strong and the lessons you learn from the items in your box will guard your heart and mind. Each item in the box is a piece of armor that will protect you from the evil in the world so that you can walk, not just *in* the light but *as* a light."

I thought about how I walked through the world before. I didn't walk. I ran. I was guarded all right, but I wasn't radiant. I didn't glow. I couldn't have helped anyone through the darkness.

"What I'm trying to say is that everyone is given different gifts because each person learns in a different way and because everyone's journey is very different. But it goes much deeper than that. We're not supposed to keep the gifts for ourselves. We look at the gifts, we touch the gifts, we come to understand the gifts, we begin to use the gifts for ourselves, and then we give the gifts to others. I had no idea that there would be a valuable life lesson to learn from each item. Like you, I received a letter before the package came and like you, the gifts inside were tailored to fit my personality. They were picked out especially for me." Mom fished into her pocket and returned with a folded, well-worn piece of paper. "I've told many people about this letter, but I've only read it to a few." She unfolded the note. It looked smooth and worn. "Whenever I'm in doubt, whenever I doubt myself, I pull this letter out to refresh my mind. It reminds me where I came from and all that I've been through. It reminds me of my journey and that, win or lose, I have not lost but gained." Mom cleared her throat and began to read. Her voice started out shaky but she finished up strong.

> *Dear Sue,*
> *Today is the day you have spent a lifetime preparing for. Every pain you have experienced has shaped you into the person you are today. The trials were a necessary part of the training, and we were with you through it all.*
> *Regardless of what you might think, we know you are finally ready. However, you should be warned: if you do accept*

this assignment, there are going to be bumps along the way. The path will be rough, but your assignment will be to make the road smooth for others. When you run into problems, please let us know so we can help. If you decide to accept our offer, it is essential that you keep the lines of communication open between us. We will be sending correspondence periodically. Often it will be through writing, but other times it will not.

So keep your eyes open, because it is the correspondence that will help you decide which path to take when you come to a fork in the road. You are a gentle, free spirit. You are kind, but naive. Your inability to see the darkness of the world has the ability to be your greatest strength or your greatest weakness. Your kindness and the openness of your heart will always send you in the right direction, but always be aware of the snares that are awaiting you around every corner. For when you get closer to the light, the darkness bites your heels. On the other hand, you will reach people that would not otherwise be reached and the genuineness of your heart and the truth in your testimony is your greatest attribute of all. Let us protect you, and you might just change the world.

Please give the offer consideration. If you do decide to accept this mission, please be at the Bursar's office at the University of Oklahoma on August 19th. When you enter the building, go to the second floor and find room 214. Upon entering the room, take a seat at desk number two. We at A-Omega are excited to extend this offer, and we have the highest hopes that you will accept. One last thing: We are aware that you have been searching for the Truth. We are also aware that you have yet to find it. If you follow us, you will find it. Please consider our offer. We hope to hear from you soon.

Arm Yourself Well,
A-Omega
Ephesians 6: 10-18

"Your letter is almost the same as mine."

Mom handed me the slip of paper and I stared at it in awe. The paper felt smooth like silk between my fingers. I re-read it silently, letting the commonality of the invitation sink in. I couldn't be certain without holding the letters side by side, but I was pretty sure the first two paragraphs were exactly the same. Midway through the letter, I began to see the difference. A-Omega saw different strengths in my mom than they saw in me. They also saw different weaknesses. But just like my letter, A-Omega accepted my Mom's weaknesses and promised to use them for a greater good.

"I received the letter from A-Omega in March. Pre-registration for fall classes began in April. I could have enrolled in April with everyone else and if I had, I might have gotten the classes I wanted, but A-Omega didn't want me at the bursar's office until the 19th of August… the last possible day to register. I had accepted their offer and I didn't want to mess up their first request, so I waited. As a result, I was forced to enroll in the only classes that were left and Psychology 101 just happened to be one of them. The rest is history."

"So what did you do?"

"Like you, when I received my first package from A-Omega, I found a letter inside. And just like you, inside the letter I found a list of names. The first name on the list was Emmie Watson. So I did what A-Omega had asked me to do. I climbed the stairs of the bursar's office with Nana by my side. When I entered the room, I took a seat in desk two and waited for nearly five minutes before a stout woman in a tweed suit materialized. She had bobbed blond hair and bifocals. You would not believe how nervous I was. This was my future. I looked at the woman's silver nametag pinned to her lapel: Emmie Watson. There was no doubt I was in the right place. I glanced back at Nana. She had a smile spread across her face that stretched from ear to ear. I accepted my class schedule and I looked forward to my future."

"What other names were on the list?"

"None that you would recognize. Oh… I take that back. You might recognize one of the names. Does Will Colbert ring a bell?"

I smiled. "Does everyone get a letter like this?"

"The invitation is available to anyone who wants it."

"But in the letter it said 'We know you are finally ready'. Was A-Omega not ready for me before? Why didn't I get the letter sooner?"

"They were ready for you. You just weren't ready for them."

Mom pushed the box toward me. "Do you want to open it?"

"Are you sure?" I hesitated for a moment before lifting the lid. I felt like I was invading her privacy.

"Go on," Mom encouraged me. "Peek inside."

After I removed the lid and looked inside the box, I tried to hide my disappointment.

"It's empty."

"Believe me, it's far from empty. It's nearly bursting it's so full." Mom noted my reservations and feeling the need to explain, she continued. "You take an item out. You use it. You learn from it. You take what you've learned and use it to help another. In return, you get another gift. Then you put that gift inside the box."

"What gift? The box is empty."

"That's because you can't see what I remember. Inside of the box you're holding is a lifetime of fear, seven years of regret and bitterness, a whole lot of hatred, some self-doubt, and believe it or not, plenty of pride."

"But none of those things are gifts."

"The gift is being able to put them in the box. To be rid of them. To finally be free."

"So what *was* in your box? When you first received it."

"A package of note cards, a list of names, a funnel, a pair of running shoes, some carabineers-"

"Carabineers?"

"I had about as much of an idea what to do with the carabineers as you did the antivirus for your computer."

"It's strange they gave you a pair of running shoes when they gave me a pair of combat boots."

"Everyone needs something different. You're a runner, Rae. You have always run away from things instead of dealing with them. I used to be the opposite. I had a hard time leaving, a hard time moving on. I find security in what I'm accustomed to. Sometimes God tells us to stay and other timeshe tells us to go. I look back now and wonder how much difference I could have made if I had started taking leaps of faith much sooner."

"What about the funnel?"

Mom closed her eyes and began to reminisce. She covered her mouth with her hand and let out an unexpected laugh before she looked me in the eye. "It was the biggest funnel I had ever seen." Mom laughed again. "I didn't know what to do with it. I figured I could either use it to cook with or use it to change my oil."

"What was it for?"

"There's a story behind that. After your father and I got married, A-Omega sent word that we would be relocating to Asia. An unfamiliar country. Totally out of my comfort zone. A different language. A different culture. And the task was dangerous. Your father and I were called to rescue women and children from human trafficking."

"How'd you save them?"

"We pulled them out with our bare hands. With the support of friends and family back home, we raised enough money to start a small non-profit. We acquired a facility to house those who had been rescued. We brought in people to teach them skills so that they could eventually make it on their own. We brought in teachers to educate them. Without a means to make a living, without the availability of an education, the chances of them falling back into the hands of traffickers was a harsh reality. By the time they were ready to leave the shelter, they were educated and had a way to provide for themselves.

"This decreased the chances of them being sold into slavery again. We had been there a year and were making progress. We had established a rapport with the locals and they respected us, protected us. A schoolhouse had just been built in the village. We had rescued sixteen girls in just a little over a year. They were finally away from their traffickers. They were safe. They were rehabilitating. They were healing. Your dad and I stood back and looked at the progress being made. We knew we couldn't have accomplished all this with only *our* strength. I could tell you story after story about how things fell into place for us. Timing. Facilities. Funding.

Support. You name it, we had it. We thanked God every step of the way for His provisions, that He trusted us, that He was patient with us. Believe me, we needed a success, no matter how big or small. We needed to know God was with us everyday. We needed to know that we weren't on our own.

"It wasn't easy being away from everything we knew. We could have easily gotten discouraged… and there were days that we did. Luckily, my down days were not Will's down days and we were able to lift each other up and get one another back on the right track. And then there was May. May was the first girl we rescued. She was fifteen and had been enslaved since the age of eight. She had never received any schooling. She couldn't read or write. Because of the abuse she received at the hand of her trafficker, she had retreated into herself and when she first came to stay with us, she barely spoke. But the transformation was dramatic. In a year's time, she went from learning to teaching, from complete silence to counseling the other girls who moved into our small home. She was the mother hen. She was the peacekeeper. She was the comforter. After a year, Will and I decided that it was time to let her go. Once again, we received funds from friends and family. It wasn't much, but it was enough to help May start a small business.

"She was eager to return to her village. She wanted to see her family. She wanted to be able to support them and understandably so. May set up a small store in her village where she sold food items and other necessities. Will and I made frequent visits to ensure she was doing well… prospering. May's goal was to buy more products with her profits and expand her small store into a family business. The next time Will and I made the thirty-mile trip to see May, we could tell that things had gone awry. May's store was only half stocked, but more concerning was the look in her eyes. The hope we had seen before was gone. With us, May had blossomed, transformed, come out of her shell. It seemed as though she had once again retreated to the place where she felt safe.

"May's father and his friends had been coming to the store and taking items without paying. Her inventory had dwindled and her source of income had disappeared. Will and I offered to take her back with us…

to come up with a new plan. She refused. So Will and I told her that we would put our heads together. We promised her we would come up with a solution. Two weeks later, Will and I returned to the small village and found that not only had May's store disappeared, but May had vanished as well. Rumor had it that her traffickers had come back for her. She had been sold again. Of course, all of the girls held a special place in our hearts, but May... well, I think you can understand. Will and I just bonded with her immediately. You can't imagine how it feels until you've been standing in those shoes. To feel that you're on the right path only to fail miserably. We had failed May. I was ready to pack it up and call it quits. Surely, I had heard God wrong. I had taken a leap of faith, but perhaps I had jumped too zealously and quite possibly in the wrong direction.

"So I called Nana, and I will never forget our conversation. I told her I was ready to leave. More than anything, I wanted for Will and me to move home where I could re-evaluate our future. I was afraid I had chosen the wrong major. I wasn't fit to counsel. But she told me to stay. She told me that even though May was gone, the other girls needed me. I screamed at her, which, as you know, is totally out of character for me. I screamed, 'Those girls don't need *me*, they need *God*.'

"And this is what your nana said: 'Sue, you are a funnel through which those girls feel God's love. Our futures are not guaranteed and neither is our prosperity, but God's love *is* a guarantee. Through you, they see hope and for the first time in their lives, they know that in God there is hope. No matter where they go or what they are doing, they will always carry that hope with them and God *will* guard their minds. God will protect their hearts.'

"The funnel was the last item in the box. It stayed in the box for over a decade before I discovered its purpose. I learned that I was to be more like a funnel than a sponge. As a child and through my teenage years, I was a sponge. I took everything in. I learned from my parents. I learned good things, but I didn't do anything with what I learned. I stayed where I felt comfortable. Maybe it was partly due to my lack of faith or perhaps my timid nature, but the good things I soaked up stayed inside. I kept everything good for myself, but God saw my potential. God wanted me to be a channel through which good things flowed."

"So did you stay?"

"We did. And we were glad for it. A month after May's disappearance, we woke one morning to find her asleep on the ground in front of the door of our shelter. The rumors had proven to be true. May had been captured by her traffickers and held against her will. Her traffickers thought they had the same girl, but they couldn't have been more wrong. Hope burned inside of May. Hope fueled her. She had been rescued before. She knew what it felt like to be free and she knew she could be free again. Hope protected her mind. May jumped out the second story window of the brothel and made her way back to us. Just think what could have happened if we had decided to call it quits."

"Where is May now?"

"Still in Thailand. She runs the mission now. When Will and I decided to start a family and come back to the States, May took over. It was her calling. You wouldn't believe how the place has grown. Over one hundred and fifty girls and boys now live at the mission."

"All because of a funnel." I smiled. My eyes were moist with tears. "I guess I'm glad you didn't change your oil with it."

Mom laughed. "Me, too."

She kissed the top of my head and then used her hand to smooth my hair. "It's funny how life works out. How even through pain we can experience such joy." Mom paused. "I'm so glad you're back, Rae."

"It's good to be here." More than anything, I meant it.

I thought about the closing of Mom's letter. A-Omega. A name I was familiar with because I had heard it growing up. My parents spoke of A-Omega, as did Nana and Papa. The name was used so often that it seemed commonplace and I let the words escape my lips without understanding... without feeling. For me, A-Omega was a synonym for relocation, discomfort, and pain, but after agreeing to follow their lead,

A-Omega looked different to me. God had freed me from some pretty sticky situations and led me in the right direction on more than one occasion. When I was with God, my situations didn't look so hopeless and my obstacles appeared easier to overcome. I was learning quickly that A-Omega was good. A-Omega had my back.

Later that night, I grabbed a blanket and slipped out the back door. I stretched out on the deck and gazed up at the stars. For the first time in my life, I felt completely still and content. My heart had been bleeding for twelve years. My parents were shrinks and my behavior was beyond them. They couldn't fix me. Alex hadn't been able to either. He had tried, and a part of my heart did belong to him. His love no doubt satisfied me, to an extent, but how could I forget that cold Minnesota morning when I was lying beside him on the sofa. Everything I had hoped for had come to pass. Chloe and Ben were gone and no longer a threat, which meant my parents were safe and so was I. But the greater gift was that I received all of this and the man that I loved was still with me. I had Alex, the world was finally on my side, but I felt emptier than I had ever felt before. I felt a deeper sense of longing.

I pulled the blanket around my shoulders. I now understood how Nana felt when she found God. All curled up and weak, wrapped in a yellow blanket, sitting in her backyard looking up at the stars, just like I was tonight. Surrounded by God's warmth in a world that could be so cold. Tonight the bleeding had finally stopped. For twelve years, I had tried with only my strength to patch the hole, but nothing had worked. I had spun my wheels until I was exhausted. And then one night, healing came so easily. I was in a pit of despair, bound and shackled, but I had been set free.

When I went to bed that night I dreamed of something different. No longer in Carl's dark basement, I dreamed that I was standing in a building looking ahead at a long, covered, crystal bridge. With me were three pieces of luggage. My baggage. I was carrying one bag on my shoulder and I was dragging the other two pieces behind. As I stood gazing at the bridge, I saw how beautiful it was, reflecting light in the colors of a rainbow. Its beauty drew me closer. I stepped onto the bridge with every intention of crossing to the other side, but when I looked down, I got scared. I could see the tips of my shoes and through the glass, I could see the ground thousands of feet below. The bridge was beautiful, but could the bridge hold all of my baggage? Could the bridge hold me? Was the bridge strong enough to take me to the other side? I heard a whisper just before I woke. "You've been traveling through a tough tunnel. Your light is coming soon."

CHAPTER THIRTY-EIGHT

I thought the evidence I found in Carl's basement would be enough to send him away, but after talking with Lavine, I realized my trip to the Pierce mansion had been a huge mistake. I had nearly lost my life and once again, I had almost taken my boyfriend down with me. And for what? More trouble. I had seen the evidence inside the boxes. Carl knew that I knew and now my life, Alex's life, my parents' lives, were all in danger. I kept thinking about Monica Bradley. She knew too much about Carl, and just look where "knowing" got her. Monica was murdered because of what she knew. To make matters worse, after the confrontation with Carl, Alex had grown extremely distant. I had spent the past week trying to find things for the two of us to do that might cheer him up: the movies, dinner, a museum, a concert. But Alex always had an excuse for why he couldn't make it. He always had plans, but not once did Alex invite me to come along. It wasn't that he was being hateful or spiteful; he was just being really weird. I thought that maybe he was embarrassed about what happened at Carl's. Maybe he was upset that he hadn't been able to save me like he had always done in the past. Maybe he was still struggling with his humanity. Whatever the reason, I decided to give Alex the space he needed.

I spent the first week of September in my studio covering old canvases with gesso while I waited for "Identity Crisis" to dry. "Identity Crisis" was a gift for Alex, a painting that would both acknowledge his internal struggle and let him know I love him just the way he is. I had hoped to have it completed in time for his birthday, but unfortunately, it was still a work in progress. Twice already, I had started out zealously, painting Alex's face onto the canvas only to cover it up with gesso. His face was the part of the painting that had to be perfect because the face was the key to it all. Half angel, half creature of the night, Alex's expression needed to portray a boy who was struggling on the inside, a boy conflicted by what the world thought of him, a boy who was searching for himself. A boy asking the question, "Who am I?"

As I painted, I thought about my mission. For months, the people I loved had been trying to tell me that I was more focused on the destination than the journey, but I hadn't listened. A-Omega had sent me a box and inside, six gifts. Each gift was a tangible item from which I was to learn a spiritual truth and each name on the list was a divine appointment from which I'd learn a valuable lesson. But I was so focused on Carl Pierce, that when the gifts failed to end in his incarceration, I grew disheartened and disappointed.

It wasn't until I was locked in shackles and facing death, that I finally heard what God had been trying to tell me all along. When everything around me was quiet, I heard him say, "It's not what I want *from* you, Rae. It's what I want *for* you." Was there a chance that I would help convict Carl? Sure there was. Did God need my help? Not really, but what God knew was this: on the journey to finding my biological dad, I would find my Heavenly father.

Earthly fathers may not love you the way you think they should, they may not say the things you need to hear, and sometimes they're not even around, but on the journey to finding Carl Pierce, I had found the Father who had been there for me all along. The One who stood beside me while I ignored Him. The One who loved me through pain and brokenness. The Father who wanted to heal my heart. The Father who wanted to give me a fresh start. I thought about my most recent dream and the whisper I heard as I stood at the mouth of the bridge. "You've been traveling through a tough tunnel," the voice said. "You're light is coming soon."

It was September 7th. My birthday was just five days away. I would no longer be a teenager. I would officially be an adult. In the past, my birthday was the day of the year I loathed most. It was the day I wished I could stay in my pajamas, curled up in my bed. September 13th made me feel guilty… but no more. It was strange. For the first time in years, I didn't loathe the thought of aging another year. I still thought of Laney, but I no longer felt responsible for her death. This year I was actually excited about my birthday; however, no one had bothered to bring it up. Not even Alex (who was always bound and determined to make me happy on the day that had brought me sadness) had mentioned it. I was about to turn twenty! This was a big deal! In less than a week, I would officially be a woman! Didn't anyone care? I was thinking these thoughts while brushing gesso onto the last canvas. It was 11:45. The TV was turned on and I was listening to a talk show when I heard Mom shouting my name.

"I'm in here!" I shouted back. A moment later Mom was standing in the doorway, huffing and puffing. The look on her face forced me to my feet. "What? What's wrong?"

"I've been running all over the house looking for you. There's a phone call for you in the kitchen. I think you should take it."

"In the kitchen? Who is it?"

"Detective Lavine."

"Why didn't he just call my cell?"

"He said he tried. He said it's urgent."

I didn't wait for Mom to explain any further. I darted out of the studio and into the kitchen. In a matter of seconds, I had the phone pressed to my ear. I caught my breath and spoke into the receiver. "This is Rae."

"The harvest is ready for reaping."

"Excuse me?"

"A situation has developed. Do you think you can meet me in Tulsa at St. John's in an hour and a half?" His voice was deep and urgent.

"St. John's… as in the hospital?"

"Yes. 1923 South Utica."

"Right. Yes. I can be there. What is this all abou-" I was cut off before I could finish. The detective had ended the conversation abruptly, leaving me with thousands of unanswered questions. Paralyzed by uncertainty, my feet were rooted to the ground and my mind began to wander for a moment as I considered what Lavine could have possibly meant. There must have been a break in the case. Was there new evidence that could lock him up for good? I pulled on my boots, said goodbye to my parents, and jumped into my car.

Once I arrived at the hospital, I realized that I had no idea where to meet Detective Lavine and that I would have to use my phone to find him. Noticing a sign for valet parking, I pulled into the horseshoe-shaped drive and shifted into park. The valet handed me a ticket, and I rushed into the lobby of the hospital as the dreamlike quality of this morning was settling around me once again. An hour ago, I had been busy brushing gesso onto my canvas. The next thing I knew, I was at St. John's Hospital, waiting for Detective Lavine to bring me up to speed. The harvest is ready for reaping. I checked my phone for the time. The drive hadn't taken as long as I thought, and I was early. I dialed Lavine, hoping he would pick up. I didn't know how much longer I could wait for answers.

Just as I had hoped, Detective Lavine answered and said he was on his way down to the lobby. I waited near the elevators and when the shiny metal doors opened, I stepped inside, feeling a rush of adrenaline as the doors slid shut. With my back against the wall, I tried to relax as Lavine pressed the button and the small metal box began its ascent.

"You look less angry than you did last time I saw you." Lavine stood tall and confident holding a cup of coffee. He flashed a friendly smile.

"I was angry with you, yes."

"I hope you understand why we couldn't use the evidence."

"I've had some time to think about it. I was mad at the situation, not you."

"Just so you know, going into Carl's basement without help was a bad idea."

"Great. Thanks."

"But what you did was brave. And just because we couldn't use the articles you recovered from the Pierce mansion, doesn't mean they weren't appreciated. I personally took the items to the Paulman house. Words cannot describe how appreciative her parents were."

"Really? I thought seeing their daughter's belongings might make her parents feel even worse."

"On the contrary, it brought them hope. We're getting close, Rae. Justice will be served. Jessie's parents can feel that."

The elevator jerked to a halt on the ninth floor. The ICU. When the doors slid open, I followed Lavine. He breezed past the nurses' station, flashing a smile and his badge.

"Detective." I quickened my pace to catch him. "Why am I here?"

Baxtor looked over his shoulder but continued to walk. "Just follow me," he said, taking a left and moving quickly down the corridor.

Not daring to argue, I followed close behind. The hallway was long and at the end, a police officer was sitting in a chair reading the paper, guarding the door. A million thoughts were swirling through my mind, but mostly, I couldn't help but wonder why an armed guard was needed at St. John's. Who was the patient and why did they need protecting. Or maybe the guard was armed because the patient was dangerous. Was Carl here? Had he been found out? Had Lavine attempted to arrest him? Had Carl gotten hurt in the struggle? Maybe Carl was cuffed to the bed. Would he go to prison after being released from the hospital?

The officer looked up as we moved down the hall. Lavine approached the guard and handed him the cup of coffee. Feeling out of place, I kept my distance while Lavine and the officer talked in hushed voices. Finally, the detective turned toward me and motioned for me to follow him into the room.

The lights were off and the curtains were drawn. Once inside, Lavine shut the door behind me and moved toward the bed. I stood by the door, too terrified to move any closer. The patient was covered with blankets.

Not moving. Lots of tubes. Bags of liquid hung above on shiny silver hooks. Machines were beeping quietly, eerie background music. Lavine took a seat beside the bed and fixed his eyes on me. It was Carl. It had to be. That's what Lavine meant when he said the harvest is ready for reaping. They had found Carl out. They had made an arrest. There was a struggle. Now Carl was dying in the hospital. Is this how it would end? He would just die? Without anytime to consider what he had done? It didn't seem fair.

Lavine motioned for me to join him. I hesitated before taking two small steps in his direction. I didn't know if I could look at Carl. I tried to be brave and took another two steps toward the bed. My legs were shaking. I couldn't look at his face. Terror. I couldn't take myself back to that place. Out of all the places I had been, out of all the things I had been through, Carl's basement was the worst. It was my lowest point but ironically, it was in his basement that I had finally found freedom. I couldn't go back. To look him in the eye would be like refastening the shackles around my own wrist. The feelings and the wounds were still fresh.

I took two more steps... and then two more. I stood at the foot of the bed and let my fingers run across the thin blanket. I tried my hardest to breathe, to calm myself as I moved closer to the patient. Lavine sat quietly, watching for my reaction. In the dim light of the hospital room, I gazed down upon the patients face; it wasn't a man at all. I turned to Lavine, waiting for an explanation.

"I got the call early this morning. 4:30." Lavine continued to speak quietly, as I regarded the girl. Wisps of blond hair poked out of the bandages wrapped around her head. "Gunshot wound, I'm afraid."

My eyes moved to Lavine. I needed more explanation.

"The call was from the hospital. The girl was thrown out of a car at the ER entrance."

"By whom?"

"Only one witness. They say it was a white sedan."

I immediately thought about the white sedan I saw at Carl's house.

"We have a team looking at the surveillance cameras right now. We should know more in a few hours."

"I might be jumping to conclusions, but do you think this white car is the same white car I saw at Carl's?"

"There's always that possibility. We're not ruling that out. Like I said we should know more in a few hours."

"So, why am I here?"

Lavine bit his lip and hesitated. He touched the plastic ID bracelet on the girl's wrist. "You're here because of the identification we found on the girl."

"Do you recognize the name?" Lavine asked. I stared at the name on her bracelet.

"Unbelievable. Gracie Lynn Abbott."

INTERCESSION

CHAPTER THIRTY-NINE

*I*t rang several times before he picked up. I envisioned Pastor Joe at his desk sifting through a heap of papers or flipping through his Bible.

"Joe!" I sighed in relief. "I was worried you weren't going to pick up."

"Rae. It's so good to hear your voice."

"Are you busy?"

"Not at all. Just had a bite to eat at Northwood's Café. Breakfast with an old friend named Rooney."

"Sounds fun. I don't think I ever met Rooney, though. Listen, Joe. I really need to talk to you, but I don't know where to start."

"It's not Alex, is it?"

"No. It's not Alex. It's Gracie Abbott. I've found another name on my list."

"That's great news."

"It would be if she wasn't in a coma."

"A coma?"

"Gunshot wound."

"Good Heavens."

"I know. It's horrible. I have a feeling she knows something about Carl Pierce, but there's only one problem: Gracie won't wake up. Detective Lavine thinks prayer is the answer, but I don't know."

"Have you ever heard of the word intercession?"

"Yeah. It means to take a break. Which is exactly what I need right now. My mind's completely frazzled. I'm exhausted."

"You're talking about intersession, with an 'S'. I'm talking about intercession with a 'C', I-N-T-E-R-*C*-E-S-S-I-O-N. They *are* pronounced the same and they share all of the same letters but one. Intersession with an 'S' does mean to take a break, but intercession with a 'C' means to intervene between two parties. In Christianity, intercession is a prayer to God on behalf of others."

"I've been hearing that a lot lately. And I do mean a lot."

"Prayer is a weapon."

"That's what I've been told. And if I were a saint, then I could understand how prayer might work, but I barely feel good enough to talk to God about myself. I definitely don't want someone else's fate to rest on my ability to intercede."

"No one's perfect, Rae."

"I've heard that before, too."

"Every saint has a past and every sinner has a future. Sound familiar?"

"No, but I like it."

"I wish I could take the credit, but they're the words of Oscar Wilde."

"I don't know."

"Look at it like this, Rae. Say, you're standing on a mountain and God is standing on a different mountain in the distance. How do you get there?"

"Wings."

"Or?"

I thought about my most recent dream: a radiant crystal bridge that connected the building I was in to a building in the distance. Worried that the bridge would not support me, I was too scared to cross. "A bridge?"

"Sure. A bridge between pain and healing. A bridge between love and hate. A bridge between heaven and earth. A bridge between God and mankind. A bridge between right and wrong. Jesus is like a bridge. He's strong enough to hold us. No matter how good. No matter how bad. He can take us to the other side."

"Because He died for us?"

"Yes, but He *lives* for us too, you know."

What Joe said reminded me of the conversation Alex and I had in his basement several months ago. I told him I loved him so much that I would die for him. Then he told me that living for someone was harder. I told Alex death hurts more. Alex told me that to love is to live. We agreed to disagree, but now Joe was telling me that Jesus did both.

My silence spurred Joe to continue.

"When Jesus died on the cross, do you think He ascended to heaven and then took a nice long *break*? Do you think it ended on Calvary? If that were the case, we would be talking about intersession with an 'S'."

"How can I be sure the bridge will hold me?"

"You get to know the bridge."

"I've heard some people say they heard God in the middle of pain. I've heard others say that God's voice comes in a gentle whisper. How do *you* hear from God, Joe? How did *you* get to know Him?"

"Listening for God is like listening to the radio. For me, the strength of the signal depends on how far I am from the radio tower. It's the same with God. The closer I am to Him, the more clearly I hear His voice, and the more certain I am that it's His. Now, I realize radios are nearly extinct and that your generation listens to music on devices that fit in the palm of your hand, but bear with me. I have a point. I still listen to my radio. I keep it on my kitchen counter. The other day, I was listening to a news program while heating up something in the microwave. All at once, right in the middle of the program, there was a huge amount of static. Are you following me?"

"Yes. So what did you do?"

"I turned off the microwave and repositioned my antenna." Joe paused. "My old radio... I have to readjust the antenna every morning. Do you get what I'm trying to say?"

"Loud and clear."

INTERCESSION

CHAPTER FORTY

*G*racie. I had finally found Gracie Abbot! But had we found her too late? Lavine told me that, according to doctors, she had a five percent chance of surviving. After a four-hour surgery, the bullet had been removed, but at what cost? Right now, the biggest concern was increased intracranial pressure, cerebral edema. It would take a miracle for the swelling in her brain to go down but even if it did, what condition would she be in? The bullet had caused extensive damage to the brain tissue. The swelling was causing even more. Gracie Abbot may never walk again… may never talk again. There was nothing we could do but wait. Gracie had been at St. John's for three days and although her condition hadn't worsened, she hadn't gotten any better either. The only reason Lavine had a guard at Gracie's hospital door was because Gracie's name was on my list. My word was good enough for him.

Lavine contacted me daily with progress reports. I could tell that he was trying his hardest to sound optimistic and to have faith, but this waiting game was taking a toll on the both of us. And there was that four letter word again: Wait. I had a progress report for Lavine, too. Things weren't getting much better at my house either. Yesterday morning on his way to work, Will noticed a car parked at the end of our road. It followed him all the way to Tulsa. Lavine offered to contact the Bartlesville

Police Department and have them patrol the road by our house if it would make us feel any safer. Will told him not to worry about it and that he had faith that we would be fine. I knew that Will was right and I wasn't really worried. I had come into contact with every name on my list but one and each person had come into my life at the perfect time. God was in control of this, not me, and that thought made me feel incredibly safe. Gracie's name was on my list. Because of this, I knew that she would wake up and when she did, she would have something very important to say.

I was so thankful to have Lavine on my side. He believed me and because of our bond, he had kept an armed officer at Gracie's hospital door around the clock for the past three days. This was an expense to the Tulsa Police Department that he wouldn't be able to justify for much longer if there wasn't a break in the case. If Gracie didn't wake up soon, he would have to dismiss the guard and Gracie would be no safer than Monica Bradley.

It was September 12th, just one day before my birthday, and I woke up with a heavy heart. I had been praying that Gracie would wake, that her wounds would heal, that God would save her. That he would turn an ugly circumstance, a horrible crime into something beautiful, but then what? What would happen once Gracie woke up? What did she know? What would she be able to tell us? Where would she go? Lavine's words rang loud in my ears. "No place for her to go. No place for her to go."

"Oh God, please be with Gracie," I prayed. "Please be with other woman like her. In the tiniest, darkest room, please comfort them; please let them know You are there. Please let them know I will come for them. Please let them know they are loved. Please calm their fears. Please God, be with Terry Dunbarr. Please God heal her heart. Take her pain away. Please God heal her heart."

Like Catchitore said, slavery has been around since the beginning of time and it doesn't appear to be going anywhere soon. I knew that I couldn't end the problem. Instead, it was the thought of helping one girl, the idea of playing a very small role in the fight to end an enormous problem that gave me a sense of peace. I glanced at the clock on the bedside table. 2:30. I threw off the down comforter and let my legs hang off the side of the bed. I rubbed my eyes. I wondered how a skinny, not so coordinated woman like me would make a difference. I flicked on the lamp and a soft glow filled my room. I glanced at my bookcase and saw my Bible on the bottom shelf, still in the box, unopened. Nana and Papa gave it to me when I turned thirteen. Slowly, I climbed out of bed and walked over to my collection of books, my prized possessions. With tired eyes, I grabbed the box that held the Bible and sat down on the floor beside my bed.

"God. Are you there? I know you are. I really feel like you have everything under control, but what do you want me to do? What do you need me to do? I'm not a strong person. Not physically. Not emotionally. What happened to Jessie and Gracie? This is hard to look at God. It's hard to face. It would be easier to walk away, but I feel you want me here. I need to hear from you. I need to know that this is the path you want me to take, and I need to know how I'll be strong enough to survive this."

I opened the box and pulled out the Bible. I held it in my hands and recalled how Papa called this book the Living Word.

"God, if I open your word will you show me the truth. Please show me how I am going to get through this."

I closed my eyes. Holding the Bible in my lap, I let it fall open. My eyes were drawn to a passage in the middle of the page.

"I can do all things through Him who gives me strength."

Tears rolled down my cheeks and I wondered why God would want to talk to someone like me. Why would He reach his hand down from the heavens to answer *my* questions?

The tears I shed the night before were cleansing, and the truth I found in Philippians gave me a renewed strength. It was an amazing feeling to know that I was not alone in this. God had my back. God was my strength. I woke up feeling refreshed and completely relieved. I was on a mission. It was 10:45 and I was in my Honda headed to Saint John's with an unlikely guest seated beside me.

When Quinn Collins shared his testimony, I learned a valuable lesson, but when I walked out the door of the computer repair shop, I thought that was it. I never thought that our paths would cross again, but last night when I was laying in bed trying my hardest to fall back asleep, a thought occurred to me. On the brink of death, Quinn had been saved when a crucifix was laid upon his chest. I knew Quinn still had the necklace. He wore it around his neck and initially, I thought I would just ask him if I could borrow it.

When I first met Quinn, I decided not to tell him about the list of names. I thought he might think it was weird… because it was, but I felt a little different now. I didn't care as much about what he thought and as I stood in front of the service counter and looked at Quinn, I thought that I might as well tell all. I might as well just tell him that his name was one of ten names on a list that A-Omega sent me. So I started at the beginning.

I told him about Mason Armishaw and Todd Catchitore. I told him about my trip to Houston and how I found Terry Dunbarr in a rundown apartment complex and how I had been sent there to save her life. I told him about Shae Simmons, the little girl who took my hand in the ally and led me to safety. I told him about Katelyn Cross, the nurse, and Steven Bellamy, the cab driver. And finally, I told him about Gracie Abbott and Baxtor Lavine. When I was finished, Quinn walked over to the window, flipped the sign from "OPEN" to "CLOSED", and locked up for the day.

"It's not the piece of gold that worked the miracle, Rae. It's the faith of the one who's wearing it."

He told me that he lived to pray for others and insisted on coming with me to the hospital. On the way to Saint John's, I called Lavine to check on Gracie's condition. She was still nonresponsive, but I was hopeful.

"Nothing new to report. Her condition hasn't changed, Rae." Lavine sounded gloomy. He had been at the hospital all night and I knew he must be tired. I told him today was the day that Gracie would wake up and then I told him I was on my way.

Twenty-five minutes later, Quinn and I exited the elevator and found Lavine waiting for us at the nurses' station holding two steaming cups of coffee in his hands.

"Care for a cup?" Lavine flashed a weak smile. His eyes looked tired. "There's cream and sugar, too. I'm sorry. I didn't realize that you were bringing a friend. I can grab another cup."

"No thanks," I said, turning down his offer.

"Well, I know you're here on business if you turn down a cup of coffee, Rae."

"Detective Lavine. This is Quinn Collins. Quinn, this is Detective Baxtor Lavine."

Lavine and Quinn shook hands to make the introduction formal and as we walked down the hall toward Gracie's room, I told him about Quinn and how he was number one on my list of names. As we continued down the corridor, Quinn started to share his testimony and had just finished telling about the snakebite and the rough ride to the town of Jesus Maria when we came to a stop at the end of the hall. Just like the last time I was here, a guard sat in front of Gracie's door.

Levine handed the officer a cup of coffee and made a bit of small talk. Quinn and I held our distance and as I looked on, I felt my stomach start to sour. I hated hospitals. I hated the smell. I hated the sounds. I hated the look of sadness on the visitors' faces. The hospital just wasn't a happy place and all at once, I was having second thoughts. I was doubting myself. What if I brought Quinn here and we prayed and nothing happened. I knew good and well that sometimes we pray for things and God doesn't answer the way we would like. Sometimes bad things happen to good people. What if this was one of those times? What if I couldn't face Gracie? The last time I saw her, she looked lifeless. The thought of being in the hospital room was making me anxious. The beeping machines. The smell of well-washed linens and Betadine. Why did the scent of sterility have to smell so terrible?

"God, please give me strength," I whispered. Lavine nodded to the officer and then pushed open the door to the room. I followed close behind. I stepped over the threshold and realized that Lavine was right. Not much had changed. The atmosphere of Gracie's room was exactly the same. Just like before, her room was dark. Sun filtered in through breaks in the drawn curtains, providing just enough light to find our way to her bedside.

A nurse was standing beside the PCA pump, pushing buttons, adjusting settings, making sure that Gracie was comfortable. As we stood beside Gracie's bed, Quinn continued his story. He told about the doctor who had written him off and then he spoke of the nurse, so filled with faith that she brought in a priest to pray for his healing. The cross. The prayers. The love. Without delay, Quinn removed the crucifix from around his neck and laid it on Gracie's chest. He offered me his right hand and Lavine his left. Making a half-moon shape, the three of us stood around Gracie. The nurse, who had just finished up her charting, put herself between Lavine and Gracie and held their hands. There was only one break in the chain. My right hand dangled at my side.

I looked at Gracie. The head of her bed was elevated and the bandage that covered her hair had just been changed. She didn't look like she was in a coma; she looked like she was taking a nap. She looked peaceful, not like I remembered her from my previous visit. I placed my hand on top of Gracie's. I closed my eyes and held them shut. The circle was complete. Quinn began to pray. He prayed for complete healing. He prayed for a miracle. A moment of silence passed between Quinn's prayer and the nurse's.

The nurse prayed for God to take Gracie's pain away. There was another moment of silence, and then Lavine began to pray. He prayed for Gracie's healing and for justice. He prayed for Jessie Paulman's family and for hope. More silence. It was my turn. I had found the words to say and was taking a moment to pray them silently before I prayed them aloud, when I heard an unfamiliar voice and felt a gentle squeeze on my hand. I looked up to find Gracie Abbott staring at me. With a soft whisper she spoke. "Carl Pierce. Emilio Hernandez. Bobby Cooper. Jessie Paulman." And then she fell back asleep.

CHAPTER FORTY-ONE

*I*t was the perfect birthday morning. My phone woke me up at 10 AM. One new text message from Alex: I love you birthday girl. I texted him back: I love you too. The sun was shining and the smell of coffee and pancakes was wafting up the stairs. I climbed out of bed and slipped on my robe. I had everything in the world to be happy about. Less than twenty-four hours ago, Gracie Abbot had spoken her first words since arriving at the hospital with a gunshot wound to the head. I knew she wasn't out of the woods yet and I knew there would be a long recovery, but she was healing. She was talking. She was doing better. And before I went to bed last night, I received a call from Lavine. Shorty after I left the hospital, Gracie had woken up again and was able to have a more lengthy conversation with the detective. She had given him the address of a house on the North side of Tulsa where Jessie was murdered. As of last night, Lavine was in the process of obtaining a search warrant for two separate addresses, one of which was the Pierce estate.

I went downstairs and found my parents in the kitchen. The table was set and there were a couple of colorfully wrapped packages in the center.

"Well, good morning, sleepyhead." Dad wore a warm smile and Mom stopped what she was doing, scurried toward me, and gave me a big hug and a kiss.

"I know. I don't usually sleep this late."

"Are you hungry?" Dad asked. His glasses were resting on the end of his nose and he was looking out at me over the top of them.

"Starving."

"Which do you want to do first, eat or open your presents?"

"Hmmm. How about presents first."

"Then presents it will be. How about we start out with this one," he said, scooting the morning paper in my direction.

"No way!" I shot back. He gave an affirmative nod. "Already! This is all happening so quickly."

"Well, are you going to read it?"

I settled into the chair and unfolded the paper. The entire front page was devoted to Jessie Paulman.

Human Trafficking Ring Suspected in the Abduction and Murder of Tulsa Teen

On February 19th, the parents of Tulsa teen, Jessie Paulman, filed a missing persons report with the Sand Springs police department after their daughter failed to return home from school. Months later, Jessie's body turned up on the shore of Lake Keystone and police were unable to explain how it got there. For months, police have been asking witnesses to come forward, but each lead has turned out to be a dead end. Last night at 9:00, Levine shared some encouraging news. A witness has come forward. Tulsa police are unwilling to release the name of the witness at this time; however, her statement has led to the arrest of three suspects. Emilio Hernandez, 45, Bobby Cooper, 27, and Carl Pierce, 61 have been identified as suspects in the death of Jessie Paulman and have been in custody in the Tulsa County Jail since six this morning. Police are being tightlipped about the investigation but have confirmed that the witness was able to lead police to the scene of the crime. Police believe that it was in a house on Tulsa's northeast side where Jessie was tortured and killed. Tulsa officers are on location looking for more clues to aid in the investigation. As for the witness, police tell us that the she is being hospitalized and treated for serious injuries.

"What ever you did, kiddo, it worked."

"Believe me. It wasn't what *I* did. I've been spinning my wheels for months trying to make this happen. It was God. It was everyone working together."

"All in His timing."

"Speaking of timing, Sunshine," Mom said, changing the subject. "How does it feel to be twenty?" She set a plate of pancakes, eggs, and fruit down in front of me and handed me a cup of coffee.

"I love it. I wish I could have gone straight from ten to twenty and skipped all of those yucky years in between," I said stirring in some cream and sugar.

"Naw," Dad said. "You learned a lot. And now you're one the wiser."

"Are you ready to open your other presents?" Mom asked hopefully.

"Sure." I reached for the medium sized package wrapped in pink foil.

"Oh, wait, this one first!" Mom hopped up from the kitchen chair and disappeared around the corner. Several moments later, she returned, pulling something behind her.

"Another bag?" I asked as I stared at the brand new lily patterned suitcase.

"Luggage," she corrected me. "I just thought, you have all of that old baggage and you're probably ready to get rid of it. This is so much better. Watch this," she said, holding onto the handle and giving it a spin. It has four wheels. It's compact. And it turns on a dime."

"You don't need to convince me, Mom. It's great. Thank you."

"You're welcome. Now you can open the next one."

I took hold of the medium sized package and gave the box a shake before peeling back the paper. Mom and Dad stared at me with eager eyes as I lifted the lid of the box. A little confused, I pulled out the figurine. "A piece of luggage and a miniature Eiffel Tower. Are you trying to tell me we're moving back to Paris or going on vacation?"

"Don't sound so excited. Open the rest of your gifts," Mom instructed.

I picked up a flat package from the table. It felt like a padded envelope wrapped in paper. I squeezed it. It didn't feel like there was anything inside. I ripped off the wrap and found that I was right. A mailing envelope. I used my finger to break the seal and pulled out a folded piece of paper. New luggage. A tiny Eiffel Tower. And... an airline ticket that had to be used within one year of purchase. The exact dates had not been set.

"Paris?"

"Well, I know how you feel about Europe, but I don't think it was Europe you disliked. The time we spent in Europe was rough. It was our situation that was hard. I want you to see a different side of Paris. The art. The history. The food. The shopping." Mom smiled. "And according to Alex, his parents left him a rather large apartment near La Bastille that isn't getting any use. And I graciously accepted his offer when he invited our family to stay."

"When are we going?"

"We can leave as soon as you're ready. With all that's been going on, you've missed enrolling for classes this fall. So I say we go right away. Stay for a couple of weeks... maybe longer. Visit all of the museums. Take a trip to Giverny to visit Monet's house. Then, you'll come back feeling refreshed and inspired. You'll be ready for art school in the spring."

"That does sound amazing, but I'm just not sure I want to leave until I can be certain that Carl isn't going anywhere."

"We'll make sure of it." Mom reached across the table, grabbed the last box, and handed it to me. "I picked this one out all by myself."

It was a dress box. I shook it. The sound of something wrapped in tissue paper softly bumping against the side.

"You are so bad," Mom scolded me playfully. "Just open the box. I'm dying to know if you love it."

This time I ripped off the paper and studied the light cream-colored gift box. "You didn't!"

"I did!"

I opened the box and pulled out the garment. A knee length dress. Soft white cotton with a yellow plumage print.

"It's perfect. It's so me."

"Just like a bird. I thought you'd love it."

At 10:45, my phone rang. I hoped it might be Detective Lavine, but it was Alex.

"Do you want to go to the park?"

"I don't know. It's hot. Maybe we could go to the movies."

"Maybe we could go to the park now, before it gets *too* hot. Then we can go to the movies later tonight."

"I don't know."

"But it's your birthday."

"I'm kind of waiting on this call from Lavine."

"They got Carl, huh?"

"Yeah. Now all we have to do is figure out if they have enough to hold him."

"They have Gracie's word."

"They have that and they have a search warrant for his house."

"Well then, it's settled."

"I know, but I just need to hear it from Lavine. He's been this close before. Carl even went to trial. I'm just curious if he found anything in Carl's basement."

"There was enough evidence hidden in his basement to lock him up for the rest of his life." Alex was trying to be encouraging but we both knew the truth.

"Yes, but he probably got rid of it as soon as he discovered we had escaped from his workshop."

"Probably, but I'll bet it killed him to do it."

"I know. He had had some of those boxes for twenty… thirty years."

"His prized possessions," Alex scoffed.

"Sick."

"Well, at least they have them in custody. Evil finally has a face. On second thought, maybe today's not the best day to go to the park."

"No. You're right. I don't know what I'm worried about. Lavine has everything under control."

It was my birthday and I did need a day to unwind. Besides, Alex was back to his old self and I was so thankful for that. We were talking. He was making plans for us. A day at the park. What could be better?

"So you're in?"

"Are you picking me up?"

"I'll be there in an hour."

I took a quick shower and slipped on my new feather print dress. I pinned the brooch over my heart and stared at myself in the full-length mirror. Six months had passed and the brooch had not returned to its original golden color, but it was getting there... slowly. I pulled on my boots and laced them up then looked myself up and down. I thought about the skinny girl who had stood in front of this mirror two years ago. Timid and a little scared to start her senior year at a brand new school. Dressed in an outfit that allowed her to blend into the crowd, to go unnoticed. The sad girl with the shell around her heart. In the last two years, I had been through a lot. Alex was right; I had changed. And for the better. Alex brought me out of my shell so that God could awaken my soul. And my heart, it was healing. And my mind, I was starting to fill it up with Truth instead of lies. And my shield, it was my faith. When I felt discouraged, when I felt the lies starting to creep back in, I pulled out my faith journal and revisited all of the truths He spoke to keep me going. And my boots. They took me where I needed to go. God gave me heavy steel toed boots in hopes that I would slow down, that I would stop running away and face life, face pain, face healing, find Him. Then there was the phone. God knew how to get my attention. I had listened to Joe and I was beginning to adjust my "antenna" every morning. Sometimes God still sent me a message on my phone, but I didn't need my phone to hear Him anymore. God spoke through nature, God spoke through people, and God spoke through His word. God didn't cause my ground to shake, God didn't cause the fiery trials, and God didn't cause the storms. His voice was a gentle whisper that came after turbulent times, the voice that said, "I've been with you through it all."

Just like he promised, Alex pulled up in front of the house an hour later and rang the bell before I was completely ready. I heard Alex and my parents conversing. My dad was laughing. My mom was giddy. Alex was using his serious voice. What in the world? I was just glad they were getting along. Quickly, I squirted on some perfume, coated my lips with gloss, and pulled my hair back into a messy bun. Twenty minutes later, we were lying on a blanket in the grass beside the bridge.

"I can't believe you invited my parents to Paris."

Alex looked up from his guitar and smiled. "I told you I would get you to Paris one way or another."

"Well, I do have a cool new piece of luggage. When should we go?"

Alex set his guitar down on the blanket and looked me in the eyes. "I think I've finally decided that it's not too bad being human. I'd like to do some human things and I'm ready for a vacation. I want to look at art. I want to relax a little. I want to spend time with you. No adventures allowed."

I laughed. I never thought I'd hear Alex say those words. "Is that what you see in our future? A vacation?"

"That's what I'd like, but maybe I should ask you. You're the one who sees the future in your dreams. So what are you dreaming about these days, Sunshine?"

"Well, I'm not having the nightmares anymore," I told him.

"That's good news."

"I've been having this new dream, though. It's a beautiful dream."

Alex was knitting his brow in a way that led me to believe he was baffled that I was capable of dreaming about something non-disastrous. When he finally spoke, he confirmed my assumption. "Beautiful dreams. That doesn't sound like you. What's it about?"

"Well, I've only had the dream twice, but it's been the same both times. In the first part of the dream, I'm standing in a dark building. Not scary, just kind of lonely. The building's empty and dark and quiet and I'm the only one inside. In my dream, I look over my shoulder and there's nothing at all… just darkness… as far the eye can see, but in front of me, I see a bridge and the bridge is amazing. It's completely enclosed. It's kind of like a glass tunnel, I guess, and it's connecting the building I'm standing in to another building in the distance. So I start walking to the bridge, but I feel so heavy. After a moment I realize that I feel heavy because I'm carrying my three pieces of luggage, but despite the weight I'm carrying around, I'm being pulled toward the bridge; and the closer I get to it, the more beautiful and colorful it becomes. So I step out onto the bridge and when I do, I look down. I'm standing on glass and below me is a never-ending drop. I'm thousands of feet in the air, maybe more. I can't see the ground. All at once, I feel scared. I wonder if the bridge can hold my weight. Is it strong enough to hold my baggage?"

I look up at Alex. He was staring at me wide eyed.

"And."

"And that's it. And then I wake up."

"Well, what's on the other side of the bridge?"

"I don't know."

"What do you mean, you don't know."

"I told you, I didn't cross the bridge."

"Why not?"

"I was too scared. The bridge was too high. I was too heavy. I don't know. I just didn't. I was afraid of the unknown."

"Okay. Next time, cross the bridge. I want to know what's on the other side." Alex paused and ran a hand through his short hair. "I have a story, too." Alex turned serious. "Do you want to hear it?"

"Sure."

"Okay then. Let me put Stella in the car, and let's go for a walk."

Alex and I started on the path. Walking beside me, he took my hand in his and made small talk. He talked about the trees and the flowers and the weather. He talked about the butterflies. He was acting all weird again. Physically he was close, he was holding my hand. He was right beside me, but his mind was somewhere far away.

"Is everything okay, Alex?"

"Yeah. Of course. Why?"

"I don't know. It's just that, ever since Carl's basement, you've been a little distant. I haven't seen much of you."

"Everything's fine." He kissed the top of my head. "I just have a lot on my mind right now."

"I thought you were going to tell me a story."

"I know." Alex began to move his thumb over mine in a nervous fashion. He took a deep breath and let it out. With his eyes closed, he began to mouth something silently to himself. He opened his eyes, took another deep breath, and began to speak. "So, there was once this little girl named Lily." Perspiration was beading on his brow. Alex cleared his throat, stood up straight, and moved his hand over his forehead.

"Alex. You're breaking out in a sweat. Please tell me what's the matter."

"Everything's fine. Just let me tell the story. When Lily was a little girl, her parents passed away." Alex took another deep breath and let it out. I looked at him. His lips were pinched shut. I had never seen him so focused.

"Alex really. You don't have to tell me. No big deal."

"It is a big deal. It's a huge deal. I want to tell you, okay. Just let me tell you."

"Okay. Fine."

Alex and I continued to walk through the woods but unlike our last adventure on that cool spring day when he took me to see the butterfly cocoons, he did not veer off into the trees; instead, he stayed on the path.

"So on Lily's tenth birthday, she went to live at an orphanage. Losing her parents was a big enough loss for a lifetime, but the sadness didn't stop there. Only six months after moving into the orphanage, Lily's closest friend fell ill and died of scarlet fever. The death struck her hard. Lily blamed the loss of her friend on the living conditions: damp and cold with very little food. Lily was never the same after that. But from the loss, she found her purpose.

"In 1931, Lily was old enough to leave the orphanage and start a life of her own. She didn't know exactly what she wanted to do. She only knew that she wanted to do something during the day that she felt good about when she laid her head down at night. Without the money to be officially trained as a nurse, she volunteered at hospitals and learned skills that would help her later in life. While she was there, she met a wealthy doctor and fell in love. In 1937, Lily Jone Baker married Charles Hill. After they wed, she began to officially study nursing and in 1942, she graduated from the Genesee Hospital School of Nursing in Rochester, New York.

"Lily and Charles had plans to start a family, but when Charles volunteered to serve as a doctor in the war, she followed him onto the field and put her dreams on hold. When World War II was over, she saw the aftermath of the Holocaust. Those who survived the concentration camps were sick, malnourished, broken, displaced, dying, and parentless. Even after the inmates were freed from the camps, they were still held behind barbed wire fences and the concentrations camps became a place for displaced persons. The number of orphaned children burdened Lily. It was enough to break anyone's heart but because of her past, Lily held a special place for these children. She wanted to do something but didn't know how to help.

"In 1945, President Truman issued a Directive that would allow refugees, mainly orphans, to enter the United States at the expense of charitable organizations. Right then and there, she decided that with the help of her husband, they would find funding to start an orphanage in the Bronx to house orphans from the war."

With my hand still in his, Alex veered off the path and came to a stop in front of a large tree with a sturdy, low-lying branch. I leaned into Alex and let go of his hand so I could wrap my arm around his waist.

"You feel tense, Alex," I whispered.

Alex's eyes were closed and his feet were rooted to the forest floor. I was beginning to think the worst. Was he going to tell me that it was time for him to leave? Was he going to leave me, after he had gotten my hopes up that he would stay? I didn't think I could bear it if he left. Alex usually went to extreme measures to cheer me up on my birthday; instead, he was acting peculiar and he was telling sad stories of orphans and war.

"I'm fine... really."

"I liked the story."

"I haven't finished telling it."

"Okay."

"I think you should sit down to hear the rest, though."

I let my arm fall from his waist then Alex took my hand and led me toward the tree. With one quick sweep, he lifted me up and set me down on the branch. My legs hovered just inches above the ground. I playfully swung them back and forth while I watched him. He tucked his hands into the pockets of his jeans and stared at his feet. I wondered if he was getting ready to give me a present. I giggled as I watched him fidget and I remembered how we had celebrated my birthday in the past. On my eighteenth birthday, he took me to the Philbrook Museum of Art in Tulsa. It was the perfect day. For a few hours, I felt peace. Just being with him, I felt happy and I forgot all about the reason why I should be so sad. During the time that we spent together, I didn't think about Laney. I didn't feel guilty. I felt love… like I was falling in love and it was new and exciting. It was the most amazing day.

On my nineteenth birthday, his approach was much different. That year, he focused more on healing my heart than making me happy and he thought that if he made me face my past then I might finally release the guilt that I had been harboring for years. So he took me to the bluff that overlooked the scene of the car crash and he told me to close my eyes and feel. Even though I wasn't happy about the idea of "feeling," Alex had been right. Feeling felt good and I learned a valuable lesson that day. While I had been trapped in the year 1990 and so focused on the tragedy that changed my family's life, the rest of the world had moved on. I realized that while I would never forget, maybe it was time for me to move on, too.

But this year I had absolutely no idea what Alex was up to. The story about Lily was bizarre and I didn't understand what Lily and her orphanage had to do with me. Not only was the story bizarre, Alex's behavior was as well. I was just about to tell him to finish the rest of the story when Alex opened his eyes and moved closer, so close that I could feel his breath on my cheek. I let my hands cup his face and then brushed my lips across his. "I love you, Alex. And whatever it is you need to -"

"Shhh." Alex pressed his finger gently to my mouth. "I brought you here for a reason."

"Really. A good reason, I hope. I'm starting to worry."

Alex forced an uneasy smile. "I've been thinking a lot about what ProfC said about history and how if we want to change the future, then we need to look at the past. When he said that history is hard to look at when the past isn't pretty, he was right. I realize that September 13th has never been a very pretty day of the year. But it's your birthday and it should be beautiful."

"Alex! I think I'm finally past that. This year feels so good. You've helped me with that."

"Well, I don't ever want to forget what happened. I want to remember my parents and I want you to remember Laney, but I want September 13th to be a day that makes us think of good things, too."

"And the story about Lily and the orphanage? Alex, I mean… I'm sorry if I'm missing something, but I just don't see how -"

"Shhh." Alex held a gentle finger to my lips and I let out a sigh. "Just let me do this." When Alex slipped his hand out of his pocket, he was holding something shiny between his finger and thumb. "Behind every piece of jewelry there is a story," he said, repeating the words of Mason Armishaw, the old jeweler who sold him the ring.

Everything was happening so fast that I didn't have time to process my thoughts and before I knew it, Alex was on a bent knee. Alex's hand was shaking and I started to cry. I wanted to shout, "Yes", but the words wouldn't come.

"I might not be the boy you fell in love with. I might not be able to protect you in all the ways I used to. I can't fix you. I can't heal you, but I will always hold you. And even though I'm not as strong as I used to be, my love for you is stronger. I love you, Sunshine. I was wondering if you would like to wear Lily's ring. I was wondering if you would be my wife. Will you marry me, Rae Colbert?"

I wiped the tears away from Alex's cheek, and he wiped the tears away from mine.

"Yes," I sobbed. "Of course I'll be your wife."

CHAPTER FORTY-TWO

Mom and Dad were as excited about the engagement as I was. They tried to act surprised, even though they had known of Alex's intentions for quite some time. They were good at keeping secrets, but I figured this was a pretty tough secret to keep.

As the days passed, evidence began to accumulate and things were beginning to fall into place. Because Lavine was unable to use any of the items Alex and I recovered from Carl's basement, I assumed that we had done more harm than good, but something good had come out of a complete disaster. When I fell from Alex's shoulders and disrupted the wall of boxes, we left Carl with a mess on his hands. Fortunately, his attempted cleanup had been rushed and the execution, sloppy. When the FBI received a warrant to search his basement, they found an earring, a retainer, a comb, some blood, and a few other items in the nooks and crannies of Carl's dark basement. All of the evidence was at the lab for DNA testing. Detective Lavine was hopeful that the items would link Carl to Jessie Paulman and possibly others.

I thought about the months I spent trying to bring Carl to justice. Alex had told me that evil takes care of evil, and he was right. Carl had literally gotten away with *murder* for years, but he was finally getting what he deserved. Now that the kingpin himself was arrested, his accomplices were falling like dominoes and with a few of them behind bars, they were making deals; they were already exchanging Carl's secrets for a lesser sentence. There was nowhere for Carl to go but down. Everything was going smoothly. I had expected a more dramatic ending. A fight. A car chase. A hostage. I felt like I should be doing something, but when I started to grow restless, I would reflect upon what God told me in Carl's basement, and His words would bring me peace. He said, "It's not what I want *from* you, it's what I want *for* you." All along, I thought my mission was Carl Pierce, but God knew better. All along, I thought I would use the items in the box to bring my biological father to justice; instead, each item taught me about God's armor. I had been trying to protect myself for years and I had grown cold and distant. It was time to let go and let God, let Him handle Carl. I didn't know what tomorrow would bring; I only knew that God wasn't finished with me yet. I was still growing. I was still learning and according to my brooch, which was now 60 percent gold and 40 percent silver, the refining process was hardly complete. Besides, I had only found nine of the ten names; I had yet to meet Peter Jovorskie.

It was midnight. I couldn't sleep. I was thinking about my future; I couldn't look at my engagement ring without thinking about Lilly and the orphanage she started. She saw a need and met it. She created a safe place, a home for children who needed to be restored and loved. I let my mind wander back to the day when I met Mason Armishaw, when I saw the ring for the very first time. I had visited his shop to learn more about my brooch, but while Mason was finishing up with another piece of jewelry, I decided to take a look around the store. It was a case of antique engagement rings that grabbed my attention, but one ring in particular stood out from the rest. Just before leaving, Mason allowed me to try it on. That was months ago. I couldn't believe Alex remembered. I couldn't believe that out of 150 rings, I was drawn to Lily's. As I thought more about seeing a need and meeting it, I tossed and turned. I couldn't stop myself from thinking about Monica Bradley and Gracie Abbott. Terry Dunbarr. Todd Catchitore's words rang loud, "There's no place for these girls to go." Lilly's story. Todd's story. Needs. Safe places. I couldn't help but think that maybe I was being led. Too restless to sleep, I climbed out of bed and descended the stairs. I slipped into my studio and sat down behind my easel. The window was open and I could hear the late summer breeze blowing the native grass to and fro. A quiet rustling. There wasn't a cloud in the sky and the stars were shining bright. I thought about the story of Elijah and how he listened for God's voice on top of the mountain. A great storm came that tore the mountains apart, but God was not in the wind. And after the storm, there was an earthquake, but God was not in the earthquake. After the earthquake, there was a fire. God wasn't in the fire, either. But God's voice did come. It came after the fire in the form of a gentle whisper. Sitting in front of my easel, surround by candy apple green walls and plenty of old canvases, I closed my eyes and whispered, "God, are you there?"

"I AM," He whispered back.

"Who am I, God? Who do *You* say I am?"

And in a gentle whisper, He replied, "You are my masterpiece."

I pulled my robe around me tight and welcomed the words that sent tears rolling down my cheeks. I had considered myself many things, but a masterpiece was never one of them. I opened my eyes and stared at my easel. My last canvas had received its final coat of gesso and it was begging for some color. I wiped the tears away and brushed my finger across the surface. I could feel the bumps and scars of the old painting beneath the heavy coat of white paint... all of my mistakes. I loved gesso. I loved its thick whiteness and how it was so forgiving. I loved brushing it on heavily over my marred canvas. It made the canvas look new and clean, without a single blemish. I always thought that *I* was the artist, but perhaps I had it all wrong. God was the artist and I was the canvas. Like the canvas on my easel, my soul had scars. I had blemishes, bumps, and bruises that I liked to call my past. I knew they were there and if others looked close enough, they could see them, too. Some might judge me based on this. Some might think my marred surface was less than perfect... not good enough. But Pastor Joe and Quinn Collins taught me a lesson that I will never forget. They told me that what God says about me is far more important than what other's say about me.

On the other hand, I knew there would also be people who would draw near to my canvas. If I allowed them to get close enough, they might brush their fingers over my mistakes. They might feel the richness, the texture, and the singularity of my scars, but with their eyes, they wouldn't see the painting of a broken girl. They would see the fresh coat of gesso that gave me a new start and they would see the beginnings of a masterpiece that only God himself could create. I thought about my soul. I thought about what God did to wipe me clean and make me new, what it cost to give my soul a coat of gesso. For years, I had tossed around the name A-Omega. I let the name escape my lips without letting the meaning of the name sink in. The Alpha and the Omega. He was my beginning and my end. He was the purity that covered my flaws. When He looked at me, He didn't see a marred soul. He saw a masterpiece. In the last six months, I have had more than one person tell me that it is not only important to know God's name for you, but also to have a name for God. According to Quinn, Jesus was the antivirus for his mind and the antivenom for his soul. Mom called God, *Healer*. Detective Lavine called God, *Provider*. And Pastor Joe said God is Love. So who is God to me? Without a shadow of a doubt, I know. If I am the canvas then God is the artist. And Jesus… He is my gesso.